LUDINGTON PUBLIC LIBRARY
5 S. BRYN MAWR AVENUE
BRYN MAWR, PA 19010

THE DEAD FRIENDS SOCIETY

PETER HALL & PAUL GANDERSMAN

Cover art by Marc Schoenbach.
Interior Illustrations by Stephen Andrade.
Greywood House blueprints by Ashley Landavazo.
Formatting and Layout by Christian Francis.

Copyright © 2022 Peter Hall and Paul Gandersman.
All Rights Reserved.

The characters and events in this book are fictitious. Any similarity to real persons, living, dead or undead is coincidental and not intended by the author.

No part of this book may be reproduced in any form or by any electronic or mechanical means, including information storage and retrieval systems, without permission in writing from the publisher, except by a reviewer who may quote brief passages in a review.

www.encyclopocalypse.com

For Christine & Ashley

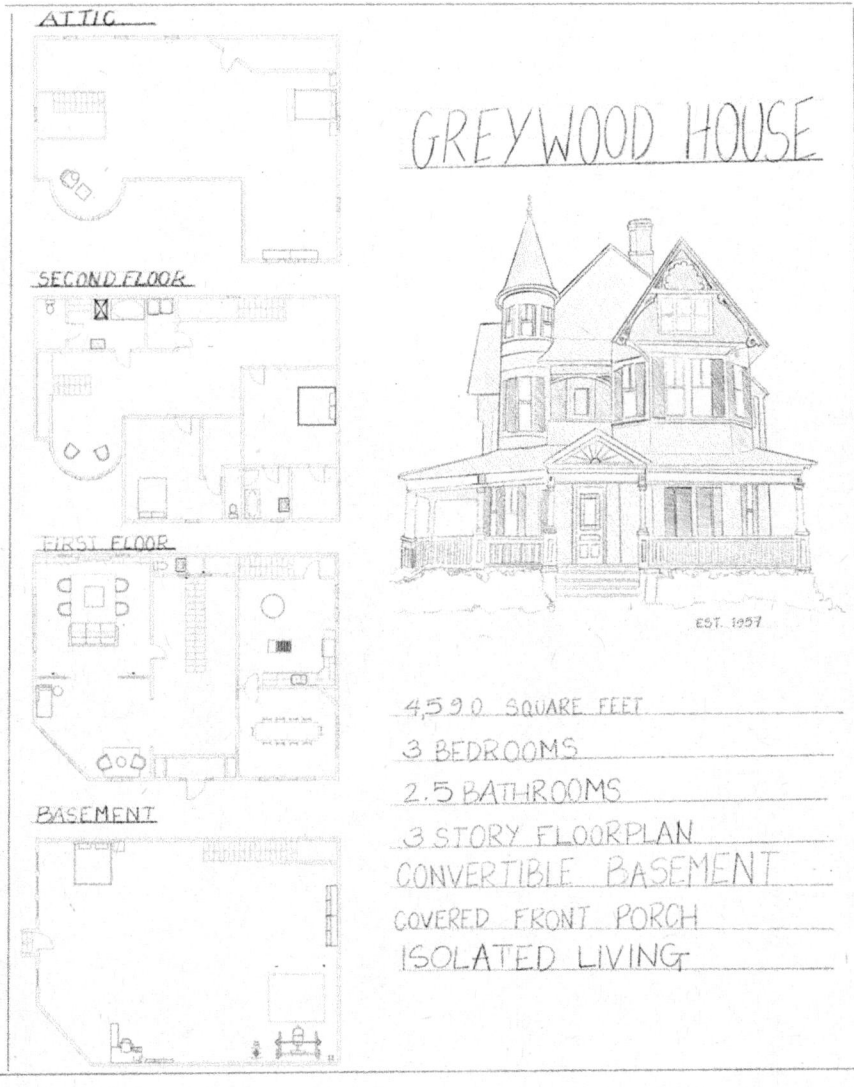

GREYWOOD HOUSE

EST. 1957

4,590 SQUARE FEET
3 BEDROOMS
2.5 BATHROOMS
3 STORY FLOORPLAN
CONVERTIBLE BASEMENT
COVERED FRONT PORCH
ISOLATED LIVING

THE FIREMAN

Chapter 1

September 14, 1998

ALL HOUSES HAVE A SOUL, AND THIS ONE WAS ROTTEN. IT HAD been rotting for decades, but the neighbors who knew what secrets Greywood House held talked only in hushed tones lest it bring down property values. It sat for years, nestled deep in the woods, its malignancy left to fester as the world refused to acknowledge that some places are truly cursed.

You would never know it from looking at Drew Denns's attic bedroom, though. She slept sprawled out in a queen-sized bed below an open window, blissfully oblivious to her future. Crisp September air drifted in with occasional gusts rattling a row of framed family photographs that lined the windowsill. Somewhere downstairs there was a low, rhythmic pounding. The last dulled wavelengths of bass from a boombox turned too loud gave the house a heartbeat strong enough to drown out Drew's snoring.

All around her were posters thumb-tacked over faded wallpaper. Kurt Cobain, Nine Inch Nails, and Garbage watched over her like angels, updating the house's '70s bones. The rockstar faces looked down on a room cluttered with abandoned art projects. A pencil sketch of a shaggy teddy bear from Mr. Esposito's Direct Observations class showed promise, but the shadow work was rough. On a nearby canvas, an aborted watercolor showed even less promise. Drew just didn't have a knack for blending colors. Bob Ross would not have been impressed. Her trees were neither happy nor little. They were jagged and severe. If that had been by design, Mr. Esposito would have given her higher marks, but Drew was too honest with her art to lie about it.

The one piece that showed the most inspiration was a sculpture. Drew had realized her true potential as an artist with clay. There was just something about shaping it with her hands, of understanding the immediate cause and effect of applying pressure here to change the shape there that made sense in her twenty-year-old brain. Give her a paintbrush and she was passable but forgettable. Give her a chisel, though, and she could really make something memorable.

The clay bust was a self-portrait. A polaroid of Drew in a mosh pit was pinned to the wall for reference. In it, Drew stood out in the crowd. Her head tilted, eyes closed, with a wave of swaying hair frozen in time. Her ex, Kris, had taken it, appreciating how totally lost in the moment Drew looked. Drew normally hated pictures of herself, but she liked this one for reasons she never quite understood. When Mr. Esposito assigned her class a self-portrait, Drew dug it out of a box of memories. It was a memento from a happier time.

Though Drew's sculpture had captured her likeness well, the moonlight distorted the shadows. Gone was the carefree girl out too late at a concert. Her parted lips were twisted into a grimace. Her head, once beautifully frozen tossing side-to-side, was now locked in a moment of violence. She didn't look like a girl at a Smashing Pumpkins show. She looked like a crash test dummy about to smash through a windshield.

That wasn't the only ill effect of the moonlight. A sole stairwell led to the attic and the moonlight stopped at the open door as if the pale light itself were afraid to creep further into the darkness. The stairs descended into the bowels of the house like an esophagus, and any light that dared go down was swallowed, fading to nothingness as the heartbeat thumped two floors below.

Then there was a sudden shattering of glass and Drew bolted upright, awakened.

Drew Denns got out of bed slowly, her mind in a stupor. She'd been in the middle of a deeply confusing dream in which the Crocodile Hunter was teaching her how to catch an anaconda and wanted to see where it was going to go, but then she'd heard the sound of glass breaking and was swept away from the rainforest and back into the attic of Greywood House. Drew stretched, her body waking up before her mind, and listened to the house.

She could hear music coming from below and figured Rose and Eli must be still hanging out. Drew glanced at the clock. It was 4:42 in the morning. She had passed out hours ago, so exhausted (or, more accurately, half-drunk) her shoes were the only thing she managed to take off before collapsing into bed. If Rose and Eli were still up, it could only mean good things. She smiled at the thought of the awkward duo sitting closer on the couch, listening to CDs. She hoped moving into the house would bring her two best friends closer together. Then she noticed something else mixed with the thumping beat of the music. It sounded like shouting, but that didn't make sense as both Rose and Eli were too mousey to be the shouting type.

Drew stepped out of bed and something sharp stabbed into her heel. She pulled it back quickly and discovered a framed picture of her grandmother shattered on the floor. Drew knelt, careful to miss the shards of glass, and inspected the broken frame, glancing from it to the curtains blowing in the wind. She felt stupid for leaving something so fragile so close to an open window. She could hear her mom's voice in her head, scolding her. *"What did you think would happen?"* Drew pushed the voice out and slipped on a beat-up pair of Converse to further avoid the glass.

She searched for something to sweep up the mess and decided on a thick piece of sketch paper. As she crossed the room to grab it, the shouting downstairs grew louder. Drew stood at the edge of the attic stairs, listening. She couldn't quite make out the words, but thought Eli was shouting for someone to "Get the hell out of here, man."

Even from the third floor, and under the blanket of music, she could hear the shakiness in Eli's voice. She took the stairs to hear better but hadn't even reached the second floor before she heard Rose. This time the words were crystal clear: "Drew! Call the police!"

Drew stopped to make sure she had heard correctly.

"What?" Drew shouted back.

"This guy broke in and he won't lea—" Rose's shouting turned into a bone-chilling scream. It was so loud, so visceral, so utterly horrified that Drew momentarily wondered if she was still dreaming, or if Rose was pranking her. But if she were dreaming, the broken glass wouldn't have felt so real. And Rose was far from the pranking type. The realization snapped Drew back to life. She turned to the attic, heart lurching in her chest.

Drew tore up the throat, bursting from the shadows in a blur of flannel. Her messy hair bound together with a scrunchy, her usually confident face filled with panic. Drew slammed the door shut as she hurtled into the bedroom. Kurt Cobain's face waved in the wind. For a second it looked like he was smiling. But no, nevermind.

Drew rushed to the phone sitting on the dresser but had too much momentum. She crashed painfully into the mahogany chest, knocking papers and books loose. A note Drew had written to her mom fell behind the dresser. She'd never had the courage to give it to her, and on any other night Drew would have dove to retrieve this private piece of herself, but there was no time. Drew's sole focus was on dialing 911.

She hastily picked up the phone, gluing her eyes to the closed door in case anyone was to suddenly throw it open. It stayed mercifully shut as Drew put the receiver to her ear and was surprised to hear voices already on the line. One was making a garbled, gasping sound and the other was talking over them.

"Ma'am? Are you okay? Do you need assistance?" the second voice said. She was calm, almost robotic. This dispatcher was well trained to manage any situation. Drew's words, in contrast, spewed out on top of one another in a trembling panic. "Uh, hello? My name is Drew Denns. I live at One Prescott Lane. I don't know what happened, but my roommate Rose just started screaming about this guy in the house and then—"

The too-calm woman cut her off. "Do you have anything to protect yourself with?"

Drew scanned the room, her eyes landing on a twelve-inch chisel sitting next to the clay self-portrait. She grabbed it, holding it tight in her hand. "I have a chisel. Like for carving." Drew's eyes returned to the door. She gripped the chisel like a knife, her imagination running wild with speculation. *Did someone just attack Rose? What the hell happened?*

"If you have to use it, use it," said the too-calm woman. "But hide until we get there. Hang up if you need to."

Click. Drew hung up the phone without a second thought. She ran to the open window with visions of scaling the side of the house to the ground, but when Drew stuck her head out, the cold wind bit at her face and the grass three stories down now looked miles away. *What are you going to do? Jump?* Drew whipped around, half-expecting this mysterious man to be there, but she was still alone. Exhaustion from her sprint up the stairs began mixing with her just-woken brain and she felt a new wave of disorientation trying to piece together what could be happening to Rose and Eli downstairs.

THUD. Drew's mind and body snapped back into sync as the sound of steel slamming into wood reverberated up through the esophageal stairwell and into the room. *What the hell was that?* Drew tip toed back to the door and gently cracked it open, listening.

Another thud. The sound was much closer this time — closer than she was comfortable with. Drew quietly closed the bedroom door; afraid the attacker might hear her. If he didn't, she'd buy herself more time as he searched the second floor. She scanned the room yet again, reconsidering her options. There weren't many.

There was an antique armoire — a handmade bit of inheritance from her woodworker grandfather — that was easily big enough to hide a person, but something about it left her feeling exposed. Drew imagined him storming in and tipping it over, trapping her inside. She fleetingly wondered if that would make it the first coffin her grandfather ever built.

Drew willed the thought out of her head. Her eyes settled on the bed. She could probably squeeze under it, but as with the armoire-turned-coffin, her head filled with the vision of a hand lifting the mattress like a child flipping a rock to look for bugs underneath.

Her eyes settled on the closet. Her mind flooded with images from a montage of horror movies she'd seen on VHS. So many girls whimpering in their closets, watching their own bedrooms in terror. She rolled her eyes as she ran toward the closet. *Jesus, you're such a fucking cliche*, she thought, but it was the only hiding place that also offered her a shot at mobility if she needed to quickly move.

Drew slipped inside and closed the closet's French doors. The hinges squeaked loudly, and she flinched with dread, but there was nothing to do about it now. This was her choice, her entire life now hanging on the hope that he... *just wouldn't check the closet? Are you stupid? Of course, he's going to check the closet.*

Had Drew ever bothered to hang up her clothes, she'd have a nice wall of fabric between her and whomever had broken into the house, but she was too lazy, opting instead to keep two carefully curated piles of dirty and not-dirty-enough laundry. She shrunk between them, and her mom's nagging voice filled her head. "If you just hung your clothes, you'd have something to hide behind." *Oh, piss off, Mom. Like you could have seen this coming.* This was as good as hiding was going to get. Drew grit her teeth and peered through the gap in the French doors.

As her brain once again tried to cope with the sudden turn the night had taken, the world shifted into slow motion. The bedroom door swept open with an odd measure of grace, like a dancer leading their partner. Drew's eyes jumped all over his frame, too overwhelmed to focus on the whole picture but instead only processing a single detail at a time.

Thick vinyl boots with a yellow stripe on the side. *Those look heavy.*

A fire axe. Wooden handle. Steel head–stained red. *Is that blood?*

A full-face oxygen mask. Only, it looked shattered. *What happened to him?*

A thick overcoat. Long. Dark. Torn to pieces in parts. *Are those bullet holes?*

Mr. Esposito would have scolded her for it. The key, he'd say, to capturing direct observations was to focus on the big picture first and then fill in the details. But Drew's mind just didn't work that way. She was always details first, big picture last. *That's why you can never finish what you start. That's why you're a cliche hiding in a closet.* Even faced with home invasion, Drew couldn't help but be hard on herself.

The Fireman strode fully into the room, a walking mountain of a man. And suddenly Drew's artist eye shifted from details to big picture. And it could barely understand. It wasn't because the room seemed to darken as he entered, as if he absorbed light. And it wasn't because she could see the floorboards bending under his weight. It was because he didn't make sense. She wasn't the problem. *He was.*

She thought The Fireman looked not just out of place, but out of time. His uniform was old, like something from the 1960s or '70s. His coat was riddled with bullet holes. Dozens of them. His mask was badly damaged, creating a shattered spiderweb in the tempered glass that hid the face underneath. *Where the hell was this guy fighting fires? Vietnam?*

Fresh blood was splattered all over him, yet none came from the bullet holes. Drew's brain tried to rationalize it as some sort of Halloween costume meant to look like he'd been to Hell and back. Until a more realistic thought occurred to her: It's not his blood.

Rose. Eli. Oh my god. What did he do to them?

The Fireman turned, his unseen eyes surveying the room. For a moment, Drew had a sense memory of the sentinels in the Saturday morning X-Men cartoon. She hadn't seen an episode in years but was hit with a vague vision of Jubilee hiding from the giant robots. Was it in a mall? What did Jubilee do? Just wait for Wolverine to save her? But Wolverine wasn't coming to save Drew. Nobody was.

The Fireman set his gaze on the armoire. Drew felt a rush of relief, a momentary vindication that, for once in her life, she'd made the right choice, as he walked casually over to the wooden cabinet. Each thunderous step felt like an eternity. She watched anxiously as The Fireman wedged his axe into the crook of the armoire's doors and pried them apart. They opened with an ugly, high-pitched screech that made Drew's skin crawl. "You should really oil these hinges," her mom once said. *Fucking mom. Always right.*

The Fireman slid his axe into the armoire, revealing where Drew kept her winter clothes. They'd been hanging for months, unused. He parted them with his axe like Moses parting the Red Sea. The Fireman tilted his head slightly, as if bemused to not find anyone hiding in the promised land between the sweaters and coats. He cocked his head back toward the room. There was an odd lightness to his movement now. It was almost playful.

Is this asshole having fun?

The Fireman glanced at the bed. And once again, Drew felt vindication.

Until he walked right past it. Right toward the fucking closet.

Drew tensed; her heart pounding as hard as it was the night she was mugged on campus. Those men only demanded her purse and left her, thankfully, alone. Drew knew this guy had no need for her purse. He wanted *her*. She was indeed becoming the closet-trapped cliche. The cops would find her dead body between her lazy piles of dirty and not-dirty-enough clothes. They'd look down at her and joke to one another. "Why do the dumb ones always hide in the closet?"

The Fireman's long gait closed the gap quickly and before Drew could process it, his axe wedged between the closet doors. *It's going to be the armoire all over again. He's going to kill me. And you'll deserve it, you dumb—*

But Drew refused to be just another cliche. She refused to be just another dead girl.

Drew gripped the chisel so tight her knuckles hurt.

The axe slid into the closet.

And Drew leapt, firing into the room like a cougar out of a canon. This time, it was The Fireman who flinched. She wished she could have seen under his mask. She wanted to see the shock on his face as she launched herself chisel-first into his hulking body. He easily had twice the mass as her, yet Drew drove him across the room, turning the chisel in his chest like a goddamn steering wheel.

She shoved outward, sinking it even deeper into his chest. The blade stopped at the hilt. Drew shoved again, but the chisel's blade wouldn't fit any deeper.

The Fireman stood a moment. He looked absurd, confused even, as if he'd just walked into a surprise party not even realizing it was his birthday. He looked from the chisel to the girl, as if trying to solve a math problem. The axe drooped in his hand. Playtime was over.

Drew screamed into his face, cursing at him, but he didn't even seem to hear her. He started teetering, a tree about to fall in the forest. Timber.

Physics took over. The Fireman teetered backwards and collapsed motionless onto the floor, his weight shaking the entire house. Drew watched in shock, her brain once again processing the details and not the big picture. She couldn't take her eyes off the wooden handle of her chisel. Just sitting there, sticking out of his chest, a tool designed to create art. And she'd used it to kill a man.

Drew stood over him, mind racing, trying to process what just happened. It was in self-defense, of course. Those words kept looping in her brain: *It was self-defense. It was self-defense. It was self-defense.* They became a mantra to rationalize having just driven a chisel into a giant, masked man's heart.

Drew looked over her shoulder as if expecting confirmation from someone else that everything had indeed just happened. She wanted to turn to someone and point. *Did you see that? I had to. It was self-defense.* The rush of adrenaline started overpowering her thoughts. The big picture started to come into focus. *Yes, you did that. But this isn't over yet. Don't stop.*

Drew bent down and put a trembling hand on the shaft of the axe. She started to pull it away, but the dead man's grip was still tight. Drew's mind pinballed from topic to topic. *What's that called? When the muscles of a dead body lock up? Rigor something? Rigor mortis?* Up until that point her only experience with it was seeing random dead deer on the side of the road, their heads and necks always wrenched backward, their once-soft bodies frozen in a horrible impersonation of a giraffe.

Without thinking, Drew kicked The Fireman's body to make sure he was going to stay down. It jiggled like a cadaver on a slab. But he didn't stand. He didn't groan. He didn't respond in any way. He lay there, motionless, his fingers wrapped tightly around the shaft of the axe.

The Fireman was dead.

Drew pried his gloved fingers off the axe. She scooped it up, marveling briefly at how heavy it was (*How does anyone use these things?*) and disappeared down the house's throat.

Chapter 2

DREW STUMBLED FROM THE ATTIC STAIRWELL INTO A LONG, narrow hallway lined with doors. The peeling wallpaper was doing its best, but no amount of decoration or attempts at modernization could ever truly hide what lay beneath the surface of Greywood House.

Drew stopped herself at the bottom of the stairs, catching her breath. She turned, scanning back up the staircase, listening intently, straining to hear any sign of movement from The Fireman. There was nothing but the increasingly loud, pulsating bass from Nine Inch Nails's "Closer" emanating from the boombox downstairs. There was something about the song, the familiarity of it, that lulled Drew into a sense of security, of normalcy. Until Trent Reznor's muffled voice started singing about feeling people from the inside and Drew thought about the chisel inside The Fireman, how it slipped inside his chest with such surprising ease. The human body was so fragile, so easy to violate. The distant song lyrics sent a shiver down her spine. Those were two dots she did not want connected. *It was self-defense, it was self-defense, it was self-defense.*

Drew re-focused on the moment and where she was. The hallway was dark, with only half of the light sconces working. She'd been meaning to replace the bulbs. Rose volunteered to do it, but Drew was prideful and insisted she'd get to it. Now she was wishing she had. The house was her responsibility, after all. Her mom entrusted her to watch over it, allowing Drew and her friends to live in the house while it was being remodeled on the condition that they take care of things. But this was still their first week living there and Drew wasn't ready to start acting like an overbearing dorm RA just yet. She was still enjoying the freedom of having moved out, even if it was into a house her mom bought to flip.

Drew whisper-shouted down the hall, calling out to Rose. Her brain knew The Fireman was dead and yet she couldn't shake the need to be quiet, to stay hidden as she swept slowly down the corridor.

The first door on the left was a shared bathroom. She poked her head in, calling out Rose's name again. The only things she found were her and Rose's toiletries, separated by their respective ownership on either side of the sink. Rose's side was lined with a dozen carefully organized bottles of various homeopathic skin care regimens. Drew's side was sparse by comparison, with a single stick of deodorant and a half-full bottle of Clearasil she needed to start using again because apparently acne refused to stop just because she'd graduated high school. Drew continued down the hall, growing more confident as she put more distance between herself and The Fireman's corpse. She shouted louder. "Rose? Eli? If you're hiding, it's safe now."

Drew wanted to add *why* it was safe. She wanted to scream it was because she killed the maniac who broke into their house with an axe, but the farther she got from his body, the more real the word kill became. Upstairs it seemed like self-defense, down here it was starting to feel criminal. She knew that was bullshit, but her head began questioning her heart with endless "What ifs?" It made her want to find Rose all the more. Rose could talk her through this. Rose could talk her through anything.

Drew arrived at the second door. It was Rose's and it was closed. She shifted the axe to her right hand and dropped the damn thing on her foot. It hurt, but she couldn't help but laugh. This night was going from normal to terrifying to ridiculous way too quickly. Drew opened the bedroom door, revealing a candle-lit room decorated with tapestries and crystals of different shapes, sizes, and colors.

A far cry from Drew's mess of a bedroom art studio, Rose Calder's room reflected her personality beautifully. It was organized, deliberate, and unabashedly feminine. Not Barbie Doll, passing around Tiger Beat in middle school feminine. There was a powerful, women supporting women quality to it all. Rose was the spiritual optimist to Drew's practical pessimist, the friend that was always there for her when she needed it most. They both thought of each other as equals, but when all else failed in life, Drew would turn to Rose for all the counsel and guidance she'd been too stubborn to seek from her own mother.

The room was empty, Rose nowhere to be found. The last Drew had seen her friend was when they were downstairs. Drew, Rose, and Eli were having a few drinks when Drew started to feel like a third wheel and went upstairs. That was hours ago, and her groggy brain could only guess as to what led to this moment.

The nagging sensation that something was wrong, that the situation wasn't under control, returned as Drew moved deeper into the room. Rose's closet door was made from the same material as Drew's. All the house's closets were. The contractor must have gotten a great deal on them.

As Drew approached the closet, she caught a glimpse of herself in Rose's full body mirror. The axe in her hand glinted in the candlelight just as it glinted off the moonlight when The Fireman entered her room. Drew hesitated to open the closet door; afraid she might find Rose crumpled on the floor of the closet like a pile of blood-soaked laundry.

Drew pleaded to the darkness, begging Rose to not jump out at her. She laughed as she said it, picturing Rose hiding in the closet just like she had. Unlike Drew, Rose hung her clothes. Her wardrobe consisted almost exclusively of maxi dresses with various floral prints. Drew couldn't remember the last time she wore a dress. She was all thin-soled Converse and tattered jeans. The closest thing she owned to a dress was the oversized flannel jacket currently wrapped around her waist, and even that was something she'd stolen from the coat check at the Fat Dragon club. It was the only thing she'd ever stolen in her life. At the time, she couldn't believe she'd done it. She wasn't even sure why she had. The cute guy at the coat check handed it to her, mistakenly thinking it was hers and she simply didn't correct him.

Drew opened the closet door, revealing nothing but the expected row of dresses. She retreated to the hall, a new wave of anxiety flooding her nerves. *Why isn't anyone answering?*

As Drew stepped back into the hall, the burnt-out bulb inside one of the light sconces flickered, as if trying to come back from the dead. The tungsten filament flared a fiery orange, briefly blinding Drew. She jumped, caught off guard, and shielded her eyes. She needn't have bothered. By the time Drew covered her face, the bulb fizzled out and the hall was dark once more.

Drew quickened her pace down the rest of the hall. As she reached the second-floor master bedroom door, she gave up all pretense of being quiet. Drew shouted as her hand hit the doorknob. "Guys? Are you in there? I really think we need to..."

But Drew couldn't finish her sentence. She screamed so loud she could feel the lining of her throat tear open.

Inside the master bedroom, Drew's fourth roommate, Wes Adams, had been impaled through the lungs by the shaft of his microphone stand. His lifeless body had started to slide down the metal but snagged the height adjustment knob in the center of the shaft. If this were a concert stage, it would have looked like Wes was in the middle of a set, bending backward and singing his lungs out.

But this wasn't a concert stage. And Wes wasn't singing. His body was oozing thick, coagulated blood that was almost as dark as the shadows around him. The top of the mic stand was covered in bits of lung.

Drew didn't know Wes well. She'd only rented him a room because he was Eli's older brother and he volunteered to pay more than everyone else just to have the biggest room in the house. The truth was she thought he was a bit of an asshole. He'd hit on both Drew and Rose the first time they'd met. They'd gone to a show he was performing at, and he'd made some crack about letting them earn their way backstage. If that wasn't bad enough, he didn't seem genuinely interested in either of them. He said it because he knew he could get away with it. That pissed off Drew more than the comment did.

Her mind immediately went to Eli and how she could possibly explain this to him. She didn't want him to see this fucked up display, to know that this was how Wes died, to know what his brother's lungs looked like, what they *smelled* like. The rational side of Drew's mind started to play catch up. *If Wes is dead, and no one else is answering her shouts...*

Drew backed out of the room. She pulled the cordless phone out of her pocket to start dialing 911 again. And then several things happened very, very fast.

First, the phone was in Drew's hand. Second, a blur whizzed through the corner of her vision. Third, the cordless phone exploded in her hand.

Drew's carving chisel embedded in the wall right next to her head. She jumped in shock. *What the fuck just happened—* But before her brain could even put a question mark at the end of the thought, she had her answer. She turned in slow motion disbelief.

At the end of the hall, at the base of the attic stairs, stood The Fireman. He stared at Drew, defiant, daring her to make a move. She looked from him to the chisel. A viscous rope of sickly black ooze dripped off its handle.

"Who are you?" She didn't even register screaming at him. It's not as if she needed to know who he was. His name and address and marital status wouldn't have changed the fact that five minutes ago he was laying on the floor of her attic bedroom, the chisel lodged firmly in his heart, and now he was standing at the end of the hall and that very chisel had just narrowly missed Drew's face.

The Fireman took a single step forward into the hallway. It was a slow, patient, purposeful step. He was in no rush. Unlike Drew, his legs weren't trembling. His hands weren't shaking. If he was breathing heavily, she couldn't tell. He looked like a statue. And Drew realized this movement, this moment was his way of answering her question: *I'm The Fireman.* End of answer. He arrived on his terms. He would leave on his terms.

That realization was both terrifying and liberating. Drew wasn't going to wait for him to make the next move. She gripped the axe tight in her hands and spun toward the first floor, racing down the sweeping staircase.

And then she was flying down the staircase.

Head over heels.

Maybe it was the weight of the axe in her hand. Maybe it was how abruptly her fight or flight response took over. Maybe it's because the man she just killed was standing at the end of the hall like nothing happened. Either way, as in senior year when she got a D in it, physics was not Drew's friend. And now it was throwing her down the goddamned stairs. *Fucking physics.*

Drew fell hard, hitting what felt like every wooden step. She lost her grip on the axe and felt a sudden, sharp pain in her back. For a second, she thought she'd fallen on its blade and had an instant flash of two police officers staring at her body and joking, "Man, how stupid do you have to be? He didn't even have to kill this one."

But luckily, she hadn't hit the axe. Her back had slammed into the newel post at the base of the banister, which sent her spinning like a top. She landed on the first floor, her right-hand slapping something large and wet as it braced her fall. She felt like she'd slipped on a banana peel and fallen into a puddle. She wanted to laugh about it, but her head had gone from aching to jackhammering. Her vision was blurring. Not from a concussion, her mind was overloaded. One second it had been standing up right. The next it was somersaulting down a staircase.

Drew tried to bring focus to the chaos, narrowing in on the details to stop the blurriness. She looked down. Her right hand was soaked in blood. Her eyes scanned the room. She screamed out Eli's name. It was pointless. Eli couldn't answer her. Eli couldn't hear her. All Eli Adams could do was lay in the middle of the floor, flooding the foyer with his blood.

They'd met in middle school but didn't become close friends until junior year when they both worked at The Suncoast Motion Picture Company. He'd actually been her boss, but you'd never know it from watching them together. Eli treated everyone as an equal, avoiding conflict whenever possible. Drew hadn't known too many guys she'd call truly good, but Eli was one of them.

Was.

Now Eli was a corpse, his body splayed on the ground, his head split down the middle. A chunky, red lake of blood and brains surrounded him. The murky mess formed a river that snaked all the way over to where Drew landed. The Fireman had made quick work of Eli. There was no sign of a struggle, nothing on the first floor looked out of place. One single chop was all it took and one of her best friends was gone forever.

Time stood still for a moment. Drew didn't know what to do, what to say, or where to go. She wanted to will herself to believe Eli was just sleeping. Maybe he was drunk. He was always a lightweight, getting drunk faster than both she and Rose. He could just be passed out, blissfully dreaming of roaming the aisles of Suncoast. But she knew he wasn't. The Adams brothers weren't just dead. They were slaughtered. That was the only word that made sense. An hour ago, they were alive and breathing. Wes was in his room, doing whatever the hell Wes did on his own. Eli was, as far as Drew thought she knew, downstairs with Rose. Now Wes's chest was inside out, and Eli's skull was cracked open like a walnut. *Slaughtered.*

Drew felt her stomach start to gurgle. Much as she wanted to, she couldn't look away from the massacre. Looking away felt like moving on, which felt like accepting this as reality. But Drew didn't have a choice anymore. She snapped back to reality to hear The Fireman descending on her, each step like thunder rolling in from the hills. She tried to stand, but her hand slipped in Eli's blood, sending her crashing back down. Her chin smacked on the floor. She bit her tongue hard enough to wonder if she'd just sliced through the tip of it. She was starting to feel like a cartoon character. Any second now Porky Pig would show up and wave as The Fireman's massive boot stomped on her chest. *Th-th-th-that's all folks!*

Drew reached desperately for a dry patch on the floor and tried again, scrambling to her feet, spitting out her own blood in the process. It mixed with Eli's, forming a brighter red island in the darker sea of his thickening viscera. She could see the blood seeping into the cracks between the hardwood slats. It looked like the house itself was drinking, pulling the crimson sea deep inside it.

She raced for the front door, her bloody hands reaching out to grab the knob, only to find that it was missing. Someone had smashed it clean off. *No, not someone. The Fireman.* The door was locked shut with no way to open it. Drew tried working her fingers into the keyhole to pinch the mechanism, but it was useless. All she could manage to do was scrape her nails on the old, rusty metal gears.

Drew banged on the door, screaming her lungs out for help. Each hit left another blood-soaked handprint. A subconscious part of her thought they looked like the Thanksgiving turkey hands she'd made back in kindergarten. She'd given her mom a card with one of those hand turkeys. Her mom said she'd keep it forever. Drew knew she hadn't. She'd probably thrown it away a day later.

Drew rammed her shoulder into the door. It shook violently but didn't budge. She screamed louder, but it didn't matter. The house was built on five acres in a subdivision full of baby boomers and retirees. There was no one out there to help her. There was no one out there to hear her. Her shouts would be swallowed by the sounds of the woods. Drew was trapped in the house. She was trapped in the house with this axe-wielding maniac.

The axe! Drew had forgotten about the weapon. She whirled away from the door to find where it had fallen. It landed halfway down the stairs. Light bounced off its shiny head as if winking at her. She smiled; her gums rimmed with the bright red blood from her tongue bite.

As soon as Drew stepped toward the stairs, The Fireman appeared at the top of the second floor. The two stood in stalemate, the axe equidistant between them.

The Fireman stared Drew down. She stared back, hoping she looked more confident than she felt. Neither moved. Drew knew he was fucking with her. He wanted her to make the first move. He wanted her to try and get the axe. But she refused to give him what he wanted. She was going to run.

As if sensing her choice, The Fireman calmly picked up the axe. He stared at it as if seeing an old friend for the first time in a long while. Absence makes the heart grow fonder.

Drew raced into the dining room nearby. She grabbed a chair and heaved it at one of the enormous bay windows. She felt like an Olympian hurling whatever those rocks were called across a field. If she couldn't go out the front door, she'd make her own damned door, thank you very much. But the house had different plans. The wooden chair bounced off the storm window with a comical *thwomp* that sounded like the house itself was laughing at her. Drew ducked out of its way as it rebounded into the nearby boom box, finally killing the music. Drew stood in deadpan shock. "Are you fucking kidding me?"

There was no time to complain, The Fireman was still hunting. He banged the head of his axe against the wall, over and over, creating a thud that echoed through the house like he was ringing a demented dinner bell.

The dining room connected through an open archway into the kitchen. It was a mess, the sink littered with pots and pans, cereal boxes open on the counter, beer cans overflowing in the trash. It was no question that this was the home of four college kids.

Drew's attention was on the kitchen's backdoor. *Please, please, please.* She raced toward it, ignoring everything around her. All she wanted to do was grab the knob, fling it open, and flee into the woods. But there was no knob. He'd smashed it off, too. Drew cursed loudly, screaming in frustration. Her already limited options were dwindling by the second.

Peter Hall & Paul Gandersman

Drew shifted toward the basement staircase; her mind too focused on escape to notice a pair of Doc Marten boots poking out from behind the kitchen island. As Drew disappeared down the stairs, the young woman's feet twitched.

Rose Calder was still alive, and Drew was too busy to notice.

Chapter 3

DREW SKIMMED DOWN THE STAIRS THREE AT A TIME, MOVING SO fast and hard that the rickety carpentry swayed under her feet, threatening to knock her off balance. But she held strong, spilling into the dank basement.

It was a cavernous space. Drew's mom told her it had once been a workshop for the house's original owner, the architect Edwin Greywood who planned the entire subdivision and saved the best plot of land for his own family, but that was decades ago. The house changed owners at least once since then and these days the basement looked like a junkyard pretending to be a young man's bedroom. Drew's mom bought it as an investment property, but she'd had such a hard time flipping it that she eventually let Drew and her friends take it over until she could find a buyer. Once Eli saw the basement, he knew he wanted to live in it. The concrete walls and exposed ceiling beams gave it a rustic, manly feel; something Eli coveted but sorely lacked himself.

Eli was an unabashed nerd with a bad habit of collecting broken electronics out of the hope that, someday, he'd get around to fixing them. He rarely did, though. He was smart enough to do it, he just lacked the ambition. He was a C student that aced every test but just never bothered to do the homework. Drew gave up on her art projects;

Eli gave up on his electronics. For both, the idea of completing the thing was far more attractive than doing it.

All of this meant that Drew had to navigate a maze of crap to get to the basement's door. There were small, safety-code-compliant windows down there, but overgrown bushes blocked most of the outside light. There was no such blockage in front of the basement door, though. The moonlight beckoned. Freedom was so close.

Drew reached for the doorknob, only, it wasn't there. Her hand passed through the air. For a moment, she felt like a ghost, like the knob was there and she was the one who was missing.

But then reality sank in, yet again.

The Fireman smashed off this doorknob, too.

Of course he had. *Why the fuck wouldn't you see this coming?*

You're so fucking stupid.

Of course he smashed this one. He smashed them all. He's smarter than you.

They're all smarter than you.

You deserve this.

You deserve to die.

"Fuck off!" Drew yelled, surprising herself.

It wasn't at The Fireman. It wasn't even at herself. She was yelling at every snide comment from her mom that made her feel like a failure. She was yelling at every piece of advice Rose gave her that she ignored. She was yelling at the universe, at the space time continuum itself. She was calling out every swirling atom that led her to this moment of self-doubt.

Drew wasn't a failure. She was a fighter. And she was going to prove it. Drew spun away from the door in a mad dash to Eli's workbench. She tossed aside fried motherboards and disassembled computer parts until she found what she was looking for: needle nose pliers.

She rammed them into the shattered lock of the door in a desperate attempt to create her own handle. She kept working the pliers, trying every possible angle. "Open, open, open, open, why won't you fucking open?"

And then something changed inside the door. The needle nose snagged on the right piece of metal. *Holy fucking shit.* Drew twisted the pliers, and the lock turned in response. She savored the click and had a flash of a half-remembered movie where some cool guy in a denim jacket rammed a screwdriver into the ignition of a stolen car and twisted until the machine roared to life, driving off into the sunset. She ripped open the door, triumphant, defiant. The cool night air kissed her skin as she took her first step, crossing the threshold of the door, stepping out of Greywood House as its lone survivor.

But then she heard it.

A cough.

It was faint and distant, but unmistakable.

Drew looked up, beyond the tall trees and at the moon. It was full and gorgeous, an impossibly bright spotlight in the night sky illuminating her path to safety. She took another step, following the path.

But the coughing continued. It grew louder, harsher.

Someone upstairs in the house was still alive. And it wasn't Eli... It wasn't Wes...

Drew clenched her fists and stepped back into the basement.

"Rose! Is that you?" she whisper-shouted. The coughing intensified in reply; a haggard and desperate struggle for air, the human equivalent of an old car engine trying to turn over. Drew's face filled with optimism. Rose Calder was still alive. But then Drew's eyes were drawn to the moonlight again. All she had to do was run and be free of this nightmare. She'd be free to reach the police, free to get help. That was the responsible thing to do, right? To go get the police. To let them deal with The Fireman. Let the professionals save Rose.

Drew knew that was a lie. There was no way she could get help in time to save Rose. That maniac was upstairs with her best friend. Drew knew what she had to do. She had to turn around, storm back up those rickety stairs, confront The Fireman (again), and save Rose. Any other choice was selfish. Any other choice was one she'd regret for the rest of her life. Just thinking about it was wasting precious seconds Rose didn't have.

Drew charged back into the house, nearly face planting into the concrete after tripping over a crate of videotapes. She cursed Eli's messiness, even though she knew her room wasn't any cleaner. The coughing intensified as she scrambled back to her feet.

And then it stopped.

The house fell silent.

"Rose!" Drew screamed, no hint of a whisper this time. Her footsteps slowed as she neared the kitchen stairs, as if her brain knew what her heart wouldn't admit. She hesitated at the base of the stairs, wilting in the silence, praying that Rose would answer her; if not by calling out her name, at least with another cough, another *anything* to prove her best friend was still alive.

But there was only silence.

Drew looked up the staircase and saw nothing but darkness in the kitchen. She wondered if The Fireman had turned off the lights. Until the darkness moved, and Drew realized the lights weren't off; The Fireman's enormous body was blocking the path to the kitchen. He advanced down the staircase toward her. His steps were no longer slow and deliberate. He moved fast, shaking the staircase. He pounded the walls with his axe as he rushed downward. *THUD, THUD, THUD.*

Drew raced like hell back to the basement door, back to the moonlight, back to freedom. She leapt like an Olympic hurdler over piles of Eli's crap. The door had drifted shut, but she grabbed the plier-handle and ripped it open again. The door was barely open an inch when it slammed back shut. At first Drew thought the house itself had come alive and slammed it shut in her face. She liked that explanation more than what was really happening.

The Fireman had thrown his axe. It pinned the door back into its frame, closing it in front of Drew's horrified face. The sharp spike on the back of the axe was inches from Drew's right eye, threatening to perform crude surgery on her cornea.

Drew tried to scramble away from the near miss, but The Fireman was no longer patient. The game of cat and mouse was over. The Fireman charged at her like a freight train.

She never had a chance. The Fireman was on her before she could react. His hand reached out and grabbed her by the throat. He lifted her off the ground, his thick gloves closing off her oxygen supply. In a split second, he drove Drew's face into the spike, nailing her to the door like he was hanging a piece of art.

It wasn't like in the movies. The end didn't last an eternity. Drew didn't see a white light. Drew didn't watch a montage of her life's best moments. She didn't see her loved ones. She just felt blinding pain as the spike impaled the center of her forehead, splitting her open like a coconut. Skull, blood, brains; crack, splash, squish.

Drew Denns was dead.

For now.

THE GHOSTS

Chapter 4

DREW SPASMED AWAKE, HER PULSE POUNDING, GASPING FOR AIR as if someone had dunked her into an ice tank. The Fireman, the chase, the axe, her face; it had all been too real to feel like a dream, yet here she was, awake and alive. It must have been a dream, a hyperreal fantasy, The Fireman some nightmare cocktail of dissociated memories. Had she drunk more than she thought she had? She didn't think so, but this would be far from the first time she woke up with a ninja hangover. All she knew was Rose, Eli, and Wes must be moving about the house, going about their business just as alive as they'd been the day before.

Drew took slow breaths, alone but embarrassed for letting her imagination affect her on such a visceral level. Drew never put stock in dreams. The truth is, she rarely remembered them after waking up. Rose would always recall her own dreams to Drew in painstaking details and all Drew could ever share back were vague recollections that were the standard weird mix of sex, death, and social traumas. Normally recalling a dream felt like trying to remember a TV show she hadn't seen in a long time. This was different, though. There was no sleepy haze, no confused feelings, no imagery up for interpretation. She could remember every step The Fireman took toward her. She could remember the moonlight reflecting off the lake of Eli's blood (an oddly beautiful sight) and she could remember the point of The Fireman's axe as it raced into her forehead.

Drew stood, laughing at how silly she felt. The laughter stopped the second she turned around and saw her own dead body face down in a pool of coagulating blood.

"What. The. Fuck."

That was the only response that made sense. As Drew stared at her own corpse, she held up her hands, expecting them to be transparent. That's how ghosts worked, right? They were translucent, diaphanous beings that could walk through walls. They were Patrick Swayze sliding his arms around Demi Moore. They were goofy, marshmallowy globs of computer animation that chased Christina Ricci around giant mansions. Ghosts weren't mundane. They were special; unearthly and unbound from physics and logic, but here Drew was looking and feeling as normal as she possibly could.

Drew's hands looked solid; her fingernails still flecked with the black polish she'd been picking at for days. There wasn't a hair or mole that looked out of place. She wasn't floating off the ground. She was alive. Or, at least, she still *felt* alive. Drew remembered reading about people who suffered from phantom limb syndrome. They'd lose a foot or a hand in some kind of accident, but they could still feel every inch of their missing parts as if nothing happened. Their brains would tell them they were wiggling toes that no longer existed. Drew found it fascinating at the time, but now she wondered if she was experiencing phantom body syndrome.

Drew bent over her corpse. She hovered her hand over it, afraid to touch it, afraid to find out if she even could touch it. What would it mean if she could? Worse, what would it mean if she couldn't? *This is so fucked.* Drew took a deep breath and touched her own dead body. Well, kind of touched it. Drew could make contact with the corpse, but something about it still felt off, as if she were touching it, but somehow it wasn't touching back? And that's when she noticed the blood.

Drew was standing right in the middle of a lagoon of her own fluids that must have been drying for hours. It wasn't the bright vibrant red she was used to seeing gush from her body after something silly like slicing her thumb attempting to make a chopped salad. This red had deepened to an almost purple hue. It looked as if the blood itself had a disease. Sickly was the only word she could think of to describe it.

A chill rippled across Drew's skin. She lifted her foot, but the blood pool didn't seem to notice. There wasn't a drop on her Converse. Drew lowered her foot back into the blood, but it didn't ripple, it didn't cling to her, it didn't acknowledge her presence in any way.

Drew's pulse began to race. She stepped back out of the blood and felt a slight pain in her forehead, in the same place where the sharp end of the axe had lobotomized her, turning her into a human hat rack. She gently rubbed the unbroken skin while looking around the basement, half expecting someone to walk over to her and explain what was going on. Weren't you supposed to see a relative when you died? Wasn't Grandma supposed to be at the top of some escalator to the clouds?

"Hello?" Drew called out meekly, but there was no one to hear her, no one to greet her, no grandmother to welcome her sweetly to the afterlife — if that's even what you could call this. Sunlight was filtering in from the basement windows. It had been dark when Drew was last conscious. She struggled to remember the exact time. It must have been around four or five in the morning. Was it morning now? How long had Drew been dead? *Is dead even the right word?* Drew looked at her corpse once again. Her white tank top had soaked up the blood like a sponge. Whatever principle of fluid dynamics caused the soaking effect must have weakened halfway up the fabric, giving the impression she'd been wearing a shirt that was red in the front and white in the back. It almost looked deliberate, like some kind of macabre tie dye fashion statement. But it wasn't. It was a horrible, terrifying mistake. *Yes, dead is the right word.* Drew thought. *Fucking murdered is even better.*

Drew maneuvered through the messy room, shouting out for anyone to come help her. Her throat had hurt from screaming at The Fireman when this all started, but she couldn't feel that any longer. There was a slight tingle to it, like she was getting over a cough, but that was all. She started to realize that her whole body felt distant, as if the events of the night before had happened to someone else and she'd just watched. Her movement around the basement slowed, growing more deliberate. She was afraid to take a wrong step, afraid to get caught sneaking around as a ghost. She could hear her mom's voice crystal clear. "God damn it, Drew, why can't you act like a proper ghost?"

Drew couldn't help but smile at the idea, and the smile quickly turned into a laugh that was so sharp and sudden it almost sounded like a bark. It was just all so ridiculous. She couldn't be a ghost. Could she? She took a deep breath. Well, it felt like breathing. She wasn't sure if air was actually flowing through her lungs, or if this was more phantom body effect. Drew wondered if she even still had lungs, or anything inside her at all.

She touched everything she could, waiting for her hands to pass through something. Eli's dirty clothes (piled just like hers), the concrete wall, the stack of VHS tapes, the TV. Drew could touch them all. Or, perhaps more accurately, it *felt* to Drew like she was touching them. But just as when she'd touched her own dead body, the contact felt one-sided. She collapsed on Eli's mattress.

Her mind circled the drain of an existential crisis. She grabbed Eli's pillow, screamed into it, and threw herself backward onto the bed. As she fell, her leg accidentally smacked the bottom of Eli's computer table. Her kick not only shook the table enough to vibrate Eli's mouse, but she felt a dull throb from her stubbed toe.

Since when can ghosts get hurt? What the fuck is happening? Am I in Hell? Did I die and go straight to fucking Hell?

Drew's downward spiral was interrupted as Eli's computer monitor flickered on, awakened by the trackball's movement. The screensaver was a scantily clad bikini model leaning over a red Ferrari. Drew rolled her eyes at the picture but couldn't help but stare. There was something about the lameness of it, the stereotype of the dorky computer kid ogling an unattainable woman on top of an equally unattainable car that gave her a comforting sense of normalcy. It was a stupid but inarguably human thing, which was exactly what Drew needed as she was feeling less and less human. Drew couldn't help but wonder how many other pictures Eli browsed through before deciding yes, *this* is the one for me. The idea of it made her laugh.

"Drew? Is that you?"

The voice drifted down from the kitchen, small, and timid, as if whomever it came from wanted so desperately to be heard but was afraid they might be heard by the wrong person. Yet for as faint and scared as the voice was, it was unmistakable. Drew's eyes went wide.

Chapter 5

ROSE CALDER STARED DOWN AT HER OWN CORPSE. SHE FOCUSED on her dead face. It looked almost peaceful, like she had decided to take a nap and simply never woke up. But then Rose's eyes drifted to the rest of the body and there was no peace to be found as she remembered all too vividly what it was like to die.

A thick phone cord was wrapped around her neck, its tangles lacerating deep into her flesh. There were even more cuts all over her skin, but they were from Rose's own fingernails as she tried to claw the cord off. Rose hadn't realized at the time how close she'd gotten but could see now the cord's plastic shielding had torn away, exposing the thin copper wires inside. It looked so fragile, so delicate, as if all she had left to do was give it a final tug and the whole thing would have broken and unraveled, filling her lungs with a life-saving rush of air.

But The Fireman had been too strong.

He pulled that phone cord so hard around her neck that Rose thought it was going to slice clean through, beheading her. Instead, it slowly cut off the oxygen to her body, and as her brain underwent hypoxia, all of Rose's senses went funny. She'd never done drugs — her aunt raised her to treat her body like a temple one should never pollute — but she'd heard enough from Drew and others to know, even if anecdotally, what getting high was supposed to feel like. And as she felt her body melt away and become weightless, as she watched the world around her tunnel to nothingness, she had a final, profoundly vivid thought: *I should have lived more. If anyone was going to destroy my temple, it should have been me.*

Rose couldn't pry her eyes away from the corpse. Her hand started twitching uncontrollably and she had the overwhelming sensation that she was dying again, that the cord was back around her neck, strangling her all over again. Her hand involuntarily shot up to her neck, massaging where the cord had been. She knew she was dead; she knew her spirit had transcended from the physical to the ethereal, but even still, no amount of rationalizing could build a big enough barrier to hold back the very real sensations and memories now crashing down on her like waves in a storm.

Drew had gone to bed, leaving Rose behind with just Eli. Rose thought they might end up chatting for a little longer and she'd go crash herself, but then she and Eli ended up hanging out together for hours. They weren't even talking the entire time. Sometimes a silence would fall, and the two of them would just sit there, nursing their beers, listening to whatever CD was in the boombox. The album would end, and then one of them would get up to put in another. It was lovely. Until he showed up.

Eli had stood to skip the track and The Fireman was just standing in the middle of the dining room, axe in hand. He didn't say anything, he didn't even do anything, he just stood there staring at the two of them like they were the ones who had broken into *his* house. At first Rose thought he had the wrong address or something, but he just stared back, chest heaving. Rose had long considered herself an empath who could read someone's aura. The Fireman had no aura though. It's not that she couldn't read him, no, he was completely empty on the inside.

That's when Rose dropped whatever polite attitude she'd managed up until that point and demanded that The Fireman leave the house. Rose tried to go open the front door for him and he reacted by lunging at her and smashing the knob clean off the door. Eli started shouting. It was almost impressive seeing Eli stand up to this giant of a man, but it proved to be a mistake. The Fireman swung his axe at Eli and the rest was a blur. Rose remembered grabbing the kitchen phone off its cradle and dialing 911, but before she could even beg for help, The Fireman was on her, choking her with the very thing she so foolishly thought would be her lifeline.

And then she'd blacked out the first time. Rose stirred back to life again at some point and called for help, but he'd returned just as she was waking and finished the job. So here she was now, staring at her own lifeless body.

Rose gripped her crystal necklace tight in her right hand. Aunt Bea had given it to Rose at her parent's funeral, telling her it belonged to her mother. Rose said she'd never take it off and had stayed true to that word for the last ten years. The crystal was a security blanket to her. Whenever she was stressed, she'd touch the crystal and imagine she was holding hands with her mom. It calmed her every single time, without fail.

Until now. Rose was too troubled by the fact that the crystal existed both around her neck and the neck of her corpse at the same time. Her left hand was squeezing the fabric of her flowy dress, drawing it together in tight balls and then releasing it, only to repeat the process again and again, both hands trying to find some sort of physical grounding when what her eyes were seeing was so unbelievable. After her parent's death, Rose had been raised by Aunt Bea to understand and respect the connection between this world and those beyond, but now that she was actually *in* the beyond, nothing was as she expected.

This wasn't what was supposed to happen when you died. She'd been obsessed with figuring out the afterlife ever since her parents' death. Bea had all kinds of theories about the afterlife, of course, but Rose had latched onto her own favorite: reincarnation. She believed in it because it seemed the least terrifying, and because she refused to believe her parents had just poofed out of existence like clouds disappearing in the sky, leaving nothing behind but a lost little girl.

Rose rubbed the crystal harder, tracing tiny, figure eight loops in its smooth surface with her right hand, balling up her dress with her left hand, unable to take her eyes off of Dead Rose, off of this intimate stranger, this woman with the pale face and the blue neck, when suddenly a dull thud filled her ears. Rose flinched, always the scaredy cat, fearing the return of The Fireman. But he wasn't there. In fact, it was a different sound entirely. This wasn't a judge's gavel, it was a stubbed toe, and it was followed by the sound of a young woman cursing.

Rose tip-toed over to the basement stairs. She peered down them but couldn't see anything. The staircase was surprisingly long, and the light faded before it hit the bottom. Rose crept as close to the edge as she could muster and softly called out. "Drew? Is that you?"

Chapter 6

Drew gazed up the wooden staircase. The kitchen above seemed even farther away than before. When she was running from The Fireman, the staircase seemed so short it felt like she practically fell into the basement. Of course, Drew had been running for her life, barreling forward without hesitation. Now, in the light of day and without a slasher chasing her, the wooden staircase seemed to stretch on and on and on before disappearing into a wall of blinding light above.

Drew was frozen in shock. Was this the heaven moment she'd been expecting? Was Grandma about to step out of the light, milk and cookies in hand? Or was Drew supposed to go up there, into the light? Or were you not supposed to go into the light? Was that the bad thing? Drew couldn't remember.

Before Drew could decide, a woman stepped into the light, and Drew felt her entire body seize up. She would have guessed her heart had stopped beating, but first she'd have to figure out if she still had a heartbeat. Drew stared up in awe at the woman floating in the light. There was an angelic airiness that surrounded her. The hem of her dress ruffled slightly in the air as if it were defying gravity. Drew's heart raced. This was it. This was the moment. She was going to go into the light. She had a good feeling about it. This was definitely the right choice. She was going to leave this all behind. She was going to heaven.

The woman took a step closer, and all those thoughts of hope, of Grandma and heaven, popped like a balloon. Rose's silhouette was unmistakable, and once again Drew felt like a fool for letting herself believe in a fantasy, believe something good could happen to her. Drew's self-deprecation was fleeting, though, as the thought of going into the great beyond gave way to the realization that she wasn't alone in all of this.

Rose took a cautious step down the stairs. Her voice cracked. "Drew? Is that really you?"

Drew stepped forward; her toe tapped nervously on the stairs. She felt her whole body vibrating from frayed nerves. "You can see me?"

Rose nodded, tears welling in her eyes. Drew's face exploded with relief, and she rushed up the staircase, which seemed to shrink in size as she moved, from a grand stairway to heaven to an old, rickety piece of woodwork. Rose didn't have time to move before Drew made it to the top of the stairs and the two slammed into one another in a deep hug. Rose felt warm — she always did — and Drew pulled her in even tighter, clinging to her friend out of the fear that if she let go, Rose would vanish just as quickly as she'd appeared.

"Rose, I'm so sorry," Drew whispered. She hadn't even meant to say it, but the guilt from being unable to save her was more profound than Drew realized.

"Don't be. This is a good thing," Rose said, taking Drew aback. She could tell Rose's life-long history of unbridled optimism had already kicked in. Unlike Drew, whose own mom inadvertently raised her to be deeply cynical, Rose had long been raised to always see the good in everything, whether it be people, places, or, apparently, the afterlife. It was something Drew often teased her about but found immediate comfort in now. Drew pulled back from the embrace, her face scrunched up in confusion. "How is this possibly a good thing?"

"We're still here," Rose replied. "And if we're here, it means something. It means we have a purpose." How was she so cool, so nonchalant about the whole thing? It made Drew feel dumb for having felt so afraid. Drew blinked back at her, and Rose smiled her perfect, sunny day of a face, and despite her best efforts otherwise, Drew could feel her shoulders relaxing, could feel Rose's optimism spreading to her like a happy virus.

"Oh yeah, what's our purpose?" A man's voice quipped from the dining room.

Drew and Rose's faces dropped in unified surprise. They turned to find Eli standing by the dining room table, looking as if he'd just woken up from a bad hangover.

Eli Adams always felt like the third wheel to Drew and Rose's friendship. Not that he minded much. He enjoyed being on the periphery of things. Just outside the spotlight was where he thrived. Drew once called him an extroverted introvert and he thought it was one of the nicest things anyone had ever said about him. That was before, though, when he was alive, and his biggest concerns were how to balance things like what his parents wanted him to do (finish his degree in Computer Science) and what he wanted to do (work at Suncoast for the next twenty years and be perfectly content). Things changed drastically the second he "woke up" staring at the inside of his own skull. He'd never felt so invisible, so disposable. He stared at his corpse and felt like he had awakened in some kind of Tales from the Crypt episode where his wish to be invisible was granted in the most fucked up way possible.

"You're here!" Rose shouted as she and Drew simultaneously ran over to him, pulling him in a tight hug. His cheeks involuntarily bloomed in a cherry blush. Eli pulled back from the hug, trying to catch his breath from being squeezed a bit too tight. "Yeah, as a goddamned ghost."

Rose's eyes scrunched up a bit. "We're not ghosts." She said.

She spoke in a defensive tone, as if Eli had just insulted her honor.

He always thought of himself as the Chandler to Rose's Phoebe; they had chemistry together, but their storylines only ever crossed when someone else was involved. Until last night. Most of the time she laughed at his dumb jokes, but every now and then he crossed a line he didn't realize Rose had. This didn't feel like one of those times, though. His brain started backpedaling, trying to figure out what to say that wouldn't offend her, when Drew pointed into the kitchen at Rose's corpse.

"If we're not ghosts, then what the hell do you call that?" Drew asked. Eli glanced behind the kitchen island to where Drew was pointing. Rose's strangled body was crumpled on the floor. He recoiled in horror. Seeing his own dead body was one thing but seeing Rose like that was making this next level real.

Rose paced and clutched her crystal necklace, her thumb running over it in circles. She looked deeply anxious. It made Eli feel like a real jerk. This was complicated, and even though they were all struggling to figure it out, he didn't want to make her feel ashamed for not wanting to admit the obvious; they were worm food and yet somehow still walking around like nothing had ever happened.

Eli began rambling, tripping over his words, trying to find the right way to acknowledge everything that happened without coming off like he didn't care, that the truth was he was starting to think all of this was pretty cool. Now that the initial shock of being dead was wearing off, he was starting to feel surprisingly alive. The world had changed in an instant, everything he thought he knew exploded in some kind of big bang moment, ushering in a new, post-corporeal universe filled with possibilities. If he enjoyed being a wallflower before, he was going to love being on *this* side of the wall. Being a ghost was just going to be the ultimate wallflower existence, right?

"Well, I just mean ghost is such a loaded word. We're more like... wandering souls," Rose clarified. Eli's eyes rolled uncontrollably. "Wandering souls" just sounded a bit too hippyish to him, like the vegan way of saying ghost. His inadvertent eye roll stung Rose a bit, and once again he felt a pang of remorse for accidentally doing something to make her feel bad. Rose turned away from him and Eli threw his hands up in defense.

"Okay, fine, call us whatever you want, but I'm going with ghost. And do you know why?" He pointed at Rose. "You're dead" He pointed at Drew. "And I haven't been downstairs yet, but I'm pretty sure you're dead." Eli pointed at himself. "And I'm mega dead in the other room. Wanna know what gives it away?" Eli raised his eyebrows, waiting for an answer. He didn't realize it, but he was grinning. Drew waved Eli to go ahead and tell them.

"It's not the fact that Rose's corpse is laying right there." Eli motioned for them to follow him as he walked over to the foyer. He peaked back just to make sure they were still with him. Drew was watching intently. Rose had gone back to idly rubbing the crystal around her neck. Eli wondered if it was more than just a safety blanket thing and if it was bordering on OCD behavior. He was no stranger to that himself, obsessively rewinding video tapes at the store. The tape deck — a not-for-retail unit that could rewind tapes twice as fast as the high-end Sony player he had at home — would stop, and even though he knew it was back at the beginning, he'd still press rewind once more just to be sure. He silently shamed himself every time he did.

Eli continued his grandstanding. He was enjoying having their eyes on him, hanging on his every word. "It's not because I now know what the inside of my skull looks like," he said, cocking his head over to his own dead body in the foyer. Drew half-glanced at it, unshocked by the state of the corpse, and Eli wondered if she'd already seen it. She must have. If Drew died in the basement, she must have come across this already. The Fireman had caught him by surprise. He shuddered, wondering what Drew and Rose went through after he'd been killed.

Unlike Drew, Rose was staring intently at Eli's body, transfixed by the jagged split down Eli's head, the shards of white bone that poked through matted tangles of hair, the chunks of brain that once had a pinkish hue but were quickly greying. Eli was surprised by the reaction. He loved to play pranks on Rose because he knew she was so twitchy and would jump at even the slightest loud voice, but this was different.

Her eyes were growing misty and distant. Eli knew she needed a distraction, knew he needed to wrap up his rambling.

Eli pointed out the farthest living room window that looked out onto the far edge of the front porch. He couldn't help but smile, knowing he was about to blow their minds. "That lady is what gives it away," Eli beamed.

Outside on the porch was a middle-aged policewoman, her face pressed against the glass, her hands cupped around her eyes to block out the light so she could see inside the house. Like Rose, the policewoman wore a necklace, but hers was Jesus on the cross. The woman lifted the cross to her mouth and kissed it, her eyes welling up with tears. Eli couldn't hear her, but he could see her lips moving quickly. He didn't know the words but was pretty sure it was a prayer.

Drew and Rose both ran to the window, waving their arms, shouting at the woman, telling her they were inside, that they were okay. Eli shook his head, explaining that she couldn't see them. But Drew didn't care, she wanted help. She wanted answers. She pounded on the window and the sound reverberated throughout the house.

Outside, the policewoman heard nothing. She couldn't see Drew, Rose, or Eli's ghostly forms, only The Fireman's bloody carnage splattered around the old house. Eli wondered if that's how the afterlife was going to work. They weren't just invisible to this living woman: she didn't even seem to exist on their plane of existence. He could see the glass window vibrate as Drew pounded on it. The lady on the porch was clueless.

The policewoman turned around, continued the quiet prayer under her breath, and walked over to three more police cars arriving on the scene. A gaggle of nosy neighbors from houses scattered throughout the sprawling subdivision had gathered to get a peek at what was going on. It was easy to tell that something was seriously wrong at Greywood House.

Drew pointed at the handful of officers that were strapping on bullet proof vests and turned to Rose for answers, but Rose had none.

Eli did. "They're coming in. They probably think The Fireman is still here."

Eli's mention of The Fireman instantly put Drew and Rose on edge. The house grew eerily still. All three surveyed it, listening for sounds, listening for his thunderous footsteps to awaken the house once more. But there was only silence. Too much silence.

A realization hit Drew. "Wait. Where's your brother?" Eli shook his head, confused. Wes had a show last night. His band, The Ruins, had been booking more and more gigs, much to the frustration of their parents who wanted Wes to just give the whole music thing up. They'd only been in the house a week, and Wes had maybe only spent the first night sleeping there.

Drew's face sunk. She looked mortified, like she knew a deep, dark secret. Eli was smart, he had a brain that was a slave to logic, but part of him must not have wanted to pick up on what Drew was not-so-subtly laying down because he just blinked back at her.

"He wasn't here." Eli mumbled, confused.

"I'm sorry, Eli," Drew said. Rose gripped his arm, showing solidarity. He didn't quite understand why. It's not like Drew just said Rose's brother had also been brutally murdered last night. He turned away from them, racing up the stairs to Wes's room, his voice cracking as he called out his brother's name. He and Wes weren't close — far from it, despite now being roommates — but he still dreaded the idea of his brother having also been a victim of The Fireman.

Rose interlocked her fingers into Drew's hand, seeking calm. "It's going to be fine," Rose said aloud, as much to herself as to Drew.

Drew pulled her hand back. "No, it isn't, Rose. We were *murdered*. That man took everything from us."

"Not everything." Rose patted her chest. "He didn't take our souls. And if we're here, we have a..."

"Oh spare me the *we all find our purpose* pep talk just this one time. I didn't believe that bullshit before, and I definitely don't now," Drew snapped back.

Rose took a moment to breathe before responding. She knew this was a typical Drew pattern. Drew lunged at things. Her aunt once called Drew a "creature of impulse," and Rose thought it was the most apt description she'd ever heard. Allowing for these momentary pauses was something she'd learned from years of conversation with Drew, years of arguments, years of trying to help Drew make the right choices.

Rose took Drew's hand again. "Look around, Drew. Maybe it's time you finally start believing in something."

Chapter 7

WES ADAMS ALWAYS FELT LIKE TWO DIFFERENT PEOPLE: THE person he was and the rockstar he wanted people to *think* he was. Before today, that divide had been aspirational, but as Wes sat on the edge of his sheetless bed, staring at his own corpse pilloried in the middle of the room, the personality split became all too literal.

Wes scanned his impaled corpse, seeing himself as he never quite had before. He'd spent so much time trying to play the part of the edgy punk singer, wearing stolen jeans that he'd rip with scissors, faded t-shirts from bands he'd never actually seen in person, with a flannel long sleeve shirt permanently wrapped around his waist, and a tattered black baseball cap that kept his long, dirty blonde hair somewhat in check. He could literally play the part, too; his guitar skills, while not Eddie Van Halen level by any means, were more than capable of nailing the noisy grunge that had become so popular in the mid '90s. But playing the part also meant acting like he never gave a damn about anything, particularly school. He certainly had to act like he didn't want his nerdy brother Eli around. Deep down, Wes loved his younger brother, but he'd spent so much time throughout high school and now the first couple years of college pretending like he wanted nothing to do with Eli that it stopped feeling like an act. A part of him regretted that, but that part was silenced by the dive bar god persona he'd spent years cultivating.

Wes's room was dark, just how he liked it. Blackout curtains blocked any light from making its way in. Strings of neon lights hung around the room, giving it a vague concert stage feel. It was a mess, but he didn't care. It was a mess that he knew how to thrive in. Surrounded by Snickers wrappers, beer cans, and a three-foot-tall stack of Ramen noodles, were shelves and shelves of CDs. He brought his whole collection with him to stay in Drew's mom's house. It wasn't even an option to leave them at his parents' place. His dad wouldn't bother selling them out from under him, he'd just trash 'em.

Plus, Wes needed access to all his inspiration at a moment's notice. He had a pair of electric guitars resting on stands, an acoustic sitting on the bed itself, and a mic stand in the center of the room, though that was currently doing its best to keep his corpse standing upright. When Wes woke up, he'd found his formerly living body arched backward, speared on the stand. He touched it, thinking he was in a dream, and the body slumped forward. It now looked like his corpse was preparing to stage dive into a sea of adoring fans.

All that work learning, practicing, and playing the part was gone in an instant, flipped off like a light switch. What did it matter now? What had it gotten him? A broken brain, that's what. For the last few years, he'd shoot or snort or drink whatever the hell someone at the party shoved in his face. He didn't enjoy it all, per se, it was just more of the show he put on for people.

Wes acted like everyone was a fan in need of entertainment and he could never let them down. But all of that karma (or "sinful behavior," as his mom called it) had caught up to him and he was now having an out-of-body experience so vivid it was really starting to convince him something might be seriously fried inside of him. *This is your brain on drugs,* the annoying commercial echoed in his thoughts. But he didn't remember taking anything other than cold medicine the night before. The Ruins were supposed to play a gig, but he wasn't feeling a hundred percent, so he grabbed a bottle of Robitussin from the 7-11 on the way home, took a few pulls straight from the bottle, and crashed for the night. The room had started to spin right as he passed out, and that was all he could remember. There had been a dream of some tall guy standing over him. But that had been just a dream. Or, at worst, a robotrip from the 'tussin. Right?

Wes took off his hat and ran his fingers through his mane of hair, muttering to himself about how this wasn't real. He sighed, exhausted even though he'd just woken up. His eyes landed on a nearby old rotary phone. It was an ancient thing that was in the room when he moved in. He didn't even know the phone number to the house yet.

Wes's foot started nervously tapping as he stared at the phone. He reached out and plucked the receiver from its cradle. He couldn't remember the last time he'd used a rotary phone. His Grandma had one growing up, and he loved dialing on it, listening to the sound of the disc as it cranked back to its default position. She used to unplug it from the wall and let him pretend to use it. The memory made him want to smile, but his mind was too toasted to register anything close to happiness. He felt like he was in a waking nightmare.

Wes put the receiver to his ear. There was a dial tone, it sounded far off, as if hearing it across a great chasm. Before he could think about what he was doing, his fingers were dialing a number. The rotor in the phone made a click-click-click sound as it settled back into place. All he had to do was dial one more number to complete the call, but he hesitated. His finger lingered over the digit and his eyes drifted back to his corpse. The dead body looked almost peaceful, like a mannequin posed in a record shop window. If it had been a picture on an album cover, Wes would have loved it, telling all his friends about how hardcore it was, and that this was what he was talking about whenever he ranted about how they needed to be bolder, how they needed to sledgehammer people's attention. But it wasn't an album cover, it was his own dead body.

Fuck it. Wes dialed the final digit. He heard the line start to ring. He crossed invisible fingers in his mind, growing twitchy and worried about what he was going to say. After what felt like an eternity of rings, a gruff, annoyed voice answered. "Who is this?" Wes breathed a sigh of relief.

"Dad, it's me. I, uh, I took something and... and I'm losing my mind. I'm scared. I'm so fucking scared, dad."

Wes waited for a response. He waited for his dad to lay into him, to berate him about how he told him the last time he called looking for a handout was the final time he was going to help his sorry ass. But instead, there was a prolonged silence until finally Mr. Adams shouted. "I said, who the hell is calling me?"

"Dad? It's me. Can you hear me? I need your help," Wes's voice cracked an octave. After another agonizing silence, Mr. Adams barked again, and his voice grew quieter as he moved the phone away from his ear. The old man's sandpaper voice shouted off to the side, calling to his wife, "Goddamnit. It's one of Wes's dumbass friends. He has the stupidest fucking—"

Click. His dad hung up. Wes stared at the phone, his eyes welling. He hadn't even consciously decided to call his old man for help, so he didn't know why he would feel so strongly about it, but there was something in that click, a finality as the dial tone hit, that was like hearing the last word on the matter. His dad might as well have said, "You're on your own, you little fucking moron," and slammed the door in his face.

Wes's legs shook intensely. The dead body in the room lost its mannequin-esque appeal and seemed to grow in size, looming over him like an anthropomorphic tombstone. Wes pictured the body coming alive, its stiff joints grinding back into their sockets as it rose upright, pulled the microphone stand out of its chest, and used it to impale him, the "real" Wes.

His chest grew tight as he remembered it happening. He could feel the metal pole sliding into his skin, piercing it with ease, sneaking between the ribs, forcing its way into a space that was meant for lean muscle, not a two-inch piece of pipe, cracking the bones like his mom's overcooked Thanksgiving turkey. Wes couldn't breathe. He collapsed off the bed, staring upright at the corpse. He could feel a popping in his chest as the metal wormed past the ribs and entered his lungs, tearing through them with a wet squish before meeting more ribs on the other side and repeating the same agonizing bone cracking on the way back out.

Wes gasped for air. He pounded on his chest, on his heart, not knowing why or what it would accomplish, just knowing that he needed to do something, that he needed to break free of this feeling, that he needed to snap back into control of his body. But he couldn't. He was failing. His movement slowed. His vision blurred. The room spun, and Wes felt it all slip away, felt the world leave him as he died all over again.

Then suddenly, the door burst open, flooding the room with light that hit Wes like a jolt from a defibrillator, zapping a tiny measure of life back into him. Someone cursed loudly, and Wes turned to find Eli standing in the doorway, staring at the impaled corpse in the center of the room.

The vision, the very real sensation, of being impaled washed away as Eli ran into the room. Wes leapt into the air, jumping into Eli's arms, his face wet with tears.

"Are you okay, man?" Eli asked, clearly disarmed by this rare display of vulnerability.

Wes instinctively pushed him away, wiped his eyes, and shifted back into performance mode. "I'm fine. I was just..." His eyes drifted over to the phone. Before Wes could finish his thought, he was cut off by something smashing so hard downstairs that it rattled the master bedroom. It sounded like the walls of the house were being demolished by a wrecking ball. They turned to one another, frozen until a second bang spurred them back to action. Wes grabbed Eli's arm, clutching him tightly.

Eli had never seen Wes act like this. For a few years now, his older brother had always been stoic, always been too cool for hugs or even high fives, and the last time he could remember anything close to this moment was when they were just kids and their parents had gone out for the evening, leaving them home alone. They'd been watching an episode of Saturday Night Live when the news cut in with an emergency broadcast. There was a tornado heading directly their way and the two of them panicked, trying to remember what to do and where to go. Wes had taken charge, grabbing Eli's trembling hand and tucking them both deep into the back of the downstairs closet right as the wind began to roar like a jet engine.

They were fine. There was no serious damage to the house, just some outdoor furniture tossed into the neighbor's yard, but from inside that closet it sounded like the apocalypse, like God himself was about to pluck their entire house from the ground and smash it to bits in a blender of wind and rain. Even then, even when they both thought their world was ending and they were still young and full of imagination and humanity and love for one another, Wes hadn't looked as scared, or clutched Eli as tightly, as he did now. The look in Wes's eyes worried Eli more than any of the afterlife insanity so far.

Chapter 8

DREW AND ROSE STOOD TO THE SIDE AS THE FRONT DOOR TOOK ITS first hit. It sounded so loud and so forceful that she was surprised the door didn't explode inward. There was another ram, and another, yet still the door stood firm, as if the house, knowing what had happened here, was trying desperately to keep anyone else from coming in ever again. Drew knew it had been built in the late '50s or '60s, back when building codes weren't nearly as strict but the materials themselves were robust. It clearly made a difference, and Drew briefly recalled that one of the reasons her mom bought the house in the first place was because it had "good bones."

The house's bones couldn't stand up forever to the miniature army of men outside, though, and a final swing did the job, knocking the enormous slab of oak off its hinges. In an instant, six cops swarmed in, guns drawn. Their hands worked in quick, silent communication as they split off in pairs to explore the murder house. Drew, never a fan of guns, felt a tingle of fear at the sight of the firearms, and Rose instinctively threw her hands up in surrender. Realizing how silly that was, she quickly put them back down, shooting Drew an embarrassed smile as she did.

The cops swarmed in with impressive speed and coordination, but all slowed to take in Eli's body, which looked like the centerpiece in an enormous area rug made of blood. One cop, the youngest of the bunch, started to vomit, throwing a gloved hand over his face to block the spew, but was a second too late. Chunks of breakfast sprayed out, landing in the blood. "Jesus Christ, Boyd. Get it together," barked his superior officer as Boyd stumbled back out the door. Another cop laughed, accusing the rookie of contaminating the crime scene.

Drew and Rose gave the remaining police a wide berth as they swept through the house in their carefully coordinated pairs. The two officers in the kitchen shouted to the others upon finding Rose's body. They called her "another vic," which amused Drew. She'd never really been around police before, her only exposure to them being movies and TV shows. She didn't think they talked like that in real life. Turns out they did. Rose squirmed. Drew knew she'd hate the idea of strange men inspecting, and inevitably touching, her body.

Eli and Wes arrived at the top of the stairs, startled at the sight of two officers approaching, and dodged out of the way. "Whoa, things just got interesting," Eli laughed.

Drew shook her head. "I'm sorry, was this too boring before?"

Eli made his way downstairs, a grin growing. "Look around you, Drew. We're ghosts. Real, no joke, ghosts! They can't see us. They can't hear us. But we're here. It's incredible!"

"I told you, we're not ghosts, we're wandering spirits," Rose interjected.

"What the fuck is a wandering spirit?" barked Wes. Eli cringed. He could tell Wes had no patience for what he called Rose's "hippie bullshit."

Rose and Drew looked to the top of the stairs. Wes stood there, defiant. The vulnerability Eli's brother had shown in his room was gone. He was back to playing the tough guy, and Eli could already tell neither Drew nor Rose was thrilled at the prospect of being trapped in the afterlife with Wes. Not that Wes cared enough about them to notice their expressions. Drew had once told Eli that any conversation she had with Wes inevitably found him spending more time looking at her chest than her face. Even though logically he knew he couldn't control Wes's actions, Eli always felt a deeply rooted guilt any time he heard something like that.

"Holy fucking shit!" Wes yelled as he finally glimpsed Eli's bloody corpse, doing a double take between the mess on the floor and the ghost standing next to him. Wes turned to Rose, a smugness growing. "My brother's head is split open like a watermelon, and you don't think we're dead?"

"I never said we weren't dead, I said we weren't ghosts. That word is too simple." Rose said.

"Oh really, Rose? Because it seems pretty fucking simple to me. Axe plus head equals ghost, not some wandering spirit bullshit." Wes laughed.

"Call it whatever you want, dickhead. We're here for a reason."

"Oh, yeah? What's that?"

"I don't know yet." Rose said, a bit sheepish at having to admit it.

"You've got all those crystal balls and shit upstairs, but you don't fucking know anything, Rose. You're just full of—"

Drew stepped between the two, giving Wes a taste of his own tough guy medicine. Eli had seen her play the anti-authority, anti-bullshit punk routine just as well as Wes. Wes turned his beady eyes away from Rose and onto Drew. He grinned.

"Screw you, Drew. This is all your fault."

"My fault? How is this my fault?"

"It's your house, isn't it?"

Drew scoffed at him, but Eli knew her well enough to tell she was caught off guard by the accusation.

"Are you serious? Is he serious?" Drew looked to Eli for back-up, and he felt suddenly awkward, like a kid caught in an argument between his parents. Eli couldn't stand conflict. Any time they had to deal with a snooty customer at Suncoast, Eli relied on Drew to step in and play the bad cop. "Are you fucking serious, Eli? You think I did this?"

"No. Not you, no." Eli said, hoping that would be enough to make Drew happy. But the truth was Wes's accusation did make a tiny, guilty hint of sense. It was Mrs. Denns's house after all, and that simple fact extended more responsibility to Drew than anyone else.

Drew's eyes narrowed at him, trying to suss out what exactly he wasn't saying. Eli knew he was a bad liar, so he often defaulted to lying by omission, which he found easier to do. It seemed Drew was seeing right through it, though.

"I've been living here just as long as you have. I know just as much about the house as you, and I know just as much about whoever the hell that psycho was as any of you do."

Eli raised his hands, surrendering. He wasn't looking for an argument. He just wanted to figure out *why* the hell they were ghosts.

Wes scoffed them both off. He wasn't the best at listening. Growing up, everyone had blamed it on his attention span, slapping him with the catch-all label of ADD. Wes used it to his advantage. Need more time to finish a test? Out came the ADD card. And since his Ritalin was to be taken at the same time every day, it afforded him a hall pass each afternoon to walk to the nurse's office. The truth was he didn't have ADD nearly as bad as he led everyone to believe. Wes just didn't care enough to focus on anything that didn't immediately benefit himself.

Wes smacked Eli's chest and pointed out the window, directing everyone's attention to the group at the bottom of the driveway. The police had strung a flimsy strip of yellow tape between two trees, which was apparently all it took to hold back the elderly neighbors murmuring amongst themselves, trying to determine what was going on. Wes thought they looked like actual sheep in a corral, with their grey hair and obedient fear keeping them from straying past a goddamned ribbon of plastic. But Wes didn't care about the sheeple, he was slapping Eli in the chest so that he'd see a trio of thin, long-haired Wes doppelgangers storming toward the house. They were the other members of The Ruins and the fact that they'd bothered to come check on Wes filled him with a joy he'd never admit to. They wove through the crowd and ducked under the tape, much to the dismay of the sheeple behind them.

The Ruins called out Wes's name. Wes yelled back to them, but they couldn't hear it. An officer leaning against a patrol car turned to intercept them, forcing them back under the yellow tape. Wes yelled at the cops, "Fucking pigs!" The cops were oblivious to him, of course. He felt ignored, unheard, and it made his blood boil. Wes slapped the wall, yelling louder. He was going to make those cops hear him. Nothing was going to stop him from reuniting with The Ruins. If he'd just gone out with them the night before like he was supposed to, he wouldn't even be there. *Fuck.* The band literally would have saved him. None of this would have ever happened.

As the big picture sank in, Wes's anger swelled. He moved quickly from the living room windows to the front door, breaking into a full sprint, shouting at the cops, shouting to his clueless friends being led away from the house. He rounded the corner, racing through the wide-open front door.

And then it happened.

Wes disappeared.

In thin air.

Poof.

Eli could have sworn he heard the sound of his brother disappearing. It was a soft swishing sound, as if the universe had sucked him up with a straw. Rose screamed, clutching her crystal necklace tightly. Drew froze, an unmistakable look on her face that said the same thing they were all thinking: *What. The. Fuck.*

And then, in a blink, Wes re-appeared.

He hurtled through the air next to Eli, as if a great force had picked him up and thrown him violently back into the house. Wes collided into the staircase, hitting the banister right in his rib cage, right where the microphone stand had impaled him. He spun like a human top before crashing into the wall and finally the floor.

Eli gawked at his brother. Drew and Rose were equally stunned. Waking up as ghosts had been one thing, and Eli had been oddly excited by it. While everyone else was freaking out, he felt like there was finally something special about him, like Eli Adams was finally cool. He'd felt a call to discovery, like they were astronauts landing on an alien world for the first time. And now this? A portal at the front door that shot you back inside? This shit was getting insane, and Eli loved it.

Wes didn't. He struggled to his feet as if he'd been thrown out the windshield of a moving car. The look of hurt on his face snapped Eli back to reality. He held out a hand to his brother to help him to his feet, but Wes shoved him away. Even in death, Wes was incapable of admitting he needed help. Wes instead locked eyes with Drew, an unspoken accusation hiding behind them. This was somehow her fault, too, which Drew picked up on immediately. "How was I supposed to know that would happen?" she said, turning her back on him and inspecting the door.

"It's *your* goddamned house, Drew."

"Oh, so I was supposed to know we were going to get killed *and* that the front door would turn into a fucking portal? You moron." Wes hopped to his feet, his eyes filling with anger. Eli flinched at the sight, knowing better than anyone what it meant. Wes was prone to lashing out, they all knew that, but only Eli knew what the word moron meant to Wes. To most people it was just a throwaway insult. In the Adams household, however, it carried a lot more weight. It was what their dad called them when he was fed up. And even though he never modified the word, never threw a profanity or adverb in front of it, he didn't need to. Old man Adams delivered it with such a signature disdain, such utter disrespect, that there was only ever one take away: "You are so fucking worthless I only need one word to say it." It was a slap in the face every time.

"Don't call me a moron." Wes's voice trembled. Eli noticed the corners of Drew's lips curl in a smile and was thankful Wes didn't notice.

"Then don't act like a moron," she shot back.

Wes's fist tightened. Eli knew his brother had been in plenty of fights in his life. Surprisingly, most of them weren't even ones he'd started. They almost always involved him stepping up for a friend, often after some crappy bar gig. All it took was one drunk person saying the wrong thing to one of his bandmates and they'd all jump in. But this was different. Eli could tell the word was stinging inside Wes's brain. *Moron.* He looked like he wanted to punch Drew, but even Wes knew better than that. So, Wes did the next dumbest thing. He swung at a nearby cop, his fist colliding painfully with the officer's chin.

Only the cop didn't react at all. He might as well have been hit with the breeze from a butterfly's wings.

Wes clutched his hand, screaming as though he'd punched a concrete wall. The cop half-smirked, like he'd just remembered a funny joke, and quickly shook it off, continuing on his way.

"Like I said. Moron," Drew said. Eli felt his entire body clench with dread, convinced Wes would wheel around and punch her too. To his surprise, Wes restrained himself. His brother trudged over to a nearby couch and rubbed his wounded fist. He looked sad. Pathetic, even.

Rose lowered her voice so Wes wouldn't hear her. "What the heck, Eli?"

"I know, I know," Eli whispered.

Drew joined the whisper-fest, accusing Wes of being a psychopath. Eli tried to defend him, that Wes had "just been through a lot." Rose, to her own surprise, laughed. It was a short, petty burst. They'd all been through a lot. Wes wasn't special. She wasn't going to give him a pass just because he was acting like a brat.

Rose could tell Eli wanted to try and talk his way out of it. And Eli was normally good at that. He was great at improvising, particularly when it came to hijacking a conversation and moving it in another direction before anyone realized what was happening. He could turn anything into a joke, and Rose usually admired that about him. She prided herself in always seeing the good in a situation; he always saw the humor. Right now, she was struggling to see either. They were only just starting to understand the mess they were in and already Wes was flying off the rails. She worried what that meant for the future.

Eli sauntered off toward Wes, taking as long as he possibly could. Rose could tell he was thinking through a conversation he didn't want to have, so she gave him privacy, focusing instead on the front door and the invisible portal that plucked Wes out of thin air.

Right next to the door, at head height, hung a Greek evil eye. The *mati*, as it was called in Greece, was a glass disc about the size of a silver dollar, ringed with concentric circles of blue leading toward a black dot in the middle, giving the appearance of an eye. Rose hung it their first day. She didn't have any Greek ancestry herself, but Aunt Bea had told her to always hang one on the front door of anywhere she stayed, even a hotel. As Rose had explained to Drew when she hung it, the Greeks believed the *mati* was a charm meant to protect someone from the evil eyes of others.

Rose stared at it and her mood soured. She wanted to joke about how much good it had done for them but couldn't find the strength. It's not as though she truly believed the evil eye worked, that it would ward off the ill intentions of others. But she liked the idea of it, just as she liked the ideas of so many other cultures and religions. Rose's belief system was a spiritual grab bag. Drew often made fun of her for it, and she secretly wished she could commit to just one way of thinking, but she found a safety in the polygamy of her beliefs. At least one of them had to be right, right?

Just not the evil eye, apparently. Rose turned from the *mati* to the doorway itself. The threshold had a strange sort of shimmer, almost like the heat wave on pavement in the middle of summer. She couldn't understand how, but she felt as if the door was pulsing. It reminded Rose of floating on the lazy river at Hawaii Falls, the waterpark she used to go to with Drew and Mrs. Denns. You didn't notice the current until you were trying to swim against it, which is when you realized just how strong it really was. She brought her hand closer to the door and felt the same sensation of a current just waiting to suck you in. Part of her wanted to walk through it just to see what would happen, but after Wes's incident, she didn't need to bother. That barely perceptible shimmer was the edge of a boundary keeping them there. Rose just hoped it wasn't permanent.

Without even realizing it, Rose's left hand drifted back up to her necklace. She began tracing that same figure eight in it, over and over. It made her feel safe. It made her feel anchored, the only thing stopping her from leaping into the portal herself.

Drew ran her hand along the edge of the front door, careful to not let her fingers cross through the threshold. But damn did she want to. She wanted to run into it, wanted to see if it would reject her the same way it rejected Wes, but she was smarter than that. She took the old, crumpled black scrunchy out of her hair.

Drew stepped back and readied to throw the scrunchy through the door. She glanced at Rose, expecting her to express concern, only to find Rose was just as fixated on the doorway. Neither was willing to run through it, but both wanted to test it for themselves. What's the worst that could happen? The scrunchy doesn't get teleported back into the house?

Drew held her breath and tossed the scrunchy at the door.

Poof.

It winked out of existence, just as Wes had. Drew and Rose both spun in unison to see it reappear in the middle of the foyer, right where

Wes had popped out. Drew couldn't help but let out a little laugh at the sight, delighted by the fact that they had access to their own personal teleporter, only this one didn't make a computer-y, whizzing sound like the transporters on Star Trek did. It was more of a soft whoosh. There was something almost gentle about it, like the universe was closing its fist around whatever passed through the door and saying, "I'll take that."

Drew's momentary smile withered as it dawned on her that it wasn't so much a teleporter as it was a barrier they couldn't pass through. What she still needed to figure out was *why* they couldn't pass through it. Was the house keeping them inside? Or was it something else? Was this purgatory? Drew wished she'd gone to church more, wished she knew what the hell any of this was supposed to be. She kept waiting for some angel with wings to show up and explain it all. *Why isn't there a tour guide in this fucking place?*

The only thing Drew did know was that barriers could be broken, and if they were trapped in this godforsaken house, she was going to find a way to break out.

Chapter 9

Eli paced nervously in front of Wes. He assumed the others thought he was afraid of his older brother, which was partly true, but not the whole truth. Most of his life had been spent looking up to Wes. Not because Wes was some bastion of good decisions. Except for The Ruins, which had begun booking bigger and more frequent gigs at some legit venues in town, Wes managed to mess up everything he tried to do. He was routinely in trouble in school. He enrolled in college to placate his parents and then dropped out in his second semester. When their parents demanded Wes repay the tuition cost, he refused, telling them they knew the risks when they gambled on him.

Yet Eli still found ways to look up to his brother. Wes may have been the black sheep of the family, he may have failed constantly — and, often, spectacularly — but at least Wes was doing something with his life. At least Wes was trying. What had Eli ever tried at in his life? He did okay in high school. He was doing okay in college. He was doing okay at Suncoast. His entire life was defined by the word okay. Their dad rarely called Eli a moron, but that's because Eli never took a risk big enough to warrant his dad weighing in at all. *You should have fucked up more in life. You should have been more like Wes. At least he's got friends out there waiting to see him, to check in on him. What have you got? You fucking loser.*

As the thoughts stampeded through Eli's brain, his pacing quickened, finally grabbing Wes's attention. "Dude, you alright?"

Eli stopped pacing. He looked down at Wes. For the second time today, his brother showed concern for someone other than himself or his band. It was a good look on Wes, but Eli still wasn't used to it. "Yeah, I'm okay," he lied.

"Do you know what the hell's going on here, man?" Wes asked. "I mean, I know we're fucking dead. I'm not a fucking moron." Wes glared at Drew, who was still whispering at the front door with Rose. The girls were out of earshot, but Wes still lowered his voice, embarrassed to ask. "Eli. Is this Hell? Are we in Hell?"

Eli laughed. He didn't mean to; it was just so funny seeing Wes be the nervous one for a change.

"Fuck you, dude. It's a valid question." Wes pushed back.

"It's not that," Eli said. "I'm not laughing at you. It's just… it's a headfuck. That's what all this is."

"No shit, Sherlock. But if we're not in Hell, then where the fuck are we?"

Eli had never been religious and had definitely never read the bible. Growing up, his family would occasionally go to church, but it was just a keeping-up-appearances thing his mom did to appease their grandmother. And when she passed, they all stopped going. Eli asked his mom about it once and received a surprisingly blunt answer. "If it didn't help her, it's not going to help me." That was as close to a talk about religion as he'd ever had with his parents, so Eli's only context for understanding Hell was how he'd seen it in pop culture, and none of this was matching up to anything he'd seen. There were no fires or brimstones (Eli didn't even know what a brimstone was), no demons poking people with pitchforks. It wasn't nearly that dramatic. Amazingly enough, Bill & Ted's Bogus Journey — one of his favorite movies — was turning out to *not* be a very accurate depiction of the afterlife.

Wes's leg began to shake again. It was like an engine piston cycling up and down, up and down, vibrating the floorboard slightly and shaking the entire couch. It was distracting for Eli, but the various cops processing the crime scene didn't register it at all. A lightbulb went off, and a grin spread across Eli's face. "We're in an alternate universe."

Wes gawked back, dumbfounded. "We're what?"

"We're in a *parallel* universe."

"Get the fuck out of here."

"No, I'm serious. That's totally what this is. The afterlife is a freaking parallel universe!"

A crime scene photographer crouched over Eli's corpse. An enormous flash bulb blasted the room with light as he took his first picture. Eli flinched at the brightness. Wes rubbed his eyes.

"See, this is what I'm talking about. It's like..." Eli reverted to pacing, but this time excitedly. "They're here." Eli raised his left hand. "And we're here." He lifted his right hand and spread it flat, hovering one over the other without letting them touch. "We can see everything they're doing, but they can't see us. So, what I really want to know is... where does our universe end and theirs begin?"

"Probably when your head gets smashed open, dude."

"I'm just trying to understand what we're dealing with. You got a better idea?" Eli cocked his eyebrows. "I'm all ears."

"So? Even if you're right and we're in some 'parallel universe' shit, what does that mean? Why should I care? What in the fucking hell does that change for us?"

Eli didn't have any answers, and Wes was rubbing it in his face. It only made Eli more curious.

Wes wanted to believe Eli, but he just couldn't wrap his head around what a parallel universe even meant. It was too Twilight Zone and, as far as he could tell, didn't have anything to do with the fact they were all murdered hours earlier.

Wes's eyes drifted over to a half-full red solo cup on the coffee table.

He imagined the taste of the cold beer he'd chugged from countless cups just like it, and Wes was hit with an existential sledgehammer. Having the front door of the house portal him back into the foyer had been terrifying enough, but the sensation of it, the utter lack of control, made his skin feel like it was made of eels. Wes reached out for the solo cup, ready to chug whatever was left inside it.

But he couldn't pick it up. He couldn't even make it wobble. Two inches of beer sat at the bottom of it, still as a frozen lake.

Eli leaned over him to watch and Wes felt like a lab specimen as he struggled with the cup, applying more and more pressure to it, trying to lift it from the table. But it wouldn't budge. It was as if the cup weighed tons. He finally gave up and growled at Eli for help. "Explain this, Bill Nye."

Eli tried picking it up but couldn't get it to budge, either. Wes felt vindicated as Eli stood back, just as dumbfounded as he was. Eli looked around the first floor of the house. Cops were everywhere now, taking notes, photos, and leaving little flags with numbers on them all around, marking the crime scene. Wes could tell the perpetual motion machine that was his brother's brain was grinding its gears. Eli's eyes went wide. "Holy crap, what if it's like Toy Story?" he asked.

"What the fuck is Toy Story?"

"Oh my god, how have you not seen Toy Story yet? It's the future of animation. You have no idea. It was created by this company called—"

"Just get to the goddamned point, Eli." Wes couldn't stand to hear Eli rant about movies.

Drew and Rose glanced over at Wes, and he could feel the distrust radiating off them like waves of heat, like he was some junkie ranting on a street corner. He knew they didn't like him, but he didn't care, not now. They locked eyes briefly, and then Drew and Rose turned away, disappearing around the corner into the kitchen.

Eli kept rambling. "Okay, well, the movie is about toys that come to life when people aren't around. When they're not being observed, they can do their own thing. Like us." Eli gestured to the cops on the first floor. Nobody was looking at them, but they were easily in the eyelines of everyone around. "I had no problem moving stuff and opening doors until they showed up. I'll bet a thousand bucks that as soon as they can't see us..." Eli dashed over to a closet on the far end of the living room. He checked his eye lines. There were no cops looking. He took a deep breath, grabbed the door handle, and twisted.

The closet door opened just as easily as it would have when they were alive. Wes hopped up, eager to try out Eli's theory, but as he started to cross the room another cop stepped into the foyer. Wes could feel all the other officers stand a bit taller in this man's presence. The crime scene photographer taking pictures of Eli's corpse gave the man a solemn nod and called him Righetti. Wes moved closer, eavesdropping.

There was something magnetic about Detective Righetti. Wes guessed he was in his early sixties, maybe even older, with leathered skin, nicotine stains on his mustache, and a pissed off look in his eyes. While the rest of the police force were in uniform, Righetti donned a long, tan raincoat. He surveyed Eli's fucked up corpse, totally unphased. Wes got the impression this guy had seen so many crime scenes that even a dude with his head smashed open barely registered as shocking.

A younger cop named Andso sidled up to Righetti. "Is it him? Is it The Fireman again?" Andso asked, without ever looking directly at the dead body. Wes's eyes lit up. Righetti didn't hesitate to answer. He turned to the naive officer. "Twenty years ago I was standing right where you are. I saw it all happen, and I promise you we killed that man. I don't know who did this, but I guarantee you it wasn't the same guy."

"You think it's a copycat?" Andso asked.

Righetti leaned over, inspecting Eli's corpse. He winced, finally showing some emotion. "All I'm saying is it wasn't him."

Wes shouted at Righetti, demanding answers, but the grizzled old man had no idea he was even there. Wes kicked the wall in frustration, but this time, with no eyes directly on him, his foot managed to connect with it. The wall shook. Not as hard as it should have had Wes not been a fucking ghost, but it was still enough to shake the nail holding up Rose's evil eye charm — and enough to make Wes feel not so impotent after all. The circle of glass came loose and fell to the floor, shattering, shards of it scattering like roaches in every direction.

"Holy shit!" Wes shouted.

Righetti and Andso both spun around, confused to find no one behind them. Righetti reached down to pick up the largest fragment. He rolled the blue glass over in his hands and looked around the first floor. Wes could practically feel Righetti looking through him. But he knew no matter how long Righetti stared, he'd never see him. Wes started to suspect no matter how hard he kicked, no matter how much he tried, nobody would ever see him again. The idea scared him more than he'd ever admit.

Chapter 10

Rose could never watch horror movies or read scary stories growing up. She was too deep an empath, so even though she knew the movies weren't real, the connection to the characters often became so strong that even a tame scare would haunt her for days. Once at a slumber party at Janet Berg's house, the group had decided to rent Little Monsters, a comedy about a shy kid who discovers a world of monsters living under his bed. The rest of the girls thought it was hilarious. Rose didn't. There's a moment in it where the young boy discovers he's slowly turning into a monster himself. She had been so scared for the boy that the very idea of him transforming into a monster disturbed Rose's sleep for months. She'd lay in bed awake, staring into the darkness wondering what it would be like to lose control of your body like that.

And yet staring at the corpse of her best friend Drew, Rose felt nothing. In fact, the absence of feeling was starting to worry her. All her fears while alive were driven by the same question: What happens when you die? What happens when you no longer exist? What does it feel like to fade from the universe? To no longer be yourself? Rose's parents died when she was nine. When Rose was forced to go live with her aunt, all anyone would say was that her parents — a doctor and a lawyer who led very different lifestyles than Rose's hippie aunt — died in a car crash. It wasn't until she was a teenager that she'd learn it was not only a drunk driving accident, but that her own father had been the drunk driver.

Now Rose knew the answer to what happened when you died. You don't. At least, she didn't feel "dead." Her best friend may be splayed out on the floor of the basement, but she was also standing right next to her. That contradiction was oddly comforting. Of course, Rose also had a whole other host of expectations for what the afterlife would look like, and while she wasn't a St. Peter at the Pearly Gates type of believer, she certainly never in a thousand years would have imagined the afterlife would consist of being trapped in a house with the mutilated bodies of you and your closest friends.

Drew grabbed Rose's hand and forced her to look away from the corpse. "Rose, I'm right here. That's not me anymore. This is me." Drew touched her chest in demonstration. Rose breathed deeply and nodded her head. She knew Drew was right. It still wasn't easy to look at, but as long as she reminded herself that the real Drew was by her side, she'd be okay.

A flash went off, drawing their attention away from the corpse and to the officer taking photos. He'd finished with Drew's corpse and was examining the basement door. He shook his head and quipped to himself, "Girl almost made it."

"Fuck you. I'd like to see you do better you fucking asshole," Drew said. Rose smirked. She didn't like to curse herself, but it was a not-so-secret secret that she loved when Drew did.

Drew stared at the basement door. It had been closed when she'd awoken but was now ajar a few inches. A slight breeze was passing through the room and Drew wondered if the officer had opened it just to let some fresh air in. When it mattered most, she literally couldn't open the door to save her life, but this man opened it just so he'd be a little less sweaty. The thought of it made her irrationally mad.

Drew watched Rose slide her hand between the open part of the door and the outside. It had that same shimmer as the front door. Rose's fingertips flirted with touching it. The boundary was a mystery, and Rose seemed upset at herself for not having any answer. Rose always had an answer for everything. The fact that she didn't was worrying. "I don't like it, Drew. I don't like it at all."

Drew thought that was a stupid thing to say. *I don't fucking like it either, Rose. Why would I? Why would anyone? This all fucking sucks.* But Drew knew better than to needle Rose now. She knew the limits of her own sarcasm.

Rose retreated from the door, but Drew didn't follow her. She fixated on the pliers jammed into the door's locking mechanism. A flood of emotion and memory came rushing back as she was reminded of her choice to go back upstairs for Rose. What if she hadn't? Would she really have gotten away? Or would The Fireman have just killed her on the lawn instead? It didn't matter though, going back was the right thing to do.

A gust of wind swept through the basement door, widening it farther, taunting Drew mercilessly, showing her the way out, but denying her an exit. Her gut told her this door was a portal just like the one upstairs, but she had to know for sure. This time she slipped off one of her sneakers. She didn't hesitate, she tossed it through the open basement door. Once more, the universe folded its invisible hands around the shoe, plucking it out of the air. Drew spun on her heels to catch sight of the shoe as it re-appeared in the basement.

But it never did.

Drew frowned, disappointed. She waited another moment, but still nothing. The subtle fear of having to go through the afterlife with only one shoe started to sink in. Rose, on the other hand, didn't notice. She was hyper focused on the basement wall.

"Was this always here?" Rose asked, pointing at the wall opposite Eli's computer. Drew squinted and could see a small, inky black splotch on the wall. Not huge, about three inches or so in diameter at its widest point. The spot was so dark that it was almost hard for Drew to process. Freshmen year, one of Drew's first professors referenced an artist who only ever worked with a special kind of black paint that they had invented themselves. It was said to swallow all light around it. Drew hadn't seen any of the artist's work, so she couldn't be sure, but all she could think about was how this three-inch hole in the wall was swallowing what precious little light there was in the room.

"I think I would have remembered this," Drew said as she reached out to touch the spot. Rose grabbed her hand in a panic. "What are you doing?"

"I don't know. I just wanted to—" But before Drew could explain why she'd felt compelled to try and touch the thing, someone upstairs yelled "Holy shit!" And then something inexplicable happened, right before their eyes.

A second black spot grew on the wall. Drew and Rose both noticed it at the same time. Rose didn't have to ask, they both knew it wasn't there before. Drew stared at the two rotten holes. They seemed to quiver in front of her eyes, a slight pulsating, as if they were alive, as if Greywood House itself was breathing.

Chapter 11

ELI WAS PACING IN THE FOYER, HOLDING A SNEAKER IN HIS HAND, when Drew and Rose returned. Drew's eyes lit up at the shoe. "Let me guess, the basement door is a no-go, too?" Drew shook her head as she slipped the shoe back on. But before she could say more, Rose noticed the shattered glass in Righetti's hand.

"What happened to my *mati*?" Rose asked.

Eli barely knew where to begin. He was sure Drew would at least know the gist of Toy Story, so he launched into the same spiel he'd given Wes. Drew was far more accepting of his parallel universe theory. Rose? Not so much. She agreed they were subject to a new set of rules in this reality but refused to call it a parallel universe. Eli sensed that wasn't anywhere in her grab bag of flower child beliefs, but appreciated Rose was somewhat receptive to new info. One thing he hated about most religious people was their refusal to even *entertain* any information that didn't fit their spoon-fed view of the world. It was something he'd argued with his grandma about all the time, but he'd given up trying to dissuade her of some of her more outlandish beliefs. It was easier to live and let live in their family.

It was one reason he was so eager to move into Mrs. Denns's house. It was his first time living outside of his childhood home. He didn't even ask for details when Drew floated him the idea. He was in. But as he walked circles around his own dead body, weaving in and out of cops as they moved about the room, he couldn't help but wonder if maybe he should have asked Drew a question or two about Greywood House before moving his whole life into its basement. Then again, if Drew knew there was any chance of a mass murder happening, she would have raised at least a teeny, tiny red flag, so logically she must not have known. But maybe Drew and her mom just didn't think of the right questions to ask? Maybe neither of them ever bothered to look into the house's history? Real estate agents lied in listings all the time. Maybe the Denns's just needed to have just dug a little deeper. *Too late now though.*

Wes waved his arms, interrupting all the parallel universe, Toy Story talk. Eli hated it when Wes did that. He could never politely say "Excuse me." Everything had to be a big performance with him. It was one reason Wes was so good on stage, but Eli found it deeply obnoxious when he wouldn't drop his 'I'm king shit, pay attention to me' act off stage.

"Look, considering we can't leave even if we wanted to, I'm pretty sure we're going to have plenty of time to figure out your precious little Toy Story rules or whatever the fuck you want to call them. What matters more is that this pig right here," Wes said, pointing at Righetti as if he were a neon sign, "this fucking squealer knew about The Fireman."

"What? They know who killed us?" Drew asked.

"Not quite," Eli said, trying to temper their expectations. "We heard them talking about some Fireman from like twenty years ago. The old guy called our Fireman a copycat killer."

Rose shivered. "Do they know where he is? Are they going to stop him from killing again?"

Eli and the rest fell silent. He'd been too busy focusing on them being goddamned Caspers to think about other people. Eli instinctively looked out the window, half expecting to see The Fireman standing in the trees like Michael Myers. *Don't serial killers return to the scene of the crime?* He scanned the edge of the woods and a mental rolodex of movies flooded him with images from countless slashers. He imagined the night before and The Fireman stalking the windows, staring into the house while they all moved about clueless to the fact he was about to break in. *Wait, if the doors were locked, how did he get in?*

But Eli's attention was pulled to a commotion brewing at the entrance of the driveway. His heart sank at the sight of Mrs. Denns struggling to get past officers holding the growing crowd back. He turned to the others bracing for a big reaction, but he was the only one who noticed. For a second, he thought about not saying anything. He hated being the bearer of bad news. Wes always made him be the one to tell dad any time they broke a plate or a glass or some cheap tool. A bent screwdriver that couldn't have cost more than five bucks had once sent their dad into a rage. Wes had thankfully drawn the brunt of that beating, but ever since then, Eli felt a deep pit of anxiety in his stomach whenever bad news was about to be delivered.

But nobody else was looking. Eli sighed. "Drew? I think you need to see this."

Drew followed his gaze and gasped. Rose and Wes finally took notice as well. Mrs. Denns fought past officers, screaming out. "My daughter lives in there! Let me see my daughter!"

Drew ran from the window to the front door but stopped short of crossing the threshold. She knew what would happen if she went through the portal and as fun as tossing objects through might have been, she wasn't about to do that with her entire body.

Eli had only met Mrs. Denns a few times but heard plenty about her from Drew venting at work. She was always pissed at her mom over one thing or another, but it wasn't like Eli's family. There wasn't an unspoken undercurrent of genuine loathing to their arguments. Eli couldn't help but wonder if the old man regretted having him and Wes. He never got that vibe from Drew's mom, though. If anything, their fights always seemed to be coming from a place of Mrs. Denns caring too much.

Now here she was, storming up the driveway like a badass, shoving aside cops, fighting to see her daughter. Eli wondered if his parents would even show up, let alone fight their way inside. He doubted it. Eli watched silently as Drew shouted for her mom. But none of the living could hear her. As Mrs. Denns hit the porch steps, she caught the attention of Detective Righetti. Eli could tell this was a guy who spent an entire career delivering bad news to people. He was about to do it again.

Detective Righetti closed the front door right in Drew's face. She slid over to the foyer windows to watch him try and diffuse the situation. "Ma'am, ma'am, please wait here."

"But my daughter and her friends live here," pleaded Mrs. Denns. "What happened? Are they okay? Is Drew okay?"

Righetti placed his hands on her shoulders. "Ma'am, you can't go in there right now."

Drew's voice cracked as she cried out "Mom! I'm right here!" She kept pounding on the windows as hard as she could. Eli could see the glass vibrate ever so slightly, and once again wondered about the science of it all. If this was a parallel universe, how much did it have in common with the living world? Was it really as simple as one layer stacked on top of the other? And if so, wouldn't that mean there should be ghosts all over the place? Were there people all over the world trapped where they died? Or was there something special about them? About Greywood House?

Rose covered her ears and fought back tears as Drew continued to pound on the windows. Even Wes seemed sympathetic to what Drew was going through. No parent should live to see their child die, and no child should have to see their parent live through it. They drifted away from the windows to give Drew space.

Mrs. Denns couldn't hear her daughter's cries, but to Eli it looked like she could *feel Drew* in her bones. He wondered if mother's intuition was a real thing. He'd never believed in any sort of extra sensory perception before, there wasn't any science to back it up, but he also didn't believe in freaking ghosts, so what the hell did he really know?

"Mom, I'm right here!" Drew and Mrs. Denns were only separated by glass and a porch, but the outside world felt miles away. Righetti leaned in close and whispered something into Mrs. Denns's ear. Eli couldn't hear it, but he didn't need to. Mrs. Denns dropped to her knees in the yard, tears streaming down her face as she screamed bloody murder into her hands.

Drew collapsed as well. Not quite as dramatically as her mom. She just kind of sank into the window, as if the futility of everything was a literal weight on her chest. Rose touched Drew's shoulder. Tears were streaming from Rose's eyes, but Eli noticed Drew wasn't crying. She was wrecked by what was happening, yet there were no tears. Now that he thought about it, he wasn't sure he'd ever seen Drew cry. She had a jaded, no-bullshit exterior, sure, but he'd always assumed that was an act not unlike Wes's. Maybe it wasn't.

Drew turned away from Rose and the scene outside. She walked up the staircase to the second floor without saying a single word or offering a single look back.

There was a moment of quiet where all Eli could hear was Mrs. Denns's labored cries outside the house. It reminded him of a trip he'd spent at his grandparents' house. They lived in a remote part of Pennsylvania surrounded by farmland. On the first night there, he awoke to the most god-awful sound he'd ever heard. It was a low, howling wail that just would not relent. He ran to find his grandma, terrified and convinced there was a monster in the field across the way. *Convinced of it.* It turns out it was a mother cow who had given birth earlier that day. The calf had been taken from her, and so the momma spent the entire night howling for her baby to be returned. He didn't know cows could make a sound like that, let alone have such complex emotions. It turned him off meat for a while, but eventually he forgot all about it and went back to scarfing down greasy Big Macs from the food court. He hadn't thought about that sound in over a decade. His life was so simple, so unremarkable that he'd had no reason to hear such grief again. Until this very moment.

Wes broke the silence. "She didn't even cry," he said, pointing up the stairs. It wasn't an accusation, just an observation, one that Eli was quite frankly stunned Wes was capable of making. Maybe he wasn't as much of an oblivious shithead as it seemed.

But Eli didn't have long to dwell on the thought. Rose stepped between the two of them. She lowered her voice, whispering that she needed to show them something in the basement. Eli was intrigued but couldn't help but laugh at Rose trying to keep quiet. "No one can hear us, dummy," Eli joked. He meant it to be a bit flirtatious, but he was terrible at it. Rose rolled her eyes at him, and he withered inside. *You moron.*

"Shut up and come with me," Rose said.

Chapter 12

DREW HAD A HABIT OF ENDING EVERY ARGUMENT WITH HER MOM by slamming a door. Any door. Once it was the wood-paneled side of her mom's '87 Station Wagon outside of the Galleria Mall. Drew was 12 at the time, going on her first real date, and all her mom wanted to do was offer some advice. Drew wasn't hearing it though. She stammered about not wanting advice from the woman who chased her dad away and then slammed the door.

Her mom didn't deserve that. But as Drew would only learn in retrospect, parents rarely deserve the bullshit kids put them through. That realization was never more profound than this moment, as Drew sat against the wall of her attic bedroom, watching yet another crime scene photographer snap pictures of the damage in her room. *Christ, how many of you are there? Why do you only show up when it's too late?*

Drew banged her head against the wall in a dull, frustrated beat. She'd spent so much of her life filled with anger and resentment toward her mom, and now all she wanted to do was hug the woman. She couldn't. She'd never be able to hug her again.

She kept picturing Righetti closing the door with her mom on the other side. Drew wanted to run through it, wanted to shove him to the side and throw herself at her, but she knew it wasn't possible. Karma wouldn't let her. It was as if her teen years spent slamming doors were now laughing in her face. *"You want to keep slamming doors shut? Fine. I'll make it so you can never even open a door, ever again."*

This stupid house was quickly becoming her coffin. Drew chewed her nails and tried to ignore the camera flashes. The policewoman was capturing the spot where Drew had broken free from the closet and stabbed The Fireman, sending him crashing to the floor. She remembered the thrill of surprising him, of driving him across the room. *I fucking killed you. Why the hell am I dead and not you?*

The photographer snapped shots of the desk and artwork knocked around during the struggle. A flash illuminated the wall behind the dresser, drawing Drew's attention to a fleck of white paper wedged in a gap between the floor and the wall. She'd written the apology note after her disastrous first semester but never had the courage to give it to her mom. Everything she'd always wanted to say was on that damned piece of paper. If Drew could just pull it from the wall, with some luck someone would find it and give it to her mom.

Drew stretched her arm as far as she could under the dresser, straining to grab hold of the corner of the paper, but it was an infuriating inch out of reach. Yesterday all Drew would have needed to do was casually bump the dresser to the side with her hip and she'd be able to reach it, but as a ghost, trying to budge the dresser felt like trying to move a skyscraper with a toothpick. Drew didn't know how much longer her mom would still be outside or if she'd ever see her again. Drew stood, gripped the dresser as tightly as she could, and tried to lift it. It was as if the dresser had been bolted to the floor. Then, out of the corner of her eye Drew saw the photographer turn her back and before Drew could react, the bolts were off. She lifted the dresser with ease but was caught off guard by the sudden movement and fell awkwardly backward, slamming her head on the wall.

The photographer jumped in fright as the dresser moved. Her eyes darted around the room, terror setting in. She froze, wild-eyed, waiting for more movement, but nothing came. The woman raised her camera and took a flurry of pictures all over the room. Drew wondered if she'd show up when the pictures were developed. She'd seen episodes of Unsolved Mysteries on ghosts and how they'd supposedly show up on film and audio tapes. The photographer reached the end of her roll of film and the camera began rewinding in a loud, grinding whir. The officer didn't wait for it to finish. She said, "Fuck this house," and ran out of the room.

Drew laughed, shouting after the woman. "Lady, you have no goddamned idea." As soon as the cop was gone, Drew dove behind the dresser for the note only to discover the sudden lurching and slamming of the dresser had caused it to sink deeper into the floorboards. Drew pried at the wood with her nails. She clawed at the trim on the wall, but it was no use. Either the contractors who built this place had done a phenomenal job or Greywood House itself didn't want to let go of its secrets.

Drew let loose a volley of curse words. Not that they'd do anything, or that anyone could hear her pain and make it go away. No one would ever hear her again. Her mom certainly wouldn't. Finally, with no one around to see, Drew allowed herself to cry for the first time in a long, long time.

Chapter 13

WES STARED AT THE TWO BLACK SPOTS ON THE BASEMENT WALL. Rose had dragged Eli and himself downstairs to see the goop in person. The way she'd described it, just looking at these spots should have made his skin crawl, but now that he was face to face with them, they just looked like shower mold. The cop down there dusting the broken doorknob for fingerprints wasn't bothered by it, so why should he care?

"It's not mold, Wes." Rose snapped back at him. He was always having to watch his mouth around her. Wes may have relished playing the bad boy around other people, but there was just something about Rose that made him walk a little straighter and stand a little taller. Sure, he thought she was hot in a hippie kind of way, but it was more than that. There was a kindness to her. She had a patience with him that few others did. Drew definitely didn't have it. She was quick to call Wes on his bullshit. Rose was different.

Eli hadn't seen the mold before either. Wes leaned in closer. The spots didn't seem that gross to him. They didn't even smell.

"Besides, mold smells," Rose chimed in.

Wes shot her a double take. *Did she just read my mind?*

"What? Why are you looking at me like that?" she asked.

"Did you just read my mind? Are you a fuckin' witch?" Wes asked as playfully as he could. He thought a girl like Rose would like to be called a witch. He was wrong. Rose screwed up her face, annoyed.

"Mold smells, right? So, if this doesn't smell, you have to admit it's not mold, right?" Eli asked, sounding as smug as possible. Wes didn't want to admit he was wrong. He never did. "Okay, you two geniuses. What is it, then?"

Eli shut up, which pleased Wes. Rose was silent, too, though Wes could tell she wanted to say something but was too shy. "What, Eli? You don't think it's intergalactic ectoplasmic globulins or some other parallel universe bullshit?" Wes asked with extra snark. Eli flicked him off. "What? I can make up shit, too." Wes added. Eli raised his other middle finger.

"It's rot." Rose declared, rubbing the crystal around her neck. She was absent mindedly tugging at her dress as well. She looked overwhelmed, like her heart was racing. "This house's heart is rotten."

Wes rolled his eyes. He couldn't help it. "Houses don't have hearts, you hippie."

"Don't call me a hippie."

"Yeah, don't call her a hippie, asshat."

It was obvious Eli had a thing for Rose, but Wes didn't know if she was clued in enough to notice. It made him want to embarrass his brother even more. There was a brief moment of silence before Wes could no longer help himself. "Rot? What the hell does that even mean?"

Rose's face hardened. She was starting to remind Wes of his mom whenever her patience was running out. "Call me a hippie all you want, but what happened to us," Rose turned to the two black spots. "That kind of violence leaves a mark, a psychic scar."

"What makes you the expert on all this?" Wes demanded.

Rose stopped squeezing her dress for a moment and said something that genuinely surprised Wes. "I'm not." She leaned in a little closer to the spots than she seemed comfortable with. "But I spent half of high school reading about reincarnation and souls and what lies beyond our mortal selves. And people like you made fun of me for it, but guess what? Look around you. We're in the beyond, so I think you need to shut up and trust me when I say I have a bad feeling about something."

Wes made a jerk off motion with his hands.

"Oh, real mature, tough guy."

Wes laughed as he leaned back in to inspect the black spots. He thought of the time he'd found a dead coyote in the woods behind their house. Something bigger had killed it days earlier. Most of the good meat had been eaten away, and the rotten remains were covered with a thin layer of black fuzz. This shit on the wall was different, though. It was so dark it almost looked colorless, like the holes were sucking in the light around them.

When he was six, Wes stole a Snickers bar from a gas station. It was an honest mistake. He didn't know that you weren't allowed to just take candy off the shelf and leave the store with it, but when his dad found out what he'd done, Wes quickly learned about theft. After a thrashing like that, any "normal kid" would have learned to ignore their instinct to reach out and grab whatever they wanted. But Wes learned a different lesson that day. Taking the candy bar wasn't the problem. Getting *caught* taking the candy bar was the problem.

Wes casually reached toward the largest of the black holes. There was something about the spot that called to him. Something about it that he couldn't understand, but maybe if he just *touched* it, it would all make sense. As he reached out, a third rotten spot bubbled up between the other two. Rose gasped. Wes yanked his hand away, startled.

Rose shook her head in dismay. "I need to go talk to someone." She raced up the stairs. "Just promise me you'll leave it alone," she said without turning back.

"We promise." Eli called up after her.

Wes stepped to his brother. They were both over six-feet tall, but while Wes had spent years performing on stage and developed a lean, muscular physique, Eli had spent all his time either standing behind the counter at Suncoast or slouching in a computer chair. Together they looked like a before and after fitness picture.

"You know, you don't have to do everything they tell you to, right?

Those girls didn't want to fuck you in high school. They ain't gonna start now." Wes said, trying to needle Eli. It was working, too. Eli stammered through some mush mouth explanation that he was "totally not interested" in them that way, but Wes wasn't buying it. He knew what Eli couldn't admit to himself: Eli would die to be with Drew or Rose. Maybe even more for Rose. There was something about her witchiness that he could tell Eli was into.

Wes grew bored of the conversation. As always, he said his piece, did his damage, and moved on. His attention was drawn to the cop dusting for fingerprints. Wes closed in on him, lingering inches from the cop's face. Wes reached out with his index finger and poked the cop on the cheek. His finger was once again blocked by the invisible barrier surrounding the living. When he had punched the cop upstairs, things were moving too fast for him to notice the nuance of what was happening, but now he was taking his time. He could see his fingertips stop millimeters from the stubble on the man's face. The cop couldn't feel or see a thing because Wes wasn't actually making contact with him. Eli's whole parallel universe theory was starting to make a bit more sense — not that Wes would admit as much to him. Wes read the cop's name off his badge. "What's up, Officer Hernandez? Can you feel this shit?" Wes pushed harder.

And harder.

And deeper.

Suddenly Officer Hernandez swatted his hand at the spot where Wes was poking, like trying to get rid of an annoying fly. Hernandez's hand passed *through* Wes's fingers. Wes yanked his hand away in a panic.

Eli's eyes went wide. "Holy shit, dude."

"I know."

"He went through you."

"I know."

"Like, straight *through* you."

"I fucking know, Eli."

"What are you two doing?" Wes and Eli whipped their heads to the stairs as if they'd been caught by their dad messing with his tools. It was only Drew. Wes frowned. "We're just having fun, *Mom*." He sarcastically drew out "Mom," just enough to piss Drew off.

"Leave that man alone."

Wes stepped away, raising his hands in surrender. Nothing appeared out of the ordinary. All his joints still moved the same way, and it's not as if Hernandez passing through Wes's body had hurt, but it still felt... wrong. That's the only way Wes's brain could rationalize it. It felt wrong. He shot Eli a look. *Keep your mouth shut.* Eli frowned, but Wes knew he'd gotten the message.

Drew zeroed in on the rotten spots, noticing there were now three instead of two. "What'd you guys do?"

"Nothing," Wes said, wondering if he answered a little quickly. Drew narrowed her eyes at Eli. "Where'd Rose go?"

Drew knew exactly what Rose meant when she told the guys she was going to go talk to someone. Rose had been doing this little "talking" ritual for years. Sometimes she'd let Drew watch, but usually it was a private moment. Drew smiled faintly. It was a reminder of happier times when Rose would perform her little seance at a sleepover. Eli and Wes gawked at her, confused. "She means her aunt Bea."

"Her fucking *aunt's* here now??" Wes asked.

"Oh, she's not here." Drew said, recognition dawning.

Wes stared blankly back.

"Then how is she talking to her?" Eli asked. Drew found herself enjoying their confusion. It was a nice distraction from what was happening upstairs. She wanted to keep their little guessing game going, so she just tapped on her temple, pointing at her brain.

"What the hell are you talking about?" Wes snapped.

Drew tapped her temple again. "She's talking to her up here."

Eli blinked, unwilling to accept that answer. "Get the hell out. Are you serious? Rose thinks she's, what, telepathic?"

Of course, Eli was a skeptic. Drew was, too. Wes seemed to be quickly losing interest in the conversation regardless and left Drew and Eli to go hover around the police officer on the other side of the room.

"I mean, I've seen her do it, but I've never *heard what she hears*, ya know? She just sits there, holding her crystal necklace. It kinda looks like meditation, but then afterward... it's wild. She knows things she didn't before, like she really was talking to someone. I don't know how she does it, but with Rose, it's always felt real. Not some bullshit gimmick."

"I knew Rose was into all that stuff, I guess I just never realized she was *into it*," Eli said, emphasizing the last part as if that explained his dismay.

"Her aunt tried to teach us all this seance, out-of-body astral projection stuff at sleepovers. Rose got obsessed and swore she could do it. I thought it was a bunch of nonsense. I guess the joke's on me, because if all of this is real," Drew gestured around the basement, "Who the hell knows what else is?"

With that thought, Drew was starting to understand why Eli had been so excited upstairs. This was a whole new world, a whole new life. She'd grown up watching movies and reading books about all kinds of supernatural stuff. She'd never Believed it with a capital B, but here they were. *Fucking ghosts*. And if they were real (and despite everything, Drew still felt pretty dang real), then maybe everything Rose's aunt used to talk about was real, too. Drew couldn't help but wonder if every second of every day she'd been surrounded by ghosts she never knew were there. There were times when she was alone and would feel a chill up her spine and look over her shoulder. Those moments never scared her, but now she knew there might have been a reason for those chills. There might have been strangers watching her entire life, just like Wes was watching Officer Hernandez.

Eli jerked his hand toward the wall, pulling Drew back to reality. "What the hell's happening?" he asked. The black spots were spreading. A bubble of darkness would form near the others, swell slightly, then sink back into the wall. It looked like the foundation of the house was *boiling*. The closest thing Drew could compare it to was roofing tar, but even that didn't do it justice. This wasn't liquid. The bubbles didn't pop, they deformed. They didn't add to the surface, they appeared to be taking it away. Reality was being deleted right in front of Drew's eyes, and the thrill she'd felt just a minute ago was morphing into dread.

Wes rejoined them at the wall. He moved closer to the holes, closer than Drew was comfortable with. She tried to pull him back and Wes wheeled on her with disgust and the unmistakable, condescending gaze of a man who thinks a woman doesn't have the right to touch him. There was a time a look like that would have made Drew sit down and shut up. That was several shitty men ago, though. Drew stood her ground. "Don't fucking touch it, Wes. I am gonna get Rose, and we're gonna figure this shit out together."

Chapter 14

Rose sat cross legged on the floor of what would have been her bedroom, had she lived in the house long enough to make it her own. She was able to decorate it with her tapestries and crystals and candles, but The Fireman arrived before she was able to truly *live* in it.

She sat as centered in the room as possible, just as Aunt Bea had taught her. Under normal circumstances, it would be best for the door to be shut, the blinds closed, and be surrounded by lit candles. Placing oneself center in a room drew focus from the barriers — the walls — to the self. Closing the blinds wasn't about darkening the room, it was about sealing oneself off from distractions. The candles weren't just for mood lighting, they were warning signs. Airports had windsocks to show which way the winds were blowing, psychics had candle flames. If one suddenly blew out, Bea said, you knew a tempest was rising.

Given her current situation, none of that was an option. She was thankful that at least there were no cops working in her room. No one had died in there, so they seemed to be ignoring it, giving her some semblance of peace and quiet in the increasingly crowded house. One of the bedroom windows was open from the night before, letting in a soft breeze and the dull sounds of people coming and going outside. She tried to close it, but it wouldn't budge. She looked down at the police cars and the small mob of people at the end of the driveway and realized it was in sight of the living. She hated to admit it, but Eli might be onto something about how and when they could interact with the mortal world. She'd have to make do with it open.

Rose carefully took off her necklace; a black quartz crystal bound to a thin chain of pure silver that had been her mother's. She'd borrowed it once in fifth grade. Kids teased her, calling her a hippie or a goth (neither of which made sense, but kids rarely know how to identify someone "different"). It was enough to stop her from ever asking to wear it again. But then the car crash happened. Her mom died wearing the necklace, and her aunt recovered it and gifted it to Rose at their funeral. Rose had worn the crystal every day of her life since. She'd even shower in it, only taking it off at times like this, when she used it to commune with "the inner self," as Bea called it. She took the necklace's chain and wove it between the fingers of both hands, creating a cat's cradle that left the crystal dangling in the middle. She kept her hands as still as possible to minimize the swaying of the crystal. She closed her eyes and spoke softly. "Please, auntie, I need your help."

Drew used to tease her about these sessions. If anyone else had called her Little Mrs. Psychic, it would have bugged her, but Rose knew Drew meant well by it. Drew didn't really understand what Rose was doing during these sessions. It didn't help that her aunt talked about all this psychic stuff as if it were real. Rose didn't think telepathy was real, but she didn't think it was a trick, either. It was more nuanced than that. It wasn't about literally talking to someone else through your mind; it was about building a world in your head. It was about looking at things from a different perspective. Being able to imagine the inner workings of someone else's mind was the ultimate exercise in empathy.

She waited. She listened. She tried to conjure Aunt Bea inside her head, but there were too many distractions. There was a commotion growing outside, a dull murmur of the crowd at the bottom of the driveway, no doubt wondering what happened in the house. There was too much distraction to focus. She'd been taught to imagine soaring above any distractions, as if viewing them from an eagle's eye, flying past them until the mind was free of their gravity. But she couldn't do that now. She started to imagine floating from her own body, drifting out the window, away from the house, rising into the clouds until the house was tiny, a doll's house below her, but always something — a footstep or a cough or an ambulance door slamming — would draw her back, sending her mind racing into her body. Rose clenched her eyes shut tighter, trying to will the distractions out of existence, to shrink them, minimize them until her mind was free to disassociate, free to commune beyond the self. Her mind began to rise, to separate, to float first above her, out the window, gazing down at the house, its roof shrinking as she rose higher, farther, untethered.

The crystal began to sway between her palms. A familiar tingle climbed up her spine. Rose spoke again, though not out loud, saying the words in her mind. *Bea, you said death was just a transition, but we're not going anywhere. We're not free. Our souls aren't wandering. We're trapped in this poisoned house.* Rose paused a moment before admitting the next part. *And I'm scared. I'm really, really scared.*

A jolt of excitement ran through her as she started to hear a faint whisper. Rose cocked her head sideways, straining to focus on the voice, to find it in the clouds she was imagining surrounded her, struggling to pinpoint where the whisper was coming from, like it was afraid to be heard. *I'm sorry, auntie, I can't hear you.*

And then Rose was falling, the clouds racing past her. Something was pulling her back to the ground. Something that felt far too real. This was no trick of the imagination, no expansion of the mind. It felt like Rose was plummeting back to earth, the once-tiny house rushing at her, swelling rapidly in size the closer she got. She knew this was an illusion, she knew she could open her eyes at any moment, but the sensation of it was overriding that part of her brain. *She was falling to her death.* She was about to crash through the roof, her precious insides once again seconds away from splattering all over this accursed house. Rose couldn't stand it. She opened her eyes.

Rose was surrounded by pure blackness. There were no open windows, no half-melted candles. The walls of the house had fallen away. The rug she sat on became an island, with the hardwood floor stretching on forever in all directions. Rose stood up. She screamed into the void, trying to wake herself up from the trance she'd fallen into, but nothing changed. She spun around in circles but found only the crushing darkness. Rose called out for her aunt, for Drew, for anyone, but her voice wouldn't travel. It was choked to a muffle by the void around her. She began hyperventilating, her lungs unable to keep up. The space around her was infinite, but it felt like she was suffocating.

Rose didn't believe in Hell, not in any kind of a Judeo-Christian sense at least. She believed in reincarnation, of a transformation the soul underwent, shifting from one mortal form to the next. But this, this unending, inescapable darkness, was Hell. Rose was convinced of it. She fell to her knees, screaming, pleading with the darkness to let her go. For the first time since she was a child, Rose prayed. She prayed to God and Krishna and Gaia and Amon and any other deity she could think of, prayed for relief, for mercy, in any way they could give it.

Suddenly, as if in answer, a faint rectangle of light flickered to life in the distance. It looked miles away. Rose didn't hesitate. She ran to it, bolting off into the darkness, afraid the light may disappear any second, trapping her in the void. Her lungs ached. Her bare feet hurt as they slapped the hardwood over and over. It was all so real, so physical. She'd never experienced anything like it before. This wasn't imaginary. This wasn't turning toward the inner self to see things from a new perspective. This was *very fucking real*, and Rose was *very fucking terrified*.

The rectangle of light grew bigger, as if a fog were lifting, and Rose found herself standing in front of a closed door, the light from within it illuminating the edge of the wooden frame. The door wasn't attached to any walls or ceiling. Rose walked a full circle around it, but it looked the same from either side, an obelisk in the darkness, only visible because of the light bleeding through the edges of its frame.

Rose opened the door. Warm, amber light flooded her face, blinding her. As her eyes adjusted, she saw the light was coming from a room at the bottom of a staircase. Rose took one last look around her, seeing only infinite floor and darkness in all directions, and reluctantly decided to descend the staircase. The wood creaked under her feet, and she paused nervously, like she was about to get caught sneaking into someone else's house. She heard faint, crackly music that sounded like it was coming from a record player. Rose couldn't put her finger on the singer's voice but was certain she'd heard him before.

Rose descended farther and found a hallway at the bottom of the stairs. The floor was carpeted, the walls were wood paneled. She followed it. The light grew brighter, the music louder, until she arrived at the edge of a living room lit by a crackling fireplace.

There was a woman laying by the fire, maybe in her thirties, Rose guessed. She was beautiful, picturesque, like she was ripped out of a postcard. The whole scene was a Norman Rockwell painting come to life. The mother was playing a board game with triplets — a trio of rosy-cheeked, eight-year-old boys — on a sheepskin rug. The game looked like Monopoly, but it was a vintage version she'd never seen before. They were laughing and smiling, and Rose could feel a sense of love and warmth in the air. This was a special place. A happy place.

And then Rose heard the rocking chair.

There was one more person in the room, but the father's face was hidden behind an opened newspaper. He was a large, imposing figure that was as stern as the woman was soft. They were an almost parody of the perfect, 1960s nuclear family. Rose half-expected to see Lucille Ball walk into the room carrying an expertly carved turkey.

"Who are you?" Rose asked, but no one responded. They couldn't see or hear her. Even here, Rose was a ghost. She walked around the room and was reminded of the first time she'd seen behind-the-scenes pictures of a TV show. It had been Jerry Seinfeld's apartment, and it was surreal to see the craft behind the movie magic, like the whole thing was some kid's diorama. But this wasn't movie magic. This was real magic. Rose had been transported somewhere, another place and time. She didn't know where or when or even how, but it was all so specific, so fully realized. She could read the headlines on the father's newspaper. She could smell the smoke from his pipe and feel the heat from the fireplace.

And then she could *feel* something else, too.

Another presence.

Rose squinted, barely discerning the shape of a person in the shadows beyond the father. He was watching the scene just as she was. "Hello?" Rose stepped between the family and the shadow and was hit with a realization. Was this some projection of Aunt Bea? Rose had obviously never performed her ritual from "the other side," and she could only begin to guess how that might change things. Had it actually worked? Had she actually formed a telepathic bond with someone? Rose looked back at the family with new eyes, wondering if maybe this was her mother's family growing up. The woman was unfamiliar, though. And she didn't recognize the boys, either.

"Auntie? Why are you showing me this? Why are you..." The words fell out of Rose's mouth as a mountainous shadow moved and time froze. The flames in the fireplace locked up as if someone hit a pause button. And then The Fireman stepped forward from the darkness.

Rose screamed at the sight of him. Before she could run, he lunged, grabbed her by the throat, and lifted her off the ground like she weighed nothing. His hand squeezed tighter and tighter, crushing her trachea just as he'd done with the phone cord. Rose's hands dropped. Her legs shook. The Fireman loosened his grip ever so slightly to keep her alive just a bit longer. He was *enjoying* it.

Rose tried to scream but didn't have any air in her lungs to power the words. She stared into The Fireman's mask, trying to see through it, to see the monster who had killed her once and was somehow doing it all over again. There was one crack — a bullet hole — over his right eye. Behind it was an unblinking eye shaking with raw, unbridled rage and power. It was a window to a soul Rose couldn't stand to look at. If this man even had a soul.

Rose's vision narrowed to a blurry tunnel and the last thing she saw before the world went black was a woman's hands emerging out of thin air — a ghostly apparition forming right before her very eyes. They reached out to her and the second their fingertips touched, the nightmare vision was swept away, replaced by the real world. In a flash, Rose was back in Greywood House and Drew was standing before her, holding her hands. They locked eyes. Drew said something to her, but Rose was too frazzled to make sense of the words. She was still trying to understand whatever the hell just happened.

Rose clutched the black quartz crystal in her hand. It felt warm. Angry, even. That crystal, that connection to her lost mother, had once given her so much comfort, but now it felt tainted, poisoned by this horror show of a house. Rose impulsively threw the crystal out of the open window. It arced through the air, passing perfectly between the billowing curtains.

And then it disappeared, winking out of existence.

Rose waited for the sound of the necklace being portaled back into the room. But it never came. She looked at the floor, an unexpected pang of regret setting in. She'd only thrown the crystal out of frustration. She hoped it popped back into the house downstairs.

Drew hurled a million and one questions at her, but Rose didn't have any answers. She didn't know where she had gone or how she had even gotten there. She didn't know the picturesque family or where they lived. She only knew one thing with absolute certainty.

"The Fireman is still here." Rose said as she rubbed her neck. It was raw to the touch, and she wondered what might have happened had Drew not pulled her out. *No.* She didn't have to wonder. She knew the truth. She could *feel* it. "And he's going to kill again."

Chapter 15

Eli paced the basement, lost in thought. Rose's story was a lot to process. They'd been arguing about it for what felt like hours. The police had bagged their bodies and left the house, leaving behind only a few stragglers who seemed to be milling about just to rack up overtime. Eli believed *Rose* believed she'd had some kind of out-of-body experience that turned into a nightmare, but she was making some serious leaps in logic to claim The Fireman was still in the house with them. There was a lot they didn't know about the afterlife, if that's what this was, but one thing was clear: a house was still just a house, right? Rose insisted it was more than that, that the house itself was alive in some way and they were all soul-bound to it, whatever the hell that meant.

"You guys aren't getting it," Rose sighed. "Killing someone doesn't just rip their life apart. It rips their *soul* apart. It's the ultimate violation. That's why we're here. And I'd bet that's why *he's* here, too. Or at least some fragment of him."

Eli wondered if this was purgatory, and the house was a waiting room to the other side. "When there's no more room left in hell, the dead will roam the waiting room," Eli joked. Only Drew laughed, which Rose didn't appreciate. Eli did, though. Thank God Drew shared his sense of humor.

Before long the group was back to bickering about the bigger existential picture, why they were still there, why they couldn't leave. Wes was uncommonly quiet throughout, which worried Eli. It wasn't like his brother to sit on the sidelines. But before Eli could ask him anything, Wes pointed to the black spots on the wall that Rose kept calling the rot. "Every time one of us does something to the people in the house, that shit grows bigger." Eli was stunned. It was such a simple, astute observation and he couldn't believe his idiot brother made it before him.

That only further fueled Rose's worry. She'd been so bothered by her struggle with The Fireman that she hadn't noticed the new spots. "If we start violating people, all we're doing is giving power to the memory of what happened here." Rose said. "That memory is what's *binding* us here. But if we stay hands off, if we let the memory of us and him and all of this fade..." Rose mimed a sort of "dust in the wind" gesture. "So will we."

The sentiment seemed logical enough to Eli. He loved to think in If-Then statements. It had been ingrained in him from his first computer class. It was the basis of all programming. If Thing A happens, then Thing B happens as a result. *If* they just stayed quiet and let everyone in the house calm down a bit, *then* the walls of the house would open up and they'd be out of purgatory. That sounded okay to Eli.

Rose turned to Wes, "We touch *nothing*. We do *nothing*. We keep it copacetic, and we'll eventually pass on peacefully. Okay?" Wes glared back. Drew squeezed her shoulder in solidarity. Wes wasn't having it, though. They'd already died once and were given a second chance as ghosts, but all Rose wanted was for them to just "fade away."

Eli tried to make it make sense for Wes. "I think Rose might be onto something. When a computer crashes, you get that blue screen of death, right? Well, before it can reboot, it has to do a memory dump to wipe whatever caused the crash." Eli could see Wes's eyes glazing over but he pressed on. "Maybe that's all this is. Maybe we're just leftover data hanging around while the world reboots. So if we let it reboot, then we'll get set free." They all looked at him like he was speaking a foreign language. Even Rose did, even though he was basically agreeing with her. "It makes sense to me, anyways."

Wes balked. "This isn't some computer crash, and this isn't some hippy-dippy, ashes-to-ashes bullshit. *If*," Wes stressed the word, knowing how Eli's brain worked, "we're in purgatory, *then* we are being tested. And *if* we don't pass that test, *then* we ain't getting out. Ever. When we do ghost shit, those holes get bigger, right? The wall starts disappearing, right? That's our way out." Wes said with total confidence, like he'd solved everything and the rest of them were idiots.

Compared to Rose's theory, Wes's seemed extra nuts. Possible, sure, but nuts. Wes could tell he wasn't getting through. "Eli. We gotta Shawshank it. The house is showing us there's a tunnel. All we gotta do is dig it."

Eli hated how much he appreciated that Wes used a movie reference that made a modicum of sense. Rose was ready to nip the idea in the bud, though. "I've seen the evil in this house, Wes. You can't *Shawshank* your way out of here. The only way to fight evil is to deny it power. The only way is to—"

"Do nothing?" Wes shouted. "Grow a pair, Rose. Otherwise you ain't ever getting out." Wes stomped up the stairs to the kitchen. Drew called him a toddler, but Eli saw it differently. Wes wasn't throwing a tantrum; he was making as much commotion as possible out of the hopes maybe someone upstairs might hear him. While the rest of them were sitting around talking, Wes was already trying to Shawshank his way to the other side. There was a logic to it that even Eli couldn't deny.

The *problem*, though, was there was logic on both sides. Rose believed they were being held and all they had to do was stop resisting and their spirits would be set free. Wes believed they had to *break* free.

Peter Hall & Paul Gandersman

Rose the pacifist, Wes the fighter. Both made their own kind of sense. Drew was standing by Rose, backing her up throughout, but Eli could tell she'd been intrigued by Wes's suggestion, too. He was hoping to talk to her about it later, when Rose wasn't around, to see what Drew really believed.

Chapter 16

Drew stared out the front window, flanked by Eli and Rose. Wes claimed his own window in the dining room. It had the best view, but no one bothered fighting him for it. The foursome watched in solemn silence as Detective Righetti, the last officer on the scene, stood by his car and stared back at the house. Drew wondered why he'd been the last to leave. Everyone else seemed eager to beat it, with car after car kicking up clouds of dirt every time they rolled out. Righetti was different. He'd hung around long after the others, just sitting in his car. Eli had assumed he was filling out paperwork. Wes insisted it was because the old man knew what was really going on here, that The Fireman had been here before, which only fueled Rose's insistence that he'd never actually left.

Drew didn't have the energy to debate either of them. Eli could go on and on about it all, rambling about parallel universes and quantum mechanics, but Drew pressed pause on trying to make sense of anything the second she watched them zip up her own body in what looked like a giant trash bag. Seeing *that* had broken her mind.

Righetti gave the house one last glance. He said something, but none of them could hear it. As Righetti got in his car and drove away,

Drew wondered if she'd hear anything from outside the house ever again.

And then Drew's mind broke all over again.

The exact moment Righetti's car left the property, the sky changed, and it changed *fast*. Day turned to night in seconds. The warm glow of the sun was replaced a second later by the cool moonlight. And then night turned to day. The sun and moon sped across the sky as if the entire world was in fast forward. Drew felt like they were at the center of a giant zoetrope and the outside world was spinning around them. Seasons started changing. Snow fell and melted in a heartbeat. Spring rains were replaced by shimmering summer heat. The leaves on the trees were a dizzying whirl of colors.

Drew turned from the hypnotic sky to see that inside the house, things were untouched. They were moving at a normal speed, talking at a normal pace. If Drew walked away from a window, it was hard to tell there was anything off about the outside world. She'd tip-toe back, though, and suddenly streaks of color flew by. She'd dated a guy who once told her she needed to drop acid to expand her mind. Drew hadn't been bold enough to try it. Now she wished she had. She wondered if it looked anything like this.

Eli had a theory for it all, because *of course* he did. It had something to do with Einstein and the special relativity of time, and how without living people present to keep time relative, they were observing it relative to something else. What that was, he wasn't sure, because Eli always had more questions than answers. Surprisingly, Rose didn't argue with him about it. Drew guessed it was because there wasn't a single one of Rose's beliefs that touched on the universe suddenly going warp speed. Instead of debating, Rose withdrew from the group.

The spinning sky started to make Drew feel a bit drunk. She and Eli turned away, unable to keep watching. Wes, however, stayed at the window, staring out, never blinking. Drew didn't know how he could stand it. Just thinking about it gave her motion sickness. She laid down on the couch, turned away from the windows, and closed her eyes, wondering if she could sleep. She tried counting sheep, but the cute fluffy animals were replaced by a parade of images repeating on a loop. For a while it was her mom on the porch right before Righetti closed the door in her face. She kept seeing that last vertical sliver of her mom disappearing over and over again as the door closed. Next it was a looping vision of The Fireman approaching her when she hid in the closet. She pictured the moment as if it were from a movie. She imagined herself jumping left to right, leaping from the closet and stabbing him again and again and again. She pictured herself driving him across the room, the chisel buried in his heart, over and over in instant replay. It was a calming thought. It wasn't sheep frolicking over a fence, but it was doing the trick. As Drew tried to count how many times she could jump out and stab him, she could feel herself growing tired, feel sleep sweeping over her body, like someone was tucking her into a warm blanket. She welcomed it, not caring if she ever woke up from it. Part of her hoped she wouldn't. She would be free of this nightmare.

Eli went from room to room, checking every window on the first floor, only to find the same sight no matter where he looked. By the time he stopped in the kitchen, he knew he needn't bother going upstairs to check. It would be the same everywhere. Outside, the world was racing by, while inside things were perfectly still. Abandoned. He'd been able to rationalize why that was happening, but that didn't make experiencing it any easier.

He rubbed his temples in an attempt to stave off a brewing headache. Eli distracted himself by trying to figure out how many days it had been since they were murdered. Every moment since the cops arrived had blurred together. Their bodies had been cleared, the blood stains cleaned (he was amazed at how they'd wiped out all but the faintest hints of what happened), the locks changed, and most of their personal belongings hauled out. Eli thought maybe their parents would come and do that personally, but he couldn't blame their families for sending crews of people to do it for them. All of that activity must have taken days, possibly weeks to accomplish, but it hadn't felt that way. Everything had felt like one really, really long day. But as he stared at the empty kitchen cabinets, Eli realized throughout all of it, at least one person had been in the house. Now that the living had left them behind, time had finally lost all meaning.

As all these thoughts hurricaned in his brain, Eli feared he was about to lose his grip on reality. Was this really all the afterlife held for them? Being imprisoned in the house they were killed in? This is what purgatory looks like? Forever? How fucking lame is that?

Eli didn't want to focus on *why* they were still here — he'd leave the philosophical stuff to Rose — but *how* they were still there. There had to be a logic to it. There had to be an If-Then to understand. And if he could just understand it, then he could exploit it.

Eli inspected the kitchen door. Someone had replaced the doorknob The Fireman chopped off. He reached for the lock and found his heart pounding. Could he open it? Should he open it?

He unlocked it. The knob turned and the door opened inward without resistance, revealing the world outside still spinning by in fast forward. Everything he'd ever experienced told him to brace for a loud, roaring sound as he watched trees whip around in the wind and day turn to night, but his ears were met with something even more unsettling: complete and utter silence. The outside world whirled by and yet made no sound whatsoever.

Drew couldn't stay asleep. The frustrating part was she couldn't tell if ghosts were literally incapable of sleep or if she couldn't shut off her brain long enough to make it happen. She opened her eyes and was surprised to find herself alone in the living room.

"Hello?"

Drew waited for an answer, but none came. A profound sense of Deja vu filled her with dread, like she was waking up in this cursed house totally alone all over again. She hurried around the first floor, desperately searching for someone and was relieved to find Eli standing in front of the open kitchen door, the world spinning on behind him. He stood completely still, gazing out, immobilized by the sight.

"Uh, Eli?" Drew asked. Eli jumped in surprise, as if woken from a daydream.

"Oh, hey Drew."

"Where is everyone?"

"I think they went up to their rooms. Muscle memory, I guess."

"Well, what are *you* doing? Drew asked.

Eli looked at the open door, confused, like he'd forgotten why he'd opened it in the first place. "I was just... testing it? I guess? I don't know what the hell I'm doing, to be perfectly honest with you."

"Testing what?" Drew asked, intrigued. She liked the idea of taking on a project. Anything to get her mind off the places it kept spiraling to.

Eli shifted uneasily, unable to hide the fact he had neither clue nor plan. If Rose had been the one to find him this way, she'd have been pissed at him for opening doors without thinking of the potential outcome. Drew didn't mind, though. She was a creature of impulse herself. She never planned her art projects, she just started carving by instinct. The trick to good art, she believed, was to let the intent reveal itself along the way.

"Well, you got the door open." Drew said.

"It was easy, but I suppose that's because we're alone."

"I thought it would be louder." Drew was disturbed by the impossible silence outside. Of all the things she'd witnessed so far in the afterlife, the complete and utter lack of sound outside Greywood House was the most unsettling, what felt the most like *the other side.*

"Me too!" Eli said, suddenly enthusiastic. "It's so fucking weird," he added.

"Are you going to go through it?"

Drew and Eli both stared at the open door, considering what lay beyond it. Drew had tried the portals at the front door and the basement, but not the kitchen. Her gut told her anything that went in it would just end up back in the foyer again, but she had to know for sure. She unwrapped the flannel shirt from around her waist.

"Now what the hell are you doing?" Eli asked.

"What could possibly go wrong?" Drew asked, shrugging her shoulders with a mercurial grin.

Drew wrapped one sleeve of the shirt around her right arm. Then she tossed the other arm at the kitchen door. The portal snatched it, pulling it taught like a rope.

"Holy crap!" Drew said, feeling the flannel pull tighter and tighter. She pulled it at an angle, but the shirt stayed in the same spot, as if glued to the dead center of the portal.

"Hold on, I want to go see if the other end is just floating in the foyer!" Eli called as he backed out of the room.

Drew smiled as she played tug of war with the void, imagining an invisible giant on the other side. She told Eli to hurry up as the portal's pull grew stronger and stronger on the shirt. She was afraid it was going to rip in half. But before she could drop it, Drew lost the game of tug-of-war, as both she and the shirt were yanked into the portal.

Eli barely had enough time to get to the foyer before the shirt and then Drew appeared out of thin air. She screamed as she slid forward, slingshotted into the wall. Eli rushed to her side.

"Are you okay?" Given the look on her face, he felt stupid for asking. Of course, she wasn't okay. She'd just experienced teleportation. Hell, she'd just violated the space-time continuum. Or at least the space part of it. Considering how fast things were moving outside, they were already violating the time part.

"Did it hurt?"

Drew struggled to catch her breath. She tried to talk but couldn't. The wind had been knocked out of her lungs and when she *was* able to get words out, her voice was hoarse. "I don't want to do that ever again."

Eli laughed. "So, you're saying that's not the way out, either?"

Drew hit him playfully in the stomach. He could tell the portal hadn't done any serious damage (or, rather, he hoped it hadn't), it was probably just disorienting as all hell.

"I'm saying that unless you want to feel like your insides are on the outside, you should probably go close that fucking door."

"Fair enough," Eli said. He dashed back to the kitchen; the door was still wide open. Outside, snow was blanketing the trees and then melting off as quickly as it had arrived. He stared at the surreal sight, hypnotized.

He wanted to go there.

He wanted to walk through it.

To feel time.

But he was too scared.

Eli closed the kitchen door. And not a moment too soon, either. Wes started shouting from upstairs, his voice reverberating throughout the house. Eli ran toward the foyer and found Wes running down the stairs, shouting "It stopped! It stopped!"

"What stopped?" Rose wasn't far behind him.

"The world. It stopped spinning!"

Eli's heart sank in his chest. When Drew asked what could possibly go wrong by messing with the portal, he thought she was just being sarcastic. He didn't think the answer was "It could break the universe." He ran to the window to see what happened and in the split second it took to reach it Eli had a vision of the outside reduced to nothing but darkness.

He was wrong, though, and Wes was right. The world was still out there, and it was no longer spinning, but back to its boring, ordinary flow of time. He pointed outside at the approaching vehicle. "See, I told you it's the people," he said, shocked that his theory had been right.

"Wait," Drew said. "What people?"

THE LIVING GIRL

Chapter 17

Abbey Moreno watched, bored, as trees blurred past the Volvo's window. Green, brown, green, brown. Freakin' endless. Occasionally a mailbox would poke out, revealing winding driveways to giant houses you could barely see through all the goddamned green and brown. Javier kept pointing out how private things would be out here, and how he could finally get a good night's sleep, but Abbey didn't care about that. Back home she could spit and hit a neighbor's house, but the lack of privacy wasn't a big deal. Even the Kincaid's screaming matches next door (they'd had to call the police on the Kincaid's more than once) had never caused her to lose sleep, and she didn't think her dad had lost any, either. Not from noise, anyway. There were plenty of reasons her dad was having crappy sleep. Privacy wasn't one of them.

Abbey joked that out here the houses were so far away they probably wouldn't even hear it if the neighbors were murdering each other. It was dead end street after dead end street. Javier laughed, a hearty, bear-hug of a sound that always made Abbey feel better. They both had good senses of humor. They'd needed 'em to make it through the last year together.

Abbey brushed hair out of her eyes and slipped her headphones back on. She turned up the volume, trying to drift away to Billie Eilish.

She felt like it was a total cliche for a sixteen-year-old to love Billie as much as she did, but on the other hand she didn't really give a damn. One of the more somber, downbeat tracks ("When the Party's Over") was playing, which brought on thoughts about her mom. She felt herself starting to fall into an emotional pit that she really couldn't handle right now, so she hit shuffle and brightened as upbeat drums kicked in.

It felt like they'd been driving for hours, but it was just because everything out here looked the same. The subdivision was called Woodbine Falls, so she'd kept an eye out for some kind of waterfall, but there wasn't even a pond in sight. Just trees. Lots and lots of trees. Green, brown, green, brown; freakin' endless. She loved nature, but more as a visitor than a permanent resident. One of her favorite memories was a road trip to Yosemite National Park to see the sequoias. She and her parents had linked arms to hug one of the ancient trees and they couldn't even make it halfway around. Those were special trees. They were older than America, for crying out loud. Her mind wandered, trying to figure out what the hell a "woodbine" even was, she could Google it but was content in deciding it was probably some kind of machine that harvested beautiful trees older than the Declaration of Independence and turned them into Ikea coffee tables.

Javier slowed the car down and pointed to a brick pillar at the end of the driveway. On top of the mailbox was a light sconce built to look like a New England lighthouse. Abbey wondered why anyone would do that this far from the ocean. *Maybe the previous owners wanted to escape the endless woods, too.* The top of the lighthouse had been smashed off. Abbey imagined a bunch of drunk teenagers driving by with baseball bats, hitting mailboxes. That was a thing people who lived out in the middle of nowhere did, right? Is that what she was going to end up doing for fun out here?

"Here we are." Javier said. "Are you ready, punk?" Abbey slipped off her headphones, making an overly dramatic sigh, playing the part of the angsty teen for her old man. Javier reached over and tousled her hair, "Bob promised a diamond in the rough, so hold onto your butts."

"I only have one butt, dad." Abbey said in auto-response. They'd been doing this back-and-forth for longer than she could remember. It was something her dad said to her forever ago, a quote she didn't understand until she finally saw that old movie, Jurassic Park. She'd called him a dork for letting her think he'd made it up this whole time. They still kept the back-and-forth going, though.

Javier turned down the drive. Unlike all the paved ones Abbey spied, this one was gravel. There was a small hill at the end, blocking the other side. Abbey was surprised to feel nervous, like she was about to show up to a blind date (not that Abbey really dated, blind or not), as they climbed the hill. And then the house came into view, and they both said "Holy shit" in perfect unison. Javier's version sounded much more optimistic.

The house was enormous, a three-story behemoth with a wraparound porch so wide and long Abbey could have sworn it alone was bigger than their current house. But it was also old. Like, *super old*. As the Volvo bounced up the drive, the details started to come into focus. The roof was missing a bunch of shingles. Wood was peeling off the sides like tree bark. The front steps were so warped they looked like an art project, as if someone tried to recreate ocean waves out of 2x4s.

"Are you serious, dad? It's in worse shape than our house."

"That's why we can afford it," Javier winked back.

A Mercedes Benz was already in the driveway and a man in a suit waited on the porch. Bob was some kind of friend-of-a-friend realtor who swore he'd be able to find them the perfect fixer upper they needed right now. Abbey didn't think a house was what they needed, but her dad sure did, so here they were, past the smashed lighthouse, at the end of a long, unpaved driveway, staring at a busted-ass house. Surrounded by green and brown, green and brown; freakin' endless.

Bob waved with a big, toothy grin and Abbey wondered if she'd seen him on a bus bench ad. He put on an expensive-looking face mask and yelled something about how the door was sticking, but Abbey couldn't make it all out. Javier parked behind the Benz, grabbed one of their homemade facemasks from the center console, and jogged eagerly up to Bob, nearly tripping on the warped steps in the process.

Abbey lingered in the car. She thought her dad was crazy for trying to move on top of everything else 2020 had to offer, but at least it was a good distraction from all the chaos. She pulled out her phone and readied for a selfie, checking her hair and making minor adjustments. Then she dropped her smile and put on as bored a face as possible before taking the picture. It was a quirk she'd taken from her mom. Any time they took a selfie, they did it stone faced. They could be in the middle of a roller coaster ride, and they'd deadpan for the camera. It was their thing. Or, it *had* been their thing. Abbey guessed it was just her thing now.

She brushed the thought away, put her mask on, and sauntered up to the house. It seemed to be alive, if barely hanging on for dear life. Its sides weren't as straight as they had once been. The huge wooden front door was decaying. It had an ornate, wrought-iron number one on it that served as both the address and a door knocker, but it was rusty, and Abbey wondered if it would fall off the hinge if she tried to use it. The windows were covered in a veil of dust so thick she couldn't see inside.

The porch steps moaned and groaned as Abbey climbed them to find Bob and her dad struggling to open the door. Bob was apologizing, rambling about how his firm had just acquired the listing from the estate and no one had had a chance to stop by yet so they should be warned he had no idea what to expect inside.

"You said you wanted a fixer upper," Bob laughed as he worked the front door open. The lock finally made a grinding sound as years of rust and grit broke free, and the bolt unlocked with a loud *shunk*. Bob swept the door open, and the men entered the dusty and dank foyer. She heard both say "Oh wow" and "Man oh man" and other things old dudes say when they're afraid of silence. "Is it that bad?" Abbey asked.

Javier turned back, beaming. "Abs, you have got to see this." *Oh, God, now what?* Abbey followed him inside. It took her eyes a minute to adjust to the darkness, but once she could see, she understood why her dad had been smiling so wide. The outside of the house looked like it was about to fall over, but the inside was shockingly well preserved. The foyer was massive, with the kind of sweeping staircase leading to a second floor that Abbey had only ever seen in movies. Standing at the door, to her right was a dining room, to her left a sprawling living room split in two parts. Whoever owned it before left behind a handful of random furniture pieces. The fabric on an old couch was dusty, but still salvageable, and Abbey briefly thought about asking if she could keep it in her room.

"I was expecting worse." Javier said, always the optimist. As much as that optimism often frustrated Abbey, she also admired him for it.

"The bones are still in good shape, and that's what really matters." Bob said, sounding so much like a salesman, Abbey started to wonder if she knew him from TV ads rather than the bus bench. He took reference photos with his iPhone, and even he couldn't hide his surprise to see the interior looking as good as it did. Bob turned to them and let out a way-too-chipper "Consider yourself blessed."

Javier whispered to Abbey. "You hear that, Abs? We're hashtag blessed." She rolled her eyes as over the top as possible, even though she secretly loved his terrible dad jokes. He bowed before her and waved his arms. "Your castle awaits." Abbey slipped her headphones back on and set off to explore.

"Hashtag you're welcome," Javier called after her as he took out his own phone and started snapping pictures. Abbey settled her eyes on the staircase. Her dad and Bob could check out the rest of the house, she only had one mission: find the best bedroom. As long as she could find her own little sanctuary, the rest of the house didn't matter. She put a hand on the railing and laughed at the soft pillow of dust that billowed. She watched the particles twinkle like stars in the dim light as they drifted back to the floor. She took her fingers and scissor walked them up the railing, creating fingertip footprints in the dust that reminded her of walking through a fresh snowfall.

She reached the second floor and wiped the dust off her fingers. She poked her head into the first door at the top of the stairs. The bedroom was huge, clearly the master so there's no way Javier would let her have it. An old bed frame had been left behind. It was missing the mattress, but the box spring remained, probably left behind by a lazy mover. The master had its own bathroom, filled with lime green tiles and out of date fixtures. Her dad would probably love it. He'd call it kitschy or something.

The next door was a laundry room that surprisingly had a washer and dryer in it, though Abbey doubted they still turned on, and if they did, she wouldn't trust them. They'd probably make her clothes smell musty like the rest of the house. A little further down, the narrow hallway made an elbow turn and she found two doors opposite one another. The one on her right was another bathroom, which had the same ugly lime green tile in it. The door on her left was a bedroom. It was smaller than the master, but still plenty big enough for her. But save for a pair of light red curtains that still hung on some of the windows, it just didn't *feel* like a room for her.

At the end of the hallway Abbey found the attic stairs. They called to her, beckoning. She stood at the bottom and gazed up. The wood on these stairs was a darker color than the rest of the house. The staircase was steep, with an oddly high ceiling that reminded Abbey of the entrance to a carnival funhouse she'd been too scared to enter. She was much younger then, and the staircase there led directly into the mouth of a giant clown. There was no screaming clown here, though, just a dull light at the top of the tunnel. Abbey turned up the volume on her music and took the first step.

Javier couldn't believe their luck. Judging by the look on Bob's face, the realtor couldn't believe it either. Even the basement of the house was enormous, and they both had to use their phones as flashlights to look around. It was an unfinished cavern that spanned the entire width of the house. Javier joked that the basement alone was bigger than their entire house. Bob admitted it was bigger than his, too.

Javier started doing the math in his head, trying to figure out the price per square foot, when he noticed the basement door leading to an exterior stairwell. Where the door should have been was a thick sheet of plywood that had been nailed in its place. The realtor didn't miss a beat. "Hey man, for the money you'd be saving on this place, you can afford all new doors."

They headed back up to the kitchen, repeating like parrots how they both couldn't believe the state of the place. Javier asked a few questions about the seller, and Bob said he'd accidentally forgotten the packet he'd gotten from the estate in their car. He'd give them a copy once they were back at the office. Javier sensed Bob was lying about the packet, but it didn't matter. He'd do his own research later.

Whatever the origin of the sale, Javier knew it didn't really matter. He needed something to focus on. He needed a project that would wholly consume him, force his mind off the hell he and Abbey had been through. He knew Abbey would give him a bit of shit moving all the way out here, but it was surprisingly still in their same school district, so she wouldn't have to leave her friends behind. He guessed the first thing Abbey would ask for was a car, and as nervous as that made him, it *would* be a must have if they lived out here. He could give her his car, though, and get a new one himself. *Volvo's are very safe cars, right?* Didn't he deserve to treat himself to something newer and nicer? A BMW? *Okay, maybe a Mazda.*

Something about the living room caught Javier's eye. It looked remarkably like the living room from Risky Business, and all Javier wanted to do was go recreate Tom Cruise's iconic slide in from the other room. It's what Abbey would lovingly call 'a total dad move.' He looked back to Bob, wanting to say something, but Bob was in the middle of looking up something on his phone. *Fuck it*, Javier thought, *I'm gonna do it.*

Javier pulled out his phone and opened his camera, switching it to video. He turned around, a smile growing on his face as he framed up his phone to look back out into the foyer. He carefully set the phone down on the windowsill, pressed record and jogged out of the room. Before he could get into place, his phone fell off the windowsill. He cursed out loud as he turned around, praying the screen wasn't cracked, suddenly feeling stupid for the whole thing. 'A totally dumb-dad move,' as Abbey would have called it.

As Javier turned around, he saw something that made his brain skip like a scratched record. It looked, for just a second, like the phone was floating off the ground, as if it had tried to pick itself up off the floor but couldn't. Javier approached it slowly, trying to rationalize it, trying to convince himself that he hadn't seen what he thought he had.

Abbey stood in the middle of the attic bedroom, imagining how she'd make it her own. Whoever had taken all the furniture hadn't bothered to take down the posters. The walls were lined with the faded faces of Kurt Cobain, Nine Inch Nails, and some band called Garbage. They were covered in dust, like everything else in the house, and barely hung to the small thumb tacks that held them in place. Abbey liked them. They felt cool. They felt vintage.

Something touched her shoulder and Abbey jumped in fright. She turned to find her dad, grinning ear to ear like a big ol' doofus. She punched his shoulder for trying to scare her. He took it like a champ. "What do you think of it?" he asked, wincing a bit at the strength in Abbey's small but furious fist.

Abbey knew that if she said no, he wouldn't move them way the hell out there. He might be heartbroken, but Abbey knew her dad would house hunt for a year if that's what she wanted. But she didn't need to break his heart. She looked around the room, wanting to smile but refusing to give him the satisfaction. She just shrugged. "It's alright."

"But is it home? Could it be home?"

Abbey turned toward the stairs, teetering on the edge. The staircase seemed somehow longer than before, even darker, with the light fading away at the top steps. But Abbey liked that. It made the attic feel separate from the house below, like it was its own apartment atop it all. *Her apartment.* She liked that idea. She liked that idea a lot.

Bob stood in the foyer, by the front door, talking rapidly into his AirPods, telling the woman on the other end that he had a feeling the Moreno's were going to buy and that she should start drafting up the papers. Normally he wouldn't jump to conclusions. It's not like they were close. They'd been connected through friends-of-friends who wanted to "help Javi and Abs out," but he knew how badly Javier wanted to get out of their old house, to get away from the memories it held.

If Javier hadn't been a friend of a friend, Bob might have tanked this sale intentionally. When the estate approached them, all they could offer were some exterior pictures and tax records. The woman who owned it had been paying the taxes for years, apparently out of the hope she'd one day have the stomach to return to it. She never did, though. Not that anyone could blame her, all things considered. Bob knew as soon as they publicly listed it, the place would be snapped up by some trendy developer who would demolish it and build something modern. Hell, they could subdivide the lot and fit a half-dozen other pre-fabs on this plot, but he hated those kinds of deals. Not because he was against flippers, people in suits just always haggled endlessly on the price, always trying to find the lowest floor they could pay. Bob knew Javier wouldn't do that — assuming Javier was still interested after he learned about the house's regrettable history.

Bob was swiping through the calendar on his phone trying to figure out how quickly they could close when he felt a tap on his shoulder. He swatted at it, trying to hit away whatever nasty bug landed on him, but when he looked there was nothing there. He went back to swiping on the phone, but not a moment later the phantom bug returned. He hated bugs. He hated houses in the woods.

But there was no bug.

Bob twisted and turned.

There weren't any bugs in the house.

It was totally still, totally silent.

But he knew *something* had touched him. *Something* had been on his shoulder. *Something* had been close to him. Very close. A sudden cold tickled its way up his spine and he felt like he'd been shoved into a walk-in freezer. "Fuck this." Bob said, stepping out of the house and onto the porch. The sun instantly started to warm him, and he felt very, very eager to make this deal and be done with Greywood House.

Javier and Abbey jogged down the stairs. He switched immediately back into sales mode. "I told you it was a diamond in the rough, didn't I?" The father and daughter followed him onto the porch, chuckling about how rough it was on the outside but how oddly charming on the inside. Bob nodded in agreement as he put his hand on the front doorknob. He stared back into the house, his eyes darting around the cavernous foyer one last time to spot whatever had just touched him, but there were only cobwebs and shadows.

Bob took a deep breath, pulled the door shut, and launched into the one part of the pitch he'd been dreading. "The estate is selling as-is, so it is an insane deal, but there is one thing you should know about this house..."

Chapter 18

DREW COULDN'T STOP HEARING THE WORDS. *"THE ESTATE IS selling as-is, the estate is selling as-is, the estate is selling as-is."* Rose, Eli, and Wes were buzzing around the first floor, moving from window to window as the girl, the dad, and the guy in the suit drove away, but Drew couldn't feel her legs. She stood, frozen, staring at the front door. *"The estate is selling as-is, the estate is selling as-is, the estate is selling as-is."*

Drew knew what the words meant but she couldn't accept them. Her mom didn't have an estate. That was a stupid thing for the guy in the suit to say, right? Only dead people had estates, right? And there's no way her mom was dead. Not now. That wasn't supposed to happen for a long, long time, when Drew was much, much older. Carol Denns was still out there, somewhere, just waiting for Drew to find her and reach out to her, to tell her everything she'd written in that damned note. A note that was now trapped under the floorboards of the attic. Trapped in this goddamn house, just like Drew. *Forfuckingever.*

The others were staring silently outside, watching the cars leave the driveway. First the Volvo, and then the Benz. As soon as the Benz disappeared over the small hill at the end of the drive, the sky went fast-forward. Eli spun from the windows, clapping his hands in excitement. Drew thought he'd never looked happier.

"Holy shit, did you guys see those fucking things?" Eli asked.

"The masks? What was up with those?" Wes asked.

"No, that was probably for dust or something. I'm talking about those screen things." Eli said.

"They were like cameras and phones and calendars all in one," Wes said. Eli touched his nose, pointing at Wes to say he'd gotten it right. That finger pointing was something Eli always did. He was probably copying from some movie Drew was sure she'd seen but couldn't remember. She didn't care. Not now. Not when her brain kept looping *"The estate is selling as-is, the estate is selling as-is." Forfuckingever.*

Eli's hands gesticulated wildly as he rambled. "Did you guys see the date on the screens? Because I sure did."

"It looked like it was from the future," Rose said.

"It *is* from the future! The screen said August third, *two thousand and twenty*." Eli stared at the group, expecting them to share his excitement. Not one of them did. Did they not understand what this meant? Did he stutter? He knew he did that sometimes when he got too excited about something. He repeated himself.

"No." Drew said.

"I'm serious, Drew. It said twenty-twenty. That's like…" Eli did the math in his head. "That's five years after freakin' Back to the Future Part 2 is set. That's… holy shit, guys. While the world was going all spinny-spin, we blew right past Back to the Future 2."

Drew shook her head at Eli. Why didn't she believe him? Why didn't any of them believe him? Hell, even if he'd somehow misread the date — which he was positive he hadn't — those people were still all walking around with technology he'd only ever seen before in sci-fi movies. None of them had ever seen a screen that thin, or a camera that slid into someone's pocket, let alone a device that had both of them built together. He'd read in an issue of WiRED how Hewlett-Packard was working on these things called "Palmtop PCs," but even those looked nothing like this. They had keyboards attached to them and green and black screens that looked like a graphing calculator. These people were carrying around Star Trek shit. Christ, even Star Trek's tech wasn't as thin and lightweight. Where'd they even fit the batteries in them?

"Look, we can all see time gets weird when living people aren't here. I've been trying to figure out how much of it has been passing, but I get too dizzy staring at it. But if days are going by like that," Eli snapped his fingers, "then it's only going to take a minute before weeks go by. It doesn't feel like that in here because--"

"Screw your special relativity, Eli." Wes said. He was pissed. Big surprise. But Eli wasn't the one making everything move fast forward. He wasn't the one who made them miss the last twenty-two years of their lives. They were all in this mess together. Or so he thought. Now they were all looking at him like this *was* somehow his fault. He was just connecting dots. *Don't shoot the messenger.*

Wes paced back and forth in front of the window, watching the sun arc across the sky followed quickly by the moon. The last time he went to sleep it was 1998. How could any of this be possible? How could twenty-two years pass just like that? He could feel his blood boiling the more he thought about it. His face felt on fire. It suddenly felt hard to breathe. Wes paced, trying to avoid the same kind of panic attack he'd had when he awoke next to his own dead body. There was no avoiding it. This was Hell. He knew he'd be here someday, but he didn't deserve it so soon. Not when The Ruins were just taking off. Twenty-two years. He'd been dead as long as he'd been alive? *Fuck that.*

Wes punched a window. A crack split the glass right down the middle, but it didn't shatter. Greywood House was too goddamned stubborn for that. It couldn't even give Wes the satisfaction of smashing a window. It couldn't give him anything. All the house could do was take and take and take. It took his life and took his future. The Ruins were going to be huge; he had *known* it. He'd never been more sure of anything in his life. He'd given everything to that band. Years of sleepless nights. He'd literally bled for the band, practicing so long and hard the guitar strings would slice through his fingertips. He didn't care. He had to *act* like it wasn't a big deal, but it was. Bleeding on his guitar was proof that he had what it takes. Until it was taken from him.

Wes wheeled away from the cracked window and saw Drew, Rose, and Eli all staring back at him like he'd just kicked a puppy. He didn't understand why they weren't just as pissed off as he was. "Don't look at me like that. I don't know about whatever the hell you guys had going on, but me? I was fucking going places. I wasn't some loser, I actually had something taken from me. I was fucking robbed. In *your* goddamned house, Drew!"

Drew locked eyes with him, looking like she wanted to rip his throat out. Wes knew Drew was a ballbuster, but he hadn't quite seen this level of intensity before. He kind of loved it. But before he could say anything, she broke contact, focused on the front door, threw the deadbolt to the side, and ripped it open.

Rose flinched as the front door slammed into the wall. She knew Drew could be impulsive, especially when it came to dealing with hard truths, but was still surprised to see her acting this way. Rose called out to her, "Drew, what are you—" but she couldn't get the words out before Drew ran at the front door, right into the portal.

FFFWWWWT— Drew disappeared, winking out of existence.

And then she reappeared, thrown sideways into the wall of the foyer. Rose called out her name again, but Drew either didn't hear her or didn't care. Drew picked herself up and readied another charge at the portal, but this time Rose ran in front of her, blocking the door. Rose pleaded with Drew, begging her to stop, begging her to just talk to them. They'd figure this all out together. Rose knew there was some way out of here. There had to be. They just needed to calm down and think.

Drew finally looked up, which was when Rose noticed her tears. She couldn't remember the last time she'd seen Drew cry. They'd been through so much together, so many break-ups and heartbreaks and drunken mistakes, but it was always Rose who was the emotional one. Drew was the rock. But Rose could tell the rock was crumbling.

"Just talk to me, Drew."

"He said the estate is selling as-is, Rose. The *estate*."

Rose had been too busy trying to keep up with everything to really listen, to *hear* what the guy in the suit was saying. Drew's lip started shaking. Rose could tell her emotional dam was about to burst, but before it could, Drew ran up the stairs. Rose wanted to run after her, but she was still in such a state of shock herself that all she could do was turn to Eli and Wes, wanting to justify why she wasn't on the same page as Drew, tell them she didn't know, she hadn't heard, but as soon as she saw the looks on their faces she knew she didn't have to explain herself. They were all just as lost and confused.

Drew sat in the attic windowsill, watching the sky in time lapse. It had been terrifying before, but she found it almost calming now. Probably because she was just too numb to care. There was no point in fighting any of this. They were in Hell. Maybe if she just gave in, she'd sink into the floor and die for real.

She heard a timid knock on the door and turned away from the sky to find Rose. Drew knew she'd come; knew she'd want to talk. Drew didn't feel like it, but not saying things out loud — not telling her mom the truth about what she meant to her — is one reason she was such a failure.

"I wasted my fucking life, Rose."

"No you didn't. Don't say that."

Rose sat next to Drew and leaned on her shoulder. It reminded Drew of how her cat, Mr. Pickles, used to always lay on her, and Drew was hit with a new wave of sadness realizing that even the damn cat would be dead by now. Rose tried to talk, tried to make Drew feel better, but she wasn't having it.

"Yes, I did. I really, really did. I wasted my mom's money on art classes instead of what I told her I was taking. I wasted her money by begging her to let us live in this house. I never finished *anything*. And then what happens? I get fucking killed. I get us all fucking killed. I literally wasted my life. *And* yours. I'm fucking useless, Rose. And now I'll be useless forever."

"You are *not* useless."

Drew ignored Rose and stared at the spot on the floor where the note had sunk irretrievably into the house. All that was left was a tiny little corner of white paper sticking out between the floorboards. It would never be seen by another living soul. Just like her. *Forfuckingever*. "And now I've wasted my chance to apologize. I wasted everything. I've been so stupid, so selfish, so fucking—" Rose placed her hands on Drew's shoulders.

She couldn't bear to look Rose in the eyes. She was doing everything in her power to hold back the torrent of tears that wanted to break free. She couldn't take that. Not now. She looked away, back to the site of the buried note. A list of missed opportunities ran through her head as Rose spoke softly.

"You're allowed to be angry. And you're allowed to be sad. But don't blame yourself for any of this. You're not allowed to do that."

Drew finally gave in and looked Rose in the eyes. They'd always had a deep connection, but in that moment, it felt somehow stronger than ever. Drew thought she could literally feel Rose's strength working its way into her, trying to help her fight off the darkness.

"I never told you this," Rose said, changing the topic, "but after my parents died, I asked your mom if she could adopt me. And do you know what she said?"

Drew couldn't help but crack a smile. "That I'd already asked."

"That you already asked."

"I found a lawyer and everything." Drew said. She shook her head at how silly it all seemed now. Child logic was a hell of a thing. Rose laughed and wiped away some tears from her face.

"Then she said something I'll never forget. She said that you and I were already sisters. Not by blood or birth but by—"

"Choice. She told me the same thing."

Rose squeezed Drew tightly. "She said that as long as we had each other, we could handle *anything*." Drew couldn't hold back the tears anymore. Rose had broken through in a way only best friends knew how.

"We are going to get out of here. Together." Rose said. So calm, so confident.

Drew wished she had even a shred of that optimism right now. Or even a shred of that selflessness. Right now, all Drew wanted was to be selfish. She wished she'd never gone back for Rose, wished she'd stayed on the other side of the basement door, wished she'd run free into the night. More than anything, she wished she wasn't thinking those things.

Wes stared deeply into the rotting basement wall. The rot's spread had continued outward, black acid eating away the wall of the real world. He was fascinated by it. So far, being a ghost fucking sucked. He was convinced that this house was just a layover on their trip to the real afterlife, and the rot was the way out, but nobody believed him. *Morons.* Why couldn't the others see it was a door for them to open? So far, sitting around doing nothing had cost them twenty-two years of their lives. What else was Rose's hippie-do-nothing-bullshit going to cost them?

Every year the Adams family took a summer trip to visit cousins at Myrtle Beach. They always flew. Never first class though. Wes was always jealous of the people in first class. They got to board the plane before anyone else. *He* wanted to be first. He'd wait as close as possible to the gate so he could be first in line when their boarding group was called. Wes just wanted the rot to open up so he could board the plane out of there. Rose and Drew were going to make them miss the flight altogether.

Wes turned to Eli, who was laying on the floor staring at the rafters. "She's wrong about all of this, you know? We're not supposed to just wait."

Eli ignored him. Of course he was perfectly content with Rose's "do nothing" plan. Eli was a sheep, just like the rest of 'em. Wes leaned in closer to the rot, his eye inches from the largest patch of darkness, trying to see through to the other side, when he thought he saw movement in the wall. He could have *sworn* he saw a swirl of motion in the darkness. He told Eli to come look.

"You're getting a little cabin fever-y dude," Eli muttered, still staring at the ceiling. "But if you just chill out—"

"Fuck off. Something's in there. And it's the key to us getting out," Wes hovered his hand over the hole. There was a similar feeling to the portal at the front door. The darkness didn't shimmer in the same way, but it radiated a presence like standing next to power lines. He was convinced it would take them somewhere. Just as the front door kept them here, this door — once they opened it — would take them somewhere else. "Someone has to man up, Eli. Is it going to be you?"

Eli sat up. He looked pissed. Wes brushed him off and leaned in closer to the hole, squinting, trying his hardest to get a peek at what was in there. He knew there was something on the other side. He'd bet his afterlife on it.

Chapter 19

HE WATCHED, SILENTLY, PATIENTLY, THROUGH THE ROTTEN HOLES. Long shafts of light from the basement stabbed around him, spears of holy illumination in the infinite darkness.

There was a man on the other side.

No, not a man. A boy, really.

He was so close to the boy. Close enough to reach out and take him.

But no. Not yet. The rot was still growing.

They were growing it for him.

The time would come, just as it had before.

The door was cracked, but not open. He felt a connection to this boy.

This boy would open the door for him.

This boy would be the key.

Chapter 20

Abbey's heart was in her throat as the U-Haul turned onto the driveway of 1 Prescott Lane. She held her breath, unsure why she was suddenly so nervous about the move. Things had gone so smoothly with the purchase, her dad said, that Abbey kept expecting something to go wrong. Maybe the house will have vanished into thin air or, more likely, fallen over, since they last visited. But as the car crested the hill at the bottom of the driveway, the diamond-in-the-rough they were "hashtag blessed to snag pre-market" (Bob's words, of course) was still standing. She let herself relax.

Sitting on Abbey's lap was a pugnacious old cat named Oracle; a handsome, defiant longhair her mom rescued. Next to her was Abbey's best friend, Willa Gordon, who insisted on helping her move. Willa adopted a preppier style in recent years, while Abbey fell into a disaffected, laid-back look. Fashion and taste never defined their friendship, though. The pair were like sisters, and since the pandemic started, they'd agreed to be in each other's bubbles, which meant spending even more time together than normal.

"This place is insane," Willa said while sliding out of the U-Haul.

"I know, right?" Abbey replied, stretching her legs, Oracle in her arm. She'd been hoping the house would impress. Willa came from money. A lot more money than Abbey and Javier had, but she never acted like it. Abbey knew she wouldn't be able to impress Willa with the state of the house, but hoped its vibe, and particularly that killer attic bedroom, would win her over. She knew she didn't *need* to impress Willa. It's not like she'd stop being Abbey's friend. Abbey just had that same desire that all teenagers had at one point or another. She wanted to be cool. *The cool girl with her own upstairs apartment.*

Javier hopped out of the driver's seat looking like a kid about to rob a candy store. "You girls ready?" Abbey nodded and held out her cat-free-hand: *Keys please.* Javier dropped them in her palm and the two girls raced to the front door. Abbey let Oracle down at the doorstep. She knew he wouldn't run away. Her mom called him the most dog-like cat she'd ever seen. His purring intensified and Abbey wondered if he was as nervous as she was.

Abbey stabbed the key into the lock, but the damn thing wouldn't turn. She kicked the door in frustration. Willa cocked an eyebrow, "You thought that would help?" Abbey playfully told her to shut up and tried the lock again, twisting the key so hard her hand started to hurt. Right as she was about to give up, the lock shuddered open. Abbey winked at Willa and brushed her shoulders off like she was a big deal.

They opened the door with a sweeping bow, a trail of dust rose off the floor as it opened. "Welcome, m'lord, to our castle." Willa began to step forward, but Abbey held her back. "I'm talking to Orrie," Abbey said as she directed Oracle, her little lord, inside first. The silver-haired cat pounced into the house and immediately froze, his beady eyes darting all over the place. He was transfixed, but then again so was Willa. Abbey smirked. The inside was such a drastic difference from the outside, even the cat couldn't help but be overwhelmed. Abbey stepped past the bewildered Oracle and began the tour in the living room, doing her best impression of an HGTV host.

"So, this is the orgy room." Abbey said, totally deadpan. Willa giggled, then turned around to find a stern-faced Javier standing behind them.

Abbey knew Willa didn't have nearly as playful a relationship with her own parents. Willa blushed a deep pink as Javier cleared his throat. "Ahem." He drew the word out as he set down a box of electronics in the foyer. Abbey launched into apology mode.

"Oh, I'm so sorry, dad." She turned to Willa, switching back to HGTV mode, "Willa, my apologies. This is just all so very, very embarrassing." Abbey turned to look her dad in the eyes. "I meant to say it's the *downstairs* orgy room."

Javier shook his head as he walked back to the U-Haul. Abbey grinned, ear to ear, proud of herself. She might have been showing off. Just a little. "Come on. I've got to show you the best part." The girls bounded upstairs, as Oracle remained behind, his head swiveling around the room, from one spot to the next, over and over.

Rose, Drew, Eli, and Wes stood in the foyer, watching as the long-haired girl from before grabbed the new girl's hand and led her upstairs. The cat stood at their feet, a quizzical expression on his face as it looked *at* each of them, one after the other. He started to purr, a low, earthy vibration that reminded Rose of Aunt Bea's cat, a needy old lady named Justice.

"Can he see us?" Drew asked. She bent down to get a closer look, but the rascal bolted into the dining room. They all watched silently as his bushy tail disappeared around the corner, and Rose was hit with a wave of melancholy as she realized she'd never cuddle with her dear Justice again.

It felt like barely any time at all had passed since the family toured the house. Rose assumed the realtor would have warned them of the murders and scared them off. He either hadn't told them or they hadn't cared, and Rose wasn't sure which answer bothered her more. She was pinning everything on the belief that their spirits were tied to the vicious memories of what had happened in the house. Over time people would forget, and the bond would be broken. Their spirits would finally be free to move on, free to wander.

Having a family move in was going to make that a heck of a lot harder.

So far, she felt validated. She couldn't quite explain it to the others, but she felt like the house was weakening. That was the only way Rose could think to describe it. The air seemed thinner somehow, the walls of the house not as claustrophobic as they'd first felt. Rose thought if they waited just a little bit longer, the barrier surrounding the house would weaken entirely. But now this new family was moving in, and she was growing more and more anxious by the second. *They are going to mess everything up.*

The realtor must not have told them, Rose convinced herself, but surely they would learn the house's history somehow, right? The girl and her dad would inevitably find out all about how a Fireman murdered the four of them, and once that happened it would strengthen their spiritual bond to the house, trapping them here longer. The idea was worming into her brain. Rose didn't want to think of being here for eternity.

Rose wished desperately that she could talk to her aunt about it. She instinctively reached for her crystal necklace, forgetting in the heat of the moment the last time she'd tried to use it had brought her face to face with The Fireman. After she impulsively threw the crystal out the window, she'd found it back in the foyer, where the house returned everything that tried to leave. She'd kept it in her pocket ever since, but she put it back on now. She wasn't ready to try and use it again quite yet, but she still wanted it closer to her heart. Rose turned to Drew, wanting to reiterate the hands-off plan with her, but Drew was already off following the girls upstairs. She turned to Eli and Wes instead, but as soon as Wes sensed her plan, he took off toward the basement. That was probably for the best, since she didn't want to get into another argument with him about the rot. Eli, though, might be able to help. But his attention wasn't on her. He was focused on a box at their feet.

The Dead Friends Society

Eli was obsessed with new technology. When he was growing up, computers and game consoles were doubling in capability every few years. Once, when he was ten, he came home to find his dad had bought the family an Apple Power Mac as a surprise. It was their first personal computer and expensive as hell, so his dad was expecting it to blow Eli's mind. Eli was disappointed because it couldn't play Doom. He tried to explain to his dad that he should have bought a Windows PC, but that just pissed the old man off.

Later, when Eli was in his early teens, he was able to convince his dad to upgrade them to a 233mhz Packard Bell that, crucially, came with Windows 95. Eli loaded up Doom, Duke Nukem 3D, and Diablo — the holy D's — and never looked back. He was a self-declared nerd from that point forward.

But right now, right in front of him, Eli was staring at something that looked straight out of Total Recall. The entire device was a screen with only a single, circular button on the face. On the back was the recognizable Apple logo in grey, a less vibrant version of the logo on the tower of the Power Mac his dad brought home. This Javier guy didn't even care about the device, though. It sat unprotected on top of one of the boxes he'd brought into the foyer. Eli wondered if it could play Doom.

Eli reached down to pick it up and Rose snapped at him to stop. He set it back down, embarrassed, like the time his mom caught him looking at a Playboy. He felt silly but knew he shouldn't. It wasn't like he was going to get caught. Not again. He'd learned his lesson when the family visited the first time and he'd been caught trying to pick up Javier's device and it fell right out of his hands.

Eli pointed outside, showing Rose the dad was in the U-Haul, well out of their eye line. They had plenty of time to sneak a peek while he was gone. "Come on, Rose. This thing is from the future! I want to see what it can do." Eli reached for the device again, and Rose slapped his hand. He pulled back, properly scolded. Rose wasn't messing around, that slap *hurt*.

"We can't risk it. They can't know we're here. We need everything and everyone copa—"

"Copacetic. Yeah, yeah. I remember."

Rose lowered her voice and gently rested her hand on Eli's. Her soft touch sent a little ghost quiver up his ghost veins and into his ghost heart. "Please, Eli. It's the only way we'll ever get out of here."

Eli wasn't sure if she was right, but he hated making her mad, so he stepped away from the device. Rose smiled and thanked him. And then a second later, the two girls came racing downstairs, passing cluelessly between them and out the front door. Rose's smile dropped in an instant. "See! They would have seen you."

"Okay, okay, you win." Eli held his hands up, once again feeling like an idiot. "I promise to leave everything alone." And he meant it. Even if he knew it would be very, very hard for him to keep that promise.

Drew followed the girls around all day as they moved in. Rose begged her not to. She had gotten so skittish about the newcomers, pleading with everyone to stay out of sight and out of mind. Drew couldn't help herself, though. Abbey and Willa were too fascinating. Drew clung to their every word, trying to glean whatever she could about the last twenty-two years by listening to them. They mostly talked about school and friends and music, but Drew did learn a few crucial things about the world after her death. Apparently, some kind of virus was wrecking the planet, and the two girls were constantly checking their pocket screens, which Drew was amazed to learn were *phones*. Eli said they were connected to the internet, which didn't make any sense. They weren't plugged in to anything, and they didn't make the horrible screeching howl Drew's old modem did when it connected to AOL.

Eventually Rose got fed up trying to police Drew and left her entirely. Drew lingered nearby, doing her best impression of a wallflower as she watched them finish decorating her old room. Willa told

Abbey how cool the house was, how she wished she had an attic bedroom, which Drew could tell brought Abbey a little bit of joy. She was being as modest as she could, but her little smirk couldn't be missed. Drew wasn't too sure about the sixteen-year-old's taste, though. Abbey and Willa looked at Drew's old posters and were utterly clueless about the bands. *The Smashing Pumpkins? Alice in Chains? Okay, that's fair, but how the hell could anyone not know who Kurt Cobain was?* Abbey wanted to take the posters down, but Willa argued she should keep 'em. They were "vintage" and "vintage was in," which Drew thought was both insane and hysterical.

Drew laughed at the idea that Nirvana could be vintage and Abbey cocked a curious head toward her side of the room. Drew froze, fearing the girl had somehow heard her. But then the living girls continued about their business. *Of course, they didn't hear you. Nobody will ever hear you again.*

Willa's phone buzzed. She groaned, complaining to Abbey that her mom was "freaking out" about letting her stay in "that creepy house."

That creepy house? Do they know what happened here? Drew assumed they didn't. After all, why the hell would anyone want to live somewhere people were murdered?

Abbey knew Willa was trying to bait her into talking about the house's unfortunate history, but brushed it off. "Oh please, it's fine. Your mom freaks out about everything she shouldn't and nothing she should."

"That's not fair!" Willa pouted.

Abbey stared at Willa, waiting to be proven wrong, and knowing she couldn't deny it. Mrs. Gordon was nice enough, but she was the kind of person who obsessively read all the updates on NextDoor, convinced every single one of her neighbors was either a serial killer or a drug dealer. Well, the non-white ones at least.

"Yeah, yeah, yeah. But you've got to give her a break on this, Abs. I mean... this place..." Willa let the words trail, as if the silence said everything, but still Abbey resisted the bait and kept taking down the old posters to make room for her mom's art. Willa wasn't going to drop it, though. They'd been dancing around the topic all day and now that it was dark outside, she could tell Willa was getting wigged out.

"Abs! Some crazy fireman *murdered* people in this house. Twice! He did it in the seventies and then he came back like twenty years later, and you don't even want to talk about it? You're for real going to just act like it didn't happen?"

Abbey just kept rolling the posters up and sticking them in a box. She finished the last one and then calmly said "Willa, you're wrong."

"I'm not wrong! Here, look!" Willa shoved her phone in Abbey's face. She'd dug up some old news article with the headline "College Co-Eds Massacred" in big, bold letters.

Abbey looked at it and smiled. She'd read that exact article weeks ago in preparation for conversations just like this one. "I'm not saying it didn't happen," Abbey calmly explained, "I'm saying you've got the details wrong."

"No, I don't. It says here—"

"You said *he* came back. *He* didn't. The cops killed the first guy. They said it was a copycat who came back in 1998."

Willa quickly scrolled through the article, no doubt trying to find a counter argument. Abbey knew she wouldn't. "They never caught that guy either, just FYI," Abbey added.

"Jesus, Abs."

"I know. It's fucked up, right?" She could tell Willa was rattled by the thought, but once again, Abbey didn't let it phase her. "Let's go, I'm missing some boxes."

Willa narrowed her eyes, unable to drop the topic. "It doesn't freak you the F out to be living in a house where all those people were killed? What if it's, you know…" Willa lowered her voice "…*haunted*?"

Abbey paused at the doorway and stared down the dark staircase just long enough to make sure she would get the words right. She had seen this entire conversation coming and practiced in her head. This was her mic drop moment. She lowered her voice, matching Willa's conspiratorial tone.

"So what if it is?" Abbey asked. "I'd rather live in a house where strangers died than stay in the house where my mom did."

Drew lingered in the corner of the attic, stunned. Too many thoughts piled up in her mind all at once. *Righetti was right? That psycho who killed us was just some fan? And what happened to that poor girl's mom? And Kurt Cobain is vintage now? What the actual fuck?*

But one thought fought its way above the rest. Drew's mind traced back to all the horror movies she'd watched (alone or with Eli, because Rose was always too scared), all the Christopher Pike novels she'd read, all the ghost stories she'd ever heard, all the stories about haunted houses, death, and exorcism, and a realization hit her with the searing force of The Fireman's axe: *This is a haunted house. And we're haunting it.*

Wes could not take his eyes off the rot. He was convinced it would be their salvation. *Those dipshits think this is mold?* This was the house showing them the way out. It was so fucking obvious, and they were all so fucking stupid for not seeing it. He hovered his right hand over one of the black holes. It was about the size of his fist. Maybe smaller. He was pretty sure his hand would fit in there — not that he particularly wanted to stick it in. When he was 14, he and Eli found a tree with a weird hole at the base of it. Wes dared his brother to stick his hand in it, but Eli refused, so Wes said fuck it, and did it himself. He blindly threw his whole arm in the hole. It sank into what felt like soft dirt. It ended up being a fire ant's nest.

The bastards swarmed him, attacking in such great numbers that he ended up passing out from the pain. The doctors said if Eli hadn't dragged his arm out and gotten the ants off him, Wes might have died. When his dad finally got to the hospital, he only had one thing to say. "Moron."

Wes could feel himself growing angry at the memory of it. He wasn't a moron. He was brave. He had balls. He wasn't afraid of some fucking deep, dark hole. He was already dead. *What's the worst that could happen?*

Wes closed his eyes and thrust his fist into the rotten hole, into the darkness. He couldn't help but expect that same feeling of soft dirt, but he felt nothing. Literal nothingness. He'd never felt such an absence of feeling before. It was an unsettling contradiction, as if the space inside the wall was so empty Wes's arm had been deleted.

He opened his eyes half-expecting to see his arm chopped off. Instead, Wes marveled at the sight of his arm inside the rot. He couldn't see inside, but he could tell his body was intact. He could even stretch his fingers out. He wiggled them around, twisting and turning, grabbing this way and that, trying to understand the emptiness on the other side. But he couldn't *feel* anything. The wall was completely empty. It was starting to make Wes feel as if he himself was hollow.

THUD.

THUD.

THUD.

Wes ripped his hand out of the hole. He spun on his heels, expecting The Fireman to be there, standing as he had right before he shoved a mic stand through Wes's chest. But there was no Fireman. There was, however, a moving dolly overloaded with weights crashing down the stairs. Wes jumped out of the way and the dolly narrowly missed him as it crashed into the wall, spilling dumbbells, weights, and a bench press bar across the basement. Wes felt stupid for having been afraid, for dodging out of the way. It's not like he would have gotten hurt. Right?

"Shit." At the top of the stairs stood the father. He was rubbing his forehead, kicking himself for dropping the dolly. He jogged downstairs and took in the mess. "Javi, you dumbass."

"Yes Javi, you *are* a dumbass." Wes snapped.

Javier jumped in fright, and for a second Wes thought the man had heard him, until he noticed a small mouse scurrying across the floor. It disappeared into a crack under the stairs. Javier laughed, "Oracle's gonna make a meal outta you."

Wes hated this guy already. He was too goddamned cheerful about everything. Everything the new family did pissed him off. The girls never stopped jabbering. It's why he'd claimed the basement in the first place, but now this asshole was down here causing a racket. He tried to push Javier away, but it was pointless. Javier, like the cop, was protected by an invisible barrier.

Wes was sick of this ghost shit. He pushed harder, angered by his own limits, but this time, Javier twitched like someone just tapped him on the shoulder. Javier spun, checking behind him. He couldn't see Wes standing right behind him. He also couldn't hear Wes muttering "What the fuck?" over and over.

Javier scratched the spot Wes had pushed and went back upstairs, leaving Wes once again alone. Wes paced excitedly, convinced he'd broken through to this guy. Then Wes noticed the wall. A new, rotten hole was bubbling and merging with another, growing softball sized. Wes had gotten Javier's attention and suddenly the rot expanded? It couldn't be a coincidence.

Wes stuck his fingers in the hole. He gripped the rim of it with both hands and tried to pull it wider. His muscles bulged, but it didn't work. He tried a different hole, straining to widen it, a demented glee spreading across his face.

Chapter 21

Eli could not stop staring at the pizza boxes on the kitchen counter. Javier left one open hours ago and the half-dozen slices of pepperoni left inside it were making his soul ache. Not that he felt hungry in the slightest. If anything, the sight of the pizza caused him to realize for the first time that he hadn't thought about eating or drinking since waking up dead. But goddamn did he want to shovel those greasy triangles of goodness right into his mouth. *Fuck, I love pizza.*

Eli had an agreement with the Sbarro guy in the food court, getting free slices in exchange for letting him use Eli's Suncoast employee discount. But more than just wanting to return to his halcyon days of popping over to grab a slice whenever the hell he wanted to, Eli was also damned curious to figure out if ghosts even *could* eat pizza. His gut told him they didn't need sustenance to survive — and his literal gut hadn't felt hunger this entire time — but just because they didn't *need it* didn't mean they couldn't *do it.*

There was no one around. Javier had gone to sleep. Abbey and Willa had been in the attic for a while. Now was his shot. He reached for the pizza.

"Eli Adams!" Rose scolded, surprising him at the kitchen entrance, Drew by her side. Eli pulled his hand back in embarrassment.

"Were you going to eat that?" Drew asked.

"No, he wasn't. Because that would be ridiculous."

"Would it?" Eli asked. "Considering it seems like we're gonna be here for a while, I vote we keep figuring out the cans and cannots of being on this side of the universe."

"We'll be here forever if you and Wes keep messing around." Rose countered.

"It's science," Eli said, hoping to lighten Rose up. "I'm just testing a hypothesis."

"What's that? If a ghost eats, then will it also have to take a ghost dump?" Drew asked sarcastically. Eli pointed at his nose: *Ding-Ding-Ding*.

"Another great question!" he said.

"You two slackers are really going to keep us trapped in here forever over a cold slice of pepperoni?" Rose said, trying to bring the conversation back to the big picture.

Eli smiled. He opened the lid of the second box, revealing a delicious-looking vegetarian pie: spinach, green peppers, red onions, roasted Brussels sprouts and cherry tomatoes, all on a thin crust with the singe marks of a woodfired oven. It was even a sauceless white pizza, just like Rose used to order. He saw her eyes glisten at the sight.

"You're saying you don't want a bite of that?" Eli asked.

Rose wanted it. She wanted it more than she would ever dare admit to Eli. She wasn't hungry, but just the look of it triggered a Pavlovian response in her mind. Pizza was such a simple reminder of the before times, of her old life, of sleepover movie nights with Drew, when something as mundane as eating a slice of cheese pizza could bring her instant comfort. She hadn't realized how badly she wanted that comfort now, how badly she wanted a reminder of the way things used to be.

"Of course she's not going to eat it, Eli," Drew said. "We have to keep things copacetic, like Rose said."

Rose couldn't believe what she was hearing. Here was Drew Denns, queen of pushing Rose out of her comfort zone, playing it safe.

Eli was stifling a laugh, but his smartass smirk gave him away. The jerk was totally right, and the worst part was he knew he was right. Rose *did* want it. Not just to eat it, but to see if they *could*. They'd done such a good job of staying out of the new family's way all day long, it was like this pizza had been left out as a reward.

Or a test.

But who was to say that having a bite would make them fail the test? If the three of them each had a slice, there was still plenty left. Or maybe they could just share a single slice? When the family finally put the pizza away, they probably wouldn't even notice. Rose had been begging everyone to not draw attention to their ethereal presence, to not remind the living that they had moved into in an old murder house, but it's not as though Javier was going to open a pizza box, notice slightly less pizza, and think "A ghost ate my pizza!" As long as they didn't eat all of it, he wouldn't notice anything. Could they interact with the world while still not drawing attention to themselves? Rose hated how much she wanted to find out.

"I'll do it if you do," Rose said to Drew.

Drew watched in utter disbelief as Rose reached out and grabbed a slice of the veggie pizza. *What the hell happened to copacetic?* She'd thought she was backing up Rose, but in truth, Drew wanted that pizza. *Bad.* She was just putting Rose's feelings before greasy, beautiful pizza. Turns out, pizza was the line Rose was willing to cross.

Drew and Eli both held their breath as Rose brought the slice to her lips. She hesitated, looking back at them for approval.

"What are they gonna do, call the Ghostbusters over some missing pizza?" Eli asked.

"Don't back down now," Drew said.

Rose bit down and her teeth sank into the pizza, tearing off the tip with ease. She closed her eyes and chewed, her face filling with ecstasy. Drew had no idea pizza could make anyone *that* happy. It was as if they'd been wandering the desert for years and finally found an oasis.

"Is it good?" Drew asked.

Rose let out a soft, subtle moan, and Drew cackled as Eli blushed a deep red. Drew grabbed a slice of the veggie as Eli went for the pepperoni. They both raised their slices in the air, toasting one another, before taking a bite.

The taste was amazing, yes, but Drew wasn't quite ready for how good the simple act of eating would make her feel. It warmed her entire body, flooding her with endorphins. She realized it wasn't the pizza that was making them feel so good, it was the rush of doing something they shouldn't and getting away with it. It was the riskiest thing any of them had done since this all started. Drew figured they'd earned it. They all had. Well, except Wes. She was in no rush to invite that dick to the first happy moment they'd had since dying.

The three of them ate their first few bites in silence, reveling in this moment that was so absurd and yet so goddamned liberating.

"Do you think we're going to have to take ghost shits now?" Eli asked, breaking the spell. They all laughed.

"Well," Drew said through a mouthful of tomatoes, "Think about it this way: We had no idea ghosts were real before, right? People like us could have been all around this entire time, and we had no clue. So, it tracks that we could have just as easily been stepping in ghost crap all along."

"No, no, no," Rose said. "That's just ridiculous. We're ghosts, not heathens." She put on a stern face, and Drew braced for another mini lecture on how that violated some random book Rose had once read about how Tibetan monks viewed the afterlife or something. But Rose surprised her.

"What you do is go to the bathroom in a toilet like a normal person. The living can't see us, they won't see your, ya' know, *business*, and then when they go flush, poof, it'll just take everything down together." Rose laughed at her own idea. "I'm not going to let death stop me from being civilized."

Eli put his pizza down and gave her a slow clap. "You, Rose Calder, are a goddamn genius." Rose did a curtsy bow with her dress, thanking him.

"I really thought you were going to chew me out for wanting to do this." Eli said.

"Yeah, well. Like you said. It's for science." Rose said between bites. "Besides, we all agree to only do things like this if we're all together and we're all absolutely, positively sure it's not going to interfere with the living, right?"

"Of course. Absolutely," Drew said.

"Positively. Scout's honor," Eli said, raising three fingers.

Suddenly they heard footsteps rushing down from the second-floor stairs. The three of them shoved their last bites of pizza in their mouths and put the pizza boxes back just the way they were. Drew's heart pounded when Abbey popped into the kitchen with an empty plate. She flipped open the box, put the remaining slices of veggie pizza on her plate, and skipped back out of the room. Not for a nanosecond did the living girl notice anything was amiss.

Drew, Rose, and Eli all had smiles as wide as the Grand Canyon. They looked like bank robbers who'd just pulled off the ultimate heist. Drew could feel muscles she didn't even know had been tense relaxing. For the first time, in a long time, she felt content, like maybe the afterlife wasn't going to be so hard, so joyless, after all.

Chapter 22

WES HAD BEEN STARING AT THE ROT FOR SO LONG HE LOST TRACK of time — not that time mattered, or even made any goddamn sense, anymore. Twenty-two years passing felt like a blink, but now that he knew decades had been ripped away from him, Wes was dying to break free of this hellhole. The rot was the key, it had to be.

He knew the living caused the holes to spread, eating away the barrier between him and the hollow side; but no matter how many times he tried to get a rise out of Javier, the damn rot would barely budge. It was as though Javier had gotten used to him. Earlier in the day, Wes jumped onto the old man's back and felt Javier stiffen underneath him only to shrug it off as a breeze and not the ghost of a murdered young man clinging to his neck. Wes then fell *through* Javier and landed on the floor. He scrambled to his feet embarrassed, like the time he tripped on stage at one of The Ruins earliest gigs.

But there was no screaming crowd here, only this asshole and his daughter and the daughter's friend, and Wes wasn't shit to any of 'em. He felt small. He felt like a *moron*. He couldn't pry open the wall. He couldn't hold on to some old dude's back. He was nothing. He'd never admit this to anyone, not even Eli, but it reminded Wes of what his dad would say whenever they'd gotten close to blows. Wes would cock back a fist, ready to knock his dad's teeth out, but every single time he'd lose his nerve and back off, and every single time his dad would say the same thing: "What's a matter? Can't get it up, ya' little limp dick?" Even from the grave, his dad was making him feel like a little limp dick. God, he hated that man.

Then a thought tore through Wes, sparking his brain like cocaine and filling him with joy for the first time since death began. *If it's been twenty-two years, dad has got to be dead by now, right?* Wes did the math in his head. The old man was in his, what, sixties when they'd been murdered? Wes didn't know his exact age — he didn't care to — but there's no way a schlub with *that* beer belly and *that* set of pack-a-day lungs was still kicking in his eighties. Picturing Old Man Adams hacking up gobs of blood and bile as cancer ate him away made Wes fist pump the air. He couldn't wait to tell Eli about it. His brother might not be as happy as he was, but even he would appreciate knowing their dad was dust.

Wes made to go upstairs but froze in his tracks. That stupid cat was back in the basement. It had been periodically checking in on him all day and Wes was convinced the damned thing could see him. But every time he tried to touch the cat it ran. This time Oracle wasn't fixated on Wes, he was staring at something *behind* him. A chill tickled the back of his neck as Wes became acutely aware he wasn't alone.

Something was watching him. Something in the hollow side of the wall. He thought he'd seen movement in it before. At one point he could have sworn he saw a figure standing back there, waiting for him. He'd called out to it, asking for help widening the hole, but then the figure, if it was real and not just a trick of the eyes, vanished.

Wes spun to the wall hoping to see whatever had the cat so worked up, but it was just the same damn wall riddled with the same damn black holes. But then he noticed the mouse.

The tiny thing wasn't in the wall, it was in front of it. Wes laughed. The two animals were in a stand-off; the mouse hoping it hadn't been seen, the cat crouching down on its hind legs, pretending to be a cheetah. Wes didn't want to give the cat the satisfaction — he hated the fury bastards — so he stomped at the mouse to scare it away. To his, and the mouse's, great surprise, Wes managed to pin the critter's tail to the ground.

The humans in the house were seemingly off limits to the ghosts, but the animals? Apparently, they were fair game. The mouse squeaked pitifully under his boot. Wes plucked him from the dirty floor. The mouse nearly squirmed away, but Wes locked his grip. He dangled it in front of the cat's face.

"Look what I've got, you little shit!" Wes said, taunting the cat. Oracle stuck up his nose and turned away, his tail raised proudly in the air as he trotted off upstairs. Wes yelled after the cat, "What's a matter? Jealous?"

Wes raised the mouse to his face, trying to make sense of everything that happened. Why could he interact with animals but not people? He could feel the rodent's heartbeat pounding in his hand. The little runt was terrified. Wes felt a minor pang of guilt and was about to set the squeaker free, until he noticed the rot on the wall. A new patch was forming, bubbling near the biggest hole, widening it. Wes tilted his head to the ceiling, trying to hear if any of the others were up to something, but the house was quiet. And besides, there's no way those cowards would even *dare* approach the living. Their big idea was to hide in the shadows like cockroaches while these assholes took their house from them. Wes thought of Rose's bullshit "dust in the wind" gesture and felt his anger growing. *We are not going to just drift away.*

Wes squeezed the mouse tighter. The rot bubbled and spread; black ink blotting out the wall. He clenched his fist so hard his veins bulged. The mouse squeaked and squirmed, trying its hardest to bite its captor. Wes squeezed as hard as he could. He could feel the mouse's ribs snap one by one like toothpicks. The squeaks stopped. The rodent's eyes and cheeks swelled, ballooning out like a stress-ball on the verge of popping.

There was no turning back now. Wes squeezed as hard as he could, until... *pop.* He felt the creature's warm insides run down his hand, a sticky mess of blood and tiny organs. Wes opened his hand, studying the aftermath, pleased with how much damage he'd done with only one hand. And just like that, Wes stopped feeling small.

He dropped the body on the ground, where it hit with a wet slap. Wes wiped the blood off on his jeans, his adrenaline surging. The rot was bubbling, spreading; the biggest hole — and the smile on Wes's face — grew rapidly.

Wes reached into hole and was thrilled to discover it was now big enough for him to fit all the way up to his shoulder. If killing one little mouse could do that, he reckoned, it wouldn't take much for him to open the rest of the wall.

Wes pulled his arm out and set his eyes on the kitchen staircase. The cat would help, but he suspected even that furball wouldn't be enough of a sacrifice to get the job done. He'd need something bigger. He'd need *someone* bigger.

Chapter 23

Rose felt guilty. That was the norm for her — intense moments of joy followed by the inevitable pounding guilt. When she was seven, she stole a sip of her mom's champagne during their annual New Year's Eve party. She'd felt that one small sip permeating throughout her body, and the weight of her choice grew and grew as the countdown to midnight ticked on and on. She didn't even make it to 11:30 before she confessed, head in hands, tears flowing like a faucet. Her mom scolded her, but there was no punishment. She just told her not to do it again, it was for grownups. Her mom knew that Rose didn't *need* the punishment. Rose would punish herself far worse than any grounding or early bedtime ever could.

Rose felt that same guilt now, the pizza permeating throughout her body just like that champagne. But the implications were potentially far more dangerous now. She was pushing the boundaries of her moral limits with every action she took in this place. She'd excused herself after eating the slice, needing some time to be alone with her thoughts. She lost track of time — it seemed to happen often in the afterlife — and when she returned to the kitchen, Drew and Eli weren't there.

She wandered the house (what else was there to do?) and was surprised to find Eli alone, sitting on the old washing machine in the laundry room. Oracle the cat was sitting below, staring intently up at him. Eli ignored the cat and gazed out the window. He greeted Rose without looking.

"I think Drew and the new girls are upstairs," he said.

"I know, but to tell you the truth, I'm kind of scared of them," Rose said.

"As someone who spent all of high school afraid to even talk to them, I agree teenage girls are fucking terrifying," Eli joked.

Rose laughed. *Freaking Eli.* Always trying to make the people around him happier. She hadn't picked up on it in high school, but lately she saw his humor as less a defense mechanism and more a service he performed for others. She admired him for that. She knew he liked her, too, but they were both way too shy to ever do anything about it. She'd secretly wished moving in together might grease the wheels on their relationship. Instead, they got murdered. Go figure.

"I think the cat is watching you," Rose said. Eli looked down at Oracle and it immediately looked the other way, as if the little runt was aware it had just been busted. Eli went back to looking out the window, and the cat returned to watching Eli, like they were playing a game. Rose was amazed.

"Yeah, he can totally see us," Eli said. "And it's blowing my fucking mind." Oracle purred. Rose bent to pet him, but he bolted out of the room leaving her crestfallen. "Don't take it personally," he said. "I've discovered he doesn't like to be touched; he just likes to watch. The little pervert."

Rose sidled up to Eli, curious to see what he was looking at outside. A stunning full moon gleamed high in the sky. Her heart stopped. She'd grown accustomed to seeing the sky in a dizzying time lapse and was awed by the stillness, the brilliance of the celestial body. She hopped up onto the dryer next to him and leaned her head on his shoulder as she moon gazed. He shifted slightly to offer Rose a better view, drawing her closer. Neither seemed to mind. They sat quietly, sharing the most normal moment Rose had had since all the chaos began, until Eli awkwardly shattered the intimacy. "Did you know time on the moon is different than time on Earth?"

Rose blinked back at him.

"I mean, it's not like astronauts see things all fast forward-y like we do, but on Earth, time is measured by how long it takes the Earth to spin on its axis, right? Well, the moon takes way longer to complete a spin on its axis, so if you're using that as your frame of reference, one lunar hour is way longer than one Earth hour, right? And so, in the '70s, at the height of the space program, this one watch company made a special watch that measures time from the moon's perspective, not the Earth's."

"Sounds useless," Rose said.

"Not if you're on the moon."

"Did astronauts wear them?"

"No," Eli chuckled. "I'm pretty sure they only ever sold them to geeks like me. I saw one of those watches when I went to Space Camp, and I've wanted one ever since." Eli sighed, wistful. "Guess I'll never get one now." It was rare to see him with his humor shields down. She wanted to cheer him up.

"Wait, you went to Space Camp?"

"Yeah!" She could see Eli's face flooding with happy memories. He playfully pointed a finger at her. "And don't you make fun of it either because it was the best week of my life. That place is fuckin' amazing. Every kid should be able to go."

"Did Wes go with you?"

And then Rose watched as the nostalgia spell broke and all those happy memories drained away. "No, he wanted to," Eli said, "but then all his friends made fun of him because of SpaceCamp the movie. Ya' know, the one with the mom from Back to the Future? God, I had such a crush on her. But they all hated it, and so he told our parents he didn't want to go."

"That really sucks, Eli."

"I wish he'd gone with me. I feel like that's the summer when everything changed. We were best friends before it, but when I got back, Wes spent all his time with his new friends and forgot all about me."

Eli looked back toward the moon, that wistful twinkle returning. "I miss that Wes."

Drew found herself unable to pull away from watching Abbey and Willa. It was like watching a live TV show. Combine that with the pizza, and things were starting to feel a shade of normal again. It was a bit hard to keep up with everything, though. The girls were speaking in a new language, referencing so many movies and shows and things on their phones that Drew just had zero clue about. She was, in her heart, only twenty-years-old, but she was starting to feel like an old lady out of touch. She was just doing her best to keep up.

She still wasn't quite sure of the specifics, but a few things about Abbey's mom had become clear. First, she died somewhat recently. Second, she was an artist. Third, she was a really, really damn good artist. So good it made Drew angry. When Abbey hung the first piece, Drew knew it was art on a level far beyond what she was capable of on her best days. Then Drew realized she'd *literally* never be capable of it. She'd never pick up a chisel or mold another piece of clay. She'd never create again. *Forfuckingever*.

Once she was able to swallow the jealousy and the flash crash of existential crisis that came with it, Drew couldn't help but appreciate the works on their own terms. Abbey had taken down all of Drew's old posters and converted the attic's walls into a gallery dedicated to her mom's art. Most were watercolors on canvas, some were oils, a few were charcoal etchings. All of them were stunners. Drew had tried her hand at painting, and while friends like Rose insisted the results were great, all she saw were the flaws. That's one of the reasons Drew loved sculpting so much. Flaws were human, flaws were shapeable. A canvas gave you finite chances. She could paint over a mess-up, but Drew would know the original flaw was still there, lurking underneath the surface. Clay was far more forgiving. A flaw could be worked out or reshaped into something else. It made her sculptures feel *alive*.

Drew wished she knew more about the artist. Abbey's mom could capture pain and beauty and introspection in a way Drew had only dreamed of, yet she didn't even know the woman's name. The showstopper in the gallery was a three-foot-tall painting Drew heard Abbey call "The Self-Portrait." It was of a woman whose head bore faces on all sides. The largest, the one looking directly at the viewer, was placid and calm. She wasn't smiling, yet presented a sort of beleaguered serenity that showed warmth and contentment. The face on the left was caught in an angry scream so vividly captured Drew could hear its primal cry. The face on the right was tilted downward in defeat and openly weeping, mascara running down her cheeks. Drew had never seen a more perfect rendering of inner turmoil. It was raw and honest and one hell of a self-portrait. It gave her goosebumps.

Drew glanced over her shoulder, afraid to get caught so close to the artwork, but there was no one looking at her, no museum guard to tell her to step away. Abbey was on the opposite side of the room, hanging more paintings. Willa was asleep on the bed, strange white drops hanging out of her ears. There weren't any wires connecting them to anything, but faint pop music trickled out from them, so she assumed they were high-tech headphones. Drew leaned toward the painting, wanting a closer inspection. There was something about the paint she couldn't quite put her finger on.

The darker hues were too textured to be normal paint. She knew some artists mixed other things into their oils. She'd read once of a Brooklyn artist who mixed bodily fluids into all her palettes, literally putting herself into the art. Drew wondered if Abbey's mom had done something similar. The screaming-happy-sad woman was surrounded by a haunting halo of red. Drew couldn't help but think of all the blood she'd seen recently, the lakes and rivers of it flowing from their corpses, and how it had started so cherry red it looked downright technicolor, but by the time the crime scene cleaners had arrived with their mops, the cherry of it all soured into a sickly black goop that made her stomach churn. Drew wondered if Abbey's mom had perhaps mixed her own *blood* in with the oil.

And then there was that texture. There were miniature mountains in the paint, casting tiny shadows that shifted depending on the angle of the observer, creating the illusion the painting itself was moving. Drew wondered if the mountains were bristles from the brush used, or if they were the artist's own hair. Without really meaning to, Drew reached out to touch the painting to see if she could tell. As her fingertips brushed the surface, the canvas began to sway side-to-side and before Drew could stop it, the painting slid off its hanging nail and came crashing down. In a panic, Drew grabbed the painting to stop it from smashing to the floor.

Abbey saw something move out of the corner of her eye. She spun, expecting Willa had woken up, but instead saw the impossible. Her mother's favorite painting, The Self-Portrait, was floating in the air.

The painting lingered a foot off the ground for what felt like eternity and then, as if possessed by a spirit of self-preservation, tilted away from the floor, and leaned safely against the wall. All Abbey could do was blink, her mind struggling to understand what just happened. The painting was falling, and then it wasn't. It was about to smash into the floor, and then it was saved.

"Uh... what the fuck? Did you see that, Wills?" Abbey asked. Willa snored in reply.

Abbey walked cautiously toward the painting, expecting it to leap from the wall. But it didn't. Abbey looked all around the room, not quite sure what she was hoping to find that could explain what happened. *A weird draft, maybe?* She held up her hand, trying to sense the air, but nothing seemed off. *Maybe the hanging wire broke?* Abbey picked up the painting and inspected it, but the wire on the back was in-tact. She checked the nail in the wall. It was missing. Abbey crouched on the floor to search for it, when something else caught her eye. A tiny fleck of white paper was poking out of the gap between the floor and the wall, right behind where The Self-Portrait had landed.

Abbey tried to pull it up but couldn't get a grip on the corner. She grabbed Willa's purse and rifled through it to find a small set of eyebrow tweezers. They were perfect for managing Willa's subtle unibrow, and apparently for plucking papers out from walls. Abbey managed to pull the whole note out on the first try.

Abbey's heart stopped when she saw "MOM" written in big letters on the front. The logical part of her knew the note could not possibly be from her mom, and yet she'd just seen the impossible happen — to her mom's self-portrait no less — which led her to the very spot in the room where she found an old note with the word "MOM" on it.

Abbey didn't believe in coincidences, so when she heard a distant voice behind her, she knew something was going on. She bolted upright like a meerkat, only to find no one standing behind her. There was only Willa, snoring softly, oblivious to it all.

The sound had been muffled, as if Abbey heard it through water, but strap her to a lie detector and she'd have sworn on a stack of bibles that the sound was someone gasping over her shoulder.

Drew couldn't hold back the gasp. It was an involuntary reaction to seeing Abbey pull her note from the wall. She thought it was gone forever, but there it was, in the hands of this new girl, waiting to be read, waiting to make its way to...

Drew's heart sank. Even if Abbey could figure out who the note was from and where it was meant to go, Drew's mom wasn't alive to read it. Drew's apology would fall on deaf ears. *Forfuckingever.*

Abbey was staring directly at Drew yet saw straight through her. The living girl squinted as if trying to see something from a great distance, but no amount of squinting would help. Nobody would ever see Drew again.

Abbey sat cross-legged at Drew's feet and unfolded the note. She began to read, and words that Drew poured out twenty-two years ago finally found an audience. The wrong audience, sure, but Drew felt a sense of relief that at least someone was discovering them. Drew knew the girl couldn't see her, but the act of it being read at all made Drew feel truly seen for the first time since this all began. That feeling suddenly overwhelmed Drew, and she began to cry. Abbey did, too. Something in the note was resonating with the girl. Drew wondered what it was.

Dear Mom,
I have to tell you something. I have to tell you so many things. I don't know where to begin, but here's a decent start.
I've been lying to you.
And I'm sorry.
I changed my major to art. And I know that's not what you want for me. And I know that's not what you're paying for. But mom? I'm really good at it. I really, really am. And it makes me happy. I'm not sure you'll ever be able to understand, ever be able to see what brings me so much joy in it. And I'll understand if you don't want to pay for school anymore. This isn't what we agreed to, after all. This isn't what I promised you. But mom? I'm trying. I'm trying to be better.
And I'm sorry.
I'm sorry for all the times I refused to listen to you, all the times I refused to see things your way, all the times I refused to recognize your experience. I'm sorry for all the times I slammed the door in your face. I've been awful to you, a truly shitty daughter that took all her bullshit out on the one person who had her back more than anyone else. But all that changes now. I promise you I will respect you, I will listen to you, and I will love you. I just ask you to give me a chance. Take a moment and try to consider my passion. Please let me show you my work, and please try to understand why it brings me such joy. I know your dream for me was to have what you didn't — a future where I could "write my

own destiny." A future where a big fat "safe" bank account was a guarantee. And I know an art major is about as polar opposite of that guarantee as I could get. But mom? Please give me a chance. One last chance. I promise I'll prove myself to you. I promise. I love you so much, and please know that when I finally have the courage to give you this note, to admit how wrong I've been about you and us, that it will be the hardest thing I've ever done. Please mom, please know that I love you.
And I'm sorry.

Drew

Abbey wiped her eyes dry. She felt like she'd just met this girl at an almost cellular level, connecting with her pain so deeply, so purely, that she believed part of Drew might be inside of her. Who *was* this mystery girl? Why was this note trapped in the floor? And why was it waiting for her, of all people, to find it? Was this note the reason she'd felt such a pull to this room and this house?

Abbey grabbed her phone to take a picture of the note. She wanted to preserve it forever. Her camera opened in selfie mode, reflecting Abbey's emotionally drained face back at her. But there was something else, too, floating over her shoulder.

The orb didn't look real. Abbey assumed it was some camera glitch caused by light and dust creating a weird cloud effect. Abbey turned to double check, but there was no cloud of dust, and there certainly was no magical orb floating behind her. Yet there it was, right behind her in the selfie.

She kept turning from the camera to the room and back again. The effect of it was disorienting. She *felt* the orb was there. She could *see it* on her phone, but every time she looked to confirm in real life, there was nothing. Abbey cleaned the screen, but it wasn't a smudge or a crack. The orb remained. She moved the phone around and the orb kept its same position, as if it was anchored to the room somehow, like it was choosing to stand still. "Holy shit," said Abbey.

"Holy shit," said Drew. It had all happened so fast. First the note, then the girl's mirror camera thing, then Drew seeing herself — some shadowy version of herself — in the image. Drew didn't know what to do, so she just stood frozen in place. The rules were changing so fast, and she didn't know what would happen if she moved and then the orb moved. The last thing she wanted to do was scare Abbey. Rose's warning echoed in her mind. She had to keep the peace; keep it copacetic. She couldn't let the rot continue to grow. They needed to become dust in the wind.

But did Rose really know what she was talking about? Drew didn't think Wes, of all people, was right about the afterlife, but she was starting to question Rose's logic as well. When Abbey had read the note, Drew felt a *connection* to her, and she believed Abbey felt it too. Drew wasn't half the spiritualist as Rose, but that connection might just have been the first truly spiritual thing Drew had ever experienced in her life.

"Am I alone in this house?" Abbey asked.

Drew's eyes went wide. *Shit. Shit shit shit.* Abbey was still holding the camera up, and Drew could see her "orb" reflected in it. Drew bit her lip gently and moved slightly to see what would happen. The orb moved too, floating in the physical space where Drew's heart would be.

"No, you're not." Drew answered.

"Am I alone in this house?" Abbey repeated, unable to hear her. Drew could see the doubt creeping into Abbey's eyes, as if she were suddenly embarrassed by the whole setup. She had the face of a girl who thought she was going crazy. Without thinking, Drew moved her body left to right, back and forth to answer. Abbey couldn't hear Drew, but she could see the orb. Drew hoped the message would be clear: *No. You are not alone.*

Abbey's face lit up. Drew wanted to leap out and hug her. "Are you a ghost?"

Drew stood up on her tippy toes, then let herself back down, and repeated it a few times, causing the orb to rise and fall as if nodding "yes."

Drew could see Abbey shaking with excitement, just as she was. The living girl took a deep breath, lowered the camera, and turned around to face where Drew was standing. The doubt that was on her face just moments ago had been squashed. She looked fearless. The girl reached out. *Rose is going to be pissed*, Drew thought, but reached out to Abbey without hesitation, desperate to not only feel seen by this stranger, but be acknowledged.

Abbey's hand extended out, reaching towards Drew.

Drew reached closer, her fingers inches from Abbey's.

They touched. Fingertips first, and then their palms pressed together, their fingers intertwining. A serene sense of oneness swarmed their bodies, uniting them.

Abbey's entire body hummed. The words "oh my God" escaped from her lips before she could catch them. Tears were welling in her eyes, and Abbey knew this moment would change her forever. She hadn't allowed herself to believe it before, but now she was absolutely certain the impossible was happening. She pressed firmly on the invisible force in front of her, feeling the shape of a hand that wasn't there. The sensation — that connection to the unseeable but undeniable — was something she hadn't felt since her mother died.

Abbey gave in, fully convinced, and threw her arms around the person she knew in mind, body, and soul was standing right in front of her. She hugged the ghost deep and hard and felt a pair of invisible arms wrapping around her, comforting her, supporting her right back.

"Oh, mom, I've missed you so fucking much," Abbey cried.

Drew was so caught off guard by Abbey's words she leapt out from under the girl's arms. She watched, guilt stricken, as Abbey stumbled to the floor, confused by the sudden withdrawal. Drew hadn't wanted this. She never meant to mislead this girl, to trick her into thinking her mom was somehow reaching out to her from beyond the grave. Drew just wanted to feel seen, to feel like she still existed. This poor girl just wanted her mom.

Drew had an impulse to reach out again, to lift Abbey from the floor and pretend to be her mom, to go through the motions and give the girl whatever closure she was seeking, but she fought it. She'd already made a huge mistake even letting the girl touch her, and now could hear Rose's voice in her ears: *"You did what?"*

Abbey waved her arms around, trying to find her "mom" again. There was fear in the young girl's eyes, and Drew could tell it wasn't because she'd just had an encounter with a ghost, but because she was terrified of losing touch with her mother all over again. Drew's heart plummeted. She'd let Rose down by breaking the barrier with the living, possibly trapping them in Greywood House forever. She'd let this girl down, possibly setting her on a path of extreme self-doubt. She'd let everyone down. All because she was stupid and selfish and impulsive. *Classic Drew.*

Abbey's arms swept through the air like she was in a pool playing Marco Polo. She called for Willa to wake up, but the sleeping girl couldn't hear her through the headphones. Abbey lowered her arms and pulled out her phone again. Drew barely had enough time to drop to the floor and scrambled backward on her hands and feet, desperate to hide from the girl's camera. Drew's back hit a wall, and she curled into a ball, trying to make herself as small as possible. When she looked up and realized she was once again in the attic closet, she couldn't help but appreciate the irony of hiding here for a second time. *You're a fuck-up*, she thought. *A total, Guinness Book of World Records, Grade A fuck-up.*

Abbey searched for Drew's orb, sweeping one arm around the room while the other pointed the camera. Her voice trembled as she called out for her mom to come back. She just wanted to talk to her. The guilt was overwhelming, and the instant Abbey turned away from the closet, Drew bolted down the attic stairs, wishing she could undo everything.

Chapter 24

ABBEY WASN'T GOING TO GIVE UP SEARCHING. THE GHOST OF HER mom had visited her in the attic, she was damn sure of it, but then something went wrong. Their connection had broken. She wouldn't let that stop her, though. She was already figuring out all the ways she could research ghosts, how quickly she could get a Ouija board off Amazon, and how many friends she'd need for a seance. But before all that could happen, she had to be sure her mom was truly gone. She wasn't quite convinced the ghost had left the house. The contact between them had changed something in Abbey. She felt like she was vibrating, like she'd been pounding Red Bull and her senses were cranked to the max. She had goosebumps all over and there was a slight ringing in her ears, a sound that was at once far away and consuming her.

Abbey searched every corner but couldn't find the orb in her bedroom and hoped the buzz in her ears meant her mom was just somewhere else in the house. One of her fondest memories from childhood was playing hide and seek with her mom. Back then their house wasn't big, but her mom could somehow always find a new place to hide. This house, though... *This* house was absolutely massive. Her mom could be hiding anywhere. This was going to be a helluva game of hide and seek.

Abbey stood atop the attic stairs, grinning like a kid on Christmas morning. "Come out, come out wherever you are," she called out playfully while descending the steps, camera held out to catch a glimpse of her mom. Abbey laughed to herself, wondering if that might count as cheating. She didn't care. She was playing a game of hide and seek with her mom again. Her entire body was electric. She'd never felt more alive.

Drew found Rose and Eli in the laundry room. She was out of breath, struggling to explain she'd not merely touched Abbey, but hugged her, too. And it had been an amazing, indescribable experience... until Drew realized who Abbey thought she was. But she didn't have time to answer Rose and Eli's barrage of questions before they heard Abbey on the attic stairs, gleefully shouting "Come out, come out, wherever you are."

Drew yanked Rose out of the laundry room. Rose in turn grabbed Eli, and the three raced down the hallway like they were playing a game of Red Rover. Eli took the turn too fast, hitting the wall and cursing profusely, but Drew didn't have time to check on him. Abbey would be on their heels in seconds and Drew needed to get away from that damned camera to the last place she thought Abbey would look for them: the basement.

Eli was, to put it mildly, really fucking confused. He wasn't the only one. Rose had been uncharacteristically quiet while Drew recapped everything that happened in the attic, leaving Eli to wonder if she was feeling some residual guilt from their pizza heist. Nothing bad had happened afterward, and they'd even shared a great moment in the laundry room. But now Drew was freaking out and the calm of their new norm was shattering.

It's not that Eli didn't believe Drew; it was just too much new information to process. He thought the rules of the afterlife were, all things considered, logical. It was Toy Story, right? *If* there were no people, *then* their universes were merged; *If* a person looked at them, *then* their universes went back to being parallel. Andy's toys weren't supposed to be able to play back with him.

"Are you absolutely sure she touched you?" he asked her.

"She didn't go *through* me, Eli."

"No, what I mean is, you know the barrier around the living? Maybe there's a barrier around us, too? Maybe she was just touching the barrier?"

Drew threw her hands up in frustration. "What's the fucking difference, Eli? I was literally holding her in my arms, man. Barrier, no barrier, I don't know what the hell you want to call it. I could *feel* her, and she could *feel* me."

"What did it feel like?" Rose asked, staring at her shoes. Her tone surprised Eli. There was a hint of jealousy to the question.

"It was incredible," Drew answered. "Just... I've never felt anything like that. It's like we were... connected... not just physically. It was more than that. It was deeper, it was like—"

"Was it worth it?" Rose interrupted.

The jealousy in Rose's voice had sharpened, giving Eli that queasy feeling he got whenever his parents argued. All of a sudden, the basement erupted into shouting, with Drew pleading that she hadn't meant to do it, and Rose accusing her of always being too impulsive. Eli retreated to the corner, wishing he could melt into the wall. He loved to argue, but in a devil's advocate kind of way; not in a "Is this going to end our friendship?" kind of way, and the tension between the two of them made his skin crawl. He wanted to talk to Wes just so he wouldn't feel like such a third wheel, only Wes was nowhere to be found. Eli realized it'd been a while since he'd seen him. *He's probably sulking by a window somewhere.*

Eli started up toward the stairs but stopped when he felt a squish under his sneaker. He knelt and discovered with horror that he'd accidentally stepped on a mouse. Or, what used to be a mouse. He looked closer at the smashed sack of bones and blood-matted fur. There was no way a normal footstep did that amount of damage. He had an immediate, gut impulse that Wes was responsible. He didn't know *how* Wes had broken the barrier with the living, but he was certain he'd found a way — just as he was certain his brother would not stop with just a mouse.

Abbey was breaking inside. She'd searched every corner of the second floor for her mother's orb but hadn't found it. She thought she'd find it in her dad's room, watching over him — not in a creepy way, but in a sweet, protective way — but all she found was Javier passed out. Hard. He'd been having trouble sleeping lately and started taking Ambien to make it through the night. Other girls her age might use that to their advantage — sneaking out late, partying, drinking — but not Abbey. She knew her dad trusted her and she wouldn't do anything to break that trust. After her mom died, Abbey and Javier only had each other. They'd become closer, both looking out for each other, and Abbey cherished that closeness. So, when Abbey saw her dad passed out from Ambien, all she could feel was pain in her heart, a connectedness to her father, and the hope for a day when he no longer had to drug himself to be able to sleep.

Having exhausted all options in the attic and second floor, Abbey walked slowly down the stairs to the dark foyer. Her arm dropped, sore from holding the phone up for so long, but she raised it as high as she could to scan for that dang orb. They'd managed to bring in most of the U-Haul's contents but gave up trying to put everything where it belonged and instead dumped an entire house's worth of crap into the living room.

The mixture of their belongings with what was left by the previous owner turned the first floor into a half-assed antique shop, with stacks of boxes and furniture and lamps forming a maze. Abbey struggled to see in the darkness. "Mom? Please come back. I need you." Her voice was cracking, but she refused to admit how pointless this was starting to feel.

Abbey slammed her knee into the sharp corner of some object she'd missed in the dark and cursed loudly. Pain shot up her leg as she stumbled her way over to an old glass lamp. She flipped it on to see what the hell she'd run into, but there was so much crap around her she couldn't tell what the culprit was. She made it a few steps into the maze when suddenly — *click* — the lamp turned off behind her.

Abbey jumped in fright and dropped her phone. She bent to pick it up and banged her forehead on a table, shaking it and knocking over a tower of books in the process. "God damn it!" She wheeled, distracted by the pain, and half-expected to find her dad or Willa with their hand on the lamp and a shit-eating grin on their face.

But she was alone.

No, not alone...

That was the whole reason she was down here. She carefully knelt to the floor, her hands searching for her phone. When she couldn't find it, panic set in. She'd lost the one way she had of finding her mom. Her heart pounded. The darkness all around her grew, steeping everything in shadow as Abbey pawed aimlessly along the ground, desperate to find the damned phone.

CLICK — the lamp turned back on.

Abbey froze on all fours, her hands and knees shaking, wanting to look at the lamp but terrified of what she might see. She tilted her head just enough to see the base of the lamp. There were no feet standing by it. There was no hand resting on it. She was totally alone.

No, not alone...

And that's when she saw a ray of light glint off her phone. The screen had cracked from the fall, but she didn't care. She snatched it up and swept the camera toward the lamp.

But there was no orb.

She wanted there to be an orb so freaking bad. She was *begging* for there to be an orb. Abbey switched the lamp back off, took a few careful steps away from it, and aimed her camera, waiting. She wanted the lamp to switch off again. She didn't really believe in God, but she caught herself praying for it to turn off.

But nothing happened. God wasn't listening.

A light in the dining room suddenly turned on, and Abbey exploded with happiness. Her mom was indeed playing a game with her. She spun 180-degrees, her camera held straight out, arm aching, eyes searching for the tell-tale orb. The spider web of cracks on her screen made it impossible to tell what she was seeing. She held it close to her face, inspecting every inch of the screen, walking as she did, only this time her throbbing knee was a constant reminder to be careful.

But still there was no orb.

What the hell?

And then Abbey felt a strange sensation on her back, like someone ran their finger from her tailbone up over her spine. She turned but was alone. *Big surprise.* And then the dining room light turned off, plunging Abbey in darkness once again. "Okay, mom, I just want to talk. This is getting a little—"

CLICK — the kitchen lights turned on, contorting the shadows all around her. This game of hide and seek was turning into a game of red light, green light. Abbey and her mom had played it when she was young, but it wasn't really *their thing*, not like hide and seek. But she so badly wanted to feel her mom again, to feel that overpowering, awe-inspiring connection she'd felt in the attic, that she ignored the small flame of doubt burning in the back of her brain: *Maybe this isn't my mom...*

Abbey ran into the kitchen. All the overhead lights were on, along with the light under the microwave and the porch light outside, which meant her mom had flipped on every single switch in the room. Abbey went around, turning them off one by one, until there was only moonlight coming in from the windows.

"Okay, mom. You win. Let's just talk, okay?"

Abbey swept the camera around, and suddenly — finally — she saw an orb. Or, thought she had. It was hard to tell with her smashed screen, but she had no doubt *something* had darted off toward the basement. Abbey made her way slowly over to the top of the stairs, camera held out like a shield. Her phone's lens struggled with the darkness down the stairs, so this time it was Abbey's turn to flip on the basement light. The filament flickered, struggling to stay alive. Abbey wasn't quite sure why. The simplest answer was the bulb was old and her dad hadn't replaced it, but there was a *feeling* Abbey was getting from the basement. She hovered her foot over the first stair a moment, her body unwilling to take the next step. That little flame of doubt growing warmer.

"No. You come to me this time. Come back to the kitchen." Abbey tried to sound calm and in control, but it was all an act. She'd been on such a high ever since the attic she hadn't really taken the time to put all the pieces together and think about what was really happening to her. But that flickering light had served as a mental reset, and she had the sinking realization just how wrong all of this was.

Abbey retreated further from the basement, but the feeling of a presence followed her. The air grew heavy. Forget the orb, forget the camera, she didn't need either to know she wasn't alone, or that this was not the same welcoming, gentle spirit from the attic.

Wes was surprised Abbey hadn't screamed her head off the first time he turned the lamp on. He couldn't believe the girl stuck around this long, playing his little game of cat and mouse, but he was so glad she had. He was starting to feel a connection to her, a flirtatious back-and-forth. At one point he ran his hand up her back, and while that fucking barrier was in the way, he knew she could feel it. She'd smiled after he'd done it. She looked like she wanted more.

He tried to lure her into the basement, but the girl was losing interest. Their flirting was over, she was ready to go back to her room. And that was fine by Wes. That preppy girl was up there, too. He could get two for one.

Abbey grew more skittish by the second. Wes didn't want to touch her again — even *he* knew that might be too much too fast — so he leaned in close and whispered in her ear. He saw her squirm, felt her body stiffen in front of him.

"Mom? Is that you?" she squeaked. He could hear her nerves fraying. Before she'd been bold and brash. Not now. Now she was quiet. *Quiet as a mouse.*

"Please, mom. I'm starting to—"

Wes couldn't help himself. He reached out and stroked the girl's hair. She froze, wide-eyed, her breath quickening. *Yeah, she felt that.* Wes moved in close, smelling her. She was intoxicating. He thought for sure that touch would push her over the edge and their game would be up, but she didn't run. He wrapped an arm around Abbey, squeezing her waist.

"Wes? Where'd you go?" A voice called up from the basement.

It was Eli. *Fucking Eli.* Always interrupting, always getting in the goddamned way. Wes knew if his brother found him like this, he'd make a big deal out of it and stop him, just like he had the one time at Alan Vempke's house party. This girl just wasn't worth the hassle. Besides, there were others in the house he could use.

Wes slipped off upstairs before Eli could find him.

Eli pinned himself to the wall of the basement stairs. He thought he'd heard Wes in the Kitchen and jumped at the sight of Abbey. She stood frozen by the kitchen island, and he was convinced she must have seen him just as she'd seen Drew in the attic. But she didn't point her camera at him. She didn't even look his direction. She was too busy trying to calm herself down. Someone else had gotten to her.

Eli sighed, knowing full well his brother had done something to her. He didn't know what, but he feared the worst. He didn't want to move a muscle lest Abbey might see him, so he waited patiently, watching out of the corner of his eye as she did a rhythmic breathing exercise — in through the nose, out through the mouth — gathering her nerves. She'd clearly practiced this before. Then she spoke to the house in a calm, clear, voice.

"I am going to find you."

It wasn't a threat, not really, but there was a matter-of-factness to it that made Eli tense. She wasn't talking to him, but even *he* felt on notice. Drew might have rattled the girl, but whatever Wes did scared the shit out of her.

"I promise," Abbey added before disappearing around the corner. Eli remained pinned against the wall, listening to the sound of her footsteps as she moved through the house, and only when he could barely hear her in the distance, did he let himself relax.

"Wes?" Eli whispered. He had to find his brother before he did something really, really stupid.

Drew sat quietly in one corner of the basement, Rose in another. Their fight had been brief but impactful, and the two retreated to opposite sides like boxers between rounds. Fighting just wasn't something Drew and Rose did, but the afterlife was dividing them. As much as Drew was trying to hang on to Rose as her North star, she was becoming harder and harder to follow. Drew's contact with Abbey had galvanized Rose. No more pizza parties, no more anything. The living were off limits and that was that. They had to start taking this seriously or they'd never fade from this place. If only Drew could buy that. If they weren't supposed to connect with the new family, then why in the hell were they still here?

Drew glanced around. A weightlifting set lived where Eli's computer desk had once been. The morning she woke up dead still felt like it had *just happened*. She'd gone from laughing at his stupid, bikini-clad screensaver to arguing with Rose about the rules of being a ghost in what felt like hours but was, apparently, decades. Her head ached as she tried to wrap her mind around it all. She rubbed her temples, a trick that had always worked when she was alive. It wasn't helping now, though. It seemed to be making things worse, as the dull throb in the middle of her head became a sizzling sensation in her ears.

It sounded like bacon frying in a pan. She closed her eyes, trying to will the sound away, but she couldn't. It nagged at her eardrums, faint enough to make her doubt she was hearing it, but loud enough to make her look around the basement. She half-expected to see Rose on the other side cooking bacon — not that Rose would ever dare eat meat, let alone pork — but of course the sound wasn't coming from Rose nor, Drew realized, was it in her head.

It was the rot.

The holes were growing before her eyes and for the first time, she could *hear* the rot. It was very slight, but undeniable. The subtle sizzling sound of the growing and merging holes made Drew's stomach churn. She couldn't smell anything, but the sound gave her a sense memory of steak searing in a skillet. She found herself suddenly hungry, and then, just as suddenly, sick at the realization the *rot* was making her hungry.

"Rose?"

Rose shook her head, refusing to turn around to face Drew. "Not now. Just give me a minute."

"But Rose I—"

"Just give me a minute!" Rose's shout caught Drew off guard. This was all so out of character for her, and Drew didn't know what to do or say, so she did the next best thing: ignored Rose. Drew approached the rotten wall slowly, listening more intently, straining to pick up on any smell, but no, there was only the dank musk of the basement and the sound of holes expanding with the faint crackle of flesh in a fire.

Drew homed in on one rotten hole in particular. It was larger than the rest, she could easily fit her whole arm through it. Part of her wanted to. Part of her wanted to just shove her arm in and wave it around just to see what happened. *It's not like some hole in the wall is going to kill me again, right?* It was the not knowing that bothered her more than anything. That's what was so frustrating about the whole goddamn situation. The rules were maddening and what little they understood was barely enough. Still, the rot was *pulling* her in. It felt like it had all the answers. Somehow, somewhere deep within it, she just *knew* she would understand everything if she could just get inside...

Something moved inside the wall.

The holes gave way to a pure, impossible blackness, but she knew something had moved. It was barely perceptible, one shade of black intersecting with another, but *something* was in there, lurking behind the holes. Hell, it might have been *making* the holes. It might have been making that sound, making the sizzle that Drew didn't want to admit made her stomach yearn.

Drew cupped her hands around her eyes to block out the light from the basement and put her face flush against the hole. It reminded her of a third-grade field trip to the zoo. She was obsessed with dinosaurs at that age and wanted so badly to see an alligator which an exhibit plaque declared a "living descendant of the great, terrible lizards." She'd rushed past her class to the gator tank, but her heart sank when she found a giant wall of plexiglass separating her and what looked like an empty swamp. She scrunched her face up against the glass and cupped her hands around her eyes like binoculars. She spotted a pair of yellow eyes staring back at her, inches from the glass. He'd been there the whole time, watching, and as soon as Drew realized it, the gator opened its enormous jaws and lunged at the glass wall, his rows of jagged teeth scraping down it like nails on a chalkboard. Drew screamed and peed her pants a little but was thrilled, nonetheless. *I survived a dino attack*, she proudly told her mom that night. Her mom laughed and told her, "Well then, you can survive just about anything, huh?"

Not anything... Drew thought while scrunching her face up like she was eight all over again, searching a different kind of swamp. She wanted to see what was hiding in the wall.

There was only stillness.

An infinite, hollow darkness.

And then Drew saw the movement again. It rushed towards her. She wanted to back away, but it came too fast. The rushing shadow opened, spreading wide, snapping toward her face. But it wasn't an alligator's jaws.

The Fireman's gloved hand shot out of the rotten hole with lightning speed, grabbing Drew by the throat and lifting her off the ground effortlessly. Drew's eyes went wide with shock and before she could even scream, The Fireman's hand was squeezing, clamping her vocal cords shut.

The Fireman's arm pushed farther out of the darkness toward Drew, until his shoulder collided with the rim of the rotten hole. That was as far as he could go before the wall held him back. But it didn't matter. All The Fireman needed was a single arm to kill Drew. Again. *For good?* His grip clenched down like a vise on her throat. Her lips turned blue as she started to lose consciousness. She slapped at his arm, but it was like hitting a tree stump. She kicked wildly trying to break free, but felt all her energy draining like sand through an hourglass as his grip grew tighter and tighter.

Rose was softly knocking her head against the wall, replaying the conversation in her mind, trying to make sure her argument was bulletproof. She was wrong to have let them get carried away in the kitchen. She should have known better. Cross one line and it becomes all too easy to cross another. She only wished her parents had practiced that. Maybe then they wouldn't have driven drunk so often.

If they just left everything alone, the house's heart would heal, and they'd be free to go. But how to convince Drew and the others of that? She wanted to say that time heals all wounds and would thus heal this one as well, but even Rose knew how dang cheesy that sounded. She wasn't going to rally anyone with Hallmark greeting card platitudes.

She tried to channel her inner Aunt Bea, who always had a quote at hand for any situation. *What was it that she used to say about healing?*

Something like "Healing is to touch with love that which was once touched by fear." Rose knocked her head a little harder, trying to remember the exact wording.

Screw it. I'm going with "Time heals all wounds, and it will heal this one, too." Rose thought. She opened her eyes, ready to dive back in for round two with Drew, and promptly screamed so hard she thought her throat would burst.

Rose couldn't believe her eyes. The Fireman's arm had broken through the rot and was lifting Drew off the ground, choking her, silencing her. Rose screamed Drew's name, but Drew went limp. Rose raced across the room and hurled herself at The Fireman's powerful arms. He barely budged. She clawed at his vinyl gloves, trying to break his grip, but it was too tight.

"Drew, hang on!" Rose pulled tighter and tighter, but his grip was inhuman. Drew's body began shaking, her eyes bulging wide, her nostrils flaring to suck in what little air they could. Drew was suffocating, surrounded by air that would never make it to her lungs unless Rose did something *now*.

Rose wrapped her arms around Drew, threw her right leg up on the wall and pushed with all her strength, trying to pull Drew free from The Fireman. Rose heaved.

Again.

And again.

Nothing.

Rose threw her left leg onto the wall. She was fully off the ground now, pressing out, her thighs burning, her arms aching as she clutched tightly across Drew's abdomen. She pushed out with every fiber of her being, screaming her voice hoarse, and suddenly The Fireman's grip broke, and she fell to the floor, Drew in her arms.

The Fireman's hand swung around wildly, trying to grab hold of them. Rose scrambled backward on the floor, pulling both of them to safety. Drew convulsed, gasping for air like she'd just swum up from the Marianas Trench. Drew struggled to speak, only a raspy whisper escaping her lips. It sounded like "You saved me" but Rose couldn't be sure.

Rose looked at the rot-riddled-wall, each hole now a small window to The Fireman on the other side. He pulled his arm back and retreated into the darkness. There was a moment of silence as the holes once again filled with that inky, infinite black. Rose got halfway into a silent prayer, hoping he was gone, when his bullet-riddle mask filled the hole where his arm had been. He stared at them, a caged beast salivating for dinner. Rose and Drew backed away further, clambering to their feet and putting as much distance as possible between them and the wall.

Rose's foot bumped against one of Javier's weights; a five-pound plate meant to go on the side of a barbell. Without thinking, Rose threw it at The Fireman. It was a perfect shot, hitting him square in the face. The bullet hole on the right side of his mask cracked wider, revealing a decrepit, diseased eye staring back at them with only the dimmest trace of white in its pupils. That evil, dead eye bore down, unfazed, and unblinking. Rose scrambled to find another weight to throw, a ten pounder this time, but when she lifted it up, The Fireman was gone.

Drew's mind flooded with emotions, but the searing pain in her throat told her so many things. Crucially, it told her there was so much more to the house, to the afterlife, than they realized. There was still a way for The Fireman to get in. There was still a way for The Firemen to hurt them.

But while that surprisingly human feeling of pain overwhelmed her, it also made something excruciatingly clear to her. She had a purpose in the afterlife. There was a reason they'd all been trapped in Greywood House. The Fireman, Drew and her fellow ghosts, the living girl; everything was connected, and they were the only thing between him and her.

"He can't get out," Drew managed to say, her voice still raspy but returning. Rose hugged her, relieved to see Drew recovering from The Fireman's assault.

"It's not big enough," Rose said.

Drew shook her head. "No, I mean we can't *let* him get out. We have to help Abbey and her dad escape this place."

"No, we need to stay *quiet*. Time heals all wounds, and it will heal—"

Drew placed her hand on Rose's shoulder, quieting her. Drew's throat burned as she struggled to speak. "We don't have time, Rose. Maybe that would work if we had more time, but we don't. We have to do something, or he'll kill everyone in this house. Us *and* them." Drew pointed toward the rest of the house and stared at Rose, pleading. "*This* is the reason we're still here. The universe isn't waiting for us to fade away. It's giving us a chance to save *them*."

Rose rubbed her crystal necklace anxiously. Everything she *thought* she understood, everything she *thought* she believed was wrong. Drew was right. They were here for a reason. They *had* to do something. She didn't want to admit it, but the sight of The Fireman made it clear she was wrong to be so passive, to be afraid of taking action.

"Okay, Drew. How the fuck do we do this?"

Chapter 25

ABBEY KNEW WILLA WOULD BELIEVE HER, SHE WAS JUST THAT kind of friend, but she hadn't had the time to think through what believing would really mean for Willa. It meant that everything her friend feared about the house was true. A bunch of people had been murdered in it, so of course it was freakin' haunted. Yes, what happened in the kitchen was terrifying, but Abbey knew Willa well enough to downplay that part and emphasize the moment with her mom in the attic. That's what would get Willa to go along with her admittedly crazy plan.

"I'm telling you, Wills, if you could have just felt what I felt up here... I know you're a church girl, so the only way I can think to describe it is holy. I had a holy experience up here."

"So, what was downstairs? An unholy experience?"

"That was... I don't think it was my mom."

"Okay, so there are *multiple ghosts* here — as in more than one — and you want me to go, what, frickin' ghost hunting with you to find them?" Willa hopped off the bed and squirmed like she'd been asked to eat a worm. "I'm sorry, Abs, but I can't do that."

"Yes, you can."

"No, I can't."

"Yes. You can."

"No. I can't."

Willa wagged her phone in Abbey's face. "Nope, nope, nope, nope, nope. Not gonna do it. I am not going frickin' ghost hunting in your big, weird, old, creepy ass house. This place is haunted AF, *Abigail*."

Abbey stared back, a coy smile spreading across her lips. She knew whenever Willa protested this much, she was about to give in. It's exactly how she acted when Abbey took her to Misato Sushi and the server brought out an octopus that wriggled its tentacles when they put soy sauce on it. Willa ate that dang octopus, and she was going to join Abbey this time, too. She knew it.

"Come on. Let's go. But we gotta use your phone, I kinda broke mine."

Abbey snatched the phone out of Willa's hand before she could say no. Willa put her hands on her hips. "Come on, Wills. I'll even let you post it." Abbey knew the lure of viral fame would get her. She stared Willa down until she broke into a reluctant smile.

"Fine, fine, but I'm not doing it for you. I'm doing it for the 'gram." Willa said, sarcastically emphasizing "the 'gram."

Abbey winked at her and then set her eyes on the attic stairs. They looked different now. Darker. Longer. Like a throat and the house was waiting to swallow whoever went down there. But Abbey held Willa's iPhone camera high. Her arm and knee still ached, but she could feel her adrenaline surging back up. They were about to film some ghosts. They might even become famous for it.

Wes stood next to Javier's bed, watching the old man sleep in *his* old bed. Literally. Javier kept the frame and box spring the lazy movers left behind and topped it with his own mattress. Wes shook his head. Even he would never sleep in a dead man's bed. That's just asking for bad luck.

Javier was snoring, a long, drawn-out nasal rattle that made Wes want to slap the man awake. He *would* make it stop, but Wes had to test something first. If Eli's Toy Story theory was correct — and it had been so far, unfortunately — Wes would have free reign to do whatever he wanted so long as Javier's eyes were closed. Wes had been able to open the door no problem, but what else he could get away with?

Wes reached down and picked up the bottle of Ambien on Javier's nightstand and shook the pills. *No limits now.* He put them back and picked up the framed photograph behind them. It was Javier, Abbey and, he guessed, Abbey's mom, all eating comically oversized burritos as big as their heads. Abbey didn't look that much younger, so it had to have been a fairly recent picture. But then why wasn't the woman here? Had they gotten a divorce?

"What'd you do to lose her, man? She was a knockout."

Wes put the picture back and Javier's iPhone caught his eye, filling him with the urge to call his parents again. Only now he wouldn't be begging for help. He'd been a chump to even think his dad would give half of a flying fuck about what was happening to his "reprobate" of a son. No, Wes wanted to call his parents' house just to make sure his dad was dead.

Wes scooped up the iPhone, knocking loose a white cable that was plugged into it. He held it in his hand like it was an alien artifact. Moonlight shimmered off the glass, but the screen stayed dark. *How the hell do you turn this thing on?* Wes turned it this way and that, but nothing happened. He was starting to feel stupid. He pointed the phone at Javier's face like a gun.

"Hey, old man, how do you make calls on this fucking thing?" Wes laughed at himself, imagining Javier waking up and seeing his phone floating in front of his face. His eyes would go wide, his mouth would drop, he'd start stammering: *g-g-g-g-g-g-ghost!* But Javier did none of that. He just kept snoring. The man was dead asleep, alright. Soon he'd just be dead.

Wes dropped the phone back onto the nightstand, climbed onto the bed and laid flat next to him. "Sup, buddy? How you doin'?"

Javier answered him with more snores. Wes smiled and took things a step further. He placed his hand on Javier's chest and watched it rise and fall with his breath. And then Wes realized something was different. His hand wasn't resting on some invisible force field. He was touching this man. He could feel the soft cotton of his shirt and the chest hairs trapped under it. His hand grew warm from the heat radiating off Javier's skin.

Javier's hand shot up and grabbed Wes's hand. Wes's eyes went wide with panic, like his dad had just caught him stealing that Snickers bar all over again, but Javier didn't do anything else. His eyes stayed closed; his snores continued as he softly cradled Wes's hand. Wes marveled at it. He'd forgotten what true contact felt like and was a little embarrassed by how much he missed it. It was almost good enough to make Wes feel bad about what he was going to do next.

Almost.

Abbey inched her way down the second floor hallway with Willa following so close, her breath tickled Abbey's neck. Willa insisted on being the one to hold her own phone, which was fine with Abbey. So long as she had Willa with her — even if Willa was using Abbey like a human shield — she felt stronger, more capable of finding her mom or, in a worst-case scenario, confronting whatever had tried to lure her to the basement.

Willa's hand was shaking despite the fact they hadn't found anything remotely supernatural yet. The guest bedroom was empty. The bathroom had nothing in it but toiletries and towels. Abbey guided Willa along toward the master bedroom. She had planned to poke their heads in there but thought better of it. It was one thing for Abbey to creep around her dad's room as he slept, but leading Willa in there would be too weird, so Abbey redirected them toward the first floor.

Willa stopped halfway down the staircase, letting Abbey take a few steps in front of her. She nodded at the living room, where high stacks of boxes looked like people standing in the darkness.

The Dead Friends Society

"Is this where the... um... ghost was messing with you?" Willa asked.

Abbey nodded and reached back to grab Willa's free arm and could feel the pulse racing through her trembling wrist. In the attic Willa had been nervous, but in a "I swear I want to go skydiving, but I'm going to need you to push me out of the plane" kind of way. But here, on the precipice of the pitch black first floor, Abbey saw the abject terror in Willa's face. This wasn't a girl who just needed a little shove to take the plunge. This was a girl who thought someone was about to rip the parachute from her hands.

"Are you okay?" Abbey asked.

Willa's wide eyes said it all: *Do I fucking look okay?*

"Do you want to stop?" Abbey asked. She hoped the answer was no, but if it was yes, she'd call it off right that second.

Willa glanced over Abbey's shoulder, reconsidering everything below her, and Abbey could tell she was trying to find the courage to keep going. She didn't find it though. Instead, Willa screamed and dropped her phone.

Eli had been scouring the first floor for Wes, but got distracted in the living room. His jaw nearly fell off his face when he saw a box overflowing with DVDs sitting by an impossibly thin TV. DVDs had just come out the year before their murders, and the tech was astronomically expensive. The discs were at least thirty dollars each at Suncoast — complete Anime sets, of which Eli was a fan, could cost over five hundred bucks — and the players themselves were north of a *thousand* bucks and weighed as much as a cable box. Eli dreamt of saving enough to buy a DVD player and start a proper collection of Neon Genesis Evangelion to replace his bootleg VHS tapes, but he didn't make nearly enough at minimum wage for it to happen any time soon.

So, when ex-Suncoast employee and ex-DVD daydreamer Eli Adams came across cardboard boxes filled with *hundreds of DVDs* sitting in the living room like they were no big deal, he was understandably distracted. Eli hunched over the box, pulling out title after title, each one blowing his mind. Some he recognized, some he didn't. *Star Wars! Alien! The Thing, seriously? They bought THE THING on DVD? This family had good taste.* He pulled out a particularly intriguing one that had digital computer code raining down and starred Keanu Reeves. *Keanu Reeves? That guy's still making movies? What the hell is a 'Matrix'?*

Eli closed the first box and moved on to the next, only this one didn't contain DVDs, it was filled with slightly smaller cases for something called a "Blu-ray." He slid out the first one. Delicately turning it over in his hands, he traced his fingers over the raised lettering: Lord of the Rings: The Fellowship of the Ring. He loved Tolkien's books growing up — *loved them* — and couldn't believe someone finally adapted the greatest fantasy series ever written into movies... and he hadn't lived to see them.

He slid the Blu-ray back with a twinge of loathing, resenting that the world kept turning, and kept filling with movies he would never get a chance to see. He ran a hand over the spines of all the Blu-rays, fanning them out and speed reading the titles. Each one was a little dagger in his heart. He knew it was stupid that discovering a box full of movies is what finally made the passage of time hit him so hard, but he didn't care. It was fucking bullshit that he'd never get to see these movies, it was total fucking bullshit that— *Wait? Is that Toy Story 4?* Eli picked up the sequel's Blu-ray, marveling at the quality of CGI in the tiny screenshots on the back.

"Holy fucking shit," he said, and all of a sudden, the Blu-ray went from weighing practically nothing to being heavier than a station wagon. Eli could barely process it before Toy Story 4 dropped out of his hand. Then a scream came from the staircase. He flipped his head around to find Abbey and her friend staring in his direction.

"Shit. Shitshitshit."

He ran to the far side of the living room and ducked to hide from their cameras. Eli scrunched up his body as small as he could and crossed his fingers that he wouldn't cause more trouble than they were already in. He *really* didn't want to disappoint Rose. He'd been so stupid to let himself get distracted by goddamned movies.

Wes carefully slid his hand out from Javier's. He waited anxiously to see if it would wake the man up, but Javier remained steadfast asleep. Wes leaned over, his face inches from Javier's. He could see the sides of Javier's nose vibrate as he snored, and marveled at how such a small, ordinary nose could make such a godawful, bone-rattling sound.

Wes pinched Javier's nose shut, sealing off his air supply. The snoring stopped, and Wes soaked up the silence until Javier's mouth dropped open and he began sucking in air again. Wes clamped his free hand over Javier's mouth, shutting off his breathing entirely.

It only took seconds for Javier's body to start shaking. Wes might not have been able to wake the man up before, but oxygen deprivation certainly did the trick. Javier's eyes flew open, and he started pawing at his nose and mouth, trying to stop whatever was suffocating him. Javier's hands passed through Wes's ghost body. The sensation made Wes's skin crawl, but he refused to give up. He didn't know if Javier could see him right now or if the old fart could only *feel* him, but it didn't matter. All that mattered was the fear in Javier's eyes as he realized something was choking him.

Wes closed his own eyes and imagined the wall in the basement, imagined rot coursing across it, tearing apart the barrier between the house and whatever laid beyond. Javier started thrashing, but Wes ignored the dying man, picturing only the rot and the freedom it would bring. It would be over soon enough. Just a few more seconds and he'd be able to go check the wall in the basement. And if Javier proved to be too small of a sacrifice to tear it down, Wes was positive the two teen girls would take care of the rest.

Abbey and Willa stood on the staircase, staring at a copy of Toy Story 4 that had seemingly just thrown itself out of a box. After Willa stopped screaming, the two shared a stunned silence. This wasn't like the game with the lamp. The light would only ever turn off when she was looking in the other direction, so Abbey hadn't seen any light switches flipped. But Toy Story 4 floating in the air and then falling to the floor? Yep, that was some straight up Poltergeist shit. On the other hand, the Pixar movie just happened to be one of her and her mom's favorite movies. That couldn't be a coincidence, right?

"I want to go home," Willa demanded.

"Right now? Are you serious, Wills? We just saw—"

"I want to go home."

"We can't give up now. Let's just find your phone and—"

"Abbey, I want to get out of this fucking devil house right fucking now. So, are you going to wake up your dad, or am I?"

Abbey starred at Willa. She'd never seen her act this way before. Willa was one of the most indecisive people she'd ever met, so for her to be so forceful was a big deal. It was as if Willa had barreled through a tunnel of fear and came out the other side having discovered a resolve she'd never known; or at least never let Abbey see before. Abbey sensed there was no use arguing about it. She couldn't talk Willa into going along with her after this. She was done. The house was haunted AF. Period. End of story.

"I'll go wake him up." Abbey said and reluctantly headed back up the staircase.

The master bedroom was only a few feet from the top of the stairs, which didn't give her much time to figure out how she was going to spin this to her dad. *Hey, uh, Dad, I know it's the middle of the night on the first night in our house, but it's totes haunted so Wills needs you to drive her home. Is that cool? Kthx.* He'd warned Abbey that her friends might treat her differently if they bought the house, but she'd brushed it off. The murders here didn't scare her. The idea of living somewhere with such a wild history was exciting to her, though now didn't seem like the best time to admit that much to Willa.

Abbey knocked softly on Javier's door. "Hey, dad? I'm coming in." She cracked the door, poking her head in first to make sure he was still in his pajamas. Then she screamed.

Eli sighed when the girls went upstairs to get the dad, but found his relief short lived when Abbey started screaming "Dad! Dad!" Eli didn't know what was wrong, but his gut knew Wes was responsible. His imagination tortured him with a slideshow of things Wes could be doing to that nice, innocent man.

Eli raced to the second floor but hung back at the door to the master bedroom. It was wide open, the lights had been flipped on, and he hesitated to rush in. If the girls were still waving that damned camera around, they could see him.

The girls shouted for Javier to talk to them, but all Eli could hear was a muffled response. He took a deep breath — Rose would be pissed if they spotted him, but so be it — and peeked around the corner to discover a mind-melting scene of universes colliding.

Willa was in the corner of the room, asking over and over if she should call the police. Javier was on the bed, his arms thrashing wildly, his face and lips blue. Abbey was shaking his shoulders, as if trying to wake him from some horrible nightmare, even though his eyes were wide open and bulging out of his head.

None of them could see Wes pinning Javier down, his hands clamped over the man's mouth and nose. But Eli could. He could also see Javier and Abbey's arms passing through Wes, unable to fight off the invisible force. The blending of realities convinced him now, more than ever, their universes (the "umbral plane" as Rose had called it) were separate, and Wes had found a way to bridge the two.

"Wes, stop!" Eli shouted.

"Oh, hey buddy," Wes looked at him with a maniacal smile twisting across his crooked face.

There was something about that smile that cut right through the thin fraternal bonds Eli still shared with Wes. He wasn't looking at his brother. He was looking at a monster. A monster who had to be stopped. Eli was all instinct, no hesitation.

He ran at the bed, and while every instinct told him he was about to run straight into Abbey, he closed his eyes and pictured himself leaping not at her, but *through* her. Eli felt a strange sensation, like moving through a waterfall, and his eyes opened as he passed through Abbey and slammed into Wes, tackling him off the bed and onto the floor. Wes rolled like a test dummy thrown from a car crash. The back of his head hit the wall hard. Eli scrambled to his feet, towering over his older brother.

Wes tried to stand, but wobbled, dazed from his crash. He lurched up at Eli. "I'm gonna give you the ass whooping dad never did."

"Fuck *you*, Wes! I can't just stand by anymore. Not this time."

Eli kicked Wes square in the chest. The blow knocked the wind out of him and sent Wes back on his ass, gasping for air just like Javier. Wes looked up at Eli, defiant but defeated.

Eli looked down at his brother, a dozen new afterlife theories swirling in his thoughts. He'd thought the rules were simple, that the ghost universe and the living universe couldn't interact at the same time. Obviously, he was wrong about that but figuring the specifics out would have to wait. As he stared down at his whimpering, rage-filled brother, he wondered if the afterlife changed Wes or if this place set free what had always been inside him.

In the past, Eli could always excuse or forgive or simply refuse to admit how much darkness was in his brother. He chalked it up to the number his dad had done on Wes and assumed, perhaps naively, that as Wes grew up and lived a life free of their dad's shadow, he'd mature. He'd stop acting like such an asshole and be the kind, decent person Eli had spent endless hours playing Sega with as a kid. But now that darkness was undeniable and Eli feared, perhaps selfishly, that no amount of mental gymnastics could excuse or forgive this.

Wes's head throbbed from smacking the wall. It was so simple to Wes, so obvious, and they were all so fucking stupid for not seeing that these people existed for them to sacrifice. He stared up at his little brother and felt sad. Eli was supposed to be the smart one, so why couldn't he understand? Why couldn't he see that Wes was doing them all a favor? "I'm opening the door, you dipshit."

Eli still didn't get it. He just stood there, huffing and puffing, and Wes realized his beanpole of a brother would never understand. Wes wasn't being selfish; he was being a hero. He was just doing what the rest of them could only wish they had the balls to do. They were all trapped in this stupid fucking house and the only way out was to use these stupid fucking people who made the stupid fucking choice to move into this stupid fucking hellhole in the first place. The girls and the old man were asking for it. They might as well have been waving flags that read *"Use us, Wes."*

"All you're doing is hurting people," Eli said.

Wes laughed. Long and hard. Eli told him to stop laughing, but Wes couldn't help himself. Everyone was just so fucking stupid, even Daddy's favorite little computer nerd.

"I said stop laughing," Eli repeated.

Eli clenched his fist in a pitiful attempt to look like a Real Tough Guy. His brother could never pull off that look. He just didn't have it in him, and the idea that Eli, of all people, would stop Wes, made him laugh and laugh and laugh. That's when Wes noticed Willa looking his direction, paranoia filling her preppy, pouty face. She could hear him. Soon enough she'd be able to *feel* him.

Wes slowed his laughter as he stood up.

"What are you doing?" Eli asked, but Wes ignored him. He couldn't take his eyes off Willa, and even though he didn't think she could see him yet, he knew she sensed him. He just needed to get closer, needed to touch her like he'd touched Javier and Abbey. Wes brushed past Eli.

"Wes! What the hell are you doing?" Eli shouted. Wes didn't

bother looking back at him. He was doing something Eli would never be man enough to do.

But Wes should have looked back. If he had, he might have seen Eli's surprisingly powerful right hook sailing toward the side of his already pounding head. Instead, all he saw was Willa disappearing into a narrowing tunnel of darkness as Eli's sucker punch knocked him unconscious.

Javier thought he was in a dream within a dream. That was the only explanation that made a lick of sense. In this dream, he'd woken up unable to breathe, with an invisible force clamping his nose and mouth shut. Once he woke up from the dream-within-a-dream, everything would be okay. Only, he wasn't waking up. No matter how much he clawed at whatever was on his face, no matter how much he pounded on his chest trying to give himself the Heimlich, he wasn't waking up. He was dying. Slowly. Painfully. But then his dear, sweet Abigail ran to his side, an angel out of the darkness, and seconds later his lungs filled with air.

"Dad! Dad, what the hell happened to you?"

"Do you need me to call the police, Mr. Moreno?" Willa asked from the corner, her hands shaking. She held her phone out, eager to dial.

"No, no, no. Don't call 911."

"Are you sure, dad? It looked like you were having a fucking heart attack," said Abbey.

"Watch your language."

"Watch my fucking *language*?" Abbey laughed. She slapped him playfully on the chest. "Watch your fucking *heart*, dad. I can't lose you, too."

Those last words stung Javier. He sat up, slowly, rubbing his face, stretching it out. His jaw and chest were sore, but his heart felt fine. Sure, it was still pounding, but that was reasonable all things considered. He tried to remember a checklist of heart attack symptoms, but all that came to mind was your left arm was supposed to tingle. He flexed his arms and hands. Nothing was tingling.

"I'm not having a heart attack, girls."

"Then what the hell was that?"

Javier shook his head, unsure how to describe it. Abbey turned to Willa. "Willa, gimme your phone. I'm calling 911."

Javier shouted "No!" a bit louder than intended and both girls flinched. All he wanted to do was calm them down, reassure them that everything was okay. The truth was he needed to reassure *himself* that everything was okay. He was feeling better by the second, but that still didn't explain what happened to him.

"You need an ambulance, dad."

"I'm not paying an arm and a leg for a stupid ambulance, Abbey." Javier could feel himself growing hot in the face. He didn't mind talking about money in front of his daughter — he prided himself on being an open book with her, especially after everything that happened with Lora — but he didn't like to do so in front of one of Abbey's friends. It was already bad enough that he felt awkward every time he drove his crappy pick-up to Willa's fancy McMansion to pick up Abbey, but he wanted that to stay *his* problem, not his daughter's.

"What I mean is, if I need to see a doctor, I can drive myself. But the fact that I can drive myself means I don't. Right?" Javier stood, stretching further, trying to reassure the girls how normal everything was. He wasn't going to tell them his chest ached, but that's because he could tell it wasn't a heart attack. It wasn't an internal pain. It felt like he'd been hit with a baseball bat. "It was probably just sleep apnea or something."

Abbey rolled her eyes, waiting for a better answer.

"Or, what's that thing? Where your mind wakes up before your body does?" Javier asked.

"Sleep paralysis," Willa answered. Abbey shot her a *you're-not-helping* look. "What? That's what it's called. I saw a documentary about it."

Javier latched onto Willa's suggestion. He pointed at her like she'd just answered right on Jeopardy. "See, Abs? Sleep paralysis. That's all it was."

"Bullcrap."

"Bulltrue." Javier countered playfully. "What are you two girls doing here anyway?"

Both the girls grew quiet, their eyes darting back and forth, having the kind of looks-only, telepathic conversation teen BFFs were adept at. The silence grew awkward, but Javier knew better than to guess what the problem was. He'd been burned too many times in the past trying to guess what had gotten them into a M-O-O-D. His default response was "Is it boys?" (It was never boys.)

Willa stepped forward. "I'll be honest, Javi, I got a little spooked and I really just kind of... could you take me home?"

"Did something happen?"

"No, no, no, nothing like that. I just..." Willa shot Abbey an apologetic look. "I just get scared easily, and with this house's history and all... I just... I'd like to sleep in my own bed tonight, if that's okay. And if I call my mom to wake her up—".

"She'll never let her come back." Abbey finished. "You know how Mrs. Gordon gets."

Willa, not wanting to be the one to bad mouth her own mom, screwed her face up into a sort of frown with raised eyebrows that looked like a bad Robert DeNiro impression. Javier wanted to laugh at it but knew better. Now wasn't the time. He stared at the pair of them. One of 'em was lying, he just couldn't tell which one. Abbey rocked back on her heels slightly, looking embarrassed and desperate for the whole conversation to be over. Javier sighed.

"Sure. I can take you home. Just give me a minute. I just had a heart attack after all." Abbey's eyes went wide and her jaw dropped. "Kidding! I'm only kidding!" Another dad joke grand slam. *Nailed it.*

Chapter 26

Rose and Drew had been arguing in circles while keeping their eyes on the rotting wall. It bubbled and spread like lava after Eli left the basement. Thankfully, it settled down before the holes became large enough for The Fireman to fit through. It was the one reason Rose was glad The Fireman was so enormous.

"We can't just wait here for him to pop back out again like we're playing fucking whack-a-mole," Drew said.

"I know that, but we also can't just go climbing in there, looking for a fight." Rose said, hoping Drew wouldn't point out the fact that *they* could fit through the largest of the holes. It'd be a tight squeeze, but not an impossible one. Either way, Rose wasn't super jazzed about the idea of worming her body through a hole in the wall and into the hollow side. She was pretty sure she knew what laid beyond there, and it wasn't some crawlspace the previous owners had patched over. It was the rotten soul of the house. It was the same black void in which she'd found The Fireman earlier. Visiting it on a psychic level had been bad enough. Rose wasn't eager to step her actual feet in it.

"Can we seal it up?" Drew asked, though even she didn't seem too confident about that idea. A new layer of drywall wasn't going to keep him out. The rot would eventually eat through it, too. *But*... an idea formed in Rose's mind.

"I think I might know what to do," Rose said, her mind racing, trying to think if she could pull this off — if she even knew *how* to pull it off...

"Talk me through it, Rose," Drew said.

Rose paced, searching for the words. "Okay, well... and please don't laugh at this, but Bea used to say the key to unlocking extrasensory potential was all about lowering the walls, the mental bricks we've been putting up all our lives. To have an out of body experience, you were supposed to deconstruct the walls inside your mind. Does that make sense?"

"Hey, if it makes sense to you, that's all that matters."

"I need you to believe me, though. That matters, too."

"I believe you, Rose. I always have. I can't do what you do. I'm not special."

Rose waved away the idea. She *was* special, but that word oversimplified the truth. There was always an invisible asterisk to the word "special" implying this was something she could do with no effort whatsoever. People who, with no musical training whatsoever, could hear a Beethoven symphony once and immediately start playing it on the piano were special. The truth was learning how to break down generation after generation of mental barriers was really, really hard work.

It took years of concerted, disciplined sessions led by Aunt Bea for Rose to have her first out of body experience. And even that episode (a silent conversation from opposite sides of the house) had still felt so unreal, so impossible, Rose secretly wondered if she'd imagined it happening. Rose knew all too well about growing up with such deeply ingrained notions about reality, about perception, about what was possible in life, and that such hardcoded notions were hard to overcome as you got older. Rose was only now starting to realize that waking up dead helped weaken a lot of her remaining mental blocks.

"Psychic experiences are only possible once we take down the mental bricks that build up the walls around our hearts and minds.

Reality is just a shared illusion. Out here," Rose gestured to the basement around them, "there's only so much we can do to change that shared illusion. There are just too many limits to our own perception of what is and isn't possible. But, if I project back into," Rose gestured to the rotting wall "I know it's not the real world. Instead of tearing down reality, maybe I can build it back up."

"You can?" Drew said, a hint of awe in her voice.

Rose knew she could sell Drew on this, but the truth was she hadn't sold *herself* on it yet. A familiar self-doubt crept back in, like her subconscious was trying to tell her this was a bad, bad plan. She turned her mind away from it. She hovered her right hand over her left as Eli had demonstrated when talking about parallel universes.

"If the barrier between us, and the living can be broken, and the barrier between us and The Fireman can be broken, that means they can be fixed, right?" Rose switched the positions of her hands, trying to make sense of everything. She pressed them flat together. "If something can be torn apart, then it can also be put back together, right?"

Drew stared at Rose a moment before responding. "Are you telling me or asking me?"

"Honestly, I don't fucking know," Rose said, surprised to hear herself cursing. Drew laughed.

Drew inched closer to the wall, smart enough to not get within arm's reach again. "What *is* in there?" she asked.

"Maybe it's his soul," Rose continued. "Or whatever is left of it."

Drew stepped back from the wall.

"And in the infinite, hollow darkness of that horrible, empty man," Rose said, "there is a single door in the darkness. Let's call that his happy place. I've seen it. If I can find it again — and if he's still there — I might be able to trap him in it." Rose's eyes drifted to the rot. She stared through it and into the hollow side. She knew The Fireman was back there, somewhere. "I'm just not sure."

Drew grabbed Rose by the hands and forced her to look her in the eyes. "Listen to me, Rose Calder. I don't know if you can do it either, but you can bet your ass I'll be right here by your side to help you. Because there's one thing I know beyond a shadow of a doubt."

"What's that?" Rose asked.

"You are really, *really* fucking special."

Abbey and Willa lingered six feet apart in the foyer. Abbey had switched on every light she could as they waited for Javier to come downstairs. Willa wasn't talking to her. She didn't need to. Abbey knew Willa would keep her secret about all the ghost stuff, just as she knew Willa would inevitably ask Abbey to forgive her for freaking out in the middle of the night. Things might be awkward for a few days, texting would grow sporadic and probably consist of just memes and emoji, but eventually they'd work their way back up to words and video calls. They'd been through this sort of thing before, and they'd go through it again, but they'd always worked through it. It's just what they did.

Javier came jogging down the stairs, pajamas traded for jeans and a t-shirt. He looked fit as a fiddle (whatever that meant), like nothing had ever happened. Abbey still couldn't shake the feeling her dad needed to see a doctor. She had to say something.

"Dad are you sure you don't—"

But anticipating what she was going to say, Javier finished her thought. "I'll go see a doctor, okay?"

"Okay, but as long as you *promise* to set up an appointment tomorrow, not next week."

Javier held up his hand in the Boy Scout's three-finger salute. "I promise. Scout's honor."

Willa kept staring down at her feet, her hands shaking ever so slightly, and chewing on her lip. Abbey was thankful her dad hadn't asked too many questions up in the bedroom, but now he was starting to notice just how freaked out Willa was. He looked back and forth between them. "Okay, what really happened to you two?"

Willa realized she'd been caught. She shifted into her high-pitched, preppy mode. "Oh, I'm totally fine, Mr. Moreno. It's just been…"

"A really freaking weird night, dad. And your heart attack certainly didn't help any."

"It wasn't a— hang on, don't pin this on me. You two came to *me*, remember? So, tell me. What happened?"

Abbey hesitated to answer out of the hope Willa might speak up first. To her great relief, Willa held up three fingers. "Nothing happened. Scout's honor," she said. Abbey smiled.

Javier let out an exaggerated "Oooooookay," and grabbed his car keys off a nearby moving box. He opened the front door and all three of them flinched at the howl of cold wind. "Alright, let's go."

Willa and Javier stepped out onto the porch, but Abbey hung back. "You're not coming?" he asked. Abbey waved away the question as if it were silly. "No, I'm tired. I'm gonna go crash." She finally made eye contact with Willa and could tell her BFF was reading her mind. Abbey nodded ever so slightly, trying to silently reassure Willa that everything would indeed be fine, that she wasn't about to go race back to the attic, grab her broken phone and start ghost hunting again.

That was, of course, a lie.

Drew chewed nervously on her nails while Rose sat in the middle of the basement, facing the rotting wall. She wasn't close enough for The Fireman to be able to reach her through the rot, but it was still close enough to make Drew uncomfortable.

"Should I sit down too?" Drew asked.

Rose shook her head. "If he finds me before I find him, I need you here to save me."

"Just like last time?"

"No," Rose said. "Because this time we're going to be ready."

Drew eyed a steel bench press bar leaning against Javier's stack of workout equipment. It was at least five feet long and had to weigh thirty or forty pounds. If she needed a weapon, this one was going to be her go-to. It might be awkward to swing, but there was no doubt it would do some serious damage to The Fireman.

Rose removed her necklace and began weaving the chain into an intricate web between her two hands, the now-cracked crystal dangled like a jewel at the center. Drew had seen her do this plenty of times before, but still found it impressive. As a kid, Drew had tried to do cat's cradle with some yarn and could never get it right, but here Rose was doing cat's cradle on steroids without batting an eye.

Rose looked up at Drew. "Are you ready?"

Drew hesitated, becoming keenly aware of how alone they were. "Should I go get Eli?"

"There's no time." Rose nodded at the wall. The rot had begun spreading again, growing dangerously large. "I have to go *now*." Rose said, and began muttering something under her breath, over and over. Rose's back stiffened. She closed her eyes, and the crystal began swaying.

Rose opened her eyes and was once again surrounded by a vast, hollow blackness. The wooden floor of the house extended into pure darkness as far as she could see, as if the world around her had stretched into infinity. If this place had walls, she couldn't see them. The first time she attempted this, the unexpected darkness had terrified her, but Rose now understood where she was. This void was The Fireman's rotten soul imprinted on the house the night he decided, for reasons Rose still didn't know and didn't really want to know, to slaughter her and her friends. You couldn't create that kind of violence without leaving a piece of oneself behind. In this case The Fireman left behind an infinite, crushing darkness, but Rose knew there was one place he'd carved out for himself. A memory he could still hide in.

Rose spun around in circles trying to find any hint of the rectangle of light and the door to The Fireman's happy place. There was nothing.

Rose closed her eyes and reached out. Not with her hands, but with her mind. She slowed her breathing, her heart rate, and *listened*. She let her body sway slightly, as if pushed around by waves in an ocean, one small step at a time, listening for the tiniest hint of any sound in any direction.

She wasn't sure how many times she'd turned, or even how long she'd been searching, but when she heard the faint crackle of fire embers in the distance, she opened her eyes. *There you are.* The door and its rectangle of light weren't far away. Rose ran as fast as she could.

Rose knew her physical body was sitting cross-legged on the floor of the basement, but she could still feel the rush of air around her face as she ran. The vibrations piercing up her shin bones with each footfall felt real. Her mind knew she wasn't really in this place but telling her body that was proving impossible. That meant if The Fireman found her again, whatever he did to her in here, the hollow side, could likely affect her out there. Rose couldn't worry about that now, though. She had to trust Drew would be there if she needed saving.

Rose slowed as she approached the rectangle of light. The door was closed, just as it had been last time, which filled her with a relief she wasn't quite expecting. What would she have done if it was open?

Rose put her ear to the door and listened. She heard the crackle of the fire, that same tip-of-her-tongue singer crooning on the record player. She imagined the scene from before, the picturesque mother laying by the fire, playing Monopoly with her picturesque children. Then she imagined the father, his face buried in a newspaper. She knew this was *his* memory she was in. It was some snapshot of happiness The Fireman was clinging to, and Rose couldn't help but wonder if his beautiful family had any idea what the man calmly reading the newspaper was capable of.

Rose wanted to open the door, to creep down the stairs to confirm The Fireman was down there, but she couldn't bring herself to. If he found her, things could get very bad, very quickly. Drew and the others would have no way of trapping him here. Rose listened more intently. She heard the newspaper crinkle as the father turned the pages. She heard dice rolling, board game pieces moving, children giggling, and the loving laughter of the mother. Rose had to hope he was down there still, reliving the moment over and over.

Rose took a few steps away from the door. She sized it up, trying to figure out how the hell she was going to seal The Fireman inside his own memory. It was easy enough to tell Drew she could figure it out, but now that Rose was here, she was at a loss. With the right training, one could learn to shape their own mindscape, but this wasn't a normal session of meditative self-care. Rose wasn't tending to her own mind, she was creeping around in someone else's, praying she wouldn't get caught. Still, she had to do *something*.

Rose stood before the door and closed her eyes. She reached out again, this time with both her mind and hands. She imagined herself grabbing the darkness, imagined what it would be like if the shadows surrounding her weren't hollow, but rather physical. She imagined what it would feel like and settled on the sticky, hot tar roofers use. She imagined pulling the tar with her bare hands, stretching it in giant ropes like it was taffy.

Suddenly, her hand felt warm. Too warm. Painfully warm.

Rose opened her eyes and found she was *holding the darkness*. It was as if she reached out and pulled a shadow from the blackness. A smoldering, sticky rope of darkness. *Damn, I'm good*, she thought, as she pulled the rope over the door, covering it in darkness. As she did, the door started to disappear; each loop of hot tar blotting out the rectangle of light coming from within.

Rose beamed, overwhelmed with how powerful she really was. Aunt Bea always told her she was capable of anything, but she'd never believed her, not truly. She thought that was just something grown-ups told kids to make them try harder. But here Rose was, pulling strands of darkness from the ether and wrapping them around the last meta-physical vestige of a serial killer's rotten soul, trapping him in his own memories.

Holy shit, it felt good.

The Dead Friends Society

Drew couldn't believe her eyes. The rot was disappearing. Pockets of it evaporated right in front of her face, revealing normal cement. Whatever Rose was doing, it was working. Drew couldn't help but jump in the air, absolutely giddy. Finally, something good was happening for them.

Drew wanted to clap Rose on the back and tell her how fucking badass she was but was afraid she might break the spell — or whatever you call it. Instead Drew paced protective circles around Rose. Her eyes darted from her friend to the wall and the continually shrinking cancer of rot encompassing it. It looked like a fire burning in reverse, the blackness dissolving off the wall, restoring the house underneath.

Rose had found a way to defeat The Fireman. Soon, they'd be free. Drew's mind drifted to the front door. She pictured standing at its threshold and stepping out. There'd be no portal, no magical rubber banding back into this goddamn house. They'd be free. To do what, Drew didn't quite know (what are ghosts supposed to do, anyway?), but they'd figure that part out later. Right now, all she could focus on was the rapidly shrinking wall of rot.

Rose, you beautiful, magical woman.

Abbey was hellbent on not giving up. *Third time's a charm.* She stood at the top stair of the basement with her phone out and recording. The screen had several spider webs of cracks running through it, making it hard to see, but the camera's lens hadn't broken, and that's all that mattered. She could look at the footage later on her computer. Right now, she just needed to get over her nerves and take the first step into the basement. She had to find proof her mom had been here with her.

Abbey's heart pounded in her chest. She'd searched the house all over and hadn't found her mom. The basement was the last place she could be. Abbey's phone buzzed and the unexpected jolt nearly gave her a stroke. It was a text from Willa: "I'm sorry. I overreacted."

"It's my fault, too. You know how I get," Abbey quickly tapped back. She waited, watching the three little dots from Willa keep appearing and disappearing. Those three dots were the cause of too much anxiety. Finally, her phone buzzed with a message: "Happy ghost hunting," followed by a string of ghost and knife emoji. Abbey laughed, sending back a string of hearts and skulls. They'd made up faster than she thought they would and was reminded once again why she loved Willa so much.

Relieved, Abbey stared down the basement stairs, which no longer seemed quite so long or dark. She pressed record and took a step. And then another. And before she realized it, Abbey was practically running down the stairs, the phone bouncing in her hands.

Rose's arms ached so badly she could barely lift them, and her hands were blistered from heat and friction. It was worth it. Sealing a severed soul in its own darkness was exhausting, but she was nearly done. Only a few thin slivers of light were still visible. It would take just a few more ropes and the door would be completely sealed off.

Rose took her mind off the pain by focusing on the future. The reason their souls had been trapped in the house was because they were tied up with the fate of The Fireman. By sealing him up, Rose was breaking that tie. The Fireman could sit in his happy place forever, oblivious to the rest of the world around his rotten soul, and their own souls would finally be free to move on.

Drew was so happy she worried she might start crying. All but a few specks of the rot had disappeared from the wall. Rose had vanquished so much of it that Drew no longer feared The Fireman lunging out of it.

Still, she approached the wall like it was a tranquilized grizzly bear. She held her hand over the newly visible cement, wary to touch it, but she had to be sure it wasn't an illusion.

Drew touched the cold cement and felt her entire body relax. It was working. Rose had done it. *Motherfucking Rose Calder. Always saving the day.*

And then the light to the basement turned on. Drew spun around in shock to find Abbey standing at the bottom of the stairs, phone held out in front of her. *This freaking girl doesn't give up*, Drew thought, as Abbey's head popped up from the phone and her eyes exploded with delight.

"I see you," Abbey said in a happy, sing-song voice.

Rose hesitated. There was just a single, hair-thin ray of light left. It was the only thing separating her from crushing darkness. It was also the only thing separating them from The Fireman. As soon as she sealed it up, they'd be done with him.

Rose pulled one more rope of darkness from the ether and wrapped it around the door. She was instantly plunged into darkness. This time, it was a relief. Rose opened her eyes. Not her mind's inner eye, her real eyes.

She was staring at a blank cement wall.

A totally blank, totally ordinary wall.

No blackness.

No rotten imprint of The Fireman's soul.

"Holy shit, I did it Drew. I really did it!"

Rose looked up expecting to see Drew beaming back down, but her face was pure dread. Rose followed her gaze and saw Abbey pointing her phone at them. Rose whispered, even though she was pretty sure the girl couldn't hear them. "Can she see us?"

Drew nodded.

Shit, Rose thought. *Shit, shit, shit.* She glanced back at the rot,

Peter Hall & Paul Gandersman

expecting it to re-appear, just as it had every time they'd haunted the living before.

But there was no rot.
She'd really done it.
She'd saved them all.

Chapter 27

HE'D NEVER GROW TIRED OF HIS BEAUTIFUL WIFE LAID BEFORE THE crackling fire, his strapping young men playing games at his feet, a 45 of Bing Crosby belting in the background.

Simple times.

Great times.

"I can see you."

The girl's voice boomed in his ears, unbearably loud.

"I know you're there," she continued.

The fire stopped crackling. His wife stopped laughing. His boys froze. The illusion broken.

She broke it.

And he'd break her.

Like he'd broken all the others.

He stormed up the basement stairs, ready to rip open the door handle like he'd rip her head...

There was nothing.

Only darkness.

The door. Where it was. Where it had been. Where it had always been. Gone.

Darkness. Nothing but darkness.

He. His family. Trapped.

He raised his axe. And swung.

The blade sank into the darkness, disappearing. Swallowed in black. The darkness, an impenetrable swamp.

He pulled the axe out. The same darkness dripped off it in thick ropes of tar.

He swung again.

And again.

And again.

She wouldn't stop him.

None of them would stop him.

Chapter 28

Drew stood statue still, though she wasn't quite sure why. What was standing still going to accomplish? Something in her lizard brain told her to do it. Isn't that what you were supposed to do when you came across a dangerous wild animal? If you showed a bear you weren't a threat, it'd ignore you, right?

It wasn't working. Drew could *feel* Abbey's heart pounding from twenty feet away. And then she heard that all-too-familiar sizzling sound of bacon on the grill. She slowly turned her head toward the wall, not wanting to look, not wanting to believe what the stomach-churning smell was already telling her. But sure enough, the rot was growing again. *Fuckfuckfuck.*

Rot bloomed across the entire wall like blackened Swiss cheese. The miracle Rose had accomplished was vanishing before their very eyes. Rose jumped to her feet and backed away from the wall. Drew panicked.

"Rose! Stop moving. It's growing *because* she sees us. *We're* opening the door for him." Drew said.

It was too late. Standing still wasn't working. Abbey wasn't some dangerous wild animal. She was a curious, persistent teenager desperate to contact her mom again. Abbey walked deeper into the room; the camera held high. She looked back and forth from the screen to where Drew and Rose were standing.

"Mom?" Abbey asked.

Drew looked around the room, trying to come up with a plan, but everything seemed hopeless. They were caught dead-to-rights, backed into a corner. There were only two ways out of the basement: the outer door and the stairs. The door would portal them right back in, so that was useless, and the stairs were behind Abbey, so there's no way they could reach them without Abbey knowing exactly where they were going. Drew knew Abbey wouldn't let herself lose track of their orbs this time, and that was a big problem considering the rot was growing, swelling, consuming the wall. Soon the whole thing would be gone and there'd be nothing to hold back The Fireman.

Abbey squinted at her phone. It was hard to make sense of things through the broken screen. She cursed at herself for always being so clumsy. If she hadn't dropped it, she'd know exactly what was going on. Now she was stuck guessing.

She knew there was one orb in the basement, she could tell that much for sure. It looked like her mom's orb from the attic, floating with that same subtle bob. But Abbey thought there might be a second orb next to it. She couldn't be sure though. The two orbs were separated by a crack in the glass, and she couldn't tell if it was real or just a glitch.

"Mom? Is there someone with you?" Abbey asked, her voice rising an octave.

The glitchy orb moved quickly, swarming toward her. Abbey's heart leapt in her throat, and butterflies swarmed in her stomach. *Okay, this is it. I wasn't crazy. It's happening again.* She prepared herself for another physical connection. "I'm here, mom. I'm here for you."

And then it came. Not gentle like last time. This time it was a violent, strong grip on her wrist. "Stop it. You're hurting me," Abbey pleaded.

Rose grabbed Abbey's wrist without thinking. Drew shouted, but Rose wasn't listening. She only cared about one thing: getting the camera out of the girl's hand. Rose had worked too hard inside that hellish abyss to have her work undone so quickly.

"You're scaring her! Stop!" Drew screamed.

Deep down Rose knew Drew was right, but they could all get out of this mess if the girl would just drop the dang camera. Rose heard Eli's voice in her head, spouting off one of his If-Then statements. *If she can't see you,* then *she'll stop being scared.* Rose tried to shake Abbey's arm, but no matter how hard she tried, she couldn't get it to budge. Rose needed to break through the barrier around Abbey. She tightened her grip.

"Drop the fucking camera!" Rose screamed in the girl's face.

She hadn't meant to yell it, only think it, but it was too late. The vitriol rushed out of Rose before she could stop it, and this time the living girl felt it; all that rage, all that anger, made the difference. Abbey's hand shook violently, her excitement and hopefulness replaced with fear and pain.

"You're scaring the shit out of her!" Drew reached out to yank Rose back. It was too late. Abbey lost control of her camera and it slammed to the floor, sending her jumping back in terror.

"I'm sorry, but I had to do it." Rose turned to face Drew, out of breath. "She was opening the wall back up and—" Rose stopped talking the second she saw what was behind Drew.

The wall now looked like hundreds of spider eyes staring back at them. The rot covered the cement top-to-bottom, leaving only a few patches unaffected. Without warning, slashes of rot ripped through the remaining wall. These weren't the normal sizzling, patches of rot, either. They were sharp, jagged lines of rot that seemed to burst outward from inside the wall itself. They also weren't random like the normal rot. There was a coordination to the slashes. They targeted what remained of the wall, hacking away at the last bits of barrier.

No, not hacking.

Chopping.

An axe.

By the time Rose pieced this together, it was too late. What little wall remained crumbled apart, giving way to a vast, infinite darkness as the tunnel to the hollow side was laid bare. Rose turned to Drew, crestfallen. "I'm so sorry, Drew. I didn't mean to—"

THUD. The sound of metal pounding on wood rang out from the hollow side. Drew stopped breathing. She knew that sound. She knew what was coming.

THUD. Abbey heard it, too. She jumped, caught off guard. It sounded like someone dropped a cannonball inside the wall, only that didn't make any sense, since there was nothing on the other side but dirt. Abbey knelt without taking her eye off the seemingly ordinary wall. She searched blindly for her phone, desperate to be able to look through the camera. She needed her window to the other side to see what was making that sound.

THUD. The final pounding echoed from the darkness. There was a brief moment of silence, of stillness, and then The Fireman stepped out of the wall, axe in hand; a moving mountain, every inch the same unstoppable murder machine as the first night he visited, the only difference was his mask. Rose had cracked it open with the weight, revealing a hideous orb of white pupil. His eye twitched, surveying the room with bloodlust, no doubt torn over who to kill first.

Drew, Rose, and Abbey stood rooted to the floor by a cocktail of fear and disbelief. "Ohmyfuckinggodohmyfuckinggodohmy—" The words spilled out of Abbey's mouth in an almost incomprehensible slur. Drew and Rose turned to her in shock. Abbey couldn't see the ghosts, but The Fireman? She could damn sure see him. Worse, The Fireman ignored the ghosts and focused on the living girl.

The Fireman lowered the steel head of his axe to the ground. He slammed it into the floor, using that bone-chilling thud the same way a hunter uses a barking dog to flush prey out of a bush. And like the poor, helpless prey that they were, Drew, Rose, and Abbey all took flight, dashing in opposite directions.

But The Fireman was too fast. He came barreling forward like a steam train, his broad shoulders knocking Rose to the side as he charged toward Abbey. Rose fell hard, her face colliding with Javier's rack of weights. The edge of a dumbbell split a cavernous gash in her forehead.

Abbey let loose a blood-curdling scream as she tore up the staircase like a bat out of hell. She could hear The Fireman on her heels. She could hear his boot crush her phone as he stomped up after her.

Rose's head felt like it was spinning around in a washing machine. She reached up to touch the searing spot on her forehead and felt warm, gooey blood. She stared at the blood on her hands and all she could think was: *Huh? Ghosts can bleed? That's weird.*

Drew reached out and took her hand, not caring that it was covered in blood. *Drew's a good friend,* Rose thought, before realizing that her mind was doing everything it could to ignore the reality around her. The Fireman was alive, her plan had failed, and he was back, about to kill the living girl.

Drew said something to Rose, an awkward orgy of words that sounded like "'whawedo?" *Huh,* Rose thought, *why is Drew singing right now? Doesn't she know she should go save the girl?*

Rose summoned what strength she could to shove Drew away. She told her "Go, go save the girl," though what little rational part of her brain remained doubted she'd managed the words without slurring. Either way, Drew understood. She dropped Rose's hand and dragged the steel bench press bar off the floor. The hollow vibration of the pipe rang in Rose's ears like a tuning fork. It was an oddly pleasant sound she wished would have stuck around, but it was replaced with the pounding of Drew's footsteps as she charged up the stairs, once again leaving Rose behind.

Rose pushed through the pain and made it to her feet. Then she took one step and collapsed.

Abbey launched up the stairs so fast she thought she was flying. Her mind was a jumbled mess of puzzle pieces she couldn't connect. One second, she was trying to talk to her mom's ghost, the next there was a goddamned fireman standing in her basement. Not just any fireman, either. *The* Fireman. The one who slaughtered those college kids in the '90s and those people in the '70s. The one Willa was so afraid would return. And now he had.

Abbey exploded from the basement into the kitchen. She tried to slow her momentum but was running so fast she collided hip-first with the island and went rolling over it in some kind of half-assed cartwheel. As she slammed into the glass cabinet on the other side, all she could think was: *Goddamn it, Willa was right. I'm about to be killed by some maniac, and freaking Willa is going to be on the news talking about how right she was.*

The shock and pain sent her falling to the kitchen floor. She landed so hard on both kneecaps she wondered if they'd shattered. She struggled to pick herself back up. Glass shards stuck in her bruised wrist. Blood flowed freely from it. She grabbed the counter, found some balance, and glanced in time to see The Fireman at the top of the basement stairs, gaining ground. She screamed at him, some jumbled mixture of "why" and "who are you" that came out like "why you?" and was aware enough to realize how stupid that sounded. What was he going to do? Stop and explain why he was there? Why her? Why all those other people?

Abbey clamped her good hand over her bleeding wrist and ran

toward the dining room. The light was off, and she crashed once again hip-first into the dining room table, only this time she was able to keep her feet on the ground. She spun like a top into the foyer and made a beeline to the front door.

Abbey grabbed hold of the lock, fumbling with it through blood-slicked fingers. "Please, please, please open." She started crying and couldn't help but look back, expecting to see The Fireman bearing down, his axe already mid-swing, but instead she found him standing impossibly tall and unbelievably wide in the doorway between the kitchen and the dining room. Something had stopped him.

It was a metal bar.

Her dad's bench press bar.

No, her dad's *floating* bench press bar.

Time slowed to a dreamlike trickle as Abbey gawked at the bar, her rattled brain failing to make it make sense. *Why is dad's bench press bar floating in the dining room? Why is this house so fucking weird?* she screamed in her head as she fumbled with the bloody lock, praying it would open in time.

Drew had never moved so fast in her life. Before she could even plan her attack, she was closing in on The Fireman. All his attention was on the girl trying desperately to open the front door. Drew flashed back to her own failure to open that damned giant slab of oak when it mattered most. The Fireman had smashed off all the doorknobs in the house, so Drew couldn't have opened the door even if she wanted to. But Abbey could, she just needed time — time Drew had to buy her.

Drew swung the steel bar. It collided with the back of The Fireman's metal helmet with more force than Drew was expecting, and the bar nearly vibrated out of her hands. The Fireman spun on Drew, towering over her, his single eye wide with disbelief. She wished she could see the rest of his face. She bet it was surprised as hell, the way a tiger looks when a monkey grabs its tail. Picturing it made Drew smile as she pivoted around him. She dodged his retaliatory axe swing and put herself squarely between Abbey and The Fireman.

You can do this, Drew told herself as she tightened her grip on the bar, this time anticipating how much the hollow steel pipe would vibrate when she smashed his stupid fucking face in. *You can actually save this girl.*

And then Abbey turned to Drew. She knew the girl couldn't see her, but what Abbey could see, however, was Javier's bench press bar floating in the air, and Drew registered what that meant a second too late, as the bar suddenly weighed two tons. She should have let it fall, but she stupidly clung to it and toppled backward. The bar fell straight down, pinning her legs. Drew howled in pain, as if a grand piano had just dropped out of thin air on top of her.

The Fireman cast his gaze down at her. Drew knew she looked pathetic, but she wasn't expecting him to look at her with such... bemusement? Was he laughing under that mask? It was as if Drew was no longer even worthy of an axe swing. The Fireman merely turned from her to Abbey, the real apple of his decrepit eye. There was nothing to stop him now.

Abbey couldn't begin to understand what she was looking at. The Fireman had stopped chasing and turned to look at a floating metal bar that then dropped out of the air. None of it made a lick of fucking sense, but Abbey was smart enough to not let the opportunity be wasted. She wiped the blood off her fingertips, clenched the lock tightly and twisted. The *thunk* of that rusty old deadbolt sliding back was the greatest sound Abbey had ever heard in her life.

The Fireman heard it, too. He stormed out of the dining room, but that impossibly tall, unbelievably wide mountain of a man was too slow. Abbey threw open the door so hard she thought the hinges might break. She leapt out onto the porch and set her sights on the driveway. It was a clear, moonlit path. This time there were no kitchen islands or dining room tables to smash into. Even she could pull this off. She was going to make it. She was going to survive. There's no way that lumbering asshole would be able to match her speed out here.

Abbey looked over her shoulder as she ran. The Fireman was running full speed through the foyer, and every ounce of confidence Abbey had built up evaporated. *How is he so fucking fast?*

But then The Fireman *vanished*.

FFFFWWWWT. Poof. Gone.

Now you see him, now you don't.

Abbey couldn't help but skid to a stop, wanting to see what the hell just happened. One second The Fireman was rushing through the doorway, and then he disappeared. Before Abbey could blink, The Fireman reappeared deeper in the foyer.

He can't leave. The house won't let him.

Abbey barked out an involuntary laugh, the kind her dad always let out whenever he had a winning hand in poker. The Fireman stood in the foyer, inches from the doorway. She could tell he *wanted* to give chase. His huge chest heaved up and down. His fists tightened around the axe. He wanted so badly to split her body in half. But he couldn't. In a matter of seconds, he had gone from being the most terrifying thing Abbey had ever seen to this weak, impotent man who couldn't even walk through a door. She wanted to run up to him. She wanted to scream in his face. She wanted to dance a goddamned jig on the porch while he watched. But even Abbey knew better than that.

"Just run," Abbey said out loud to herself. She turned away from the house and ran off into the night, laughing as she did. Abbey knew she probably looked insane, but she didn't care. She'd just become the first person to ever survive The Fireman.

Chapter 29

Eli sat against the wall, rubbing his aching fist as he waited for Wes to regain consciousness. His brother was still breathing, but he hadn't moved an inch since Eli decked him.

Eli had never punched anyone before. He'd seen it a million times in movies, of course, but that was always fantasy to him; something reserved for "real men." Sure, he'd long dreamt of punching people. The dickwads who kept slipping expensive DVDs into their jackets at Suncoast. Their dad, naturally. And then there was Wes, but he never thought himself capable of doing it. Not because he was a Zen-like pacifist, he was just a string bean of a guy. The truth was Eli never got into fights because he was afraid he'd lose them.

Yet there lied Wes Adams, dropped by a one-punch knockout. He hadn't even meant to do it, he'd just seen the ravenous look in Wes's eyes and knew if he didn't act, his brother would do something unforgivable. So, he clenched his fist, swung, and boom— Wes dropped like a marionette with its strings cut.

Eli was pretty sure Wes wasn't going to get up too soon after a blow like that, but he'd stayed by his side just in case. He watched silently as Abbey and Willa slunk out of the room. He looked the other way as clueless ol' Javier changed out of his sleeping clothes and into a fresh pair of jeans, but other than that, Eli kept a vigilant watch over the ticking time bomb sitting next to him. He was in the middle of trying to figure out how to explain this all to Drew and Rose when he heard screaming from downstairs.

Eli cracked the bedroom door open ever so slightly so he could hear. The screams grew louder. They started from the basement but were spilling up to the kitchen. He wanted to see what was going on but was afraid to open the door fully and risk waking up Wes. He was hoping Wes might sleep off his anger, but then there was an enormous crash and the shattering of glass, and Eli couldn't sit back anymore. He flung open the door and ran downstairs.

And then Eli Adams promptly shit his pants.

Not literally, thank God, but seeing The Fireman back in the house, back in the foyer, standing in the almost identical spot where he split Eli's skull like Gallagher splits watermelons, Eli finally understood how someone could crap themselves out of fear. His entire body was in revolt, rejecting all his brain's commands and replacing them with its own. His inputs and outputs were all mixed up. Eli *wanted* to yell for Abbey to run away, but his mouth wouldn't open. He *wanted* to run, but his legs wouldn't work. He *wanted* to turn into a ball of fire and blast off like a rocket, leaving behind this wretched, wretched house, but the best his body could manage was to not shit itself. At least that was some measure of a win.

None of it made any sense. This maniac should *not* be here. Why was he here? Why was he back? It had been twenty-two goddamned years already. Hadn't this guy gotten the memo to move the hell on?

Eli watched, his stupid body not processing anything, as Abbey flung open the front door and ran out. When The Fireman tried to chase her, he blinked out of existence with that familiar *FFFFWWWT* and was portaled back into the house. And then it all clicked for Eli.

This motherfucker is a ghost just like us!

"WHAT" Eli yelled. It wasn't even a question, nor a statement, it was the only thing his collapsing brain could output. The Fireman either didn't hear him or didn't care, he just stood at the threshold to the front door, chest heaving as the girl stood on the porch, so close and yet impossible to reach.

Drew shouted Eli's name from somewhere down below and before he could tell his legs not to, they were carrying him down the stairs, searching for her voice. His autopilot legs were at least smart enough to give The Fireman a wide berth — not that the undead psychopath was even paying attention to him. He could tell The Fireman only had eyes for Abbey.

Eli rounded the dining room corner and found Drew trying to squirm her way out from underneath a metal pipe pinned across her legs. He tried to lift it off Drew, but it was like trying to lift Thor's hammer. No puny mortal could do it.

"What the hell happened here?" Eli asked.

"He came back!"

"I can see that, Drew! How? *How? How* did he come back?"

"First we have to save her."

"I'm pretty sure she's safe."

Eli pointed out the dining room window to Abbey on the porch. Drew had to twist her body to be able to see, but he could feel her relax once she saw Abbey turn from the house and start limping down the driveway. As soon as the living girl was looking the other way, the bench press bar lifted effortlessly off Drew. Its release caught Eli off balance, and he stumbled backward into the wall. The bar clattered to the floor at his feet, ringing out like a gong. *Or a dinner bell*, Eli mused, as The Fireman turned away from the front door and set his sights directly on them.

Wes woke up with his brain feeling two sizes too big for his head, leaving him to wonder if it was possible for a brain to pop inside its skull. Though he'd blacked out plenty of times from drugs and alcohol, he'd only ever been *knocked* out once when he was nine. He was climbing a tree to get Eli's frisbee back. A branch snapped and Wes plummeted headfirst into the street below. All he could remember was asphalt rushing toward his forehead and then total blackness, as if the sun switched off. He couldn't believe Eli, of all people, was capable of literally knocking his lights out like that. It made him want to find Eli and throw his ass head-first out a tree.

Wes clambered to his feet, doing his best to ignore the nuclear explosion in his skull. Javier and the girls were gone, but so was Eli. Wes called out his brother's name as loud as he could. He wanted Eli to know he was coming. He wanted that skinny fuck to know he was about to get the beating of a lifetime. But as Wes stumbled down the first-floor staircase, he switched from wanting to kill his brother to fearing for his own life.

Somehow The Fireman returned, and he had Eli and Drew cornered in the dining room. None of this made sense. He wasn't supposed to be here! None of them were! Wes was so, so close to getting that stupid rotting door in the basement to open up so he could leave these idiots behind, but now The Fireman stood in the way of all of that.

The sight of his killer caused Wes to stumble, and he fell down the remaining stairs, spilling into the foyer just feet from The Fireman. Wes panic-scrambled backward on his hands and knees to the living room as The Fireman cocked his head toward him, amused to have another victim fall into his lap. Wes's arrival seemed to overwhelm The Fireman, though. The giant stood between everyone, unable to decide who to kill first. The momentary pause was enough to give Eli time to help Drew to her feet.

"Forget her, Eli!" Wes yelled as he backed into the maze of crap that filled the living room. Wes wanted to grab one of the boxes and throw it at The Fireman but was too scared. The Fireman had already killed him once, sentencing him to the Hell that was this shitty, old-ass house. Wes didn't want to think about where he'd be sent after that psychopath cracked open his ribcage a second time, so he stayed quiet and hoped The Fireman would go after *them* and not him.

Eli had some kind of weapon in his hand. It was longer than The

Fireman's axe, and Eli held it awkwardly. His arms were shaking, though Wes couldn't tell if that was from nerves or just the weight of the metal. Eli cocked the bar back like he was readying a baseball bat for a swing, but Wes could tell his brother had no idea what he was doing. Unlike Wes, Eli never spent a tear-filled summer playing T-ball with their dad drunkenly yelling "Choke up on the bat, ya' moron!" from the stands.

Wes knew Eli didn't stand a chance. Not against The Fireman. Nobody stood a chance against The Fireman.

Drew stared at The Fireman, his axe raised high above them, ready to kill again. Only this time, Drew was oddly at peace. Ever since "waking up" in the basement, the *why* of it all ate away at her. *Why* were they still there? *Why* hadn't their souls gone to heaven (or even hell), as she'd been raised to believe? If Rose was right, *why* hadn't their spirits been free to wander on their way to re-incarnation? If Eli was right, *why* hadn't their memory files been deleted, and the world rebooted? Now the *why* of it all was crystal clear.

They were here to save the living girl.

It was so simple it made Drew mad she hadn't realized it from the jump. They were the only thing that could have possibly protected Abbey and Javier. They'd done the job they didn't even realize they'd been hired for, and now she was ready to move on. She wished moving on didn't have to happen at the end of The Fireman's axe, but she was okay with it. Abbey was safe. That's all that mattered.

Drew wanted to tell Eli all of this. She wanted to help him understand he didn't have to try and fight back. She wanted him to be okay with knowing they'd never be able to kill The Fireman — hell, they probably couldn't even do any real damage to him — they just needed to be able to slow him down long enough to save the girl. They'd done that. Job done, game over. Hallelujah, bring on the *real* afterlife.

And then Eli swung at The Fireman, and once again everything Drew believed to be true blew up in her face.

Eli knew he wasn't the strongest guy around. Shit, after Drew and Wes he was only the third strongest person in the room— not counting The Fireman, whom he was now doubting was even a man. Had Rose been there with them (where was she, anyway?), he'd have been the weakest. But Eli wasn't worried about muscles right now; he was worried about physics.

Eli always had a natural gift for the sciences, but there was something about physics that clicked with him. Angles, geometry, the mechanics of motion; they were a language he was born understanding. When he was eight, their dad bought a used pool table for the rec room. Eli won the first time he played. It was almost too easy. He could see all the angles and knew just where to put the ball. The trickiest part had been figuring out how much force to apply with the cue. Once he'd gotten that down, he cleared the table.

Old Man Adams scoffed and called him "special," and not in a nice way. Eli instinctively knew the right amount of pressure in the right place at the right angle was all it ever took. He could see the invisible geometry of it in his mind, like chalk lines drawn in the air, connecting dots, showing him where to aim the tip of his pool cue.

Eli saw those same chalk lines right now, only they weren't showing him how to sink the eight ball, they were showing him where to hit The Fireman. The right amount of pressure, in the right place, at the right angle. In this case, the right place was The Fireman's bent leg. He was wearing thick pants made of some kind of synthetic polymer, but Eli could still see the little bump of the kneecap underneath it, sticking out.

Like a cue ball.

Eli swung the metal bar.

It didn't matter that he was the weakest person in the room. It didn't matter that The Fireman was easily twice his size. All that mattered was the right amount of pressure in the right place at the right angle.

The Fireman realized too late what Eli was doing. He tried to back away, but the physics were already in motion. The metal bar collided just below The Fireman's kneecap. Eli had, for the first time in his life, missed the eight ball. But that didn't matter, either.

The Fireman's leg *shattered*, and he collapsed onto his good knee. A jagged, pearlescent stalagmite of broken femur pierced through and tore The Fireman's pants.

Eli looked from the bone to Drew to The Fireman, feeling like a kid whose first swing had cracked open the birthday party pinata, only it wasn't candy that spilled out, it was a volcano of putrid, viscous black ooze, as if the Fireman's cursed body had long forgotten what blood was supposed to look like.

Wes couldn't believe it. For the second time in a single day, Eli was making Wes look weak. Here he was cowering in the shadows, hiding behind a stack of goddamned books, and there was his twerpy, skinny, annoying virgin brother, standing up to The Fireman, doing what Wes wasn't man enough to do. He could hear their father's voice booming in his head, "What's a matter, ya' little limp dick? Can't get it up?"

Wes stood up. He wasn't going to let Eli take The Fireman down. That was *his* job. That was *his* right. Sure, he'd gotten a little scared, but who wouldn't? The Fireman had killed him once, but now he knew The Fireman could be hurt. He could bleed (if that was blood), and, as a very wise movie once told him, if it can bleed, it can be killed.

Wes ran over to Drew and Eli, who were still too stunned by Eli's surprise move to realize they should be taking advantage of the moment. Wes grabbed the bar, but Eli wouldn't let it go.

"Give it to me," Wes hissed. "I'll finish him."

Eli loosened his grip and Wes took the galvanized steel in his hands. He held it from the bottom like a baseball bat, hand over hand, correcting his form. He hated that even now Old Man Adams's voice was in his head. He hated that he still wanted to make the man proud.

The Fireman looked up at Wes, and Wes stared right back at that goblin eye. How had he ever been afraid of this chump? He was pathetic. The Fireman was on bended, broken knee, looking like he was about to propose. Wes pulled the steel back, high and tight, giving his hips a little waggle as he settled into his batter's stance.

Wes closed his eyes and pictured decapitating The Fireman with a single swing, sending his head sailing out of the ballpark, a roaring crowd chanting Wes's name as he took a victory lap. He readied his swing, soaking up the moment — and then Wes felt a familiar feeling he couldn't quite put his finger on. A warmth spread from his chest outward, his shirt grew damp, and his ears filled with screams.

Wes opened his eyes.

The Fireman's axe was in his chest.

Drew was fifteen when she wanted to become a forensic pathologist. She liked the idea of being a doctor without having the pressure of saving people's lives. Her mom didn't think that was a practical goal though ("Real estate is the family business, Drew"), so she arranged a hospital tour. Drew knew her mom was trying to scare her out of her new dream job but didn't want to give her the satisfaction. The last stop on the tour was the morgue. It was the first time Drew saw a dead body (if only that would have been the last).

It wasn't the sight of death that scared Drew off a medical career path, it was the *sound*. Specifically, it was the sound of the rib spreader the pathologist used to crack open John Doe's chest. It was a surprisingly primitive tool with a hand crank. The pathologist turned the crank, the gears let out a chilling TINK-TINK-TINK sound as they spun, followed by a dark symphony of bones cracking, one after another.

TINK-TINK-TINK, CRACKCRACKCRACK.

The pathologist would rest her arm, and then start cranking again. TINK-TINK-TINK, CRACKCRACKCRACK.

It reminded Drew of pencils snapping, only there was a wetness to it that flipped a switch in her. *Yep, nope, not doing this job.* She, of course, wouldn't admit to her mom that the morgue had cured her of her "silly dream," she just stopped bringing it up and eventually stopped thinking about it all together. Until now, until she heard that same, wet CRACKCRACKCRACK as The Fireman's axe snapped Wes's ribs.

Drew backed away. To her dismay, Eli did, too. She thought he might have tried to leap forward and save his brother, but he didn't. Drew suspected Eli knew how pointless it would be. There was nothing anyone could do for Wes. The axe was, after all, another primitive tool, its head a perfect wedge that could split whatever was in its way: a piece of wood, a door, or a human ribcage.

CRACKCRACKCRACK.

Eli watched helplessly as The Fireman used the axe in Wes's chest like a hand rail to pull himself back up and shift his weight onto his good leg. The Fireman studied Wes's face as if silently telling him thank you, and then tossed him to the side. Wes's body slid across the floor into the foyer and came to a stop in almost the exact same spot Eli had died twenty-two years ago. *Huh*, Eli thought, *that's funny*.

Eli felt detached from the entire situation, like it was happening to someone else. He pictured himself in a movie theater, tossing popcorn into his mouth, marveling at how the gore effects were so real. *How'd they do that?* he'd silently muse as the silver screen flickered, reflecting the red torrents of blood on his face. Eli wondered if this was what Rose's out-of-body experiences were like. He'd have to ask her later. If there was a later.

The Fireman was bored by Wes. He turned to Eli and Drew. He didn't attack, though. He just wanted to make sure they were watching, make sure they knew exactly what he was capable of. As Eli stared back, enraptured by his power, The Fireman reached down to the shiny, white bone sticking out of his leg, and began shoving it back in until it snapped crudely into place. Eli imagined the camera pushing in on the gnarly wound, seeing the finer details of the gore FX as The Fireman's body appeared to heal itself.

No, *heal* was the wrong word. That implied a humanity. It was more like The Fireman's body was in repair mode. Eli could see a rotten flap of skin cover the broken bone as a thick, black ooze congealed over everything, sealing it up. The Fireman took a step, testing the repair job. He limped, and Eli felt relief that even The Fireman couldn't hide the wince of pain, but the leg was holding.

Eli grabbed Drew's hand and held it tight. There was nothing romantic about it, he just needed to feel human contact in that moment. He needed to ground himself back in the room. He didn't want to be in this movie theater anymore. He didn't want to be watching the sequel to the night they were murdered. He didn't want to be thinking about what The Fireman was repairing himself for, and he definitely didn't want to see what The Fireman was capable of in the third act. Eli just wanted to turn the whole thing off, rewind it, and pick out a rom com instead.

The Fireman grabbed the axe in Wes's chest and yanked it upward. The wedged blade slid easily out, lubricated by fresh blood. Eli squeezed Drew's hand tighter, and she squeezed back. They braced themselves for The Fireman's assault, but he merely took his axe and turned away, lumbering off toward the kitchen before disappearing down the dark basement stairs. It reminded Eli of when a triumphant but beleaguered Godzilla would stomp through city-wide carnage on his way back into the ocean; a living God returning to his eternal slumber. Eli wanted to smile at the image, until he realized *they* were the destroyed city.

Drew was thankful for Eli's hand. She didn't know she needed it, but that contact, that reminder that she wasn't truly alone in this moment, was a heartbeat telling her she was alive. Maybe not alive-alive, but at least still not truly dead. Not like Wes. And if they weren't truly dead yet, it meant their job still wasn't done.

They couldn't just save the girl, they had to *kill* The Fireman. How they were going to do that was a big ol' question mark, but Drew hoped Rose could help figure that out.

Rose! Drew had almost forgotten about her in all this chaos. She dropped Eli's hand and ran into the kitchen, shouting as loud as she could. "Rose! He's coming back!"

Rose was deep in a kaleidoscopic dream of memories that didn't belong together. Her parents' funeral giving way to her first kiss morphing into Aunt Bea teaching her meditation shifting into Drew driving them on the highway, windows down, speakers blaring. Drew had earned her driver's license before Rose, and the two of them spent countless nights just driving around, listening to music. It was bliss. Rose would give anything to be back in that passenger seat, not a care in the world.

"Rose! He's coming back!"

Drew's voice splashed over Rose like ice water. She bolted upright; her head rang like a gong as she tried to remember why there was blood on her hands. As she started piecing it together, The Fireman lumbered down the basement stairs. Rose covered her mouth with her hands so she wouldn't scream. But he didn't even look her way. He headed straight toward the rotten wall, straight toward the hollow side.

Rose barely had time to notice there was something different about him. His movement was off. Before, The Fireman had been a towering powerhouse that moved like he had Pennsylvania steel for a spine, but now there was a hunch to his back and a painful slump in his step as he disappeared into the wall. Rose knew where he was going. She managed to get to her feet. She had to get back to Drew. They needed to regroup. They needed to trap him back in the hollow side before it was too late.

Rose climbed the basement stairs to the kitchen, her strength returning with each step. Until she became keenly aware of how quiet things were. Before she'd passed out, the house had been full of screams. Now it was dead silent. Something was very, very wrong.

Eli knelt over Wes's body. His brother's glossed-over eyes stared at the ceiling, small flickers of movement the only indication he was still alive, though Eli supposed those could just be biochemical reactions. The human body could do that, right? Muscles could be stimulated even after death. Wes's jittering eyes and quivering lip didn't mean he was alive, it just meant his biology was lagging. The twitches were just the last blast of inputs from a dying brain.

Drew put her hand on Eli's shoulder. It was soft, caring. She had barely known Wes, didn't even *like* Wes, but she was there to support Eli all the same. And then Eli felt a second hand on his other shoulder. He glanced back to see Rose looking down at him and he felt a surge of reassurance, as if everything was going to be okay. Eli put his own hand on Wes's face and closed his brother's eyelids. The eyeballs twitched slowly underneath. He looked like he was dreaming. Eli knew he wasn't. Wes already looked so small, so diminutive, simultaneously the boy he'd grown up with and the man he'd grown to fear.

"What do you think happens now?" Eli asked the others. He didn't direct it to either of them specifically, but he hoped Rose would answer. She didn't. She just squeezed his shoulder. "I mean, what the fuck happens now? How does somebody die when they're already dead?"

Eli started laughing. He didn't even realize he was doing it. He knew he was supposed to be crying, not laughing, but he couldn't bring himself to do it. It was all just so absurd. The truth was, he felt like he'd said goodbye to his real brother years ago. Telling Wes about Drew's room for rent was Eli's last-ditch effort to rediscover whatever fraternal bond they had left. All it managed to do was turn Wes into a roommate who happened to have once been his brother.

As if sensing Eli had finally, truly acknowledged the truth of their broken relationship, Wes's body started to fade away. Drew and Rose gasped. Eli was, for once in his life, speechless. It reminded him of how JPEGs loaded on his 56.6k internet connection, appearing line-by-line, only this was the opposite? Wes was getting removed line-by-line? But that wasn't quite right, either. It almost looked as if Wes's corpse was... sinking into the floor? Or dissolving, like a cross-fade between two shots in a film?

As his mind jumped to a dozen different comparisons, failing to find precedent for the unprecedented, Eli Adams got his answer to what happened when you died in the afterlife. One moment you're there, the next you're not. If it could happen to Wes, then it could happen to any one of them.

Wes could feel Eli's hand on his face.
    It was warm.
    And then it wasn't.
    And then he wasn't.

Chapter 30

Rose was glad she'd been able to see Wes pass. Not that she was happy for his death (yet again), but because of *how* it had happened. He'd literally passed on, completely moving out of the umbral plane. To where he went, she didn't know, but it confirmed the one belief Rose refused to give up on: This place was transitory. She still wasn't convinced there was only one way to the fabled *other side*, though. Wes had found the *wrong* way to pass. There had to be a *right* way.

Rose wanted to talk about it, but couldn't quite figure out a polite way to say, "*Hey, Eli, you know how your brother just died? Well, actually, that's a good thing!*" She was struggling to find the words when Eli held out his two hands, hovering them over one another.

"We're here" Eli said of his left hand, "the living are here," then hovered his right hand over the left. "And now, Wes is..." Eli thought for a moment, then moved one hand way below the other. "He's down here. Or up. I don't know how these universes are oriented in geospatial planes. Hell, they could be sideways for all I—"

Rose reached out and held Eli's hand. She locked eyes with him and could feel his entire body relax with her touch. "He's dead, Eli. He didn't go to some other reality. He didn't drop below us or above us. He's..." Rose made her dust-in-the-wind gesture. "He's gone. For real this time."

"How do you know?"

"I just do." Rose said. And that was the truth. She didn't know how she knew, but she was certain of it.

"None of us have wanted to admit it, but this house *is* purgatory," Drew said.

Rose raised her hand to object, the entire concept of purgatory was a Judeo-Christian creation she felt wasn't nearly nuanced enough. Drew waved her down, anticipating the objection.

"Call this whatever word you want; the point is it's not just some waiting room. We're not late for some appointment in Heaven or Hell. And Eli, if this place was a true parallel universe, then the walls of the universe wouldn't stop at the fucking front door."

Drew moved to the center of the foyer, taking center stage. Rose couldn't help but admire how confident and purpose-driven she looked. Gone was the indecisive, waffle-y friend who Rose used to chastise for being so non-committal about everything. This Drew was taking a stand. It was a good look on her.

"Wes was right about something," Drew continued. "This place is a test. We can either pass it or we can fail it. And, no offense Eli, but I'm pretty sure Wes failed it."

Wes hadn't been entirely wrong. He gained access to the hollow side with violence; Rose did it with magic. Both were violations of the natural order that brought about the wrath of The Fireman. Rose had just been luckier. She shuddered at the realization.

"So, if this is a test, how do we pass it?" Rose asked, crossing her arms. She could feel herself growing unnecessarily defensive; not because Drew was wrong, but because Rose didn't like having anything in common with Wes.

"It's simple. We save Abbey."

"Didn't we just do that?" Eli asked.

"No. We saved her from *that* attack. The only way to truly save Abbey and her dad, and anyone else who comes to this godforsaken house is to—"

"Kill the son of a bitch," Rose said, much to the surprise of the other two. Rose laughed, the irony of her entire belief system hitting her. She'd spent her whole life being passive, being a fountain of love and compassion. All that earned her was a horrible, painful death and an afterlife that was all prison and no heaven. It was time for a change.

"And how do we do that?" Eli asked, a tremor in his voice, and before the others could answer — if they even had answers (Rose didn't) — the front door opened and they heard Javier storm in, shouting "If there's anyone in here, you need to get out, right now."

Abbey fought off tears as she stood on the porch. She knew she looked like a cliche; the pouty sixteen-year-old putting on a big show to try and get her way. She didn't care. She wasn't trying to get her dad to buy her a car, she just wanted him to *believe* her. Javier said he would search the house for The Fireman, but if he really believed her, he'd have called the cops. Instead, he acted like Abbey was five years old and he just needed to go look under her bed to prove a monster wasn't there.

Abbey also desperately wanted to go to sleep. It had been a hell of a night and she was just so, so freakin' tired. She'd made it halfway out of Woodbine Falls when her dad found her on the side of the road, borderline delirious (his words), and she told him all about the ghost and The Fireman and he just gawked back at her like she was some conspiracy theorist nutjob online.

Javier jogged down the second-floor staircase into the foyer. She could tell by the look on his face that he was about to drop a lecture on how dehydration and stress can cause hallucinations or whatever else made it easier to not believe her. She was way too tired for that. She knew how insane it all sounded, and maybe she had gotten some of the details wrong in retelling it, but just because it *sounded* insane didn't mean that she was crazy. She hated that word, and she wasn't about to let her dad talk her into feeling that way.

She just wanted the night to be over. She just wanted to be alone. She just wanted to be believed. Abbey crossed the threshold back into the house and ran up the stairs.

"Where are you going?" Javier shouted after her.

"To lock myself in my room."

"We need to talk about this."

"What's there to talk about? I told you the truth. Either you believe me, or you don't. So. What's it gonna be?" Abbey crossed her arms and tapped her foot impatiently, waiting on the stairs for an answer.

Javier squirmed through his words, trying to be careful not to give her any live ammunition to toss back his way. "Abs, it's just... what you're saying is.. So... I mean. A haunted house? *Really?*"

Abbey held up her wrist. Blood had seeped through the torn-shirt-turned-bandage covering her glass cuts. "So you think I just did this to myself?"

Javier's hesitation told her everything. If he believed her, there wouldn't have been a nanosecond of doubt, but it felt like the entire world was in slow motion while she waited for him to answer. The pause *was* the answer.

She turned her back on him and then let loose the one thing she knew would hit him hardest. "Mom would have believed me. But you would have called her crazy, too."

"Hey!" Javier shouted. It was a forceful, booming voice. Not a normal, *we need to talk, young lady* dad voice. This was a declarative, *Shut the fuck up and listen* dad voice. "I never once called your mother crazy!"

But Abbey kept storming the stairs, knowing full well she'd crossed a line. She just wanted him to feel a fraction of the torment she did. He hadn't yet, but he would. Abbey stopped on the top step. She couldn't look him in the eyes but delivered the final twist of the knife all the same.

The Dead Friends Society

"If you don't think she was crazy, then why'd she kill herself?"

Drew had spent most of the Moreno's first day in the house spying on them. She'd loved being a fly on the wall observing these fascinating people's lives. But *this*? This felt wrong. They shouldn't be watching this conversation.

And yet Drew couldn't look away. She'd been so intrigued by the artist who created the absolutely stunning array of work now hanging in her— no, Abbey's bedroom. She'd gathered the mom's name was Lora and that she'd died a few months ago (or was it a year?). But Drew had no idea it was a suicide. Her mind flooded with questions.

Drew thought of suicide often. Not that she was, herself, suicidal, but it was a topic she found her mind jumping to far more frequently than she'd ever admitted to Rose, let alone her own mom. But to Drew, it was more of a thought experiment. She couldn't step onto a roof without imagining what would happen if she jumped off it. She couldn't drive her car without wondering what would happen if she just drove into a brick wall. She couldn't rub the veins in her wrist without feeling keenly aware of how little skin kept those veins safely inside her. She'd never act on any of these impulses, Drew told herself, she just held a morbid fascination with the thin line between life and death, and how anyone could cross that line a hundred different ways every single day.

Drew couldn't fathom willingly crossing that line and knew that anyone who did must have been in tremendous pain. It made her want to run up to Abbey and hug the poor girl. That would just make things worse, though. Drew wondered if any of this would have even happened if she hadn't touched Abbey the first time. It was a train of thought that sent Drew tracing back the cause-and-effect of everything that had happened that night. She pulled Rose and Eli into the kitchen, away from the father-daughter heartbreak.

Eli was thankful for any excuse to not watch Abbey lay into her dad like that. He just felt too bad for both of them. He was reaching out; she was lashing out. It was unbelievably private, and he felt unbelievably awkward watching it.

"This is all my fault. It's all my fault." Drew let loose a flurry of confession.

"This *isn't* your fault," Rose said.

"Yes it is! Yes it fucking is! If I hadn't made contact with Abbey, then Abbey would have never thought the ghost of her mom was trying to reach out to her. And if Abbey had never gone looking for her mom, then she would have never gotten scared. And if she'd never gotten scared, then the rot would have never—"

"Whoa, whoa, whoa." Eli waved for both to be quiet. "Maybe you guys scared her, but whatever you thought you were doing wasn't nearly as bad as what Wes *actually did*." Both Drew and Rose eyed him confused.

"What did he do?" Drew asked.

Eli knew she was hoping he'd say something that would invalidate every ounce of self-loathing she was clearly melting under. The truth was he'd planned on telling them all about Wes trying to suffocate Javier, but then the shit hit the fan and Wes took an axe to the chest and so what was the point in telling them his brother was an attempted murderer? Wes was dead. He couldn't hurt anyone now.

Eli rubbed his knuckles. The skin was still raw from where he punched his brother.

"It doesn't matter. Just trust me on this, please. Wes did something bad — very bad — and it would have been even worse if I hadn't stopped him. So that rot... that hole in the wall... I'm sure we all had a small part in cracking it, but Wes was the dynamite that blew it up. Trust me."

Eli eyed the dark basement steps, and a chill shot up his spine. The Fireman was now free to come and go as he pleased. Hell, he could be standing at the bottom of the stairs, just waiting for one of them to walk out and...

Rose started taking the stairs and Eli reached out. "He could be down there." Eli said, eyes pleading.

"I know," Rose said, calm as ever. She tried to take another step and Eli grabbed her.

"He could kill you!"

"I know," Rose said. "That's why we have to go kill *him*."

Rose disappeared down the dark staircase, not a care in the world, and Eli felt his heart do backflips in his chest.

Rose was fucking terrified. She tried to put on a brave face to convince Drew and Eli that they'd already proven they could hurt The Fireman, so obviously they could kill him, but the idea of walking through the rotten hole in the wall equipped with nothing but some blunt objects to swing at him suddenly seemed like a very, very bad idea now that they were inches from the crushing void that was the entrance to the hollow side.

Drew held up a hammer and a crowbar, offering them as choices to Rose. "They're the biggest, hardest things I could find. Take your pick."

"That's what she said," Eli could *not* help himself, and Rose couldn't help but smile, until she looked back at the tools. What the heck were they thinking? These were for housework, not battling demons on the umbral plane. Eli held out the bench press bar, offering it to Drew.

"Here, I'll trade you," he said, taking the hammer.

"Are you sure?" Drew asked.

"God yes. You're stronger than me." Eli said.

He wasn't being self-deprecating; he was just a man unafraid to admit he was weaker than the women around him. Rose loved him for that. Drew offered the crowbar to Rose, but she waved it away and lifted the crystal around her neck. "I've got my weapon."

Eli raised a doubtful eyebrow. "Are you sure that's enough?"

Rose turned back to the rotten wall. She imagined the hollow side just beyond and remembered how she'd managed to pull its seemingly infinite darkness out of nothing and use it to bind The Fireman's door shut. Yes, he'd still managed to get out of it, but that was just her first try. This time, she knew what to expect. This time, she was ready.

Rose turned to Drew, who nodded back *I'm ready* before Rose could even ask. Rose moved to Eli next. She sized him up. He was practically shaking. Rose and Drew were ready to take a step into the deep, dark unknown. Eli wasn't. He'd only be carried through by their confidence. Rose knew she needed to give him a boost.

"Oh, Eli. Eli, Eli, Eli." Rose said, a sly smile curling her lips.

"What?" he asked, blushing.

"When you see what things are like in there, what we can *do* in there, I am going to blow your fucking mind."

Rose took her first full step out of the basement and into the darkness. She looked over her shoulder. Drew followed first, and then Eli. After just a few steps, the three of them were completely swallowed in darkness. Rose looked back toward the basement. The entrance already looked hundreds of feet away. The impossible geography of this place was sinking in faster than she thought it would.

Drew and Eli both put a hand on Rose's shoulder like they were kindergartners following a line leader. She could feel Eli's hand shaking, his nerves threatening to overpower him. His anxiety was surprisingly infectious. The blackness around them was so oppressive it started to feel physical, like it was pressing down on Rose from all sides, filling her eyes and ears and lungs, and for a moment she wondered if it was possible to drown from pure despair.

But then she saw it.

A small, familiar rectangle of orange light grew on the horizon. Rose smiled at the sight. She started jogging toward the beacon in the darkness. But as they arrived, Rose's heart sank. Her confidence imploded.

She'd been so sure she could lead them to The Fireman's happy place, but that door was gone, replaced by another all-too-familiar door that filled Rose with a sickening dread. Rose searched around, desperate for another rectangle of light on the horizon, but there was nothing. They'd found the only island of light in an ocean of darkness, and it was the wrong door.

THE HOLLOW SIDE

Chapter 31

DREW, ELI, AND ROSE STOOD SLACK-JAWED OUTSIDE THE FRONT door of Greywood House. The hand-made, wrought-iron number one stared back, taunting them. Drew had once marveled at the custom metalwork that went into it. Now she wanted to rip it off the door.

After all that running through the infinite darkness of the hollow side, they ended up back at the front door of goddamned Greywood House? Was this some kind of cruel, cosmic joke?

"I don't understand," Rose said, voice quaking. "Last time it was a different door, and it certainly wasn't the door to *our* house."

"It's not our house," Eli said matter-of-factly. "Look closer at the address. It's not all rusted."

Drew had to squint in the darkness to see, but sure enough Eli was right. When she'd first toured the house with her mom, there'd been a thin layer of orange rust on the metal. Two decades later, when Abbey and Javier moved in, the rust had spread from the brackets to the hinges of the door knocker. But right now, there was barely a hint of rust. In fact, the entire door looked… younger?

"Do you hear that?" Rose asked.

All three of them pressed their ears against the door. There was a dull thump of rock music coming from within. Rose reached for the doorknob but hesitated to turn it. She glanced at Drew and Eli, looking for permission. Both nodded. The door to Greywood House swept open effortlessly, as if its hinges had just been oiled.

As they stepped in, Drew was hit with a sense of Deja-vu so profound it felt like an out-of-body experience. This was indeed the same Greywood House they knew — the same foyer, the same hourglass shaped living room, the same railing leading to the second floor — and yet, it was all wrong.

"What the hell's going on?" Drew asked, though it was clear the others were also wondering. The first floor was filled with furniture that reminded Drew of her grandma's house from the 1970s. She was a stubborn old lady whose refusal to update anything turned her house into a living time capsule. Every time she visited; Drew couldn't help but marvel at how retro everything was. Unlike Grandma's, however, this house was filthy. Beer cans were all over and a potent smell of weed hung in the air. A record player in the living room blasted Led Zeppelin's Houses of the Holy. It was on Side B, early on in "No Quarter," near the end of the record, filling the house with drums and guitars.

"So, am I going to be the asshole who has to say it?" Eli asked, positively giddy. "We just fucking time traveled!"

His grin grew. Eli was loving whatever the hell was going on. Drew just wanted it to be over.

"It's not time travel," Rose said sharply. "We're inside a memory."

Eli scoffed, like Rose might as well have just said they were on the moon. It didn't sound too crazy to Drew, though. She glanced out the open front door to the crushing horizon of hollow darkness that stretched off into infinity. Nothing seemed off the table at this point.

Drew closed the door.

Eli laughed. He couldn't help himself. Every time he thought he had a handle on this whole afterlife thing, something insane came along to add new wrinkles. By the looks on their faces, though, laughter was the last thing on Drew and Rose's minds.

"It's just..." Eli motioned all around the foyer. "I thought when you died, *you died*. That was it. End of line. No heaven, no hell, just... nada. Zip. And here we are, motherfucking ghosts motherfucking Quantum Leaping our way through the afterlife."

Both Drew and Rose laughed; polite, quiet chuckles that made him feel a little less insane for finding it all so absurd. "I mean, why wasn't any of this shit in the bible? I'd have gone to church way more often if the priest said, 'Before you get to heaven, you'll be a time-traveling ghost.'" Eli said as he got a closer look at the '70s furniture in the living room. Then his entire body locked up in fear.

The Fireman was pacing back and forth on the far side of the living room.

"He's here!" Eli whispered.

Drew and Rose huddled next to him in the foyer, as if that would somehow protect them. Eli became acutely aware of the hammer in his hand. Back in the real world, it seemed like a decent enough weapon. Holding it now, he felt like an idiot. What good would a hammer be against *him*?

But The Fireman didn't attack. He didn't even notice them. He paced back and forth on the far side of the living room, constantly readjusting the grip on his axe. He looked like a nervous batter waiting to step up to the plate.

"He can't see us," Drew whispered. *Then why the hell are you whispering*, Eli wanted to snap back, but stopped himself. They'd been standing in the foyer for a good minute before any of them even realized The Fireman was twenty feet away. He had the element of surprise the entire time, so why hadn't he attacked? Was Rose right? Was this just a memory?

That's when Eli noticed differences between *this* Fireman and *their* Fireman. Like the front door, this '70s version looked younger, newer? There were no bullet holes in his coat. His mask wasn't shattered. There wasn't a drop of blood on that damned axe.

"It's not him," either Drew or Rose said. Eli couldn't be sure; his mind was too fried by the time travel to keep up.

"I mean, it's him, but it isn't, you know?" Eli said.

"He hasn't killed anyone," Drew guessed.

"Yet." Rose said what they were all thinking.

Rose clutched her crystal so tightly its sharp edges stabbed into her palm. She knew in her gut the axe-wielding man stalking back and forth at the end of the living room wasn't their fireman. Not yet. Tonight, was the night he was going to *become* The Fireman. The thought sent a chill up her spine.

Rose led them into the hollow side expecting to find his rotten soul hiding out in that Norman Rockwell family memory. She felt stupid for assuming that fireside vista was the only good memory someone like The Fireman would cling to. *Of course* a psychopath would come back to this, what she assumed was his first night of carnage. Rose didn't know how many people he'd killed in the '70s, or even why, but she feared they were about to learn it all firsthand.

As if reading her mind, the '70s Fireman stopped pacing. He set his sights on the front door directly behind them. He marched toward it, his heavy steps sounding like another set of drums on the Zeppelin record. Drew and Eli moved out of the way, but Rose stood her ground. He's just a memory, she told herself, but knew she had to prove it to the others.

"Rose! Hide!" Eli whisper-yelled, but Rose didn't budge. She stood in the path of the '70s Fireman. And he walked right through Rose, passing through her as if she didn't even exist. She was perversely proud to be right, even though she knew that being right about this being a memory also meant things were about to get very, very violent.

Right on cue, the '70s Fireman used his axe to smash the front door-knob clean off. The massacre was about to begin. The group huddled at the back of the foyer, watching with bated breath. Rose suspected the people in the house heard The Fireman's axe break the doorknob and would come running.

But no one came. Even '70s Fireman seemed a bit surprised. He gripped his axe tighter, waiting for a fight that wasn't coming.

"Where is he? Where's the real Fireman?" Drew asked.

Rose took her eyes off the '70s Fireman and scanned the rest of the first floor. When she'd (accidentally) entered his memories the first time, The Fireman had been standing in the shadows of his own basement, watching his family. Rose became suddenly aware of every shadow in Greywood House. There were dark nooks and crannies all over the place. He could be in any one of them, re-living the memories of his first kills.

"He's somewhere in the house, I just know it," Rose said. She sensed The Fireman was a peeping Tom, only instead of creeping through some neighbor's window, he was lurking in the shadows, getting off on his own memories. Right now, the memory wasn't juicy enough to lure him in. Rose figured that once the killing started, the real Fireman would reveal himself.

And once again, as if reading Rose's mind, the '70s Fireman sprung to action. He'd grown impatient waiting for his prey to show up and pounded the head of his axe against the floor over and over, creating the THUD-THUD-THUD the three of them knew all too well. He hit the ground hard enough to shake the record player. The needle scratched out of its groove and there was no more Houses of the Holy, only the quiet stillness of Greywood House.

Until the footsteps started.

The '70s folks hadn't heard him smashing the doorknob, but they'd definitely heard him banging on the floor. "What the hell are you doing?" A woman's voice shouted from upstairs.

Drew's heart raced when a woman appeared at the top of the stairs. She had feathered blonde hair and a pair of bell bottom jeans that looked uncomfortably tight around the waist. The woman buttoned her blouse up as she bounced down the stairs. She had the glow of someone who'd either just finished or just started having sex. Whichever it was, she looked pissed about being interrupted.

Right behind Bell Bottoms came a shirtless, muscular man with a mustache that would make Tom Selleck jealous. The Mustache man was grinning ear to ear. They'd *definitely* been fooling around right when '70s Fireman rang the proverbial bell. Drew felt even worse for them. They looked like such a bubbly, happy couple. They didn't deserve what was bound to happen next.

Bell and Mustache slowed down on the steps when they spotted '70s Fireman, but they were more bemused than outright angry. "Hey buddy, ain't no fire here." Bell said. '70s Fireman stood at the front door, his breath quickening as they approached.

"I think one of your pole pals sent ya' to the wrong house, Jack." Mustache joked. Bell Bottoms giggled. '70s Fireman didn't laugh. He stared at the two of them, sizing them up. He looked disappointed. Drew suspected they weren't who he came here for. '70s Fireman thudded his axe against the floor a few more times.

"What's your malfunction?" Mustache shouted, placing himself between Bell and The Fireman.

"What's all the goddamned racket?" another man shouted from the kitchen. "You two better not be fucking out there." The man trotted in through the dining room, head tilted back as he chugged a Pabst Blue Ribbon. He looked like Mustache's brother, only with a thinner head of hair and a shaggy pair of mutton chops that reminded Drew of Quint from Jaws.

Not-Quint wasn't nearly as bemused by the interloper as the others. He skidded to a stop in the dining room and jabbed an angry finger at his brother. "Did you let this motherfucker in here?"

"Do you know this guy?" Mustache fired back.

"What, are you too fucking stoned to put it together? He's *the guy!*"

"What guy?" Mustache asked.

The Dead Friends Society

"What guy?" Not-Quint repeated, shocked his brother could be so clueless. "He's the guy, numbnuts. He's the fucking *husband*."

Mustache's brain caught up and in a second his entire body tensed and he held his hands defensively in the air to show how unarmed they were.

"Hey, hey, hey, buddy. That wasn't our fault."

What the fuck is going on? Drew thought.

"What wasn't your fault?" Bell asked nervously, though the men ignored her.

"The cops cleared us, man. They got no proof we had anything to do with any of that."

"No proof!" Not-Quint shouted.

"I'm sorry about your family, man, I am, but—"

"Don't say another fucking word to this asshole." Not-Quint interrupted. "He's just trying to trick us into saying something we shouldn't, because he knows they've got—" Not-Quint stepped toward '70s Fireman, all drunken bravado "—No Proof!"

Not-Quint threw the can of PBR at '70s Fireman.

But '70s Fireman was done listening.

He raised his axe high.

Bell screamed.

Eli felt like he'd Last Action Hero'ed his way into a movie. He was too embarrassed to admit it to Rose or Drew, but he was kind of enjoying it. Eli blamed the part of him that could never quite divorce the real world from the movies constantly looping in his pop-culture addled brain.

Until '70s Fireman raised his axe and the screaming started and slammed Eli back to reality real fast.

'70s Fireman swung at Not-Quint but missed. His axe lodged in the floorboard at the drunk man's feet. Not-Quint shouted to his brother to get the hell out, but '70s Fireman was blocking the path to both the front door and the dining room. Mustache and Bell had no exit.

"Where's your gun?" Mustache shouted.

"I don't fucking know!" Not-Quint yelled back.

Mustache slapped the wall in frustration. He grabbed Bell and took off for the second floor of the house. Eli presumed he was going to go look for the gun, which was when he remembered *their* Fireman was riddled with bullet holes and found himself excited at the prospect at least one of these yokels was going to blast the hell out of The Fireman. Eli couldn't wait to see that happen.

"Does anyone see him? Does anyone see the real Fireman?" Drew asked.

"He's not here," Rose said, drawing Eli back to the reason they came. If he *wasn't* there, why the hell did they even come?

"He's not here because no one's died yet. I'll bet you anything he's somewhere, waiting for the real murders to happen." Rose theorized.

Eli watched Not-Quint run from '70s Fireman into the kitchen. '70s Fireman dislodged his axe and pursued. Rose followed the pair of them, but Drew and Eli hesitated. Rose shouted, "Come on!" over her shoulder as she headed toward the kitchen and—

FFFFFWWWTT

Rose disappeared into thin air.

Drew and Eli both screamed.

Rose was running into the dining room one second and the next she was falling into the basement. The sensation of teleporting made her want to vomit, but she was too overwhelmed to even manage that basic bodily function. Her head was spinning. This journey into the hollow side was nothing she expected. Her trip to The Fireman's happy place was linear, this was anything but; then again, Rose admitted to herself, memories themselves are rarely linear. They were more dreamlike, crashing into one another without much reason.

There did appear to be a reason for her sudden teleportation, though. Rose hadn't merely been teleported to the basement of Greywood House, she'd been brought to the precise moment Not-Quint was stumbling away from '70s Fireman, begging for his life.

Upstairs, Not-Quint had been all drunken bluster, but down here, alone, he was as scared as they'd all been in the face of death. Curiously, he wasn't the only one who looked nervous. The axe was shaking in '70s Fireman's hands, and Rose's gut told her this was the moment of his first kill. This was when he went from being a man who could hypothetically kill someone to being a *killer*. That's a Rubicon that, when crossed, tears a person's soul apart. And Rose was about to see it happen.

Not-Quint held up his hands. His face was a blubbering mess. Rose couldn't make out the precise words, but he was saying something about how it was all an accident, how they honestly didn't know anyone was in that house, how they'd never kill those little kids on purpose. Rose believed him. Nobody could lie like that in the face of death. But '70s Fireman was too rage-filled to care.

He swung the axe. Rose wanted to look away, but something was telling her not to. She clutched her crystal and squinted her eyes as the blade penetrated the crying man's neck and travelled halfway through his collarbone. Not-Quint stumbled backward into the center wall of the basement. As '70s Fireman yanked his axe out of the dying man's neck, a geyser of blood erupted, painting the wall a deep, dark crimson. Rose gasped at the sight. The blood spray covered the exact spot the rot had formed back in their world.

That's why this moment was so important to him. This *was* his first kill. This was what bound his murderous soul to this house.

Rose couldn't take her eyes off the wall, each successive splash of blood darkened it just as the rot had. It was all clicking in place. Then someone touched her shoulder and Rose screamed, fearing The Fireman had found her before she could find him.

But it was just Drew and Eli, out of breath and bewildered from the teleportation. Eli immediately threw up, though she couldn't tell if it was due to jumping from one memory to the next or the sight of Not-Quint's mangled, partially decapitated body.

"Rose, what the fuck is going on? Why did we get portaled from up there to down—"

Rose held up her hand, silencing Drew. She didn't want to be rude, but she was on a mission. "Does anybody see our Fireman?" Rose asked.

Drew and Eli followed her searching gaze around the basement, but there was nothing but '70s Fireman staring at Not-Quint's limp body slumped against the wall.

"Shit. Okay. We have to just keep jumping from memory to memory until we find him. He's hiding here somewhere. I know it. I can feel it." Rose grabbed Drew and Eli's hands. "Are you guys ready?"

"For what?" Eli asked.

But Rose didn't answer. It was easier to just show them. She pulled them behind her and took the first step up the kitchen staircase.

FFFFFWWWWTT—

Drew lost her balance. She thought she was about to climb the basement stairs but instead found herself landing in the second-floor hallway. '70s Fireman was in the middle of chopping down the master bedroom's door.

Drew could see Bell and Mustache through the cracks. Bell was screaming into a rotary phone, begging for them to send the police. Mustache was tossing dresser drawers, desperately searching for a gun. All the while '70s Fireman kept chop, chop, chopping. Drew couldn't help but notice that he looked energized. Killing Not-Quint had given him the conviction he needed to keep going.

"Shit! He's not here either." Rose said.

It made Drew want to laugh. Not because there was anything funny about the nightmare they were trapped in, but because Rose so rarely cursed when they were alive. Now that they were dead, though,

Rose's potty mouth was quickly catching up. Drew guessed that once most of Rose's spiritual beliefs got blown-up, cursing no longer seemed that taboo.

Rose pointed toward the attic and grabbed their hands. Drew's arms were starting to ache from lugging the damned bench press bar all over the place, but at least this time she was ready for the portal they were about to jump through. As soon as they crossed the threshold of the hallway and stepped on the attic stairs — *FFFF-FWWWTT* — they portaled into the attic, landing in an instant at the top of the staircase.

And then, for what felt like the gazillionth time since all this started, Drew saw something that broke her mind all over again.

Eli had just been getting a handle on all these memory jumps (though he'd still prefer to think of it as time travel) when they skipped from the '70s hallway to Drew's attic bedroom in the '90s.

"Holy fucking shit!"

The Fireman — *their Fireman* — was lying face down in the middle of the floor and Drew, or the memory of '90s Drew stood over his body. '90s Drew kicked it and The Fireman's body wobbled like a cadaver on a slab.

"I told you I fucking killed him." Drew said, a hint of glee to her voice. Eli would have been happy if he'd stabbed The Fireman, too. The three of them watched '90s Drew run out of the room, passing right through them on her way down the attic stairs. But the memory didn't end there.

The ghosts of Bell, Mustache, and Not-Quint all emerged from the closet, utter shock on their faces. Eli pointed at the new trio; his face just as shocked as theirs. He turned to Rose and Drew.

"Wait, they were ghosts, too? Just like us?" Eli asked.

This was so much more than just parallel universes. Or purgatory. This was some all-time, what-the-actual-fuck, seriously, why-wasn't-this-in-the-bible shit. Trying to make sense of it all was giving Eli a high. There was still so much to discover about the afterlife.

"Shhhh, shut up. I want to hear them." Rose whispered as she crept closer.

"She killed him! She actually fucking killed him!" Ghost Bell said.

"I told you she would." Ghost Not-Quint said.

"No you didn't!" Ghost Mustache argued.

"Shut up, the both of you. Does this mean we can finally leave?" Ghost Bell asked.

The '70s ghosts looked toward the attic stairs, and Eli instantly understood. The '70s ghosts must have been trapped in the house just like they were, watching their every move just as Eli watched Abbey and Javier's. The realization made him queasy. If the '70s ghosts were watching the whole time, especially when he was alone in the basement... *yikes*.

But why hadn't the '70s ghosts been around when Eli, Drew, and Rose woke up dead? Then it hit Eli. *They must have gotten out.*

Maybe Drew stabbing The Fireman cleared the portal surrounding the house. If it had, then maybe killing him again really was all it was going to take to get out of there. Suddenly the hammer in Eli's hand felt considerably more useful.

But then The Fireman's dead body stirred.

The '70s Ghosts jumped back in shock. Not-Quint slapped Mustache in the chest, insinuating he'd been right all along. Bell threw herself onto The Fireman, trying to pin him to the ground. She screamed for the men to help her, but they were too slow to act. The Fireman got to his knees before they could stop him. He threw Bell off him with ease. She crashed to the attic floor, clutching her ribs in pain.

Mustache stepped up, finally finding some courage. The Fireman was ready for him. His huge hands sprung out like a bear trap and clamped Mustache around his head. The Fireman dug his gloved thumbs into the muscular ghost's eye sockets.

Mustache screamed louder and harder than Eli had ever heard a man scream. It thankfully didn't last long. There was a wet crunching sound and Eli could see Mustache's orbital sockets break like eggshells under the grip of The Fireman and then the poor man's entire skull collapsed inward like a rotten jack-o-lantern.

"Jesus fucking Christ," Eli said, completely unaware the words were aloud and not just in his head.

It was almost like The Fireman had somehow grown *stronger* in death. That's the only way Eli could rationalize his ability to literally crush a man's skull with his hands. The amount of pressure must have been enormous. Eli ran calculations in his head, trying to recall the figure he'd once read for the pounds-per-square-inch pressure of an alligator's bite. Not because he was particularly interested in quantifying The Fireman's brute force strength, he just wanted to distract himself from the fact that he was standing in the memory of his own killer, watching that killer pop the head of a former ghost like it was a grape. *Jesus, what a mindfuck.*

If The Fireman could do that so easily... Eli had a sinking fear the reason they'd never met the '70s ghosts wasn't because they'd escaped the house; it was because The Fireman killed them all. They'd found a way out, alright, only it was the same "out" Wes found.

The Fireman dropped Mustache's body to the floor and squared off against Bell and Not-Quint. The Fireman didn't say anything to them. He didn't have to. The message was clear. Try it again, and I'll destroy you, too.

Everyone in the room — '70s ghosts, '90s ghosts, and The Fireman — watched as Mustache's body faded into nothingness, just as Wes's had. Then The Fireman pulled Drew's chisel out of his chest and stalked off down the attic stairs.

Eli wanted to talk to his friends about it, to share with them all his new theories, but Rose and Drew were already on the heels of The Fireman, which meant Eli had to brace for a—*FFFFFWWWWTT—*

Drew closed her eyes, hoping that would help the jump between memories. But she could sense the world around her warping. It reminded her of a coaster cresting the top of a hill before plummeting to Earth. Her stomach lurched, her eyes opened, and they dropped out into the kitchen.

She recognized the memory immediately. In front of her, '90s Drew raced to the kitchen door only to discover the knob had been broken off. '90s Drew gave up on the door and tore down the basement stairs. But the memory didn't end there.

'90s Fireman entered the kitchen, banging his axe against the wall, over and over again, like a battlefield war drum. Drew had heard each of those thuds on the night they happened, but she hadn't seen what happened next. As '90s Fireman pounded the wall, Bell and Not-Quint crept up behind him.

Not-Quint jumped on the '90s Fireman's back, his right arm wrapped around the man's enormous throat, putting him in a chokehold. Bell grabbed the shaft of the axe, trying to wrestle it from his hand.

Not-Quint and Bell had a decent attack plan: he was cutting off the '90s Fireman's air supply, trying desperately to drive him to the floor; she had a good grip on the axe, enough so that '90s Fireman was struggling to hold it while simultaneously fending them both off.

Drew wished she could jump in and give them the extra hand they needed to take him down but knew she couldn't. She just had to watch them be outmatched.

As if bored of playing tug-of-war over the axe, '90s Fireman simply let it go right as Bell was pulling with all her strength. The momentum sent the axe straight into the woman's very surprised face.

"Holy shit, she killed herself." Eli exclaimed. Drew almost shouted the same thing herself. The Fireman wasn't just some dumb, mindless killer. He used Bell's own momentum against her. That realization scared Drew more than anything. They'd come here to kill The Fireman, but now she knew they wouldn't be able to brute force him. They'd have to learn from the '70s Ghosts and outsmart him. How exactly they were going to do that, Drew had no fucking idea.

Not-Quint screamed at the sight of Bell's self-inflicted axe wound, which the '90s Fireman used to his advantage. With both arms freed, '90s Fireman reached back and grabbed Not-Quint by his head and power slammed him into the floor.

The axe was still stuck in Bell's face when '90s Fireman grabbed the handle and used it to lift the woman as if she were weightless. He swung her body toward Not-Quint. At the apex of the swing, the axe dislodged from Bell's head and sent her crashing into Not-Quint. Her limp body pinned him to the floor. Not-Quint tried to worm his way free, but '90s Fireman was on him in an instant. His axe swung down, decapitating Not-Quint, and sending a wave of blood spraying out.

Drew couldn't help but think of Splash Mountain at Disneyworld and that feeling *just* before you were soaked. She held up her hands, ready to block the wave of viscera, but there was no splash. The blood was just another memory that passed clean through her. When Drew opened her eyes again, the bodies of Bell and Not-Quint were fading to nothingness, just as Wes had.

And still, the memory continued. There was something else Drew hadn't been privy to the night she died, and she dreaded seeing it.

A cough started filling the kitchen. It was soft at first, almost imperceptible, but quickly gave way to loud hacking. It came from behind the kitchen island, a spot Drew had been too distracted to notice as she ran from The Fireman.

Drew knew that cough, though. She'd heard it from the basement. She knew back then that it belonged to Rose, but she had no idea Rose had been so close. She'd run *right past* her that night. If she'd just been more observant, she'd have seen Rose. Drew could have saved her, then. Drew could have carried her into the basement, could have gotten them both out. *Maybe we'd be alive right now.*

'90s Fireman stood over '90s Rose, staring down at her while she gasped back to life. Her cheeks flushed red as her body oxygenated. He paused, watching long enough to see her recover. The fucker was letting her try and call out for help. '90s Fireman cocked his head toward the basement stairs. He listened to see if Drew would come back for her.

The real Rose put a hand on Drew's shoulder. "He was using me as bait, Drew. And I am so fucking sorry you came back for me. It's my fault you're here. You could have gotten out. You could have—"

Drew pulled Rose in for a hug. "No. We're here *together* for a reason." Drew grabbed Rose and Eli's hands. "Come on, we have to end this fucking thing once and for all."

Chapter 32

ROSE WAS PISSED. SHE WAS PISSED BECAUSE SHE HAD NO IDEA THE '70s ghosts ever existed. She was pissed because she was being forced to relive her own death. But more than anything she was pissed because there was a *reason* they hadn't found The Fireman yet: these memories weren't special to him. The deaths of Rose and her friends were just more forgettable notches on his murderous bedpost. *That* was infuriating.

Rose's face hardened as Drew led the group from the kitchen into the next memory. The house spit them out in the basement. It was Not-Quint's murder all over again.

"We've already been here." Eli complained. Rose didn't want to dwell in these moments. She didn't want to see the moment she was used at bait. She didn't want to think about Drew being lured back from safety, back into the house, back to her death.

Rose was ready for this fucking nightmare to be over. She took the lead this time and pulled them back. They spilled out into the foyer, at the memory of Eli getting killed. She already knew the aftermath and didn't care to stick around to see it happen.

Rose broke into a run, each entry and exit from a room teleporting them all around the house. It felt like a Rubik's Cube, with each twist shifting them from one side of the house to the other. Unlike a Rubik's Cube, though, there didn't seem to be any logic to the puzzle. It was random. Sometimes they'd leave a memory only to end up right back in it again. Sometimes they'd be taken to a string of new memories (Wes's death was particularly unpleasant to see) only to end up back at one they'd already seen.

"This isn't working, Rose." Drew pleaded, out of breath. But Rose pressed on, jumping from one haunted vignette to another, until finally they arrived at a surreal scene that stopped them all in their tracks.

The bodies of Bell, Mustache, and Not-Quint were piled at the base of the stairs. '70s Fireman stood over them, pouring gasoline on the corpses. He was surrounded by nearly a dozen police officers, all with guns drawn. One officer stood slightly ahead of the rest, a young Detective Righetti.

"We all know what happened to your wife, to your *kids*, was wrong. And if you think these people deserve to burn for what they did, I swear to God, I don't blame you. But they're dead now. They can't hurt anyone else." Righetti said.

He was calm and cautious, but Rose knew there wasn't going to be a negotiation here. They'd arrived at the moment the police were about to gun down the '70s Fireman, and in so doing, binding his rotten, murderous soul to Greywood House forever.

Rose whispered to Drew and Eli. "He's here. I know it."

They looked around, frantic to find him, but the foyer was crammed full of people. It was hard to see through the swarm of officers, and even though Rose knew their memories couldn't hurt her, her entire body still tensed at the sight of so many guns drawn. In particular, she noticed the youngest rookie in the unit struggling to keep it together. He was so scared, his revolver rattled in his hand.

"I have an idea," Rose said, stepping forward. She couldn't find The Fireman lurking, but she sensed he was there. This was the moment he was reborn; the moment he was set free. He *had* to be hiding in this memory.

"You failed your family," Rose shouted to the room. "You're the reason they're dead. I don't know what they did to your family, but I do know you *didn't* save them. You weren't there when they needed you."

Rose waited a moment, then shouted louder. "You weren't there when you could have made a difference."

Rose squinted through the crowded memory trying to spot any movement beyond the terrified cop with an itchy trigger finger. Righetti moved closer to '70s Fireman. The other officers all stood firm, guns ready.

Righetti asked the '70s Fireman to not do anything stupid, to just come with him and end this peacefully. '70s Fireman cocked his head toward the detective, like a dog trying to understand his human.

"I've seen your wife." Rose shouted louder. "She was beautiful. And those three boys... I bet they would have grown up to be really strong young men. But you failed them."

Rose couldn't imagine herself saying these things to any decent human being, but she was hoping — praying — they'd get a rise out of The Fireman. *What is he waiting for?*

"If only you'd been there to protect them."

And then too many things happened all at once.

The '70s Fireman started turning around toward Righetti.

The scared rookie fired his pistol.

He had such poor aim that he missed his target entirely, but it didn't matter. Rookie pulling the trigger was like firing a starter pistol in the air, and the rest of the cops were off to the races. They all fired. Over and over. The sound, memory or not, was absolutely deafening; a cacophonous roar of explosions that echoed throughout the vast, open first floor of the house. Smoke from the guns quickly filled the space, but that didn't stop Rose from seeing the '70s Fireman's body spasm over and over as dozens and dozens of bullets ripped through him.

The smoke *did* stop Rose from seeing their Fireman — the *real* Fireman — rush at her from the shadows of the dining room.

She'd been right. He was lurking in the memory. *This* was his defining moment.

Rose hated being right.

Eli felt like everything was playing out in slow motion. The gunfire drowned out any sense of reasonable thought, and the smoke nearly blinded him. But he *was* able to see Rose backing away toward the wall, her hands outstretched, attempting to block something rushing toward her. It lifted her in the air, like a ballerina performing a soubresaut.

Eli's heart sank into his stomach as The Fireman's axe thrust Rose upward. Eli and Drew screamed her name in unison so loudly he was convinced the Memory Cops would somehow hear them through the layers of reality, turn, and shoot them, too.

And then through the smoke, *he* came. The *real* Fireman. He was huge, impossibly so, and Eli had the terrifying thought The Fireman was somehow growing larger. The Fireman held Rose in the air a moment and then yanked his axe back. She collapsed in a heap at Drew's feet.

Rose was still alive, still breathing... barely. Eli braced himself for The Fireman to swing at him next, but then something unexpected happened.

Righetti screamed at the officers to stop, and one by one they all lowered their weapons. Strangely, the real Fireman stopped, too. He shifted his attention away from Eli to Righetti standing over his past self's bullet-riddled corpse. Righetti stared down at the bloody, broken mess and shook his head.

"What have you done?" Righetti asked, though Eli wasn't sure if he was talking to the other cops or to the mangled murderer at his feet. *Maybe both?* There'd been no trial, no procedural justice. One officer pulled his trigger, then the rest dutifully followed suit, turning the foyer of Greywood House into a literal firing squad.

The real Fireman swung his axe at Righetti in a high, powerful arc that looked like it would chop a redwood in half. But it passed right through the memory. The Fireman turned to the next officer, swinging his axe futilely through him as well. His anger boiled over as he worked through the room, swinging at every cop, one by one. Eli, Drew, and

Rose might as well have not existed in that moment. The only thing that mattered to The Fireman was the memory of the men who executed him.

Rose whispered for help. It was barely audible.

"We have to get her out of here." Drew pleaded. Eli was sucked back to reality. Rose's dress covered the wound, but judging by how much blood was gushing out and how Rose was clutching her stomach, Eli was afraid vital organs might spill out of her. Things were dire, but he had no idea where the hell they were supposed to take her. Until he noticed the front door.

The police had broken the door down with a battering ram, revealing the hollow, infinite darkness beyond it. Before Drew could object, he dropped the hammer in his hand and grabbed Rose by her shoulders. Drew followed suit, trading her weapon for Rose's legs, and together they carried her toward the door, toward the darkness.

As they stepped out onto what should have been the porch, the rest of Greywood House faded away. All that remained was that free-floating rectangle of the open door. Inside it, Eli could see The Fireman still swinging his axe at the cops, over and over. He looked pathetic. And for a moment, just a moment, Eli felt pity for his murderer.

Then he took one look at Rose and any empathy he had was swallowed by seething rage.

Drew spent one summer as a lifeguard. She'd turned sixteen but didn't have a car and The Splash Pad was the nearest place she could reach by bike. It was a largely forgettable job spent dodging skeevy comments from the sixteen-year-old boys (they thought they were men; they weren't) and sitting in tall, white chairs watching hordes of kids go nuts in the pool.

To land the job, Drew had to go through a rash of safety certifications that covered everything from CPR to broken necks, but never once needed to put that knowledge to the test. As wild as the kids could be, she only had to dive in a handful of times. Each one was a false alarm, and in the intervening years, any first-aid knowledge she knew had faded.

Looking down at Rose, Drew desperately wished it would all come rushing back. She stared at her best friend, utterly clueless what to do. No amount of chest compressions and mouth breathing would help the gaping wound that stretched from Rose's belly button to her heart. Drew knew to put pressure on bleeding wounds, but she feared if she did her hand would slip inside of Rose.

"It's okay, Drew." Rose said, quiet as a mouse.

Rose smiled up at Drew and Eli. Her teeth were stained a soft red, and Drew had a flashback to the time she and Rose biked to 7/11 and spent all their money on dozens and dozens of cherry-flavored Pixie Sticks. Their ten-year-old teeth were red for days.

"Put me down." Rose said.

"We have to get you out of here." Eli said.

"No, Eli. Please. It's okay."

There was such softness, such kindness to Rose's voice. She was more worried about hurting their feelings than her own survival. Drew looked over her shoulder, trying to see how far they'd gone. The doorway to Greywood House was a faint rectangle. They *seemed* safe. It would be hard for The Fireman to find them here. Hell, she was pretty sure they'd been carrying Rose in a straight line, and yet the doorway was now off to their right. This hollow hellscape was just as disorienting as the whole trip down memory lane had just been. The current of the hollow side was pulling them in whatever direction it pleased, and they were in no position to fight that current.

Drew lowered Rose's legs, Eli followed by carefully lowering Rose's shoulder. Drew cradled Rose's head. She looked beautiful, even with her blood-stained teeth.

"Rose, I am so sorry. I don't know what to do. I don't know how to fix this."

"You can't," Rose said. There was no sadness to her voice. Just acceptance. "And I'm okay with it. Honest." Rose tried to raise her hand and do Eli's three-finger Boy Scout salute, but she couldn't muster the energy.

"I love you, Rose. I love you so fucking much." Drew said.

"Me, too." Eli added. Drew glanced at him. His face was wet with tears. He hadn't even cried when his own brother died.

"I love you both."

"We know, Rose. We know."

"Do me a favor." Rose reached behind her neck and unclasped her necklace, then folded Drew's hands around the crystal. Drew didn't want to take it. She wanted to put it back around Rose's neck. She didn't want to acknowledge what Rose was doing. She didn't want to acknowledge what the hollow side was taking from her.

Rose tried to sit up, but her body wouldn't let her, so Drew had to do the lifting. Rose leaned in and whispered in Drew's ear.

"Break the cycle." Rose said.

Rose wanted to tell Drew so much more. She wanted to tell her about all the little moments between the two of them that still meant the world to her. She wanted to tell her to not be scared, that this was just another transition. Rose wanted to tell Drew that she knew they could kill The Fireman. The memories confirmed it. Outside, in their world, The Fireman seemed like a supernatural killing machine, but he was *human*, almost maddeningly so. If she could get under his skin with just a few words, it meant he was exploitable; it meant he was vulnerable. Drew and Eli just had to do the same thing. They'd have to be smart about it. They'd have to work as a team, but if they could, they could do what the '70s ghosts tried to do and failed. They could *break the cycle*.

Rose couldn't tell Drew any of this, though. Her energy had drained entirely. The Fireman took it all, leaving her with just enough life to stare up at the infinite darkness.

When she'd first found her way into the hollow side, Rose had been terrified, but now, there was something inexplicably comforting about it all. Before Rose was born, there was nothing. Soon there'd be nothing again. That wasn't such a bad concept, right? That's all the hollow side was: nothingness. And why should anyone be afraid of nothing?

Rose felt Drew's hand on her face.

It was warm.

And then it wasn't.

And then she wasn't.

Eli watched Rose fade away in Drew's arms. First, she was there, then she just... dissolved. Wes looked terrified when it happened. Rose looked at peace. She looked ready.

Eli wasn't. Rose seemed like the only one who had half a clue as to what was really going on in the afterlife. Hell, she knew how to bring them to the hollow side. Without her, how were they going to get back?

Drew stood. Eli half-expected her to collapse in sobs, but Drew just hugged him. Long and hard.

"This is so fucked," Eli said.

"We're going to break the cycle," Drew said.

"How?"

Drew's face was wet with tears, though Eli didn't know if they were hers or had rubbed off from him. He'd never seen her cry. He always thought she was too tough for that.

Drew clutched the crystal in the exact same way he'd seen Rose do countless times before. He always thought it was a bit of an OCD thing for Rose, like some kind of security blanket she always had to have with her, but now he wondered if it really *was* special. Shit, if ghosts were real, why not magical crystals? Why not werewolves? And bigfoot?

Drew closed her eyes and rubbed the crystal. Eli watched silently. Maybe this was how Drew was going to grieve. Not with theatrical sobs, but a quiet moment with something that meant the world to Rose.

But then Drew started walking with her eyes closed, one foot after the other into the darkness.

"Where are you going?" Eli called after her.

Drew didn't answer, just kept walking. Eli had to jog to catch up, and when he did, he saw a faint rectangle of light materialize in the distance. He recognized it immediately. It was the rotten wall back to their basement. Drew had found her way back. *Freaking magic crystals, man.*

"We are going to go back," Drew said, not missing a step. "We are going to go back and do whatever it takes to get Abbey and Javier out of the house. I don't care if we have to haunt the ever-living shit out of 'em, we are going to get them the hell out."

"And then?"

The tunnel back to the basement had seemed so far away, but was suddenly close, like they'd traveled a mile in mere footsteps. As if sensing it, Drew stopped walking. She opened her eyes and turned to Eli.

"And then we rip out his fucking heart." Drew said, taking the last step out of the hollow side and back into the basement of the real Greywood House.

THE FIREMAN RETURNS

Chapter 33

ELI AND DREW EMERGED IN THE BASEMENT, ONLY TO DISCOVER everything changed. When they'd left, the place was a mess, with stacks of moving boxes and weight-lifting gear scattered everywhere. Now the mess had been entirely cleaned up, with half the space converted into a home gym, while the other half looked to be an all-purpose rec room assembled out of old, mismatched furniture.

"Shit." Eli lost track of time while they were in the hollow side, but it still only felt like a few hours at most. The basement now looked like a sitcom coffee shop collided with a gym. There's no way Javier could have transformed it in the middle of the night.

"Time must work even weirder in there," Eli said, pointing back to the rotten wall that was now a permanent, gaping tunnel to the hollow side. "Like, if they left the house while we were in there, everything went *extra* fast-forward-y for us."

But it was obvious Drew wasn't interested in the mechanics of intra-universe time flow. She collapsed to her knees and fell into deep, heaving cries. They'd been on too much of an adrenaline rush to really process Rose's death as it was happening, but now that they were back, the finality of it was setting in. Eli joined her on the floor.

"Sorry, that was stupid of me. I just... I have to distract myself with all this afterlife bullshit because I don't want to admit what's really happening." Eli said.

"It's so unfair. It should have been me." Drew said.

Eli shook his head. "And if it had been, Rose would be here right now saying the exact same thing. You know that."

"I just can't believe she's gone."

"Is she, though?"

Drew's breathing slowed. She glanced at Eli, her face red and unable to maintain eye contact. She looked mad, probably because she knew he was about to try and spin what happened, to take away the pain with some movie reference or scientific theory.

"Don't get me wrong," Eli said. "She's gone, as in she disappeared in *there* and is not currently out *here*, but is she gone-gone? I mean, who the fuck knows what happens when you 'die' in the afterlife. Maybe it's permanent. Maybe the death of the body is the first death, and the death of the soul is the final death, ya' know? Or — or — maybe it's just a transition. That's what Rose believed."

"Do you really believe that?"

Eli took his time to respond, knowing full well the wrong answer might piss off the one ally he had left. He couldn't say the words, though. He wasn't sure he *did* believe it, so saying yes aloud would have felt like a lie, and Eli was a terrible, terrible liar. Instead, he gently nodded. That was a good middle ground, Eli thought. He *wanted* to believe it but was still fighting the science side of his brain at every turn, even though science, as far as he knew, was out the window.

Drew nodded back at Eli. She sensed he was just agreeing with all this transition talk to make her feel better, but she didn't care. Lie or not, it made her feel better. The death of the body and then the death of the soul. That made sense. It also suggested that maybe the second death was avoidable.

Drew turned her attention to the rot, the wide-open tunnel loomed

The Dead Friends Society

like a gaping maw. Somewhere on the other side was The Fireman and all he had to do was walk through and start claiming more victims, continuing the cycle of violence that Rose begged Drew to break. She realized she was unconsciously rubbing Rose's crystal, hoping it would bring her answers. She could hear Rose's voice in her head, not with any specific instructions, just her voice, the lilt of it, bouncing around in her brain. It was calming. Comforting. Eli was right. Rose wasn't here, but she was far from gone.

"I don't get why they're even still here," Eli said, gesturing to the newly furnished basement. "I mean, Abbey was fucking *attacked*. Why didn't they bug out?"

"Her dad didn't believe her."

"That's messed up."

Drew wanted to roll her eyes at him. Of course, Eli would just assume he'd be believed if he said he'd been attacked. Drew knew better. Without solid, incontrovertible proof, nobody was going to believe Abbey, not even her own father. Even with proof, people probably still wouldn't believe her.

"So how are we doing this?" Eli asked. "How do we get Abbey and her dad out of here?"

It was a good question. Drew made contact with Abbey once before. Sure, it was accidental, and Abbey mistook Drew for her dead mother, but they shared a connection. Maybe they could do it again. Maybe she could speak to her that way and convince Abbey that they needed to leave. Permanently.

"Okay, well what do I do while you're doing the Patrick Swayze on her?" Eli asked.

"I don't know. Scare Javier out of here, Beetlejuice style?"

"Let's not mix our movie metaphors, Drew." Eli scolded, pushing up a pair of imaginary glasses as if he were a disapproving professor. He was trying to break the tension of the moment, and Drew was thankful for it. She cracked a smile, but it quickly lowered upon hearing voices upstairs.

The sound was muffled, so she couldn't tell if it was Abbey or

Javier, but either way it meant there was no time to plan. They had to go wing it. One way or another, Drew was hellbent on saving Abbey's life.

Once again, Drew made her way up the basement stairs of Greywood House to try and save someone. But this time she had Eli with her and was glad he didn't require much convincing. She guessed it was because he knew they were out of options.

The voices grew louder, clearer as they entered the kitchen. Drew's heart sank. She could tell Abbey was up there, along with what sounded like a crowd of people.

Eli's jaw dropped. He couldn't believe Abbey was having a party. A fucking *party*. A minute ago, they were trying to figure out how to convince *two people* to leave before The Fireman returned. Now there were at least *six teenagers* (an even split of three girls and three boys) in the living room, and God knows how many others were spread out in Greywood House.

Eli and Drew stood at the back of the dining room, watching silently, trying to inventory the scene. It wasn't just the party that was throwing Eli off, there were so many other changes, too.

The cluttered maze of boxes and furniture were gone, and all that remained was a tastefully organized living room. Well, not just organized — *decorated*. At the back of the living room was a giant Christmas Tree and the foyer and staircase were draped with tinsel. Eli quickly did the math in his head. The Morenos had first shown up in August of 2020 (*Jesus, 2020 sounded so sci-fi just to think about*), but now the whole house looked like it was auditioning for the North Pole. Had they really been in the hollow side for four months? Or, worse, was it possible more than one Christmas could have passed since they left?

Eli supposed entire years could have passed while they were in the hollow side, but Abbey didn't look drastically older. Her hair had a deep streak of blue running through it that wasn't there when they left, but it was hard to tell if there was anything else different about her since she was wearing an ugly, oversized Christmas sweater and a cotton face mask with a bright red Rudolf nose in the center. That's when Eli registered most of the party were wearing face masks, too. Only two people weren't: a muscle-bound jock and his clearly stoned pal. The four others, including Abbey, seemed to be mad at the other two over their lack of masks.

From the beginning, the afterlife had been, to put it mildly, weird. But this? A Christmas party? With kids in masks? *Did Halloween and Christmas merge since the '90s?* Eli finally turned to Drew, his jaw still slightly agape.

"The future is so fucking weird," Eli said.

Chapter 34

ABBEY DIDN'T EVEN WANT TO HAVE A FREAKIN' PARTY. IT WAS Willa's idea.

It was the last night of Javier's work trip, the last night of Abbey having the house totally to herself, and she'd been looking forward to doing nothing. There was no homework over Winter break, no endless schedule of Zoom class meetings to log on to, no dad to give her random remodeling projects. All she had planned was glorious, not-putting-on-pants, not-doing-a-goddamn-thing nothing. Lockdown somehow kept her busier than before the whole world crapped the sheets, but this week had been bliss. There was jack for her to do, and after the hell that was their first night there, Abbey had been enjoying the peace, quiet, and total lack of obligation to anybody but herself.

Of course, Willa saw things differently. The things Abbey saw as self-care, Willa saw as anti-social. To Willa, it was downright criminal to have a big house to yourself and not throw a party. After enduring a barrage of endless texts, Abbey finally gave in. She said yes to a party on one condition: everyone had to mask up. It was a simple rule. So why the hell couldn't Travis and Nick follow it? She knew Willa would wear one. She was happy to see Danni and Ben each wearing masks even though they no doubt had their tongues down each other's throats before putting them on. But Travis and Nick were just too damned self-righteous to do it.

"I told them they had to," Willa whispered to Abbey.

Travis mimed trying to drink a beer through his mask. "How am I supposed to have any fun like this? Huh?"

"Ever heard of a straw?" Danni quipped and pulled out a metal straw from the neon pink fanny pack around her waist. Danni slid the straw under her mask and modeled using it.

When the new (virtual) school year started, one of the first assignments they'd been given was to write a paper imagining what the world was going to look like in five years. Since then, Abbey couldn't help but turn that future-gazing lens on her friends. She imagined Danni and Ben would still be together (they had the strongest relationship she'd ever seen), off living in some coastal city with jobs in marketing or design.

Abbey was less sure about Willa. If she was being honest, she'd guess that Willa would be married to the first guy to ask. Not that Willa was easy, she was just too ready to slide into domesticity, too eager to follow in her mom's footsteps. Travis and Nick were much less predictable. Nick was a lovely person — when he was sober. When he was high, as was now, he would cocoon himself in vape smoke and become a much more paranoid, twitchy personality. Abbey bet he was either going to invent the next bitcoin or go on some hike and never be seen from again.

Travis, though? He was a bit of a wildcard. Normally he was a smart, sensitive guy; the exact opposite of the meathead vibes his barrel chest and swollen biceps gave off. So why was he being such a dick tonight?

"Look, you two smooth brains. I'm going upstairs. If you feel like doing the responsible thing, you know how to reach me." Abbey said, waving her phone in the air.

"I thought the entire point of tonight was to be irresponsible,"

Travis said, voice raised like he was creating some mic drop moment. Abbey rolled her eyes.

"That's literally what Willa said!" Travis laughed. "It's on the text chain. There are receipts. Don't act like I'm the dick here."

"No, I said we were going to have a *responsibly irresponsible* night," Willa corrected him.

"Responsibly irresponsible is a contradiction." Nick said. "You can't do it. No offense, Wills, but it's like, an oxymoron or whatever."

Ben shook his head at the other guys and let out a simple, baleful "Bro..."

Ben was the master of the word "bro." He could take those three letters and spin them off into hundreds of unsaid sentiments, his face and inflection always finishing the thought for him. Right now, the unsaid part was "Bro... don't be such a fucking tool."

Danni motioned for Willa to go up with Abbey and turned her attention to the defiant dipshits still lingering in the foyer. Even from the stairs, Abbey could hear her whisper "Go cheer her up, I'll deal with these two."

Abbey watched, a small smile blooming, as Danni shoved Travis and Nick outside and told them they needed to man up and mask up if they didn't want to spend all night on the porch. *Damn, I want to be like Danni in five years*, Abbey thought as she rounded the stairs to the second floor.

Drew remained frozen in shock, unable to process. She was counting on only having to deal with two people, not a half-dozen. At least now that the party was spread out, reaching Abbey seemed a bit more doable.

"If I can get through to Abbey, she can convince the rest of them." Drew said, though she wasn't sure who she was trying to convince: Eli or herself. By the look on Eli's face, he wasn't buying it, either.

"If The Fireman comes back tonight — and considering there's still a wide-open hole to his fucked up little memory world, I'd say it's a damn good chance he does — then each one of these kids is going to have a very, very, very bad time." Eli said.

"I know that Eli. Jesus!" Was he really trying to argue with her now? She headed up the stairs after Abbey.

"I know, I know, I know. I'm just... Trying to Beetlejuice Javier out of the house was going to be hard enough on its own, but now we've got the cast of Can't Hardly Wait to deal with. I don't even know where to start."

"You can start by not mixing your movie metaphors," Drew said, trying to put him at ease. "You figure out something with them, and I'll figure out something with these two."

Eli blinked back at her like he'd been told to fix a Space Shuttle with a roll of toilet paper and some sticky tape. She knew he needed more encouragement.

"Just remember, you're the one who broke his fucking leg. Not me, not Rose, not Wes. You, Eli Adams. You did that, and you're going to break a helluva lot more next time."

Eli smiled. Half-hearted, but at least he wasn't as despondent.

Drew ran upstairs, hoping to find Abbey in the attic.

Eli felt a small sense of pride. Drew was right. He was the one who hit The Fireman. He was the one who gave them a fighting chance. *Yeah, but you're also the one who had a front-row seat to The Fireman popping his bone back in like a LEGO.*

Eli became hyper aware how alone he was; how defenseless. They might have left The Fireman attacking his memories, but with this many people in the house, they were *begging* him to return. Eli wanted to run down the basement stairs just to make sure The Fireman hadn't already emerged, but even if he had, what was Eli going to do about it?

As long as these people were in the house, he wouldn't be able to fight back.

Eli stood atop the basement stairs, nervously listening for The Fireman's booming footsteps. But all he heard were a few literal crickets chirping.

Satisfied for the moment, Eli returned to the foyer and eavesdropped by the front window where Danni, Ben, Travis, and Nick were arguing on the porch.

"What's your deal, Travis?" Danni asked, hands planted firmly on her hips. Ben stood behind her, shaking his head at Travis and Nick.

"Yeah. Come on, bro."

Nick finished a long hit off his weird electronic joint thing and coughed a little while exhaling. "It's not a big deal, *bro*. We've been staying in a bubble. We don't have it."

Nick patted Travis on the shoulder, looking for backup. Travis nodded, a bit over-enthusiastically. "You know Abbey always blows shit out of proportion. She always has to make everything about *her*. She'll get over it in a few. Just watch."

Eli looked around the foyer, trying to find an object he could use to get their attention. He eyed a beer bottle, checked his eyelines to make sure no one on the porch was looking in his direction, grabbed it, and tossed it against the wall. It shattered on impact.

The foursome on the porch jumped at the sound. They peeked in through the window, eyes darting around for the source. "Doesn't Abs have a cat? Probably knocked something over. Cats do that shit. It's like their superpower." The stoner joked. Eli stared in disbelief as Nick bent over and imitated a cat knocking stuff off a table.

Danni took a deep breath and collected herself. She reached into her fanny pack and pulled out some disposable face masks. She tossed them to Travis and Nick. "Please. Just put them on. Abbey's been through a lot and the least we can do is respect her wishes. Okay?"

Travis scoffed. "That was, like, months ago." Nick nodded in agreement mid-toke. "I asked her about it. She said she's over it."

"Just put on the masks if you want to come back in." Danni turned her back on them, grabbed Ben by the hand and led him back inside with her. Eli didn't move out of the way in time and the door swung open right through him. He hated that. It felt so invasive. Ben shut the door behind them and rubbed the back of Danni's neck. "You okay, babe?"

"She is *not* over it," Danni said.

"You know what I'm not over?" Ben said. He leaned in and kissed her gently on the side of her neck. He whispered something in her ear and her eyes lit up. She smiled and pulled Ben toward the kitchen.

"Are they seriously about to go make out?" Eli asked aloud, turning to see Drew and Rose's reaction, only to be hit with the sad reminder that he was both alone and would never see Rose's smirk again.

Ben squeezed Danni's butt and she giggled. "Jesus Christ, not now people!" Eli yelled at them, but the bubbly pair of teens were too clueless to heed his warning.

Eli set his sights back on the porch. Travis was taking a hit off the digital joint now, and neither he nor the stoner looked like they'd be heading back inside any time soon. *At least The Fireman can't get to them out there*, Eli thought, as he set off to follow the make-out couple.

Eli flashed over all the horror movies he'd seen, all the scenes of couples getting it on only for the killer to rip them to pieces in their most vulnerable state — the same vulnerable state Danni and Ben were surely about to be in. *Christ, they are begging The Fireman to return.*

Drew found Abbey in the attic sitting at her computer desk with Willa hanging off the edge of her bed, head upside down and staring at her. Oracle the cat was laying on the floor between them. He perked up as Drew entered, looking directly at her.

The attic bedroom was fully decorated while they'd been in the hollow side. There were more pieces of Abbey's mom's art hanging now, and there was even an easel set up in the corner with a half-finished charcoal sketch on it. Abbey was following in her mom's footsteps, it seemed, and it warmed Drew's heart to see.

"Abs, we're all just worried about you." Willa said. "You're up, you're down. You're happy, you're sad."

"They're called emotions, Wills. You should watch Inside Out some time. It's very educational."

Drew wanted to reach out and shake Abbey but was worried about being too forceful too fast. She didn't want to scare the hell out of the girl. Fear made people irrational. Drew knew that all too well. Hell, it was the entire reason she was a ghost. If she had let her brain make choices instead of her heart, Drew would never have turned back to save Rose. She knew if she scared Abbey now, it could mean the end of the girl's life.

Drew gently put a hand on Abbey's shoulder only to be blocked by that damned forcefield that surrounded all living people. Abbey's guard had gone back up in the last few months.

"You know what I'm talking about. You get trapped in these downward spirals and all you want to do is push people away." Willa said.

"I didn't push anyone away, you're the ones who started treating me differently. Like I'm some fragile, porcelain doll." Abbey said. But there was a tiny hint of dishonesty in her voice and even Drew could tell that wasn't the whole truth.

Willa cocked a disbelieving eyebrow. "How? How did we treat you differently?"

"You treated me like I was crazy!"

"I never called you crazy. Don't even pretend I called you crazy."

"You thought it."

"You're projecting, Abs."

"No, I'm not. You all thought I made it up, like I was trying to get attention."

"I didn't."

"You sure acted like it."

This is all my fault, Drew thought to herself, feeling like shit. Of course people would think Abbey was crazy. Drew remembered high school all too well, and while 2020 was no doubt very different from when she graduated in 1996, she doubted the social side changed that much. High schoolers would *definitely* gossip about the girl who said she touched her mom's ghost and then got chased by an axe-wielding fireman who miraculously vanished afterward.

Drew couldn't worry about all that right now, though. She couldn't control what happened in the past. She *could* control, however, what happened tonight. And since she couldn't break through to Abbey, she'd have to go to Plan B.

Drew looked around the room for something to knock over that was out of both Willa and Abbey's eyelines. She didn't have too many options but settled on one of the small paintings hanging on the wall: a watercolor of the family's cat, Oracle. Drew looked from the painting to the real cat, who was still watching Drew wherever she went. The painting captured a remarkable likeness, and even in the heat of the moment, Drew found herself jealous of Abbey's talent.

Drew tried to move the painting. It was heavier than she expected it to be. The damn cat was watching her. Despite the extra resistance, Drew managed to lift it off its wire and drop it to the floor.

Both Willa and Abbey jumped at the sound, their eyes wide as saucers. Even Oracle hissed at Drew. She had their attention, now Drew just had to figure out how best to use it.

Eli stood at the top of the basement stairs, listening to Danni and Ben giggling down in the darkness. They were no doubt inadvertently putting on a peepshow for The Fireman.

Fuck. Fuckfuckfuck. Eli ran down the stairs, letting out a silent curse with each step. He thought they'd have more time to get these people out of the house. Why couldn't they have gone up to the guest bedroom like normal people? Why, of all places, did they have to choose the one room in the house with a giant gateway to a supernatural serial killer's inner sanctum? *Fucking teenagers.*

Eli spilled out into the basement half-expecting to see The Fireman already there, but there was no sign of him. There were, however, two recklessly horny teens mere feet from the rotten wall. Both of their shirts were already off as they ground into one another on the couch. Eli yelled for them to get out, which was pointless. He did the next thing that jumped into his head and started flipping the light switch, flashing the lights on and off like a bartender telling drunks it was closing time. Danni popped up like a meerkat. She was still wearing a bra but used a couch pillow to cover herself.

"Hey, get lost you pervs!" she yelled.

"Not cool, bro!" Ben shouted.

Danni looked through Eli, up the empty staircase, then back to Ben.

"There's nobody there," she said, more amused than scared.

"They're just fucking with us. Travis is probably still salty about the mask thing. Ignore 'em. Don't let 'em ruin this."

Danni smiled and sauntered back over to him. "Oh, we weren't in the middle of something, were we? You didn't want to—" she straddled him "keep going, did you?" Ben squeezed her waist and she let out a howl of a laugh.

Eli sighed and scanned the room for something to knock over. He landed on Javier's workbench. There were a ton of tools to choose from, but one object stood out among the rest: a 12-inch circular saw blade. Eli briefly wondered if it could cut him, but he didn't have time to ponder how the real world could affect the ghost world right now. He picked the blade up and scraped it against the metal side of the bench, creating a high-pitched screech of metal-on-metal.

Both Danni and Ben bolted upright. They looked directly at the source of the sound, causing the blade to fall out of Eli's hand. It spun on the ground like a quarter.

It worked even better than he hoped. There was no way they didn't find *that* creepy as hell. He was a good ten feet away but could practically hear their hearts pounding. It was exhilarating in a way he wasn't expecting, and he wondered if this rush was why Wes had been so eager to haunt Javier and Abbey.

Eli didn't want to have anything in common with his brother though and told himself he was only scaring the innocent couple in order to save them. But he was going to have to channel his inner Wes to get the job done.

Chapter 35

HE COULD SENSE THEM THROUGHOUT THE HOUSE.

Their voices, their very heartbeats, jackhammers in his ears.

He needed them silent. They were distractions keeping him from finding the way back to his family, back to the memories they'd torn him from.

He'd make them silent.

He'd make them all silent.

He stepped out of the darkness, into Greywood House.

It felt good to return.

Chapter 36

ABBEY JUMPED WHEN THE PAINTING FELL, BUT SHE WASN'T scared. Startled, but not scared. Willa sure was, though. She screamed like she did when they were ten years old watching The Conjuring for the first time. But Abbey didn't scream. Abbey felt *comfort*.

This was the moment she'd been waiting for, thinking about for months. The ghost finally returned. She was finally going to prove she wasn't crazy.

But after the momentary feeling of relief, the self-doubt started to creep in. Was *this* really her mom? If it was, why hadn't she returned sooner? And if it wasn't, who was it? Abbey rubbed her wrist, the cuts from the shattered picture frame barely visible, but she could still feel them beneath the surface of her skin. *This* was the energy she'd felt in her room all those months ago. *This* was the ghost she'd connected with. Abbey knew it deep within her soul.

The moment felt endless, but in reality, was merely a second. "Oh my God, what was that?" Willa shouted, backing up against the bed's headboard. She grabbed a pillow and hid behind it.

Abbey approached the fallen painting. With each step, she could *feel* the ghostly presence get closer. She didn't bother to use her phone to find the orb. She didn't need to anymore. The signal was stronger now and Abbey was dialed right in.

Drew had no clue what to do as Abbey approached her. The living girl couldn't see her, but Drew felt Abbey could somehow sense her, like they were playing a game of Marco Polo and Drew had nowhere to hide.

She didn't know what changed. Had dropping the painting caused Abbey to "wake up" to Drew's presence? Was this something Abbey had been waiting for the whole time? Had their last encounter left her more open to a new one? The rules of the afterlife seemed to constantly be in flux, constantly surprising her. Navigating layers upon layers of reality, deeper and deeper connections, was all so confusing, all so endlessly exhausting. *Forfuckingever.*

Break the cycle.

Rose's last wish echoed in Drew's mind, and she wondered if she even *could* stop the cycle of violence. She wasn't sure how she'd missed it before, but it was obvious now that Greywood House was fueled by a hatred and pain so ugly, so powerful, it crossed layers of reality. How could anyone break that cycle? The ghosts of Bell Bottoms and Mustache tried, and the Fireman killed them just as easily as he'd killed Drew and her friends in the real world. How the hell was Drew supposed to stop him?

Drew didn't think. She acted on instinct. She reached out and grabbed Abbey's shoulder. This time there was no barrier. Drew was touching Abbey, the living girl. She was warm. Alive. Intoxicating. Drew felt goosebumps spread across the girl's soft skin.

"Abbey... can you hear me?"

Abbey stopped in her tracks. An invisible force pressed against her shoulder. She heard the voice. She heard the question. Not out loud. Somehow... in her mind? Maybe she *was* crazy? Maybe it *was* all in her head? She knew that's what the others would say, but for the first time in months, Abbey didn't doubt herself. She didn't care. This was real enough for her.

She nodded slowly and raised her hand, hoping to relive the connection she'd made months ago in this very room.

Drew's heart was pounding. *This is happening. Again.* She knew things were changing. Nothing would be the same after this. But it felt right.

Drew raised her hand and pressed it against Abbey's.

Their hands touched and they both melded, the living and the dead, defying the layers of reality that kept them apart. In that moment, they were of one heart, one mind, one idea: *Break the cycle.*

Chapter 37

Eli's stunt with the saw blade earned him Danni and Ben's full attention. The trouble was he didn't know what the hell to do with it. They were scared, but they weren't doing anything about it. Instead, they just walked over to the blade and stared at it, as if the metal disc would suddenly stand up, apologize, and explain why it decided to leap off the work bench.

They stood right next to Eli, oblivious to the real cause of its fall. He thought about reaching out to shove them away. His mind flashed through all the moments when Wes touched the living. His brother tried to punch a cop and had nearly broken his hand in the process, so obviously sudden force wasn't the way. Maybe a more subtle approach was necessary.

Eli hovered his hand over Ben's shoulder. He didn't touch the skin but was close enough to feel its warmth. Eli held his hand there a few moments before Ben shivered like walking through a cold spot.

"What? What's wrong?" Danni asked.

"It's, uh. It's nothing, babe." Ben said, rubbing his shoulder.

Eli hovered his hand in the same spot on Ben's other shoulder. A few seconds later, Ben did the same squirmy dance. Eli let out an involuntary "Holy shit," delighted to make contact. Danni's head swiveled toward where he was standing, a quizzical look on her face. *Did she just hear me?*

Danni squinted into the darkness and reached out. Her hand traveled through Eli, and he couldn't help but squirm. It's not that the living passing through him even really felt like anything, it was the mental angle that bothered him. So much of the afterlife felt more or less like being alive that Eli could convince himself he was just in some kind of parallel universe; a hand passing right through him was an unnerving reminder that he really was dead. As if Danni could somehow sense Eli's squirming, she quickly pulled her hand back and held it close to her chest, like she'd just touched a block of ice.

Eli laughed. It was like the world's weirdest threesome. Both Danni and Ben's faces filled with dread.

But they weren't looking at Eli. They were looking behind him.

They looked upward.

They were looking at someone much taller.

Someone much scarier.

Eli didn't need to turn and see The Fireman for himself. He could feel him there, the same way oceans felt the pull of the moon.

"Get out!" Eli screamed, but the two were frozen in shock at the sight of The Fireman. Only Danni could muster a mumbled "He's real." Ben just stood there; his brain undone.

The Fireman tilted his head down at Eli. That horrible white eye studied him through the cracked mask, compelling him to run. But Eli stood his ground. He planted himself between The Fireman and the teens. And then The Fireman kicked out like he was knocking down the door to a burning building.

His foot landed square in Eli's chest and launched him through Danni and Ben. Eli collided painfully into the workbench. All the tools rattled, and even in his daze, Eli couldn't help but note The Fireman's kick had been so powerful, even the real world had to acknowledge it.

The sound of the rattling tools startled Danni and Ben out of their stupor. Ben stepped forward, placing himself between The Fireman and Danni. It was a noble, but costly move. The Fireman cross-checked

Ben with the shaft of his axe. The wood caught the handsome teen right in the jaw; teeth went flying, Ben went sailing backwards. Eli managed to scramble out of his way right before Ben collided with the workbench. Danni ran to his side to help her beau to his feet. Eli wished she'd have just run up the stairs. Maybe then she'd have stood a chance.

The Fireman took one step toward the couple and swung his axe sideways in a wide arc. It collided with Danni's temple first before passing through and bisecting Ben's forehead. *Good lord, what a violent end for such pretty people.*

But The Fireman wasn't done swinging. He redirected the momentum of the axe toward Eli. He tried to spin out of the way, but The Fireman was even faster than before. The tip of the axe carved a line diagonally across Eli's chest, nearly slicing off his nipple in the process. Eli screamed out in pain and blood started flowing. He didn't know yet how bad the slice was, but it felt like The Fireman had peeled him like an apple.

Eli scrambled backward on his hands and feet until he touched something familiar. He grabbed the circular saw blade and threw it like a frisbee. Throwing had never been his strong suit, but it turned out that didn't matter when the entire rim of your disc is lined with metal teeth built to tear through wood. The saw blade lodged in The Fireman's hip, and he staggered backward. Eli couldn't believe his eyes. For the second time, he'd done some serious damage to this asshole.

That feeling of pride didn't last long.

The Fireman wheeled on him. Eli was thankfully a touch faster this time, spreading his legs wide open. The steel head of the axe narrowly missed his crotch and slammed into the floor between his legs. The blade embedded deep in the concrete, which gave Eli the precious seconds he needed to get to his feet. He yelled out Drew's name. It was a futile call for help. He knew she wouldn't hear him from all the way down in the basement. Eli just didn't want to die alone.

Not again.

Drew thought she heard Eli's voice, but it was too faint to be sure. Whatever it was would have to wait. Drew had managed to reconnect with Abbey. If she broke it off now, she might never be able to reach her again.

"Abbey, what are you doing?" Willa asked.

Abbey ignored Willa. Drew could tell her entire focus was on the bond between them. Drew thought she heard Abbey say, "Not now, Willa!" but Abbey's lips never moved. The connection wasn't just a one-way street from the dead to the living.

"Why did you leave me?" Abbey thought.

"I didn't mean to. It's complicated." Drew said.

"Who are you?" Abbey thought.

"My name is Drew Denns and I'm here to save you."

Abbey felt like being underwater, like when she used to sit at the bottom of the deep end of the pool and the only thing she could hear was the dull thump-thump-thump of her heart. But this time her heartbeat was joined by a voice.

The voice wasn't crystal clear, not at first, but it swirled around in her head until it came to the surface. The words "I'm here to save you" echoed over and over. Even though it felt like she was both flying and drowning at the same time, they were the most calming, reassuring words she'd ever heard.

Then the echo changed. "Save you" morphed into "Get out." The voice said it, over and over. "Get out, get out, get out, get out, get out."

The voice remained oddly calm, reminding Abbey of the time she was nine and their flight to Mexico experienced a sudden drop in air pressure. The oxygen masks deployed, and the plane erupted into screams. And yet the flight attendant confidently took over the intercom, reminding them to stay calm and secure their oxygen masks.

Abbey's mom had to put it on for her. The attendant smiled at Abbey and then turned to her mother and said, "She's a brave one, isn't she?" Abbey hadn't felt brave. She thought the plane was going to crash into a mountain, but the sound of that stranger's voice, the confidence and serenity of it, soothed away all her fear.

"Get out, get out, get out, get out, get out." The words just kept pinballing around Abbey's mind. She turned to Willa and said, in her best impression of that flight attendant, "We have to get out of here."

It must have been a bad impression, though, because Willa didn't look calm — not one bit — as she yelled, "No fucking shit, Abbey!"

Eli couldn't help but marvel as The Fireman pulled his axe out of the basement floor. He hadn't dislodged the blade — instead he pulled out the jagged chunk of concrete it was stuck in, like Arthur pulling the stone from the earth along with the sword. *How is he so goddamned strong?* Eli looked for something to fight back with when he heard a voice upstairs in the kitchen.

The Fireman must have heard it, too, as they both stopped to listen. It was a young man's voice; one of the guys from the porch. They'd come inside. *Idiots! You were safe!* Eli glanced over at The Fireman, feeling like they were both runners on the starting line. Eli didn't wait for the pistol to go off, though. He bolted for the stairs. Out of the corner of his eye he could hear The Fireman smashing his axe head on the floor, trying to break the concrete off it.

Eli launched into the kitchen to find Nick, the stoner kid, with Travis, the jock. Neither had masks on and were mid-conversation.

"You don't really believe Abbey and all this haunted house stuff, do you?" Nick asked, handing Travis a beer from the fridge.

"All I know is, I will fuck up a ghost. For real. I will rip a ghost in fucking half." Travis said, flexing his muscles as he walked out of the kitchen and back to the porch.

Eli shook his head. He felt significantly less sympathy for these two morons than he had for the couple downstairs, but he still didn't want anyone else to die. Nick pulled out his phone and a speaker no larger than a soda can started blasting out a rap song louder than the biggest boombox Eli had ever heard. He resisted the urge to grab the speaker and figure out how it worked.

The Fireman's axe-pounding from the basement picked up. Nick turned the volume up and muttered something about Ben going to town on Danni. This clueless dolt was practically begging The Fireman to silence him.

The pounding from downstairs stopped. The Fireman had cleaned his weapon and was ready for his next victim. *Fuckfuckfuckfuckfuck.* Eli quickly scanned the kitchen for weapons. He had a flash of pulling out a twelve-inch butcher's knife for self-defense. But twelve inches had nothing on The Fireman's size. Eli couldn't fight. All he could do was delay the inevitable.

Nick leaned back and opened a Dr. Pepper. Before Nick had a chance to close the fridge door, Eli slammed it shut with all the force he could muster and the cut across his chest seared with pain from the quick movement. Nick spun around, dropping the soda. Sticky liquid spilled all over the kitchen floor, but he didn't run. He didn't even blink. He just stood there, slack jawed. "Holy shit. I am so fucking high right now."

"God dammi—" Eli stopped mid phrase when The Fireman stepped into the kitchen. Nick heard it too and turned to face the monstrous man. Nick's slack jaw somehow slackened further. Nick's speech slurred. He was, indeed, very, *very* high.

"Cool cosplay, bro. What are you, like, a ghost or some shi—"

Nick didn't finish his question.

In one fluid motion, The Fireman yanked the circular saw out of his hip like he was starting a lawn mower and flung it at Nick. The stoner's head separated from his neck; severed by a single, perfectly perpendicular slice of the circular saw. The blade traveled through his spinal cord and lodged firmly into one of the kitchen cabinets. Blood dripped from its edges onto the laminate countertop below.

Nick's decapitated head slid off the stump of his neck and landed with a gruesome *plop* on the soda-soaked-tile floor. Eli's hand was still frozen on the fridge's door handle. The whole moment played out in a frenetic burst of anime-like violence.

Once again, Eli screamed Drew's name, telling her to get Abbey out of the house, hoping she could hear him this time. The Fireman tilted his head upward, listening for a response. They both heard the faint shuffling of feet upstairs. Eli couldn't see a face through the mask, but if he had to guess, he thought The Fireman might have been smiling.

The Fireman had to get through Eli in order to get upstairs. If he had time to think about it logically, Eli most likely would have come up with another — literally *any* other — plan, but he was acting on pure instinct now. The Fireman raised his axe and rushed at Eli. Using a lightning-quick physics guess, Eli threw the fridge door open again. He held it in front of him like a shield as the axe came down.

The door redirected The Fireman's swing away from Eli's head. The wedged blade instead slid down the edge of the door, peeling the metal like a can opener. Eli couldn't move his hand out of the way in time.

The tip of the axe sheared off Eli's left pinky and ring fingers. The pain rang through him in bright, blinding flashes as blood sprayed all over ice cream sandwiches stacked in the freezer.

Eli tried to back away, but the shock of losing his fingers short circuited his senses. He staggered, staring at his mangled hand. The Fireman shoved the fridge door outward, smashing into Eli. He fell to the floor next to his severed fingers and watched as the blood mixed with sticky, sugary soda. Eli stared at them, trying to remember an episode of E.R. he'd seen about a construction worker with two amputated fingers. He wished he could remember how they were reattached. He knew you were supposed to keep them on ice. But then again, he was dead. And Eli had serious doubts about a ghost ambulance taking him to a ghost E.R. where Ghost George Clooney would sew his ghost fingers back.

Peter Hall & Paul Gandersman

You're losing it, dude. Eli snapped back to reality. He looked up to find the Fireman lording over him, a king staring down at his conquered subject. Eli didn't want to die for a second time looking at The Fireman. He wanted to go out with a happy image this time. Eli closed his eyes, pictured Rose smiling in one of her flowing sundresses, and braced for the axe to come down.

Chapter 38

DREW DRIPPED FRUSTRATION AS ABBEY AND WILLA RESPONDED with panic instead of action. The two teens debated what to do, what to take, like they were planning for a vacation. They should have been running from the house like it were the building from The Towering Inferno. Instead, they were hesitating and itemizing.

"Go! Just go!" Drew yelled at them. Abbey jumped as Drew's voice boomed in her mind. She grabbed Willa's hand and the two ran down the stairs into the heart of the house. Drew followed eagerly behind them, but as soon as they landed on the second-floor hallway, all three stopped.

THUD.

It was loud. Metal on hardwood.

"He's here!" Drew screamed.

"He's here!" Abbey echoed.

"Who is here? Who?" Willa shouted back, completely out of the loop.

Drew moved in front of the girls, her mind a whirlwind of thoughts while trying to figure out how to get them out of the house without The Fireman seeing them. Drew wasn't quite sure where the thud had come from, but it sounded like maybe the kitchen. Drew grabbed Abbey's shoulder and said, "Wait here until I come get you." Abbey nodded slowly and then turned to an exceedingly confused Willa. "We have to wait here until she comes to get us."

Willa blinked. "What?"

Drew beamed. Abbey was a great listener. With a little luck, they were going to survive this thing after all.

Drew heard Willa yelling behind her. "Wait for who, Abbey?" That poor girl. She has no clue what's going on. Drew thought it might be better that way. Willa already looked on the verge of having a total mental breakdown; if her sixteen-year-old brain truly understood what was happening, she might go catatonic. Drew didn't have time to try and manage that situation, though. All she could do at this point was hope Abbey would keep Willa in check.

Drew rounded the corner of the hallway and carefully surveyed the first floor. Someone had turned off the overhead lights, so the first floor was illuminated by the Christmas tree and strings of lights that bounced off the tinsel like colorful disco balls. The front door was closed. There were no partying teenagers. There was no Fireman.

That would have been great news, but the absence of both the living and Eli filled Drew with dread. Something was wrong.

Drew crept down the staircase. Her eyes darted all over the first floor, scanning the corners for hiding teenagers, but she came up empty. She whisper-shouted Eli's name, praying she was quiet enough for The Fireman to not hear her but loud enough that Eli might from wherever he was hiding. *If* he was hiding...

THUD. Drew flinched at the sound of The Fireman's axe striking the house. By now she knew all too well what it meant.

The Fireman was back on the hunt.

Eli pictured Rose on the day they moved into the house. She always had a smile that could brighten anyone's mood, but it was twice as infectious that day. Rose's optimism spread to Eli and the others like a virus.

They were starting college lives. They were all living on their own for the first time. They were living the dream. It was a glorious moment in their lives, untouched by the future.

Eli wished he could live in that memory, that moment, forever. Maybe the final swing of The Fireman's axe would make that possible.

THUD.

Eli flinched.

But it wasn't the killing blow. The sound wasn't even in the same room.

Eli opened his eyes. The Fireman was gone. Eli tried to stand and was hit with the painful reminder he was missing two fingers on his left hand. He held his hand up, examining it closer. The fingers had been severed between the first and second knuckles. White bone shone amid shreds of pink meat.

Eli's hand no longer hurt though. There was just a dull, distant sensation, like his fingers had fallen asleep. Eli wondered if he was experiencing trauma-induced shock. He heard it was possible for a brain to become so overloaded that it decided to simply not feel pain anymore. He'd only ever read about in books, though, and even then, it involved a soldier in war not realizing a mortar shell had blown off their arm. Two fingers weren't nearly as bad as losing an entire limb, yet here Eli was, feeling oddly content about his dismemberment.

Adrenaline is a hell of a drug, Eli thought. Of course, he also knew from that same book that the shock would eventually wear off and his mangled hand was going to hurt like hell all over again. He'd deal with that when it happened.

Eli shifted his weight to his good hand and stood up. Nick's decapitated body was still standing in the kitchen. The stoner had been leaning against the counter when The Fireman decided to play fucked-up-frisbee, and while the poor guy's head had fallen to the floor, the body remained propped up by his elbows. It looked comical, like an over-the-top Halloween decoration. Eli couldn't help but laugh at the sight, and the sound of his own laughter confirmed he was indeed in shock. His brain chemistry was trying to protect him from the reality around him. It was doing a damned good job of it, too. Eli wished he could find some way to thank it.

THUD.

Eli tilted his head, trying to pinpoint the sound. *The living room?* He cradled his bleeding hand and limped toward the sound.

Abbey could feel Willa shaking like a leaf. Not that she could blame her. As far as Willa knew, Abbey was having some kind of psychotic break, hearing things and talking to people who weren't there. Willa hadn't heard the dead girl's voice. She hadn't experienced the calmness of it, the assuredness. The spirit wasn't there to hurt them, it was there to help; to protect, even.

Abbey's mind had been going warp speed since hearing Drew's voice, since feeling her presence. Things hadn't slowed down enough for her to truly acknowledge *why* Drew was telling them to get out of the house, but as they huddled in the hallway, all Abbey could think about was the night The Fireman appeared out of thin air in the basement and tried to kill her.

There'd been no sign of either him or the orbs in the months since. Abbey had started to doubt her own memory of the night. She knew other people, including her dad, said they "believed her" but nobody ever *acted* like they did. Over time she started to doubt herself, too. Everything that happened was so impossible, so illogical that there must have been some other explanation for it. Nobody thought Abbey was making it all up, per se, they just thought maybe it was some kind of stress-induced hallucination. She'd almost convinced herself it was.

THUD.

Another one, this time from the living room.

This was no stress-induced hallucination. The Fireman was back. Abbey felt an almost cocky wave of relief at the thought. It meant she wasn't crazy. It had all happened. Now Willa would understand. Her dad would understand. They'd all understand.

If they survived the night, that is.

Abbey wanted to run. She wanted to go dive out a freaking window, but that's not what Drew's voice told her to do. Drew told her to wait, and, despite every impulse she had to run, that's what Abbey was going to do.

Willa pulled out her phone. Abbey thought she was going to call the cops but was surprised to see Willa turn on the camera and hold it out, just as they'd done on that fateful night, months ago.

Abbey clutched Willa tighter. At long last, someone believed her.

Drew pinned herself against the staircase wall as The Fireman continued to pound his axe against the downstairs floor. She had a flash of the first memory from the '70s that they'd been thrust into. The '70s Fireman had lingered at the rear of the living room, trying to psych himself up for murder. Drew wondered if he was doing the same thing right now. Was he still trying to build up his confidence?

Drew crept further down the stairs. She froze when she spotted The Fireman in the living room. Drew realized what he was doing but was too late.

The front door opened and in walked the meathead, Travis. "What's that banging sound? What the hell are y'all doing in here?" he shouted.

"No!" Drew shouted back. But even if Travis had been able to hear her, it was too late. He'd fallen for The Fireman's bait. Had he stayed on the porch, he'd have been safe and out of reach, but the jock didn't know that and instead came to investigate, dooming himself.

Something flew out of the darkness from the living room.

Travis's beer-free-hand shot up and caught the object with shockingly fast reflexes. He beamed like he'd just scored the winning touchdown.

Until he realized the football in question was Nick's severed head.

"What the fuck, dude!" Travis shouted, throwing the head back from where it came. It sailed into the shadows of the living room. The head bounced off The Fireman's chest, which didn't slow him down one bit as he powered toward Travis. His axe arced high through the air in another one of his signature killing swings.

Only, Travis's hand shot up and grabbed the shaft of the axe. The blade stopped just inches from his face.

Holy shit, Drew thought. *Who the hell is this guy?*

Eli was dumbstruck. One moment The Fireman's axe was soaring through the air about to split this jock in half, and then in the blink of an eye it stopped.

This wasn't possible. Nobody could stop The Fireman. He was too big, too powerful. Yet here he was, in a deadlock with some popped-collar-polo high schooler. Granted, said high schooler looked like he could bench press a bus, but still — the dude wasn't even using both hands to stop the axe. The jock still had his beer in the other.

Eli found himself stumbling from the dining room to the foyer, trying to get a closer look. He needed to confirm this was really happening, that it wasn't yet another side effect of shock.

That's when he saw Drew rushing down to him from the stairs. Her eyes went wide at the sight of Eli's three-fingered hand.

They watched together in awe as Travis threw his beer into The Fireman's face and grabbed the axe with both hands. The Fireman bore down on Travis, but, for the first time ever, had found his match in this high school Schwarzenegger. The two were nearly as tall, and with both arms now in action, Travis was winning their tug-of-war. The teen's muscles bulged, and Eli could have sworn they were doubling in size in front of his eyes.

Travis planted one of his legs on The Fireman's chest and kicked it outward like he was doing an 800-pound leg press. The Fireman fell backward into the shadows as Travis ripped the axe out of his hands.

"Holy fucking shit!" Eli and Drew both shouted in unison. He could feel Drew gripping his arm; feel the same exhilaration coursing through her.

They were about to see The Fireman defeated. It was fucking euphoric.

Travis held the axe in the air like a trophy and shouted, "That's what you fuckin' get!"

God bless jocks, Eli thought, for the first time in his life.

Abbey had no clue what Travis was shouting about, but based on the sheer joy in his voice, it had to be something good.

Had he somehow caught The Fireman before things got out of hand? Travis was a big dude, after all. Coach had him doing two-a-days since June, turning Travis into a sentient stack of muscles. He might have been a dick earlier, but Abbey was suddenly very relieved he'd come to the party.

"Travis! Is everything alright?" Willa called out, her voice trembling.

"I got his fuckin' axe!" Travis shouted back from the foyer.

Abbey wanted to wait, wanted to do what the voice told her to, but this changed everything. Abbey nudged Willa, and together they rushed down the hallway, phone out and recording just in case.

Drew was on cloud nine. This entire time she'd been panicking about how in the hell they were going to get Abbey and the others safely out of the house. Never once had she considered one of them could stand up to The Fireman. It was such an absurd idea it didn't even register as a possibility. But the guy with the tree trunk forearms had not only overpowered The Fireman, he made it look *easy*.

But then The Fireman returned.

He charged out from the living room, rushing from the shadows like a freight train from a tunnel. Travis's arms were still raised high in foolish celebration when The Fireman collided with him, knocking him face-first into the front door. The jock's forehead hit the oak so hard Drew thought he'd crash through it and onto the porch, but the damned thing held upright, trapping Travis inside.

The Fireman attacked Travis from behind. He grabbed each wrist and pulled his arms wide like Travis was Jesus on the cross. Still, Travis refused to drop the axe.

The Fireman pulled Travis's arms wider and wider and wider, until Drew heard a soft popping sound as both of the poor boy's shoulders dislocated from their sockets. He howled in unbelievable pain.

"Stop!" Drew shouted before she even realized what she was doing.

The Fireman tilted his head in her direction, listening.

"You don't have to do this. *He* didn't kill your family. *He* had nothing to do with it."

The Fireman relaxed his pull and Travis slumped slightly. A welcome relief swept over his face. But The Fireman hadn't let him go completely. He was merely waiting to see what else Drew had to say. Drew shot Eli a *now what?* face but he was as unprepared for any of this as she was.

All Drew could think of was Rose in the hollow side, and how she successfully taunted The Fireman with how he'd been unable to protect his family. If she could distract him, maybe The Fireman would spare Travis and turn on Drew instead? That was a win in her book.

"You've already made the people who killed your family pay. I've seen it. *You've* seen it. They paid with their lives. Twice!"

Drew took a step toward The Fireman. She felt like a hostage negotiator taking small steps to prove how harmless she was, how vulnerable she was. She studied The Fireman to see if it was working, but it was hard to tell. He hadn't made Travis a double amputee yet, so that was *something*.

Drew took another step and pressed on.

"So many people have paid for what those men did to your wife and kids. It's time for this to end. You have that power. You. No one else."

The Fireman turned his head straight at Drew.

All she could see through his shattered mask was that one horrible eye, but even that looked as if it somehow softened. She was getting through to him. She just had to bring it home.

Rose's voice welled up inside of Drew.

"You can break the cycle." Drew said. "I know you can."

Chapter 39

HE STARED AT THE GIRL, THE ONE WHO'D PUT UP SUCH A FIGHT.

Her pretty face was filled with tears.

She was talking to him, saying something, though the words were lost.

All that mattered was her face. She was pleading.

Begging.

Not for her life, but the life of the man who had taken his axe.

He relaxed his grip. The man's arms slackened.

He considered her again.

She was selfless.

He relaxed further.

So pretty. So selfless.

Just like his dear Elizabeth had been.

Elizabeth was pretty. Elizabeth was selfless.

And Elizabeth would have begged, too.

He tightened his grip. He pulled harder. The man started screaming again.

Elizabeth would have begged those men to spare her boys.

Spare his boys.

But those men didn't spare his boys. They didn't spare his Elizabeth. They showed no mercy. No guilt.

He pulled the new man's arms as hard as he could.

The man was strong.

But he was stronger.

He turned to the pretty girl. He'd show her just how strong he was.

Chapter 40

ABBEY FROZE AT THE TOP OF THE STAIRS, LOCKED IN HORROR AS The Fireman pulled Travis's arms apart. As they ripped free of his body, torrents of blood sprayed out in every direction, staining his shirt red, giving Abbey the image of a steamed crab's claws sliding out of their sockets. Sinewy tendrils of flesh stretched taut, holding Travis briefly upright, before they too snapped and Travis's screaming body collapsed on the floor. His legs shook violently, his feet tapped on the floor over and over like they were trying to remember the beat to a song.

The tapping stopped and the house filled with an eerie silence before Willa let out the loudest scream Abbey had ever heard in her life. It was as if Willa's entire essence was escaping out of her throat. Then Willa collapsed and her body tumbled down the staircase. Abbey impulsively ran after and grabbed Willa by her hair before she reached the bottom of the stairs. A clump of hair came out in her grip. She hoped Willa would forgive her.

The Fireman turned on them. He held Travis's severed arms wide, showing off his handiwork. Travis's hand still gripped the axe tightly as The Fireman threw the severed arms to the ground. He didn't even bother to pry the axe from the dead man's hand. He didn't need it. If he could do that to Travis, the strongest person Abbey ever met, she didn't dare imagine what he was going to do to her and Willa.

Abbey grabbed Willa tightly and tried to drag her back up the stairs, but Willa's limp body made it a struggle. Every time she thought she had a good grip, Willa would slip and slide down another step. Two steps up, one step down.

The Fireman would be on her in seconds, eager to finish what he'd started months ago. Abbey flashed back to that night, to how The Fireman stopped chasing her as soon as she was on the porch. At the time, it didn't make any sense, and her inability to explain it was just another detail that no one fully believed about that night.

But now the pieces were clicking into place. The Fireman didn't *want* to stop that night; he *had* to stop. Drew's "get out" echoed once again in Abbey's head. It wasn't advice, it was an explanation. She wasn't being told to merely get out of the house, she was being told to get out of his *reach*.

It was a sudden, maddening revelation; a glimmer of hope shattered by the further realization that she had no way of reaching the front door. Abbey was trapped on the staircase, Willa passed out in her arms. She could maybe drop Willa, use her as bait, hop the banister and make a run for it while The Fireman chopped her preppy BFF to pieces. But how could Abbey live with herself if she did that? She couldn't.

But then The Fireman stopped chasing her. His head whipped back in a strange way, like he'd just walked into an invisible wall. His hands — those powerful, unstoppable hands — clawed at the air around him, trying to grab something Abbey couldn't see.

Then Abbey felt it. That same, goosebump-y chill she got whenever the ghost of Drew Denns was nearby.

Eli watched, incredulous, as Drew leapt onto the back of The Fireman. *What in the hell is she doing? Did she not just see him rip that dude's arms off like they were nothing?*

They stood no chance against The Fireman. Eli broke the giant's leg and it barely slowed the monster down. He'd sunk a goddamned saw blade into The Fireman's hip only to watch him pull it out like a splinter. The jock getting pulled apart like Laffy Taffy sealed the deal: no one could stop The Fireman.

"Help me!" Drew yelled at Eli, but she might as well have been speaking a different language.

The words "help" just didn't make sense. Helping implied there was an attainable goal. *If* there was help, *then* there was hope. Eli couldn't conceive of either of those things. There was only death in their future. Real, *permanent* death. At best they could delay it, but inevitably it would come. They'd failed whatever test this afterlife had given them. The Fireman would extinguish whatever semblance of a soul was still in them, and then they'd fade away, just as Wes had, just as Rose had. What was the point in fighting it?

The Fireman swatted all around to grab hold of Drew, but this was the rare instance where The Fireman's size worked against him. His arms were enormous, but the bulging muscles and broad chest made it harder for him to reach Drew. Eli found it oddly comical, like The Fireman kept trying to pat himself on the back but couldn't quite reach. He spun this way and that, trying to throw Drew off. The Fireman's thrashing shifted him from the base of the staircase toward the living room.

Eli realized Drew's plan. She wasn't trying to hurt The Fireman; she was just trying to distract him. She was steering him away, clearing a path for Abbey to get to the front door.

Eli wasn't sure what to do. He couldn't hop on The Fireman's back, too, and any frontal assault was out of the question. The Fireman would snap Eli like a twig. He needed something to hit The Fireman with.

He needed the axe.

Eli ran to Travis's severed arm still clutching the shaft of the axe. He tried to lift it with his good hand, but it was impossibly heavy. Eli looked up at Abbey and cursed as he realized he was in her eye line.

She'd have to move before he'd have a chance of prying the axe from the dead man's hand.

The Fireman changed tactics. Instead of trying to grab Drew, he ran backwards, slamming her into the wall that separated the foyer from the living room. He slammed her again and again.

Drew grunted in pain but refused to let go. Abbey called out Drew's name right as The Fireman threw his back at the wall a final time and both he and Drew smashed through it. The entire house shook, and Eli had the panicked thought that the wall must have been load bearing and the whole place was about to collapse.

Abbey watched, confused, as The Fireman started throwing his back at the living room wall. It was an insane thing for anyone to do under normal circumstances, but there was something particularly bizarre about the way he was doing it.

From her high angle on the staircase, Abbey could see The Fireman's back never quite touched the wall. His body always stopped short, as if there was something sandwiched between The Fireman and the house.

"Drew!" Abbey shouted, the name leaping from her throat while her brain was still connecting the dots.

It had to be the ghost girl. She must be clinging to The Fireman's back. *She* was the one who lured The Fireman away from the stairs, away from the front door. *She* was also the one getting beat to hell by The Fireman. Why? Why was this strange ghost girl helping her?

The Fireman gave one final, enormous slam against the wall and this time he crashed through it, landing on the floor in the living room. Abbey could see a thick wooden beam in the wall snap in half. It reminded her of the way trees looked after a hurricane.

The first-floor ceiling above buckled as the support beam fractured, which was only slightly as worrying as the orange sparks that started flying from a bundle of frayed electrical wires inside the wall. Abbey didn't know if the house was going to fall down, catch on fire, or both. She didn't want to stay and find out.

Abbey thought all the noise would wake Willa up, but so far it hadn't. That might have been for the best. The Fireman was no longer standing between them and the door, but to get there, Abbey would have to carry Willa over Travis's corpse and the ocean of blood pooling from his bloody stumps. Even though the two of them had broken up (it was mutual), Abbey knew that Travis was the first guy Willa ever told she loved. Nobody should have to be dragged through a seeping fire hydrant of their first love's blood.

Abbey managed to ease Willa safely to the base of the stairs. Just a few more feet and she'd be able to rip open the front door and they'd be free.

Abbey eyed the front door. Its knob was badly damaged, likely during The Fireman and Travis's battle. Abbey just prayed it would still turn. She knelt and tried to hoist Willa to her feet, but her body was still limp, and she slid back to the floor. If Willa couldn't stand, Abbey had no choice but to drag her across the room, through the blood, over Travis's body. *Jesus, how the hell did it all come to this?*

Abbey lowered Willa to the ground and started to pull her toward the front door. The Fireman must have sensed her, because as soon as she moved, he began stirring to his feet in the living room.

Drew felt like she'd been run over by a steamroller. Her vision was blurred. Her hearing had gone out, replaced by a high-pitched ringing that drowned out the rest of the world.

She rolled on the floor, unintentionally balling up into a fetal position. Drew wondered if that was a muscle memory. Or was it a sense memory? Her brain couldn't even focus on the words. All she could think was The Fireman hit her so hard, her entire body was shutting down, reverting to one of the first shapes it ever knew. She wanted to close her eyes and just fall asleep, to let herself disappear and follow Rose out of existence.

But The Fireman stirred to his feet, leaving Drew no option but to follow suit.

Drew rolled onto her hands and knees and tried to stand, but her body collapsed. She tried to do a push-up, telling her biceps to press down on the floor, but her muscles were in revolt, ignoring everything they were instructed to do. Or maybe they weren't receiving the instructions. Had The Fireman truly broken something inside of her? Drew tried to push-up again but collapsed. Her eyes closed. He'd won.

And then Drew felt like she was floating. Her hands could no longer feel the floor. She felt like a cloud drifting upward and wondered if this was what floating up to heaven felt like. Drew opened her eyes. There was no heaven, just Eli's shit-eating grin as he hoisted her to her feet.

"What the hell were you thinking?" he asked. She didn't have the energy to respond. All she could do was look past The Fireman limping across the room to Abbey desperately trying to open the door.

It had all been for her. Drew was fading, but at least the girl would live, at least Drew's choices would finally have mattered. Abbey would drag her friend onto the front porch, and they'd be safe. The Fireman would no doubt redirect his rage at Drew and Eli, and that would be that. But at least he wouldn't get Abbey. At least she'd get away. She'd *live*. Drew was ready for it to be over, finally.

But the front doorknob didn't turn. Abbey couldn't get it open. And The Fireman was closing in. Drew did the only thing she could. She pushed away from Eli and threw herself at The Fireman.

Chapter 41

HE WAS SO CLOSE TO ENDING IT ALL. THE LIVING GIRL WAS TRAPPED. She'd be silenced in seconds.
    Then she threw herself at him.
    The dead girl who refused to stay dead.
    She clung to his leg like a toddler. Like his boys used to.
    His precious boys. The ones taken. The ones ripped from his life.
    He lifted the dead girl.
    She was screaming. They were all screaming.
    He squeezed her throat.
    He felt her bones.
    Felt them grind under his gloves.
    He gripped harder.
    Soon the screaming would stop.
    Soon he'd go back to what he wanted. Back to the memories of her.
    Back to being alone. Forever.
    The dead girl turned her head, looked at the living girl.
    She looked happy.
    He choked her.
    Tighter.
    And tighter.

Chapter 42

ABBEY WAS TOO FLUSTERED TO FEEL THE TEARS STREAMING DOWN her face. The goddamned front door wouldn't open. The knob had been bent sideways when Travis slammed into it. She could feel the lock inside twist. She could tell it was close — so freaking close — to unlocking.

The Fireman lumbered toward her, a single white eye gazing at her from under his shattered mask. She screamed and lost her focus. He quickened his pace, his hands outstretched, ready to ruin her the way he ruined Travis.

Abbey darted backward to avoid his grasp, but she didn't need to. The Fireman halted, distracted by some invisible thing at his feet. He reached down with both hands. Abbey felt those all-too-familiar goosebumps as the space between The Fireman's hands started to darken and fill, like blowing smoke into a bottle. A shape started to form between his hands.

The shape of a woman.

Abbey's heart leapt as Drew Denns started to materialize before her very eyes. As the ghost took shape, she could see The Fireman's hands were wrapped around Drew's throat, squeezing it tight as he lifted her off the ground. And yet Drew still somehow managed to turn to Abbey. She didn't say anything, but Abbey knew what Drew was telling her. *Go. Get out.* Drew was sacrificing herself.

Abbey doubled her efforts on the door, twisting the doorknob so fucking hard she feared she might break her hand.

SHHHUUNNKK— The door unlatched and flew open, flooding the first floor with the early rays of dawn. Abbey reached down and grabbed Willa's wrist. She glanced back up at Drew, who had a faint smile on her face despite the fact she was dying (*if a ghost could even die*, Abbey wondered). Drew's eyes rolled into the back of her head.

Abbey dragged Willa out to the porch. As they crossed the threshold to safety, she looked back. The Fireman's grip on Drew's throat slackened. A second ghost was materializing. A tall, scrawny guy was pulling on The Fireman's arm. He wasn't nearly strong enough to break The Fireman's grip.

But then the lanky guy did something truly unexpected. He hooked his arms around the Fireman's elbow, and then he leapt sideways, right toward the front door. Abbey watched in awe as the new guy's foot crossed the threshold of the front door and was immediately pulled upward to the center of the door. The guy was suspended sideways, as if being sucked into a wormhole. He screamed in pain, and then in a blink, the doorway swallowed up his legs, pulling him, The Fireman, and Drew all into thin air.

Abbey jumped back in fright as the three of them then popped back out into the foyer from nowhere.

Eli gave up trying to lift the axe from the ground. It was just too complicated with Abbey in the room. He looked around for another weapon, but there was no time. The Fireman was draining the afterlife from Drew. She'd be gone in seconds. Eli didn't have the strength to stop this fucking monster.

But the house did.

The Fireman was close enough to the front door, all Eli had to do was feed him to the portal. He wrapped his arms around the killer's arm and threw himself sideways. His lanky legs were just long enough to put his foot through the threshold of the front door.

He immediately regretted it. As the portal grabbed him, Eli felt like he was Stretch Armstrong about to snap. He could have sworn he felt his cells being flattened like spaghetti. Thankfully, the feeling was over almost as quickly as it started, and the three of them were hurtled through the door and crashed back into the house like skydivers landing without parachutes.

Eli staggered back to his feet. He called out Drew's name, but she didn't answer. That's when he saw she wasn't moving, either. The Fireman was, though. That asshole was quicker to recover than either of them. Eli could see The Fireman's hideous eye glaring down at Drew's still body, soaking up the view, savoring the fact that he was about to finish her off once and for all.

Eli didn't think. He leapt onto The Fireman's back. He wasn't trying to steer The Fireman away like Drew had. Eli had a softer goal. He wanted that goddamned eye. Eli's remaining index finger slipped into the hole in The Fireman's mask.

Eli was always a squeamish kid. One time at a Halloween party, Jacob Rafferty's mom prepared a bunch of gross ingredients for them to touch. He knew the bowl of eyeballs were really peeled grapes, and yet his hand recoiled in horror. Eli had nearly thrown up at the sensation. Mrs. Rafferty cackled and asked if he liked that.

Eli, always the gentleman, responded with a politely restrained "No, Ma'am, I did not like that." But even at seven, he wanted to tell her to fuck off. He'd always had a fear about his eyeball being touched. It was just such a vulnerable part of the body. So soft, so easy to damage. Even touching a grape pretending to be an eyeball made his skin crawl.

But Eli's skin didn't crawl as his fingernail sank into The Fireman's eye, popping the cornea with shocking ease. The eyeball was just as soft, just as easy to damage as he always feared. But Eli's hand didn't recoil in horror this time. He pushed further, sinking a good four inches into The Fireman's skull.

Eli didn't know what was in there. He didn't know what The Fireman was made of. But The Fireman's reaction made it very clear: No, Ma'am, he did not like that. Not one bit.

The Fireman dropped Drew and grabbed Eli's wrist. He gripped it so hard Eli thought his bones would break, but he refused to give up. He moved his thumb around, squeezing, performing exploratory surgery inside The Fireman's eye socket. Eli felt a bit of resistance under his finger and then it broke through to a new soft, squishy spot, leaving Eli to wonder if he'd reached the other side of the eye socket. He didn't know anatomy well enough to be sure. Either way, there was no way The Fireman was just going to pop his body back together this time.

The Fireman yanked Eli's hand, pulling it free from the mask. Foul-smelling black rot gushed from the hole as The Fireman flung Eli to the floor like a ragdoll. Eli hit the hardwood and felt all the air punch out of his lungs. The pain didn't stop him from laughing. The Fireman would surely still kill him, but at least that goddamned goblin eye wouldn't be staring at him when it happened. At least he'd fucking *hurt him.*

Drew spasmed awake. Early morning traces of sunlight streamed in through the front door. She'd lost consciousness before getting to see Abbey escape, but the sunlight at least told her the girl had gotten out. Abbey and Willa were safe, no doubt running down the driveway, screaming their heads off for someone to come help. Just the thought of it filled Drew with so much joy it started to override the pain. Until she took in the scene and was reminded just how dire things were.

Drew's vision swirled like the world around her was being flushed down a drain. She thought her hearing had returned but the only thing she could hear was Eli laughing. *Why is Eli laughing? What'd I miss?*

Drew propped her head up just enough to see Eli in the middle of the foyer, rolling around like he'd just been told the funniest joke ever. The Fireman was a good five feet away, stomping his foot on the floor like he was trying to put out a campfire.

As Drew's vision stabilized, she realized the fire was Eli. But The Fireman couldn't see him. The Fireman couldn't see anything. Eli had done some serious damage to him this time. It looked like the eye underneath The Fireman's mask had been carved out with an ice cream scoop. All that remained was an oozing mess of rotten flesh.

"Eli!" Drew tried to call out, but her throat burned as air passed through it. Eli stopped laughing and an enormous smile spread across his face. He scrambled over to Drew and helped her stand up.

"I thought you were dead," Eli said.

Drew smiled back at him, even though every muscle in her face hurt. "We are dead, dummy," she said, and Eli barked out a laugh. Neither of them could turn down an easy punchline. Here they were, at the end of their afterlives, laughing. If nothing else, Drew was happy they had each other when it was time to fade away.

The Fireman continued to blindly stomp around in the living room. And then something in the corner of Drew's eye caught her attention.

Drew thought she'd exhausted her capacity to be surprised a literal lifetime ago, and yet the sight of Abbey holding out The Fireman's axe still did the trick.

"I think you need this" Abbey said, waiting for Drew to take it.

Abbey stood at the base of the porch, out of breath. She looked back at the house and could hear a thousand voices telling her not to go back, telling her she was safe. And the rational part of her knew all those voices were right. She shouldn't go back. She should keep dragging Willa down the driveway and onto the road until they found someone to help. And yet nothing about her experience in Greywood House had been rational. Only one voice helped her this entire time, and Abbey felt inexplicably drawn back to help the ghost girl.

"I'll be right back," Abbey told Willa, who stirred but still didn't quite wake. She crept up the porch steps, taking them one at a time. Her gut was telling her to return to the house, but she wasn't going to be an idiot about it. She promised herself she'd bolt at the first sign of trouble. But as the doorway came into view, she felt the impulse to run fade. The Fireman was still in the house, still alive, still enormous. But something was different. He was stomping around, confused.

No, not confused.

Blind.

They blinded him!

Abbey's steps quickened and she arrived at the door to find Drew standing, leaning on the ghost whose name she didn't know but who she suspected was another one of the college kids who'd been killed in the '90s. The two ghosts were huddled together, sharing a moment of relief. But Abbey knew it wasn't over. The Fireman might have been weakened, perhaps permanently, but he was still a threat. He could still kill.

Abbey saw The Fireman's axe on the floor near the front door. The sight of Travis's hand still clutching it made her gag, but she knew what she had to do. Abbey took a deep breath, stepped back into Greywood House, and pried the axe from Travis's hand.

Drew took the axe from Abbey without even really thinking. The living girl was staring right at her, and yet she was able to hold the axe. Drew knew then that something had fundamentally changed between them. She and Eli were no longer the toys hiding from their owner. They were equals. As equal as the dead and the living could be.

The axe was heavy in Drew's hands, just as it had been the first time she'd taken it from The Fireman decades ago. But she wasn't going to let him take it back this time.

The Dead Friends Society

The Fireman dropped to his hands and knees, searching in desperation for the one who had blinded him. The juggernaut's movements slowed, though Drew couldn't tell if it was because he was exhausted or if he was giving up. She felt an odd pang of pity. He almost looked lost, like he was waiting for someone to help him.

The pity didn't last long, though.

Drew stepped toward The Fireman. She looked back at Eli and Abbey, who both gave her a subtle nod to continue.

Drew looked down at her murderer, at the man who had taken everything from her, from Wes, from Rose— from so, so many people. She didn't hesitate.

Drew swung.

Chapter 43

HE COULDN'T SEE HER, BUT HE COULD HEAR HER.

He couldn't see the axe, but he could hear it.

He knew what it sounded like arcing through the air.

He knew what it sounded like when it connected with bone, splitting it like firewood.

He knew these things all too well. He'd done it himself so many times.

But he never knew it so well as this moment.

The already darkened world around him grew blacker as he felt the axe enter his skull.

The metal was cold.

And then it wasn't.

And then he wasn't.

Chapter 44

ELI WATCHED IN AWE AS DREW SPLIT THE FIREMAN'S HEAD IN half with a single stroke. A stream of liquid, black rot bubbled out of the wound. Drew yanked the axe back out. Streaks of the black ooze splashed off the end of the axe and splattered the broken foyer wall. They dripped down the house in viscous ropes.

Drew raised the axe for another strike, but Eli could already tell a second one wouldn't be necessary. One look at The Fireman made that obvious. The titan had been felled. Black rot flowed from his head like crude oil from a broken pump.

Drew looked to Eli, seeking confirmation he was seeing the same thing she was. She didn't smile. She didn't frown. Her face was expressionless. But Eli knew what she was thinking, what she felt. She'd finished it. The nightmare was over. The Fireman was dead.

"Who are you?" Abbey's voice caught Eli off guard. She was no longer looking *through* him. No, the living girl was looking *at* him.

"I'm Eli?" Eli asked, so thrown off by the girl's ability to see him he couldn't even be sure of his own name.

Abbey nodded, smiling. Eli gave a small, impulsive wave. *What is happening? Stop waving at her, you dork*, he thought to himself, forcing a smile back. Abbey was visibly shaken, and not just from the trauma of the night. Eli could sense a different kind of nervousness welling up in her.

"I'm not crazy?" Abbey asked.

"No, you're really, really not," Drew said with a sigh.

Eli could tell the adrenaline rush was wearing off and Drew's body was starting to catch back up to all the damage done to it. So was his. He'd almost forgotten The Fireman had sliced off two of his fingers, but the strobes of pain slowly returning to his left hand were a reminder he could have happily done without. Eli tucked his mangled hand behind his back, deciding he'd ignore it as long as possible.

"I mean. This is all pretty fucking crazy if you ask me. But you? You're not crazy." Eli said.

Abbey laughed. The moment almost felt normal, until the sparks from the broken electrical cables landed on the thick ropes of black ooze, igniting whatever the hell had been inside The Fireman. Fire spread outward from the wall, leaping from one strand of liquid rot to the next as if the flames themselves were alive.

"You gotta go!" Eli shouted to Abbey. He instinctively shoved her out the front door, and to both his and Abbey's surprise, his hands actually made contact with her. Eli had grown so used to being invisible to Abbey and all the others, he wasn't expecting to be able to touch her.

Something had changed. If Abbey could see them, did that mean their universes were no longer parallel? Eli looked down at Travis's dead body. *And why the hell isn't he a ghost?* The Fireman was dead, but he still had so, so many questions. The all too familiar existential crisis of their ever-shifting reality returned, joining the renewed pain from his severed fingers. *At least we saved her*, Eli thought.

Abbey stood on the porch, looking back at Eli and Drew, confused. Eli could tell she was expecting them to leave with her. Abbey didn't know Greywood House was their eternal prison.

As the flames spread, licking up the walls to the second floor, Eli thought it was at least a fitting end to things. He didn't know what kind of funeral his parents had held for him out in the real world, but here, where it mattered, they were going to get a Viking Funeral. Eli felt like they'd at least earned that much.

Drew placed a hand on Eli's shoulder. He didn't have to look at her face to know she resigned to their fate, too.

Drew looked at Abbey's silent, confused face. It reminded Drew of Sir Hops, the bunny she and Rose nurtured after it had been run over by a lawnmower. Once his leg had fully healed and he could survive in the wild, they found a nice field on the edge of a forest and let him go. Sir Hops didn't run away immediately like they expected. He'd just stared back, confused as to why his protectors were walking away from him. It was one of Drew's earliest heartbreaks. And that was just a silly rabbit. This was a living, breathing girl that Drew had to release back into the wild. She couldn't bear the heartbreak again and turned away from Abbey to the burning house.

The Fireman's body lay on the ground, now utterly lifeless. But she'd seen him that way before. She'd once stabbed him in the heart with a chisel and he'd still managed to get back up. Drew had to be sure that wouldn't be the case this time.

Drew took the axe and dipped it in the black seepage, coating its blade. Drew stepped toward the spreading flames. The heat was magnificent and rising fast. She had to will herself to step further into the growing furnace.

Drew held out the axe and the flames latched onto the blackened rot like a torch. The heat radiated against her hand, and she could tell, she *knew*, there was no surviving this fire, even as a ghost. Even as whatever the fuck The Fireman was.

Eli moved to Drew's side. They didn't talk. They both knew what had to be done.

Drew tossed the flaming axe onto The Fireman's corpse. It was like tossing a lit match into a swimming pool of napalm. The Fireman set ablaze so quickly it caught Drew off guard. She'd never seen flames move so fast, and she and Eli both jumped back as the fire grew with a fury, culminating in what felt like a small explosion — though Drew couldn't tell if the house was shaking, or it was just her body starting to crash from its endocrine high.

Drew shielded her face from the onslaught of heat. Through her fingers, she watched as The Fireman was consumed by flames. He would never hurt anyone again. *We got you, motherfucker. We got you.*

The flames spread from his body to the rotten bile surrounding him. It was difficult to see clearly through the smoke and flames, but Drew sensed it wasn't merely the floor burning.

Just as the rot had once consumed the wall in the basement, turning it into a tunnel to the hollow side, the ground itself seemed to be melting from reality, giving way to that same infinite darkness. The Fireman's flaming body sank into the pit.

Drew and Eli both moved to the edge and watched as his burning body fell into an infinite abyss, the bright orange growing smaller and smaller as it fell, until the once giant Fireman was reduced to a pinprick of orange light. And then he was gone, swallowed by the darkness.

Drew teetered on the edge of the pit and found herself fighting off a sneaking urge to jump in after him. Not out of a suicidal tendency, but because she wanted to follow him. She wanted to see where he ended up. She wanted to see what true Hell looked like. She wanted to make damn sure he'd stay there. But before she could act on the impulse, a hand grabbed her wrist and started pulling her away from the hole, away from Greywood House.

Abbey didn't understand what the hell the ghosts were doing — one moment they were standing over The Fireman's burning body, and then he vanished into thin air — but she didn't want to waste time asking them.

While those two fixated on the spot where The Fireman disappeared, Abbey watched the rest of the house erupt into flames. She had a fleeting desire to run up the burning staircase, to go to the attic and rescue all her mother's art before it was too late, but as soon as she took a step back into Greywood House, a tidal wave of heat crashed onto her. She knew that was pointless. They had to get out, and they had to get out right now.

Abbey grabbed Drew and Eli's hands and yanked them toward the front door. They both pulled back slightly, resisting as if she were asking them to do the unthinkable. But Abbey wasn't asking. They'd saved her, now it was her turn to save them, whether they wanted it or not. Abbey pulled hard, dragging them through the front door.

The second the three of them hit the front porch, Abbey felt Drew and Eli stop resisting. They looked at her, bewildered, like Abbey just pulled off some Herculean task. All she'd done was get them out of the freakin' burning house. She was no hero. Besides, they were freakin' ghosts. Why the hell were *they* the ones acting so strange?

She was the one who should be freaking out right now. She was the one who was going to have to explain all this to the police. She was the one who was going to have to tell her dad. And thanks to whatever the hell had just happened in the foyer, it's not like she had The Fireman's body as proof she wasn't crazy. She'd have to hope Willa could vouch for what happened. *Oh God, Willa!*

Abbey looked down the driveway to where she'd left her friend, but Willa was gone. Abbey's heart sunk, fearing The Fireman had somehow escaped; that he'd somehow snuck out amid all the flames and smoke and killed Willa, too. But then Abbey spotted her at the end of the driveway. Willa was on her phone, no doubt talking a mile a minute to a very overwhelmed 911 dispatcher. As soon as Willa spotted Abbey, she dropped to her knees. For a second Abbey thought she'd passed out again, but she was just in shock.

"Oh my god, Abs, I thought you were dead!" Willa screamed as Abbey ran toward her. Willa would have been right, were it not for the intervention of two complete strangers, both of whom were willing to die all over again just to save her.

Abbey looked back at Drew and Eli as they walked in a daze away from the inferno that was Greywood House. Abbey waved her arms at them, signaling them to come closer.

"Who are you waving at?" Willa asked.

Drew had to shield her eyes from the morning sun. She'd spent twenty-two years trapped in the house she and her friends died in. Time had become meaningless within its walls, but out here the sky was no longer spinning in time lapse. This was the real world. They were free. Eli stared back at the fire, but Drew refused to look. She wanted to walk away from Greywood house and never turn back.

"Where do you think he went? Or Rose? Or Wes?" Eli asked, his mind surely filling with a thousand new theories now that Abbey had pulled them out of their purgatory.

"Because if we're here," Eli raised a hand, hovering it over the other. He pointed at Abbey and Willa at the bottom of the driveway. "And they're—"

Drew grabbed his hands and lowered them. Eli said sorry, but Drew didn't want to hear that, either. Something told her they'd have all the time in the world to figure everything out.

Drew rubbed Rose's crystal dangling from her neck. A smile formed on her face as she and Eli walked away from Greywood House. Rose might have been wrong about the way out, but she was right in the end. Their souls were finally free to wander.

THE BEYOND

Chapter 45

ABBEY HATED CEMETERIES. SHE'D SPENT FAR TOO MUCH TIME IN them for a sixteen-year-old. Both sets of her grandparents had died by the time she was twelve, though their funerals weren't nearly as devastating as her mother's had been. Abbey hoped that would be the last funeral she'd have to go to for a long, long time. But The Fireman had seen otherwise and now she was at her fourth funeral in as many weeks, and Travis's was proving even more awkward than Nick's, Ben's, or even Danni's.

Travis's family had waited weeks to hopefully recover some of their son's remains, but the excavation of Greywood House proved fruitless. Everything had been reduced to indistinguishable ash. The insurance inspector who came out said he'd never seen anything quite like it. He'd never seen a house burn with such ferocity before and told the Morenos it was as if the entire house was a crematorium.

Abbey lingered in the back of the procession with her dad and Willa as Travis's empty coffin was carried to its final resting place. Throughout the service she could feel everyone's eyes on them, knowing full well that even though people *said* they believed Abbey and Willa about what happened, so few did anything to prove it. Classmates were treating them like lepers, keeping even more distance than socially necessary, as if the spectre of death was following Abbey, ready to leap on anyone who got too close.

Not that she really blamed any of them. What happened at Greywood House was ripe for scandal and conspiracy. Abbey Moreno and her friends had been the third set of victims to be attacked by an axe-wielding maniac. Everyone had a theory about what happened. Some thought it was a brother of the original '70s Fireman who'd sworn to take revenge on anyone with any connection to the house where his brother was executed. Others thought it was yet another copycat killer who learned about the '70s and '90s murders and leapt at the opportunity to become *the* urban legend for a new generation.

Naturally, Abbey knew all those people were freakin' wrong, but she didn't have the energy to set the record straight. She knew doing so would condemn her to a life she'd never be able to escape; a life where everything she ever said or did would be called into question. It was less painful to let people gossip and whisper in hushed tones. The truth belonged to the survivors of that night and no one else. It was theirs to share or not, and both Abbey and Willa agreed they'd keep things private for now.

Willa did tell her parents but neither believed her, saying that anything "supernatural" that happened was just a trauma-induced hallucination. Eventually Willa gave up trying to convince them. Since then, and despite the protest of her parents, Willa had been spending more and more time with Abbey and Javier (who, thankfully this time, believed Abbey) at their temporary apartment, which, as far as any of them knew, was most definitely *not* haunted.

But Abbey's life wasn't entirely ghost free.

Drew watched Travis's coffin lower six feet into the earth and wondered if this was what her own funeral had been like. Crying, confused parents. A sea of former friends all whispering among one another in a death-obsessed game of telephone where no one person had any of the details right.

"Do you think this is what it was like for us, too?" Eli asked, his voice lowered despite the fact the mourners couldn't hear him.

"I was just thinking that." Drew whispered back.

There'd been a lot of that synchronicity lately. Drew just assumed it was because they were spending so much time together. After they left Greywood House, they were both free to go anywhere, and yet they decided to stick together while trying to get a handle on the afterlife beyond the walls of their prison.

The sky no longer went into time lapse if they were ever left alone, but they still weren't able to openly interact with the living world if people could see them. There was one notable exception, though.

Abbey could not only see and talk to both of them, but Drew and Eli were also able to interact with the world while the living girl was watching. That final night at Greywood House had bonded them together in ways none of them could quite articulate, and so it just made sense that the three of them would spend a bit more time together as they figured out what that bond meant not just for them, but for their unseen role in this increasingly bizarre existence.

The mourners stood up and turned toward them. Drew could feel Abbey and Eli both tense up, as if they'd just been caught doing something illicit, but the priest simply ended the service while Drew was lost in thought.

"Maybe hanging at the back wasn't a good idea," Abbey said softly. She was right. Soon everyone would file out right past them. "We can go now."

Willa nodded, as did Eli. Drew smiled slightly. In the past two months Abbey had grown quite adept at saying something in response to both the dead and the living at the same time, even if the latter had no idea the former was still hovering around. Abbey told her dad and Willa about Drew and Eli's existence but said only that they were simply "still around." She hadn't specified that Drew and Eli were also their new roommates. That would come in time.

Javier led Abbey and Willa down a small path away from the funeral. When they were well out of earshot of the mourners, Abbey told them she needed a minute. Willa and her dad didn't ask any follow-up questions as they went to wait by the car. Drew and Eli sidled up to one another as Abbey turned to them, a somber look on her face.

"There's another reason I asked you guys to come with me today," Abbey said.

"Oh God, what is it?" Eli asked, rubbing the now-healed stumps where his two fingers once were. Eli had been on edge since the attack, always saying that this was all too good to be true, that they didn't deserve to survive the afterlife. It was like they were fugitives on the run and Eli was expecting the grim reaper to show up and take them back to jail.

Drew didn't feel that way. She thought they'd been given a new lease on life. She didn't know *why* that was. She didn't think they deserved to get out while others were left behind, but those things were out of their control and Drew vowed to make the most of the chance they were given. They'd managed to not only help Abbey, but break a cycle of violence that had torn too many lives apart. Maybe there'd be more people like Abbey to help, more cycles of violence to bring to an end.

"Don't worry, it's not bad," Abbey said, leading them down a row of progressively older, weathered tombstones. "I didn't mean to spring this on you, but earlier today I found out there's something here I think you both should see."

Abbey pulled out her phone to check a map and then took a sharp turn, leading them deeper into the cemetery. "I think it's over here," Abbey said, pointing at a section of tombstones that lay underneath the largest willow tree Drew had ever seen.

"Please don't tell me I'm buried over there," Eli said. "I'm not sure I want to stand over my own grave. That's just... that ain't right."

"None of this has been right for a long, long time," Drew said.

"I'm just sayin', I feel like if a ghost stands on its own grave that's like when a time traveler touches themselves in the past. Universes shouldn't collide like that. That's just asking for trouble."

"It's not your grave, Eli," Abbey said. Her eyes settled back on Drew.

Drew's heart started racing.

She began absentmindedly rubbing the crystal necklace around her neck as she drifted toward the cluster of tombstones. Eli followed silently behind her, while Abbey remained at the edge of the path to give them space.

Drew's mind whirled, trying to anticipate how she'd feel standing over her own tombstone. She was pretty sure universes weren't going to collide like Eli joked, but she still had butterflies in her stomach as she stepped into the shade of the picturesque willow tree.

The willow's canopy covered over a dozen different headstones. Eli moved from one to the next, scanning the names. Drew didn't need to search, though. She held the necklace tight, and just as it had in the hollow side, she felt it speak to her, nudging her in the right direction.

Drew stopped walking and looked down. She gasped when she saw the name.

Rose Calder
1978-1998
"The dead are always speaking to those willing to listen."

Drew dropped to her knees. Tears welled up in her eyes. Eli sat down next to her and placed his good hand on the gravestone. He said something under his breath that Drew couldn't hear. She knew it was for Rose's ears only, but she could feel the love and loss emanating from Eli.

Eli withdrew and Drew leaned her head against the tombstone. She didn't know what to say as tears gently fell from her face, wetting the marble like rain. She wanted to tell Rose that they'd done it, that they'd broken the cycle just like she asked her to. Drew wanted to say that she wished they could switch places, that Rose was the one who deserved the afterlife, not her. But in the end, Drew found herself too speechless to articulate any of it. She took off the black quartz crystal necklace, kissed it, and laid it gently on top of the tombstone.

Eli laid his hand on Drew's shoulder. "I miss her so goddamn much," he said.

"We wouldn't be here without her," Drew said.

"I know. Goddamn it, do I know." Eli said.

The two ghosts leaned on one another as they stared down at Rose's tombstone. Drew couldn't bear it. Eli had been right. Drew wasn't standing on her own tombstone, but this still felt like the universe collapsing in on itself. Drew was in the present. Rose was in the past. Their meeting like this was a reminder the two would never again co-exist.

But then the black quartz crystal twitched, jumping slightly on the tombstone. Drew felt Eli grip her shoulder tightly.

"Did you see that?" She was almost afraid to ask. She didn't want to open the door to the possibility she'd imagined it. But Eli nodded in awed silence. They both leaned in closer, staring at the crystal, their eyes begging for it to move again.

"Rose? Is that you?" Drew asked.

The crystal began vibrating, doing a happy little tap dance on top of the tombstone.

Oh Rose, you beautiful, magical woman, Drew thought, plucking the crystal off of the tombstone. *Tell me how to find you.*

The crystal grew warm in her hand, and as Rose's voice called to her, Drew listened, ready to follow. She'd send every monster she encountered back to hell if it meant finding Rose again.

Acknowledgments

The Dead Friends Society was supposed to be a movie. We started developing it years ago, when the world was very different. We wanted to create something that had horror, had stakes, had characters you could relate to, but at the end of it all, we just wanted people to have *fun*.

When the pandemic hit in March of 2020, it became clear that our plans for bringing Drew and her friends to the big screen weren't going to happen any time soon. We never stopped thinking about this story, these characters, their lives and afterlives, though. We decided to do something we'd never done before. We wrote a book. And now it's in your hands – or in your ears – and we hope it does for you what creating it did for us: melt the real world away with a blast of good, old-fashioned, midnight movie madness.

We have so many more stories to tell in this universe – be it more books, shorts, comics, or hopefully one day bringing these ghosts themselves to life. *Thank you* for sharing this story with us. Most of all, we hope you had *fun*.

Thank you first and foremost to our amazing families for supporting us through this whole process. Christine Hall, Tigh Hall, and Dean Hall. Ray Hall, Liz Hall, and Adrian Hall. Ashley Landavazo. Rick Gandersman, Nancy Gandersman, and Andrew Gandersman. We couldn't have done this without you.

To Alex Euting, Cameron Burns, and Aaron Koontz, thank you for encouraging our original pitch back in the day. You helped light a fire in us for this story that is still burning.

Thank you to Will Goss, Emily Hagins, Ben Hanks, Jay Rosenkrantz, Rod Paddock, Aaron Morgan, Tyler Mager, Kyle Bogart, Glen Oliver, and Beau Farrell for always giving us the honest feedback – whether on this book or the screenplay before it – we needed to hear.

To C. Robert Cargill, thank you for giving us the push we needed to finally pull this book out of its drawer and show it to the world.

To everyone that worked with us on our short film, Givertaker, whether you knew it or not, it's part of the same universe The Dead Friends Society exists in. Thank you for your talents in the first tease of this world we're creating.

To Joshua Fields, thank you for replying to Paul's tweet and alerting Encyclopocalypse to our manuscript.

To Sean Duregger and Mark Alan Miller, thank you both for seeing something in this story and agreeing to publish it. We're in this together now!

This project has been shapeshifting from one medium to another over the span of the craziest years we've ever known, so if your name isn't here, we apologize for our broken brains. Thank you to everyone who helped and everyone who read.

And lastly, thank you to the horror writers and directors who seeded countless ideas and images in our minds. There are too many to name, so we'll just end with the most obvious.

Thank you, Wes Craven. We never met you, but your movies met us.

About the Authors

Peter Hall and Paul Gandersman are writers and filmmakers living in Austin, TX.
This is their first book.
It won't be their last.

About the Authors

Peter Hall and Paul Gunderman are writers and illustrators living in Austin, TX.

This is their first book.

It won't be their last.

CPSIA information can be obtained
at www.ICGtesting.com
Printed in the USA
LVHW091541021122
732204LV00021B/725/J

2/23
LUDINGTON PUBLIC LIBRARY
5 S. BRYN MAWR AVENUE
BRYN MAWR, PA 19010
30043012198648